HOME
BY
DARK

HOME
BY
DARK

Tish Knapp

To order additional copies of this book, contact:
Xlibris Corporation
1-888-795-4274
www.Xlibris.com
Orders@Xlibris.com
15416

To Mama, Velma, Mamee,
Grandma Caldwell and all my ancestral voices-

ACKNOWLEDGEMENTS

MANY THANKS TO my husband, Gene, and my family who always made my writing a high priority even when I forgot to. Special thanks to Jake Knapp, whose art is on the cover and Stan Moldoff, who took my picture. Thanks also to my Wednesday night writing group who would not stop their encouraging, suggesting, prodding and pushing until this book was finished. Publishing a first book is as scary as going to the grocery store without your clothes on and this one would never have come to completion without the encouragement of all those people who wanted it to happen.

PROLOGUE

1929

NOT LONG AFTER the last bit of summer daylight had deserted the rich, delta farmlands of Mississippi, in the drab front room of Deedove's cabin, the time for watchfulness and guarding had come, just as the ancestors had said it would. The conjure woman, descendant of countless African conjure women before her, stood tightlipped and big in the lamplight. She fixed her eyes on the wall somewhere behind the four white men and a boy who had knocked loudly at her cabin door just after dark and shoved their way into her house. Five of them. One older man in his Sunday clothes, the younger three in their shirtsleeves, and a half-grown boy.

The ancestors had tried from the beginning to warn Deedove, whispering in her head as they had done since she first breathed life. This time, they insisted, was mean and ill-omened for the baby. They had prophesied the kind of danger that was standing in her cabin right now long before the child spirit began her journey into life, the next generation of the conjure. The child might be lost, they cautioned, Deedove's child whose earthly form rested now uneasily in her belly. But she hadn't listened to a word of it. Now . . .

"You two check in the back room," the gray-headed one said. "Kaleb can get the front here." The white man's voice was controlled and cold. His pale eyes turned toward her. "Deedove, we want you to know we here tonight in the name of God Almighty."

She pushed words out at him between her teeth.

"What your Mr. God Almighty got to do with the business of a fifty-year-old, colored woman?"

"Got nothing to do with your color, Deedove. Has to do with that voodoo foolishness you people love so much." His voice was like sweet cyanide.

She drew all her strength into her chest and spoke silently in her inward conjure-voice to the sweet, small thing inside her, the child.

"Be calm, baby. Everything gonna be alright."

She cast her eyes warily about the room, thinking hard. She hadn't needed the women's warnings; she'd seen the omens, herself. But she had risked the loss of the child-spirit anyway. Why? she wondered now. But she knew. She had hungered for the child, had already heard in her visions the sound of the baby calling her, "Mama", the small girl-child listening for the reassurance of Deedove's voice alone. The sweetness of that.

And she believed her power was strong enough to protect the baby. Hadn't she coaxed the child-spirit out of the mists all by herself? And because the women refused to help, hadn't she alone forced her body to conceive the fragile form that would house the spirit of the child on earth? Without a man forcing her down, demanding that she spread herself beneath him like a plowed field ready for planting. No, none of that. She had done it by herself. All by herself.

There came a troubling in her womb, an anxious hesitation of the child's journey into life. Deedove called silently to the conjure women who had lived before her, whose voices had hummed in her head since the day she was born. Before even. They knew very well what was creeping up around her door right now. That terrible, dark, ghost-of-a-thing that had always threatened to swallow up the conjure.

Mama, all of ya'll, I needs you to quiet the baby for me.

Her attention turned outward again. The violating of her house, the sounds of rummaging and shuffling, unwrapping and sniffing, the clinking of jars on the shelf in the rough, gray cupboard above her stove pinched at her calm, but she kept an arrogant tilt to her head. The men didn't have any idea what to look for, she reassured herself. Ignorance. Scary stories and fairy tales were all they had to go on. As suspicious of a bottle of dried peppermint as the gray and musky ragwort.

She recognized the gray-headed man. Earl Fowler had been the Sunday school superintendent at the Calvary Church for at least forty years. Her jaw tightened and her eyes narrowed. That church had its history with the conjure, taking a stand against the work of the women for as far back as she could remember.

The two younger ones in the back room yelled out.

"Think we got something here."

They crowded back into her front room, nervously placed a bundle on the table, and then dissolved back out of the light into the shadows.

Deedove watched carefully and read the faces before her. She recognized those two standing back now. They were the great grandsons of the men who first railed against the conjure. They were the fourth generation standing here now in her house. The scary stories they had heard since they were children made them anxious, quivery and uneasy with what they were about.

The third man unwrapped the bundle on Deedove's old, wooden, kitchen table. He was thin and wormy, and his skin was splotched and shiny from too much washing. He was an Owen; she knew because of his freckled skin and red hair. She wondered what in the world he was doing spending time with *this* group. She never heard of any Owen taking up with a church gathering before. Minding a still was Owen religion. Must be a recent convert led to the baptismal font in the Calvary Church by some sweet, young lamb in the flock whose daddy wouldn't let her spend time with an unbaptized man.

Deedove's cabin filled with the smell of white men shifting

and breathing heavy, but the boy hung back just outside the door, fresh and frightened. She didn't know who he was except he had soft, young eyes. She could feel his nervousness and his fear and his young boy gentleness.

Earl Fowler looked at the contents of the bundle and rubbed at his upper lip and shook his head slightly. The Owen poked at the things on the table nervously, trying to convince the others by what lay revealed now in the lamp light, dried marigold and nightshade, swamp milk weed, clematis and foxglove, squirrel paw and the gray powder she made from the dried up genitals of stag.

Voodoo stuff, they thought. But the women had nothing to do with voodoo. It was the great mystery of being alive that fascinated the women, that they reveled in. From the beginning of time, they watched and wooed that mystery until it revealed its secrets to the sisterhood, how to bring babies from the mists beyond time into this world and then, when the time came, how to see them back out of it again. They learned to read life signs, mix healing concoctions, love potions, revenge oils. They could help the barren come with child or the too successful rid themselves of an indiscreet or inconvenient sowing.

The gray-haired man rubbed his forehead. The fidgety, razor-thin Owen spoke.

"What you think, Mr. Earl?"

"I don't know. Got no idea what to look for. But seems like you maybe come on some things might be evidence. I wouldn't imagine these the kinda things you gonna find laying around most cabins."

"I told you, didn't I? Didn't I tell you, Mr. Earl? That there old black bitch. My mama been knowing about that woman for a long time. Use to tell me stories I wouldn't dare to speak in Christian company. Babies born into her black hands with big, ugly, red birthmarks about their faces or heads so big they about popped open. Swear to God, I can't say it all, but you can believe it. That one still practicing, Mr. Earl. Just like her mama."

The gray head turned toward Deedove and spoke in a nail-hard voice.

"Woman, hear me now. Who is the father of that child you carrying?"

Deedove drew her lips in tighter and shook her head slightly. The rank foolishness of trying to explain to this gathering how she had tantalized the child-spirit with the fire of life, until it's own unique form came to be housed in her womb.

He spoke again.

"If you don't tell me right now what man you been with, Deedove, we gonna be inclined to believe the child to be something abominable in the sight of the Lord."

He stared up at her with his watery eyes, but still she remained silent. The child-spirit trembled.

"Now, see there, Mr. Earl. She can't say who done it to her. Lord God, you think we got us a witch here been screwing around with the devil?"

He laughed nervously and began to shift from side to side in his excitement.

"That sure woulda been something to see," he muttered.

Mr. Earl nodded gravely in reply. Deedove felt the Owen's excitement. For the first time in his life he was standing with the honorable side of the community at the very threshold of gaining respect from the people of Hart County whose language his daddy had never been able to understand. The people his father had outwardly scorned and inwardly envied all his life. The excitement turned his nervous shuffle into a dance of eagerness.

The old man spoke again.

"Well, she never took up with no man anybody knew about."

The other two stood silently, fascinated, watching. She could hear their uneasy breathing.

The boy stood back by the door, young and untaught.

The Owen spoke again.

"That's the truth, Mr. Earl. Coming up with a pickaninny old as she is. And that pore, little, old baby of preacher's found cold dead in its bed, looking like it was just sleeping. Now you know ain't no preacher ever done nothing to deserve something like that. Gotta be a connection."

"But that don't necessarily say for sure that Deedove some kinda witch," said one of the two who stood back away from the table.

Deedove remembered the way that one had looked as a child when she dipped up cracklin' for him out of the pot where she was rendering his daddy's lard.

"Hey, ain't you ever heard about her mama and her grandmama?"

"Well, stories. Yeah. But I ain't ever heard of anybody seeing anything out right."

"Well, she ain't gonna let you see anything for sure," the Owen said with a stab of laughter. "But everybody know her mama was a conjure and her grandmama, too. When I's a little boy I wouldn'ta passed by her on the sidewalk, I's so scared of her." And then he paused and huffed and added quickly, "'Course I ain't scared no more."

Deedove knew at once how deeply his man-spirit recognized her powers and how he hated her, because it placed her over him.

"What we gonna do with her?" he asked licking thin, dry lips. She could smell his eager sweat.

"She got the right to speak in her own defense," the gray-headed one prompted as he stepped forward into the center of the lamp light and placed both his hands firmly on the table.

Deedove lightened. Along with the fear and hatred that shoved through her door tonight, Earl Fowler had been civilized enough to bring a sense of justice with him. That justice might serve as the balance she needed.

"Now, Deedove," the older man was saying, "On Friday the church gathered for the funeral service of the preacher's baby. One of our members saw you laying something down in front of the parsonage during that time. That person believes 'cause of who you come from, you were performing some sorta voodoo curse there. What you got to say for yourself?"

Now she understood. Somebody had taken notice when she leaned over on her way into town to see what looked to her like a nickel caught in the sidewalk. She remembered seeing the black hearse parked in front of the church and crossing over to the far side of the street to stay away from any troubled spirits.

The Owen shifted nervously from side to side. "You's thinking nobody saw you, but somebody did."

"Weren't no nickel though. Were a button," she mumbled to herself.

"What's that?" Earl Fowler leaned closer.

"I's reaching for a button," she said out loud to him.

The young boy watched nervously from the flung open door. He had not discovered yet the ways grown men use to ease their fear and she felt his need to bolt and run.

"A button?" the Owen snorted.

The gray-headed one frowned at him and spoke.

"Deedove, what you mean by a button? The man that saw you said you did some kinda ritual out there in front of the church."

She turned to her apron hanging on the wall and reached in the pocket and drew out something.

"I ain't done nary thing to no white preacher's baby. I stop on my way into town to pick up a nickel I see stuck in the sidewalk. I rise back up, rub away the dirt on my apron, hold it up to the light to get a good look at it. It warn't no nickel. Was a button. Still worth something though, so I puts it in my pocket. Here."

She laid her hand flat on the table in front of the men and when she withdrew it a round, silver button lay in its place.

"A button?" the skinny one snorted again. "Mr. Earl, you know that old front-heavy woman ain't gonna stoop clear over to the sidewalk for no button. Everybody know what it was she done in front of that church. Was a voodoo curse, Mr. Earl. How else you gonna explain that baby up and dying? Not even sick."

Back in the shadows the other two men struggled within themselves. A disbelief rumbled and boiled inside both of them, insisting on being heard and they wrestled with the need to speak the disbelief aloud. Finally, they kept it to themselves and eased the guilt they felt with the pride they took in who they were, had been before they were born, and the assurance the Calvary Church gave them that they were doing God's will.

Deedove spoke again.

"What I do ain't got nothing to do with no curses," she said, folding her arms over the swollen abdomen.

"Well, then maybe you gonna tell us who give you that belly?" the Owen said, walking around the table, jabbing a long finger at her middle. "I bet the devil give it to you for delivering the soul of that dead baby over to him." Then he said over his shoulder to the others, "I heard of stuff like that."

She could smell the excitement on him. Because he counted violence to be better than eating or lying with a woman or breathing because it was the deepest human feeling he had ever known. The gray-haired man narrowed his eyes in thought, and the Owen saw it and knew he was being listened to and it fed his intoxication.

Still restrained, the old one asked, "Deedove, that true? You still practicing your African black magic? Even though the church of God forbids it?"

One of them coughed nervously. And the boy moved to the porch and stood back watching through the opened door.

"Hey, Mr. Earl, this ought to be a public thing we doing here. We ought to take her across the river up by Worthey Brothers where all of them can see. Make an example of her, so won't any more of them think all they gotta do to cause white folks grief is to work some of their mumbo jumbo."

Deedove's look of disdain changed slightly. The young one on the porch jumped and called through the opened door.

"Hey, ya'll. Ain't we been here long enough?"

It was the first time she had heard him speak. His voice was high and young.

"I bet she could do most anything she wanted to anybody bothered her," he muttered.

"Boy, if you need to go on home to your mama, you do it by yourself," said the one in the back who had found the bundle. "I told ya'll I didn't think we ought to bring that boy along?"

"No, now," the gray-haired one said. "All ya'll listen. That boy's the next generation. Children got to learn how to deal with these kinda things. Else this country be ruined for every God fearing man, woman, and child in Mississippi." Then turning toward the door he said, "William, I don't wanta hear any more of that from you. You understand?"

The boy lowered his head.

"Mr. Earl, please. Lemme go," he begged quietly.

"Hush, boy. I'm ashamed of you. No need to be afraid. God Almighty will protect us all from the black power of this woman."

"I ain't afraid. I just don't want to see what ya'll . . . " he said almost to himself.

Then before she could correct the motion in the room, the gray-haired one nodded slightly toward the Owen, relinquishing his sense of order and justice to the baser man. And that nod ushered a sudden and terrible coldness into her house that threatened to engulf her. She heard with bone-chilling terror the approach of the dark thing, a creeping through the cracks around the door and windows, something larger than the men, monstrous, that commanded their mouths to move and their hands and arms to follow. A sliding through the walls into the close air of the room, a settling with anticipation into the dark corners. Her great power turned to ice, and she began to shake.

She could hear the whimper of the child spirit turning now to a low moan and despair grew heavy inside her. And then finally she heard the old familiar murmur in her head and her heart lightened.

Mama, she called.

The voices of the conjure answered her with a mournful shudder. None of them, not even Deedove, would be able to protect the child now. Their nullified, collective power caused a horror that rose up bitter in Deedove's mouth. She reached out frantically with her mind, trying to read the air.

"You wanta go down town with us, woman? Down to the front of Worthey Brothers to see your friends?"

The question came from the Owen.

"I ain't got no friends," she answered.

The lamplight reflected off the faces, grotesque now with deep shadows.

"Come on, ya'll. Leave her alone."

It was the boy again. She reached out with her mind to him and saw that he alone among them recognized the presence of the darkness and feared it.

The child spirit was trembling now. Such easy prey. Deedove's realization now at what she had done to the baby overcame her. The powerless ancestors were gathering one by one in an endless, silent congregation to bear witness to the taking. The child spirit, the next generation, the new, small, shifting daughter whose earthly form fluttered tiny fingers beneath her mother's heart would be lost in the darkness. And none of them knew what it would take to find her and bring her back home to them again.

The old man spoke again. "Well, I don't like this kinda thing, but I know something has to be done."

The freckled hand shot out and grabbed her forearm.

"Come on, woman. We gonna take you into town. And when we finish ain't no nigger in Hart County ever gonna give credit to a conjure again."

"No," she said, backing away from them. "I ain't going nowhere."

But the younger men didn't listen. They were reaching out toward her, grabbing her arms now, the boy and the old, gray-haired one holding back, standing behind them, she pulling against them, holding on to anything, trying to wriggle free, flailing arms and kicking bare feet. But they tore her hands loose from the table, drug her through the door, disregarding the bare feet and the ripping of the cotton nightgown, revealing the full breasts. Dragging her out of the lighted kitchen into the night, across the new bridge that spanned the dark Big Black River right up into town. Right out under the cold streetlight. The Owen yelling out, "Voodoo woman," to the night so that anybody in listening distance would know what the commotion was about. And Deedove, trying to run, to pull away, to save the child, but stumbling because of the heavy belly.

The crowded Saturday night street was emptied in a moment as word spread and people of all ages disappeared from the storefronts and sidewalks to whisper in shadowed alleyways or tremble behind darkened stores or lay breathlessly under wagons.

The older man, the gray-haired one, yelled into the empty streets, "This woman here put a curse on a white man's child. Ya'll hear? And in the name of the true God Almighty we here tonight to put an end to her devil business forever. Amen."

And right out there in the light of the street lamp where anybody could have seen if they wanted to, the heavy fists and boots of the men shot out from the darkness striking at whatever delicate parts they found, hard knuckles and boot leather against woman flesh again and again until the jerked out gasps and groaning stopped and the sound of muffled thumps was all that broke the thick night air.

At last when the terrible hunger within them was satisfied, they walked away and left the crumpled form moaning softly in the street. The Owen laughing, the other two astonished and sickened by the fierceness of their own violence, salving their troubled consciences by reminding each other they had done it for the Lord.

And finally the street was quiet. The Saturday night street strangely quiet and deserted. Except for the mules and the wagons in the vacant lot next to Worthey Brothers General Store. And a boy's face, small and dark, peering cautiously over the top of a wooden wagon rail.

CHAPTER 1

1949

JUBILEE HORNE HURRIED down the dusty road that ran along the Big Black River two miles north of Tula, Mississippi. The late afternoon was fast turning into night and she was uneasy. When Benny came home and found the cabin dark and no supper waiting on the table, the creases between his brows would darken with anger. He'd really be mad if he found out she'd gone to visit Deedove. She walked faster, clutching a paper sack full of field peas the old conjure woman had given her.

The summer sky was still light but starting to fleck with stars. The swamp glittered with the throb of lightning bugs under thick sycamores and cottonwoods. Her brown skin was sticky and damp in the mid-July heat and sweat ran down between her breasts. Dust from the road clung to her old shoes that were run over at the sides and cracked across the top. Her swollen belly pushed against the waistline of the oversized housedress Sis Riah had loaned her. It was because of this child inside her that Deedove had sent the message for her to come. And because of who Deedove was that Jubilee had put down everything and hurried to her cabin.

In the gloom of that place the wide-opened, cloudy eyes of the old conjure woman fixed on her, and the mouth with the snuff stained and missing teeth announced the prediction. The baby was a girl-child whose mission on earth was veiled and heavy laden.

"Heavy laden?" she'd asked, suddenly worried. "What that mean?"

The wellbeing of the little one would be watched over.

"Watched over?" Jubilee echoed.

By a legion of women who were ordained to help her finish the work she came to do.

"Watched over? Why she need to be watched over?"

But Deedove refused to tell her any more, even when she insisted on an explanation. Jubilee sat across from the heavy, silent woman at her scarred-up, kitchen table as if she were paralyzed. In her ears hummed the strangeness of that place and what seemed like the far away chime of foreign music. And she forgot about where she was and what time it was until she noticed the scarcity of light beyond the dusty cabin window and jumped up to go.

Benny would surely be upset when she got home.

As she hurried along she wrapped her free arm across her belly, embracing the tiny child within. She should tell Benny about the baby, that it was a girl. But he'd ask her how she knew and she couldn't lie to him; she'd have to say that Deedove told her. But every time she mentioned that name, Benny went into a rage. She grimaced. Maybe she'd just keep the news to herself for a while.

The silhouette of their cabin appeared off to the right against the lead-colored, evening sky. It sat on a knoll that divided two fields of young knee-high cotton filled with green boles ripening in the hot, dry summer. She was surprised to see the windows dark. She smiled, realizing she had beat Benny home.

She turned onto the rough tractor trail that led up to the cabin. On either side of her, green cotton leaves were covered with a thin layer of dust. She climbed the steps to the cabin porch and turned and strained her eyes up and down Highway 51. Nobody in sight. She stood for a while listening.

The call of frogs and night birds echoed across the rich bottomland. To her right she could see the fields and pastures Benny worked that belonged to the Montgomerys, father and son. To her left lay the edge of the Big Black River swamp. She caught the thick, musky smell of it, the rich, warm dirt and thick undergrowth, the welcomed coolness in summer. She knew the way through the dark tangle of trees to a place where muscadines were ripening and a bend in the river caused a deep hole in the riverbed where she could set a trotline and catch the big river catfish. She breathed in the rich swamp air. So much life in that place, she thought. If she were buried there she'd just rise right back up out of that black loam alive and laughing again. She smiled and turned and went inside to get supper ready.

It was a small unpainted two-roomed house with a stove to heat and cook by in the forward room and their bed and trunk in the back room. She carried water from a well about half a mile through the field and their nature needs were taken care of in an outhouse out back. There was a front door and a back door and on warm July nights like this she opened them both, so the swamp breezes could blow straight through the place.

Behind the cabin was a small pasture where they kept their little red mule and six white-faced Herefords. Benny brought day-old calves whose mothers had died or deserted them home to her and she bottle fed them until they reached weaning age. Mr. Luke gave them all the calves she could save that way.

She sat the bag of peas on the floor and hurried to the little kitchen table. She struck a match and lit the coal-oil lamp sitting on it. The wood stove felt warm. It wouldn't take long to get supper ready. She hurriedly put a few chunks of wood into the firebox and blew onto the coals. She meant to heat up the last of the ham and sweet potatoes and the breakfast biscuits. Benny would be starving and irritable when he got home.

But Jubilee always kept in her mind the way he was three years ago when they were courting and right after they married. She remembered him in the evenings tired from work, sprawled out at the small wooden table watching her as she did the things that brought his supper to him. He'd talk to her back then about his day. The things that had made him mad or that tickled him and she'd offer comfort or laughter while he talked. And if the work took her too close to him he'd reach out and grab her and pull her protesting into his lap. They dreamed back then about a bigger house to live in, more money, a better life. Benny said she'd changed his luck. Things were gonna be different. But in the last three years, nothing had changed and she knew it stung him every time he thought of how he'd let her down.

But none of those things mattered to her. She was happier than she ever remembered being in her whole life. She was proud to be Benny's wife. He was one of the most respected colored men in Hart County, partly because of the way he lived and partly because of who he worked for. Everybody in town knew Mr. Luke trusted Benny and that was good enough for them. When he drove the green, Ford pickup in to get cow feed at the farmers' co-op, Mr. Charlie McKay would give him whatever he asked for. Merchants in town extended credit if he needed it for sugar and flour and soap. Everybody knew Benny was Mr. Luke's boy.

In all his thirty-five years Benny had never given any of them any cause not to trust him. What ever he said he was going to do he did. What he borrowed he paid back. He came home every payday with his pockets full of the money Mr. Luke and his wife paid both of them for a week's work. Jubilee would tie it up safe in a handkerchief and stuff it into the bottom of the old molasses can in the cabinet above her cook stove until they needed it.

Supper was heated and cooled down again and she was imagining all sorts of drownings and upturned tractors when she finally heard his steps on the path.

"Benny," she called. "You alright? Where you been so late?"

He stomped dirt from his shoes on the porch and then pushed open the screen door. He took off his straw hat, slapping it against his leg, and hung it on a nail.

"Trying to fix that goddamn old tractor," he said. Without looking at her, he headed through the kitchen toward the back of the house.

"Couldn't you fixed it tomorrow?" she asked.

"Nawh," he called. "Gotta have it first thing in the morning while the dew's still out."

"How come?" she called to him. She could hear the sounds he made washing cotton poison and grease off his hands and face in the wash basin out back. He didn't answer until he came back into the room glistening from the soap and well water.

"How come?" she asked again.

"Gotta poison the cotton up at the Nance place."

He pulled up a chair to the table.

"Mr. Luke ain't hiring Mr. Abbot Lee to do it in his airplane?" She set a full plate of food in front of him.

"Cotton's short enough to do it with the tractor," he answered, picking up the fork.

"You must be starving," she said.

He dug into the ham and potatoes taking big bites. After a while he nodded toward the paper sack near the cupboard.

"What's in the bag?" he asked her, his mouth full.

Her eyes darted in the direction of his nod. She didn't answer right away.

"Jubilee?"

"Field peas," she said.

"Where they come from?" he asked.

His voice was lighter now and calmer with the food, but she could tell by the angle he kept to his shoulders that he was still irritated. She hated to interrupt the pattern he kept that brought the food from the plate to his mouth.

Finally, he looked up at her waiting for an answer.

"Deedove give them to me," she said, turning back toward the stove, so she wouldn't have to see the look come over his face.

"What? Deedove?" He stopped eating and smacked the tabletop with his free hand. "Ain't I put food enough on this table without you taking peas off of that woman?"

"Course you do, Benny, but Deedove mean it for a kindness," she said turning toward him.

"Kindness? Good Lord, Jubilee. How many times I gotta forbid you to go visiting that woman?"

The look on Benny's face made her stomach sick.

"Benny, please don't fuss. She so lonely."

"And I'm saying you don't know what you hanging around with. Ask anybody in Hart County, colored or white. Ask Sis Riah. She tell you the same thing."

"But it's a silly idea everybody got. Deedove can't hurt nobody. She just a pore old woman, can't hardly see. Ain't got nobody to take care of her."

"You just do like I say. She shame us all with her foolishness. I'm telling you for the last time, stay away from her. You hear?"

Benny looked hard at his wife, waiting for her to answer.

"Jubilee?"

"I hear," she said finally.

He looked at her a moment longer. Jubilee took a deep breath and waited tensely. After a bit he bent his head and began eating again and she let the breath go slowly, realizing the worse was over. She sat down gently across from him and watched as he ate.

She wished he wouldn't be quite so hard and closed minded about the old seer. She remembered it was right after she and Benny got married and she started cooking and cleaning for Miz Mary Alice Montgomery when she first met Deedove. The old seer shuffled up the driveway to Mr. Luke's house one frosted November day during hog killing. She settled down in the back yard on a round of unsplit firewood beside the hanging carcasses and tossed chunks of fat into a huge footed iron pot. She kept the fire going by shoving short sticks of kindling into the red coals under the pot, and so she rendered up the lard.

Mr. Luke's children hung around Deedove begging her for cracklings. Every now and then she'd dip down into the bubbling pot and scoop up the browned skins and put them, dripping, on newspaper to cool. But she never said much to the children, the way most colored women did. Some people thought she was touched in the head. A few said she was some kind of seer.

There she sat out by the smokehouse silently stirring and dipping up the hot lard into cans. Jubilee was filled with curiosity as she watched from the kitchen window. Finally when noontime came, she took dinner out to Benny and Hippy, who were butchering the hog carcasses, and to Deedove, too.

""Here your dinner," she said as she set a plate of fried chicken and turnip greens beside Deedove on a piece of upturned log. "Mind if I eats with you?" Without waiting for an answer she sat down beside the bubbling pot with her own plate in her lap. "That kitchen too stuffy to eat in."

Deedove looked at her carefully for a long time, squinting her gray veiled eyes as if she were about to ask a question, and then without saying a word she looked back into the bubbling pot in front of her.

"My name Jubilee. I Benny's wife, Miss Deedove," she offered.

"Humpf, so you the one," Deedove responded without looking back up. Then silence.

Finally, when Jubilee was beginning to feel uneasy, Deedove spoke up.

"The grease'll burn you."

The sound of the husky voice made Jubilee look up in surprise. She didn't know exactly what Deedove meant. Maybe she was crazy like everybody said. A close look at the wrinkled face did not tell her anything, but she had been raised to be polite to her elders.

"Yes, ma'm. It sure will," she said and added, "You gonna have cracklin' bread for supper, Miss Deedove?"

"Humpf," the old woman grunted again. Then silence. Jubilee was used to the casual call and response of women talking together. She wasn't sure exactly what to do now. Just as she thought she might remark on the cold weather, Deedove looked directly into her eyes and spoke again.

"The grease'll burn you."

Jubilee looked up in confusion and finally muttered, "Yassum," and lowered her eyes back to her plate.

Deedove just kept sitting there heavily on the old stump, her legs apart, covered with brown cotton stockings, men's muddy work shoes on her feet with the laces dragging, an ancient oversized wool, field coat hanging over her faded print, work dress, a kerchief tied around her head with kinks of black and gray straying out here and there, leaning forward, her face shiny with sweat. Occasionally she looked up at Jubilee and studied her, but mostly she seemed intent on the view in front of her of the bubbling pot, sending steam into the cool November air.

Jubilee tried talking about different things to her, about working for Miz Mary Alice, about the possibility of her and Benny having a baby, about church and the new Negro preacher, hoping to get the old woman to talk. But Deedove didn't say another word— just looked at her hard occasionally and then leaned back over the pot and the work before her. Finally, Jubilee finished her dinner in silence and got up to leave.

"Bye, Miss Deedove," she said.

As she walked away she heard the husky voice again from behind her.

"Remember what I told you."

That was all. And when she turned and looked at the old woman it seemed like she had imagined the words. Like she had heard them inside her own head and not from the wrinkled tightly shut mouth.

"Told me?" she asked herself on the way back into the kitchen. "What did she tell me?"

She thought about it during the afternoon as she did the ironing and couldn't get the sweating old face and clouded eyes out of her mind. She kept hearing the voice almost like Deedove was in the room with her.

That night when she tried to explain to Benny the effect that Deedove's words had on her, he just teased her about spending time with a crazy old woman who never said anything anybody could figure out anyway.

The next day when she spilled the hot chicken grease all over her hand, and Miz Mary Alice had to take her to Dr. Ingram to get a dressing on it, and then she couldn't go to work for over a week, she was reminded of the strangely prophetic words. She told Benny again what Deedove said to her.

"She saw it, Benny," she told him in wonder while they ate the supper he had to cook for them. "I thought she's just talking about the lard heating up in the pot that day, but she was warning me. I know it now. I couldn't get her out of my head all afternoon."

But Benny laughed at her. Maybe he didn't believe like she did, that the old woman had real conjure powers. But she had heard the words and seen the face, and something more, too. During the times she had visited in Deedove's cabin down by the town bridge, times that Benny didn't know about, sometimes she had come back in the late afternoon with the sounds of strange voices echoing in her head.

"Next thing she gonna be asking you to pay her for her seeings. You better not let me hear you done give her money," Benny warned.

But Deedove had never asked Jubilee for anything, though, heaven knows, she had offered it plenty of times, inspite of Benny's disapproval. She sat now across from her husband, watching him finish eating. And she felt the desire that always filled her heart, to do for Benny what pleased him. But at the same time something more powerful had begun to stir deep in her, something that wanted to know everything there was to know about Deedove. He looked up and caught her expression, but before he could ask her about it, she spoke up.

"Benny, day after tomorrow Saturday."

"Yeah. You planning on going into town with me?" he asked her. The tone of his voice had changed.

"Sure am. I hope it don't rain. Me and Sis Riah planning a tea party."

"She say Sweet Boy coming in, too?"

"I imagine he will. Only time he don't is when Mr. Matthew work him on Saturday."

After supper Benny watched her clearing up the supper dishes. He sat back in the chair and pulled a book of cigarette papers and a white muslin pouch of tobacco out of his overalls pocket. He rolled a cigarette on the bare table top and licked the paper shut, then leaning forward, removed the glass chimney from the lamp and lit one of the twisted paper ends.

"You get a lot done in the field today?" she asked him.

"Nearly finished up the work in Miz Olivia's fields," he answered looking at the curve of her back. "Except for the tractor."

She asked about the cotton poisoning, how long it would take, and the tractor, what he had done to fix it. He knew she was trying to make it like it use to be between them, simple and easy, but he resisted. And then she began the kind of dreamy talk she sometimes drifted into when she thought about the baby and the future, and without realizing it a kind of comfort slid over him and a warmth swelled inside him. And then suddenly he caught himself moving with her in the dream and he wrenched himself back, cursing and counting it as a weakness in himself.

She had almost done it to him again. Pulled him into that sweet fog of mindless, sightless trust. What was it about this woman that didn't seem to understand that there was no time for dreams in this place? He had to get away from the sight of her softness and roundness. He stood up and walked out onto the porch and looked beyond the fields to the highway.

The gentle sounds of her humming came through the screen door behind him. She was so goddamn happy. It seemed like growing up colored in Hart County had taught her absolutely nothing. She had no idea how ignorant happiness was in this place. In this place you guard against wishing and wanting every minute of your life. You don't dare ever count on anything good coming to you beyond the sucking in of your own breath. Better not to want or hope for anything except what you have to have to live. And then better learn to take nothing more than you barely need to survive and tell the world you had a plenty.

CHAPTER 2

NEXT MORNING JUBILEE could barely tolerate the heat from the wood cook stove in the kitchen of the big house where she worked. She wiped sweat from her face with her apron while she prepared the midday meal for the Montgomery family. She fixed stew meat in her own homemade sauce and picked, shelled, and cooked field peas.

In the middle of the morning, Mr. Luke's little girl, Anise, slammed the back porch, screen door and ran into the kitchen calling, "Jubilee, come see what I made. Come see my house in the bushes in the back yard."

She was out of breath and her short brown hair stuck to her face.

"Just a minute, hon. I'm making butter. Let me finish."

Anise sat down impatiently at the kitchen table while Jubilee pressed the last of the whey out of the fresh butter with a wooden paddle. Anise talked as she sat. She had gone down to the pond and cut bitter weeds to lay across the upper branches of the bushes for the roof and she'd found some pretty pieces of glass to be her dishes and she had even made a shelf to put them on.

"How come you playing in all that dirt when you got a toy box full of pretty things you ain't hardly touched?" Jubilee asked her.

"Cause it's fun," Anise answered with her eyes on the butter Jubilee was working.

And the truth was, when Jubilee finally left the kitchen, crossed the back yard, and crawled with great difficulty through the old bushes behind the little girl and at last entered the dim cave between the lugustrums, she understood why Anise loved it so much. They sat quietly together in the wonder of the soft green interior and the magic of the cool filtered sunlight.

"You like it?" Anise asked after a long silence.

"I loves it," Jubilee answered.

When she crawled back out, Anise helped by holding back the branches, so she could maneuver her awkward size through the small corridor. Finally when she got out, the little girl hugged her and she returned to the kitchen smiling.

Mary Alice Montgomery drove Jubilee home in the afternoon and later on Anise rode the new horse across the two pastures that separated the Lexington highway from old 51 to visit Jubilee. She only stayed a little while because she wanted to ride the new rhone to the Gage Place and back. When she left, Jubilee took a blue, speckled bowl and the paper bag full of field peas out to the cabin porch and sat down in the swing to shell them. The air was heavy except for a cautious breeze that came up from the swamp bringing a fragile cooling to her neck. In the distance over the cotton fields she heard somebody singing.

"Sowing in the morning. Sowing seeds of kindness".

The notes of the old song rose faintly at first and then stronger.

"Sowing in the noontide, and the dewy eve."

Jubilee looked hard across the field as the singer approached down the highway. She recognized the voice before she could make out the face. It was Sis Riah, stepping in time to the music and swinging her arms as she walked along. Jubilee joined in harmonizing on the old song.

"Waiting for the harvest, and the time of reaping-
We shall come rejoicing, bringing in the sheaves."

As she sang, she squinted her eyes with her hand up to shade them. When the song ended she whooped a welcome and watched as the figure returned the wave and walked toward the dirt path that led to the cabin.

"Need a visitor?" Sis Riah's voice called across the field.

Jubilee put her hands around her mouth and yelled back, "Sho' do." She leaned into the swing and smiled and watched the older woman's progress toward the house. Sis Riah was a born storyteller, and Jubilee was always happy to have her visit.

The first time Sis Riah came by was right after Jubilee and Benny married. She told her about how she was raised on the old Russell place when Mr. Luke's grandparents lived out there. The site of the big house was up on a rise of ground to the north of where Jubilee's cabin stood right now and she pointed toward the roof of the old smoke house that was still standing that could be seen from their backyard.

"All your family gone?" Jubilee had asked her in a quiet moment.

"Ain't got no children and my folks long gone. Daddy die right after the war. I was still a nursing baby then. We'd a been in bad trouble if Mama hadn't a lucked up and got a job cleaning house and cooking for Mr. Frank and Miz Helen Russell, Miz Olivia's mama and daddy. They let Mama live in a cabin right out back of the main house, so there was a roof over our heads. And Mama up and had the spit to beg them to allow her to keep her baby girl in the kitchen with her while she work. That was me."

"They let her do it?" Jubilee asked surprised.

"Yeah, they did. Miz Olivia's folks was fine people. Honest with they coloreds. Benny's great grandaddy sharecrop for them, too. Them was funny times back then. No such thing as masters and slaves no more; so nobody know who they suppose to be."

Jubilee visited Sis Riah a few weeks later to bring her a caramel cake for her birthday. They were drinking coffee in her front room when Olivia Montgomery drove up in her new Buick to bring Sis Riah a present. It was a new red wool winter coat.

"How come Miz Olivia so nice to you?" she asked after Olivia left.

"Can't resist me, I reckon," Sis Riah answered. "Nobody can. You want a slice of this cake with your coffee?"

Jubilee laughed while her hostess passed a plate to her.

"You want to hear that story?"

"About Miz Olivia? Sure," Jubilee said with enthusiasm.

So Sis Riah sat down in the comfortable old chair across from her guest, so she could enjoy the telling of the story as much as her listener.

"When I was about two years old, living out on the old place with mama, the Russell's had they selves a little girl. That was Olivia. And later on when the baby grow to walking, Miz Helen give me a dime a day to watch out for her and keep her out of trouble. I thought I was rich. Told my mama she could quit working and get on home."

"How long that last? A dime a day."

"Right long time. And from the very first me and Miss Olivia just flat out love one another," Sis Riah said. "Day in and day out, up until the time Olivia turn fourteen, we be together. 'Til it come time for her to go off to boarding school. Have another slice, hon?"

Jubilee shook her head, so her hostess continued. She said, for a going-away present she had given her friend a little white figurine of an angel. Olivia said she'd kept the pretty thing on the table by her bed at school. It reminded her of home, and it kept her from dying of homesickness.

"But after a time," Sis Riah said, "Olivia make friends at the school and pretty soon things change and through the years I hears less and less from her and finally it just settle down like it ought to."

And now Sis Riah's husband worked in Tula for Olivia's husband. The only thing that remained of the friendship was the way Olivia always made sure Sis Riah and Sweet Boy had everything they needed. And when Sis Riah came into town and sat and visited with Saphronia, who cooked and cleaned for Olivia, the white woman always found a reason to come into the kitchen and talk. Everybody in town knew they talked as friends even though it put Saphronia out of sorts and caused her to complain to anybody who would listen that Sis Riah was not in proper respect of her employer.

"But you can see how come we feels different about one another than most folks around here," she said. "We got plenty proper respect."

Now Jubilee could see Sis Riah clearly as she turned off the highway onto the dusty path that led between the cotton fields. She wore a cotton dress printed with big blue and pink flowers and she carried a small parcel under her arm wrapped in newspaper.

"Sis Riah," she called, "What you doing walking up and down the highway this time of day?"

"Coming to see you. How you feeling?" She walked across the cabin yard past the brightly colored zinnias and marigolds that Jubilee planted along the bottle path and she climbed the two steps to the porch. "You looking good, girl. Having babies fortifies you," she said.

Jubilee laughed and patted the seat on the swing beside her.

"Set down here and visit. You want a glass of tea?"

"No, thank you. I can't stay but a little while. Darkness coming on, and Sweet Boy hit the ceiling if he catch me out walking past dark."

Sis Riah had already smoothed her housedress over her ample behind and was aiming it for the space Jubilee had made for her. She had a great pink rose pinned to her collar, and the scent of it floated past Jubilee.

"Who you think you fooling, Sis Riah? Sweet Boy never get mad at you," Jubilee said as she breathed in the sweet spice of the flower.

Sis Riah began rocking the swing gently to and fro by swinging her legs back and forth underneath it. Jubilee's tired back began to relax with the motion.

"Umm, umm," she said, closing her eyes. "That's nice. I always forgets to rock."

"I loves rocking," Sis Riah said. "My mama use to stop work every now and then when I was little and rock me in a old chair in the kitchen and sing me all her old-timey songs. I remembers that."

Jubilee couldn't remember her own mama ever rocking her or even holding her for that matter.

"Don't put that dark skin next to me," she use to say. "Might be catching."

And Jubilee's aunt who raised her didn't rock her own children much less the little waif her sister had abandoned to her care. Jubilee vowed to herself that her little girl would remember being rocked when she was as old as Sis Riah. Older even. She began to swing her legs in rhythm with Sis Riah's and they laughed when the peas threatened to roll out of the bowl if they didn't slow down.

Then a funny thing happened. A scene etched itself onto her mind's eye. She was on the porch of another house much nicer than this one and bigger that belonged to Sis Riah and Benny and her. The sensation of ownership permeated everything. The field behind it ran flat and even, until it was divided by a stream from a sister field. And those two fields belonged to them, too. Sis Riah sat beside her as she did now, but she was rocking a baby girl in her lap. It was Jubilee's baby, but not the one she carried now. Not her firstborn. And she was shelling peas there, too. In a swing, rocking, on the porch of this other house.

Sis Riah's voice lightly humming one of her old songs interrupted Jubilee's day dream and gently brought her back to the moment again. But everything seemed a little different because of the clarity of the vision.

And finally the vision drifted away from her and she thought it was just her imagination and the July heat. Or maybe it was the result of too much wishing. Hadn't she thought since she first met Sis Riah that this wise woman was just what she needed in her life? Just the right person to teach her how to be the kind of mother she wanted to be for this baby and the others to come. The kind of mother Sis Riah would have been if she'd had the chance. Someone who could teach her those sweet, gentle things Sis Riah's mother had taught her so long ago in the warmth and assurance of the Russell's kitchen. The rocking and singing, the hugging and talking. All the things that were so much a part of Sis Riah that they were the only way she knew how to live. She would teach Jubilee those things.

Sis Riah saw the sudden thoughtfulness on Jubilee's face.

"What you thinking about, honey?"

"Nothing much. Sis Riah, you gonna help me with the baby." It was a statement, not a question.

"Don't you know I am, sugar."

"You and Benny gonna have a beautiful child," she said to the young woman.

"Thank you, Sis Riah."

Jubilee watched her hands now as the pale peas fell from the pods into the bowl in her lap.

"I just wants her to grow up and be everything the good Lord meant her to be. I wants her to have everything she need, Sis Riah. I wants her to have some things she don't need, but take pleasure in."

"How come you so sure you having a girl, hon? Just wishing?"

Jubilee took a deep breath and breathed out the words in a sigh. "Oh, ain't necessarily wishing. Benny want a boy. He gonna be disappointed at first."

"So what make you think it ain't no boy?"

Sis Riah raised a soft, full, brown arm and leaned it against the chain that held the swing and rested her head back against it. Jubilee kept her eyes on the peas and hesitated to say anything more.

"Jubi? I say, how come you know it's a girl?"

"Well, you might not believe it, but Deedove tell me."

Sis Riah leaned forward and put both her feet on the porch floor and stopped the swing's rocking.

"When you see Deedove?" she asked.

"She send me a note to come see her yesterday evening by Quilla's littlest girl. She say Deedove have some field peas for me and some knowledge to pass on about my baby. So I go across the old bridge to see her late afternoon yesterday. I was almost dark getting home. Lord, I hates to cross that old bridge at night."

"Deedove tell you the baby gonna be a girl?"

"Yes, m'am, she did."

Sis Riah was leaning forward in the still swing.

"She say anything else?"

"Well, I wouldn't say this to nobody else, but you like my mama, Sis Riah, so I feel like I can boast a little to you. Deedove say she gonna be a specially blessed child."

"What you think she mean by that?"

"I don't know exactly. But I do know she gonna be wonderful."

Sis Riah rose from the swing and walked quietly to the other end of the porch, looking out over the late afternoon cotton fields toward the dark swamp.

"I wonder what that woman think she doing messing with your baby," she said resting against the porch post.

"She just took interest in her, Sis Riah. She even ask could she help me when my pains come on. She say she want to be there. You know she a midwife? She say the women in her family been midwifing since time begin."

"Well, she telling the truth there. Back before the war all the babies around here, white and colored, brought forth by her grandmama."

"Sure enough?"

"That the way it start out. But times change. People think different about Deedove's ways now. What you tell her?"

Sis Riah walked back over to the swing and sat down beside Jubilee in the twilight.

"Well, I tell her about how Benny and me saving, so we can pay the colored doctor in Lexington and how I'm going to the hospital up there when it come time. I tell her Dr. Kitchen ain't gonna allow her in the room with me, I know. Just him and a nurse maybe to help out, I reckon."

"What she say?"

"Something about how a hospital a place for dying not for being born. She say since the old times it always be the right of womenfolk to greet new life into the world and it be asking for trouble to give over that job to men folk, even if they is doctors. Something about what she say make me wonder is she right. But Benny and me decide to do it this a way. So I try to be nice. I don't want to hurt her feelings. Seem like she all alone, Sis Riah. Got nobody that cares for her."

"She all alone, hon, because she want to be. Many times she turn kind deeds away from her door. Them what tries to befriend her find out soon they might just as well keep on walking."

"She don't treat me like that. She always seem glad when I come to visit."

"That the very thing got me puzzled, baby."

The hot day was cooling down and a chilly breeze had begun to blow off the swamp. Jubilee's hands were still, the pea shelling forgotten. Her eyes were on the serious face next to her. She had never before seen Sis Riah lose her sunniness and it frightened her.

"Now, listen here, Jubi, what I'm gonna tell you," she said leaning closer and putting a soft, warm hand on Jubilee's arm. "You got to take caution about Deedove. People thinking her funny ways due to what happen to her long time ago. They discount her and say she crazy."

"You think she crazy, don't know what she saying?"

"No, honey. I believe she have her mind. But I think Deedove spend her whole life looking for some kinda way to get back everything been taken away from her. I think she willing to use any thing and any body to do just that. I think she know exactly what she doing. And that what worry me the most."

"You think she might hurt me or maybe the baby?"

"I don't know, honey. I don't see a connection right off. I sure don't want to scare you unnecessarily. But I get chills when I think about her living way out there by herself, right next to that old burnt up mansion all alone. And when I sees her waddling over Town Bridge on her way to render lard somewhere. She have lots of time to brood and plan."

"But she can't cast no spells on me or the baby, can she?" Jubilee said reading the concern on Sis Riah's face carefully.

"Aw, honey, I don't know. I just don't know."

Jubilee listened with all her heart. She knew the wisdom this woman had was sound and under most circumstances she would not hesitate to heed Sis Riah's advice and avoid Deedove whenever she could. But there was something about that strange old woman and that forlorn little cabin that sat off by itself in the shadow of the burnt up remains of the past. There were things far more important than the gender of her unborn child to be revealed in that place. And she knew the next time Deedove sent her word to come talk to her, she would take the risk and go.

Jubilee searched her mind for another subject to talk about and saw the package Sis Riah had put between them on the swing seat.

"What you got with you?" she said nodding her head toward the bundle and directing her own attention back down to the enameled bowl in her lap.

Sis Riah leaned back slowly in the swing again and resumed the gentle rocking.

"It ain't for you, honey. It's for your sweet, little ol' baby."

Jubilee put aside the bowl again and picked up the small neat bundle wrapped in newspaper and tied with cotton string. When she untied the bow-knot, baby gowns and embroidered jackets, caps and socks and diapers spilled out onto her lap, too small for anything to wear, it seemed. Not new but carefully mended, washed until they were stain free and ironed and folded.

"Sis Riah, where you find these?" Jubilee said.

"I been wandering all over this here country side looking for people with babies grown too big for them. They all glad to help you out."

"Oh, Sis Riah. They wonderful. Thank you so much."

"Thank your neighbors, honey," she said. "One of the good things about living in Hart County."

"You right. It is good to live here, ain't it? I wouldn't ever want to live no place else. Would you, Sis Riah?" Jubilee.

Sis Riah noticed the gathering darkness creeping from the swamp up over the cotton. She pushed herself up from the swing with a grunt and started down the steps.

"Well, I don't mind saying I done thought about it."

"Leaving Tula? How come?"

"Just to see what life be like some place else?" She looked out toward the swamp again. "Getting dark. I got to go."

"Right now?" But Jubilee looked across the fields testing the light and said, "You right. It's getting late. We'll talk some more when I see you in town tomorrow."

"Alright then. I better be hurrying on. Sure don't like to be walking on that old bridge this late." She grabbed hold of the porch post and steadied herself. "And you better stay off it all together. We don't want to be fishing you out of that muddy old water."

Jubilee was glad to hear the teasing come back into Sis Riah's voice.

"Yes m'am, I be careful."

"Fine then. Bye, hon."

"Bye, Sis Riah. Come back soon. And thank ya'll for the baby things."

"Not me, honey. Thank your neighbors."

She waved back over her shoulder as she walked down the path. When she was too far away to see anymore Jubilee could hear the singing begin again.

> "Bringing in the sheaves, Bringing in the sheaves.
> We shall come rejoicing, Bringing in the sheaves.

CHAPTER 3

DEEDOVE WAS AWAKENED in the middle of the night by the distant sound of a whimpering child. And now in the early first light of day she grunted and stumped around the one room of her cabin, her legs swollen from too much salt and the summer heat and her high blood pressure.

"Mama, you hear me?" she said to the empty room.

She listened for a minute but heard what she expected to hear from her ancestors. Nothing. Even though she often resented the mutterings and advisings of the women, the silence in her head was driving her to distraction. Sometime during her teen years the women had learned that their stony sudden silence was the only effective way of dealing with their mule-headed descendant when she was up to something they didn't approve of. But the voices she often heard lately arose from the disagreement between the women about what should be done. It certainly seemed to Deedove that something had to be done about the child, and quick.

"What else you suggest?" she said impatiently to the silent room. "You got a better idea you tell me," but nothing answered her except the scratching of crows' feet on the tin roof.

She took bottles off the shelf above the stove and carefully shook some of the contents into her hands, measuring by the weight on her palm, and then she sprinkled dried herbs and other things into the iron kettle on the wood stove. She stopped every now and then and listened briefly. She knew they were watching her, disapproving of the way she figured to use the things. But curiosity would draw them hovering somewhere about the room anyway, sniffing and whispering around and, at the same time, trying to act like they weren't the least bit curious about what she was doing. She knew they were there and pretty soon they would not be able to resist the urge to give her some kind of advice and judgement on the proceedings.

The thick curtains were drawn over the windows, and she had laid a pole across the jamb and the door. Even in this lonely place she felt the need to keep out anybody who might be nosey about what was going on inside her cabin.

"Mama, I know you here if you speaking or not," she muttered. "The baby close right now. I hear her in the night. Ain't you gonna help me?"

Deedove's hair was tied up in her kerchief and her face beaded with sweat shown in the lamplight that faded into dimness in the far corners of the room.

"I know you can hear her, too. That pitiful little whining every now and then. Wake me up two or three times every night. Can't get no sleep nor peace no how. Mama, come on now. You know you gonna help me. Looka here. What things gonna do the job? See here what I got in my kitchen? I need anything else?"

She waited a moment, her full hands held out toward the empty room. A short "humpf" stirred in the air around her, then settled back into the dimness and silence again. They didn't know any more than she did, she thought. She studied the bottles above the stove and listened; she added a few more things to the steaming kettle and waited for a kind of satisfaction to sit comfortably inside her.

Finally, after the measuring and sprinkling she brushed her hands together over the pot and turned her back on the concoction and waddled to a crude chair in the corner drawn up to a small wooden table with green and black linoleum tacked to the top.

She sat upright in the chair, not leaning back and relaxing, but waiting, not wanting to get too comfortable, so she would have to heave and push to get back up.

"You know what I'm doing I gotta do. Don't need to shut your mouth on me forever. Now, you tell me, ain't it what I'm suppose to be about? Bring back that child to ya'll?" There was a murmur in the air for a moment. Deedove hesitated and listened. "Well, I know you laying all this mess at my door, but ya'll know you was part of it too. Everyone of ya'll forever meddling in my business."

She leaned on the table and watched the steam from the kettle rise in the air and fill the room.

Presently she pushed herself up and returned to the kettle, picking up a folded up cotton rag and wrapping it around the handle and lifting the pot off the hot fire. She set it down on the back surface of the stove where it was cooler. The steam subsided, hissing back down into the pot. She stood waiting, testing the sides now and again with her hands until the contents cooled enough for her to hold both hands on the sides.

"Well, Mama, it don't matter if you and all them others goes with me or not. I's the one here right now. I's the live one and you ain't. And you know I got to get her back some how same way she went."

But she hesitated, thinking about the sacrifice that must be made. The women had never paid such a price. It ran against everything they held dear. For a moment her eyes glittered, and she thought she heard them say something to her.

"Oh, Mama," she moaned.

But nothing. She shook her head and wiped at her eyes and went on working.

Again she reached up to the bottle shelf and brought down a small empty one and carefully poured the thick liquid from the pot into it. When it was utterly full the pot was completely empty and clean as though it had been scrubbed and shined, without a trace of the former contents.

"Mama, I don't know no other way to do it. I can't help who gonna get hurt. She won't even know. This way. Ain't no other way

I can see. So. I'm going now. I'm gonna give this to the mama," she said into the empty cabin.

She slipped the bottle into an apron pocket, hobbled to the door, put on the wool field coat she wore winter or summer and, disengaging the door pole, she left, letting the cabin door bang carelessly shut behind her. And when she was too far away to hear it, the sound of murmuring and whispering disturbed the silence of the room and from very far in the distance came the trembling cry of a child making the voices hush and listen.

CHAPTER 4

LATE FRIDAY EVENING, Benny drove Mr. Luke's old tractor down between rows of cotton, spraying insecticide on the thick green plants on both sides of the row to kill the boll weevils. Usually, Mr. Luke hired a pilot this time of year to do the spraying by airplane, because the cotton plants would had gotten too high by midsummer for the tractor to do the job. But the spring had been so dry this year that the cotton was still short enough for the tractor to do it. The Montgomerys would save money by having Benny do the work this way. Benny's eyes and nose stung, and he choked on the smell of the chemicals the tractor was distributing. He had almost finished with the field by the river and was planning to spray the one across the road on Monday when the fine mist of insecticide spewed sporadically and then quit. He stopped the tractor and got down.

"Goddamn it," he said, looking back down the row to analyze the white misty pattern sprayed on the dusty leaves.

It looked like the main nozzle had stopped up. He walked back to the spraying apparatus and hit the tank hard enough to make his hand sting, cursing to himself as he thought of the time it would take to fix it. He'd be late getting home again.

He carefully disassembled the parts and found as he predicted that the rubber gasket on the spray head was badly worn and had clogged the passageway. He'd need the thing in working order first thing Monday morning. Best thing to do was drive on into town and get the replacement part before the stores closed.

The only place in Tula that might have the part Benny needed was Owen's John Deere Dealership downtown. Benny had worked hard over the years to earn a kind of respect from the merchants in Tula, but he knew that wouldn't do him a bit of good in the Owen place. There wasn't a colored man in the county that didn't dread going in there. But it was the only place north of Canton he knew about where he could get replacement parts for the old tractor.

Mr. Sam Owen was what everybody in the county called white trash because of the way he treated Negroes. Unlike other businessmen in Tula, he and his son didn't depend on colored trade to insure their prosperity. The only farmers in town that owned farm machinery were the well-to-do white men, who bought tractors and combines from the Owens. Nothing would keep the father and son from hassling the colored men that were unlucky enough to be sent to the equipment store to do the business of their white bosses.

Mr. Luke knew about the situation and most of the time he wouldn't send Benny on an errand there, but Luke was in Jackson at the cattle auction that day. If Benny didn't go get the part, his employer would know it was because he was scared of the Owens and he couldn't stand that. So late in the afternoon he drove Mr. Luke's pickup down town and parked it in front of the dealership.

The store was in a new building near the end of the main street of town. On the lot that separated the dealership from the dry cleaners, new and used farm equipment waited to be sold to the plantation owners of Hart County. He stood on the sidewalk beside the parked pickup and took a deep breath and let it out slowly with a sigh through his lips and walked through the door of the place. He passed lawn mowers and wheelbarrows and shelves full of seed and fertilizer in sacks with spare tractor parts hung up behind them. The counter at the back of the store where customers ordered or paid for the things they needed was deserted.

He took off his straw hat and suddenly became aware of how dirty his overalls were and that he smelled like insecticide and sweat from working all day in the heat and humidity. He knew that these were the kind of details that the owner would not miss. He set his teeth and his mind and determined to let any harassment they directed his way roll over him. It was a survival technique that he had learned at an early age. He stood back a foot or so from the edge of the counter. The door behind suddenly opened and Mr. Sam's son, Wynn, came in and looked at Benny.

"Well, what you want?" he said grinning at the colored man in front of him.

"I needs a replacement gasket for the sprayer on Mr. Luke's old John Deere."

Benny meant to say as little as possible. Again the door opened behind the counter and Mr. Sam came through red faced and yelling.

"What the hell you do to Mr. Putnam's lawn mower? You dumbass. You messed it up so bad he's saying I'm gonna have to buy him a new one."

Sam Owen was a short, fat man dressed in a plaid shirt straining over his abdomen and khaki work pants riding beneath his belly and sagging in the seat. Benny saw the reflection of his own body in the window behind Mr. Sam. He was taller by several inches than both men and his muscles were rock hard from the everyday physical labor of farming. But his stomach tightened and his mouth had gone dry with fear. He was disgusted at himself.

Wynn Owen leaned against the counter.

"Shoot, Daddy," he said grinning at his father's anger, "You the one said to fix it with used parts. Must not a held up, that's all."

Wynn motioned toward Benny.

"Hey, Luke Montgomery's boy wants a new gasket for the sprayer on that old tractor."

Benny felt a hot flood rise up his neck to his face behind his eyes and pound at his ears. He stood silently and looked at the counter by the old cash register.

"Well, get the damn thing for him, if you think you can do that right." Mr. Sam wrote something on a pad by the cash register. "Jesus, it's hot today."

He walked over to a cold drink box back by the catalog books and bought himself an Orange Crush. As he drank it the red started to leave his face. His eyes fell on Benny's back and his expression changed. "Whew, sure smells ripe in here."

Benny was watching Wynn look through packages of tractor parts in the front of the store. He had let down his guard, because he thought the father's anger at the son would divert attention away from him.

"Didn't smell bad 'til that nigger walked in here," Wynn said.

He had found the gasket and was sauntering back toward Benny.

"Now don't tease the boy, Wynn," the older man whined. "That nigger is Luke Montgomery's pride and joy. I imagine he's about as proud of that boy as he is that good line of bird dogs he raises out at the old Gage Place. Luke always did take pride in raising a good line of dogs. Once he gets him a good bitch and a stud he breeds them, so they'll get him a new generation of good dogs. Now you take this here nigger. Luke Montgomery just carrying out his daddy's habit of breeding a good line of boys for the next generation of Montgomerys. You seen that yella girl of Benny's lately?"

Wynn grinned. His father continued.

"That belly on her? See, it's working. And it's a smart thing on Luke's part, too. Once you get a quiet, respectful bird dog that'll find the birds the way he's suppose to and won't give you no trouble like shitting in your house or wanting to sleep in your bed when you ain't home, well, you want to use that bird dog as a stud. This here's just another one of Luke Montgomery's bird dogs."

Wynn was laughing and writing out a charge on a book that he'd taken from below the counter. Benny gritted his teeth. An image of himself as a little boy came into his mind. He was looking up at his daddy's face that was filled with pride for his bright, young son, the boy he believed would someday make him proud beyond his sweetest dreams. The son who would someday let him down, let them all down.

Benny took the gasket from Wynn's hand. With his teeth locked shut he walked out of the store leaving the sounds of mirth behind him. When he reached the street he could barely breathe. He stood still for a minute, trying to make the anger pass over. He knew the way it was with these men. Mr. Luke said it was fear or ignorance that made people say things like that. But the thing they had said.

He shook his head to get the idea out of it. He had to let it roll over him. Couldn't pay attention to it or he wouldn't be able to live. They were wrong, what they said. His life was his and nobody else's. He didn't belong to Luke Montgomery or any body else. He was a free man.

Oh, there were differences all right. He knew that well enough. He thought about how Mr. Luke talked to him, standing out by the pickup leaning against the tailgate. He had never set his foot inside the big two story white house the younger Montgomerys lived in. And Mr. Luke had always called him Benny. But he knew since he was a boy that he better not ever forget and call his boss, Luke. He didn't even like to think about it.

He pushed his breath through his nose and tightened his lips. That was just the way things were. His father had tried to challenge it, the old ways of thinking, for his boy's sake, believing this unusually smart son would prove them all wrong once and for all. But as things finally turned out it didn't do any good. And Benny thought it had destroyed everything he counted on as a boy.

The anger moved within him. He thought of the time he had found out about the woman his daddy had in town that his mama didn't know anything about. It was on a Saturday night when his mama was at home sick in bed and he had ridden to town on a mule the way he liked to do, because he was almost a man. He was surprised to see his daddy in town standing with his back to the street out in front of the colored juke joint talking to a woman in a dress that was the color and texture of crepe myrtle.

"Daddy?" he had called and his daddy had turned toward him quick and solemn and after a minute laughed and motioned to him to come there.

"Benny, Jr.?" he said, smelling of whiskey with his arm draped over his tall son's shoulder. "This your brother, Little Man."

He was dumb struck. He looked down at the little boy who was holding on to the legs of the woman who smelled like the toiletry counter at the Variety Store.

Why had his daddy done that? Introduced him to that woman and her child. Why hadn't he just kept his little secret to himself? His daddy said it was his way of showing Benny how to survive in this place. But he thought it was a meanness in him, and it had changed his love for the old man from that day on.

CHAPTER 5

"HOWDY, MR. BENNY."

He jerked his head toward the voice and discovered he had almost run into a young woman who was standing right in front of him. He turned his eyes quickly toward the street for a moment and struggled to regain his calm. The town was almost deserted except for two women coming out of Dr. Ingram's office across the street, fussing over a crying baby.

"Mr. Benny?" she said again.

"Evening," he said and touched the brim of his hat and stepped toward the curb and out of her way.

Instead of walking on down the street she stood looking at him with a kind of smile on her face.

"What you doing down town this late, Mr. Benny? It's past five thirty."

She tilted her head to the side. Benny recognized who it was. Her hair was done up in a new kind of style like she had just come from Mae Brown's Beauty Parlor and she had on a blue dress that looked store-bought and patent leather shoes with high heels.

Nan Hawkins worked at the dry cleaners instead of picking cotton in the fields or cleaning somebody's house like the other women, and she always made Benny feel uncomfortable on the few occasions he had a reason to say something to her.

"What?" he asked.

"What you doing, Mr. Benny?"

"Oh, uh, . . . I come in to get a part for Mr. Luke's tractor." There was a pause. She just stood there in front of him with her hand on her hip and her eyes right on him waiting.

"The gasket on the spray nozzle stopped up the main hose," he explained. "I had to get another one before Monday."

He thought immediately that it was a dumb thing to say. What did she know or care about the gasket on a main hose? It was the kind of thing he'd say to a man. But she acted like she was listening.

"Mr. Luke depend on you, don't he, Mr. Benny?"

"Yes, ma'm. I reckon he do."

"Sometimes folks talking in the cleaners say you smarter than Mr. Luke. Say you ought to be the boss instead of him."

"I don't never think about nothing like that, Miss Nan." Then he added quickly, "Well, I gotta go. My supper be waiting."

She was smiling, sassy and impudent, looking up at him. He could feel a nervousness begin to agitate his middle where the anger had just been. Every time he breathed he could smell fresh laundry soap and some kind of perfume. He remembered the chemical odor and the sweat on him and he stepped back from her and shot his eyes sideways.

"Miz Jubilee had her baby yet?" she was asking.

"Uh, nawh. She not due for a few more weeks," he answered. There was another uncomfortable pause.

Then she said, "Miz Sis Riah come by the shop with some baby clothes wanting to know the best way to get out some stains. She say they for your baby."

"Oh, that's nice. I know we be proud to get them."

Benny felt more agitated by the minute standing on the sidewalk talking to this young woman. Nan Hawkins was not like any other women in Tula. She didn't need a man. Had her own money. Knew how to do stuff in the dry cleaners, run that big equipment even Miz Maude Jones didn't know about.

"I ain't never talked to Miz Jubilee, but I reckon she a pretty special woman," she was saying.

"Why you say that?" he asked, surprised.

"Well, ain't many women around here that's gonna have a baby got a husband, especially one nice as you, Mr. Benny."

"I'll tell her you say that."

"I meant to say it for you, too. Made me start to wondering just what kind of man you is, Mr. Benny."

She wasn't smiling now, just looking at him steadily. Benny didn't know exactly what to say. She saw his nervousness and looked away from him down toward the railroad.

"Well, I'm headed down for a cat fish special at Grapes Camp. You ever eat they catfish there?" she asked.

He had never been into the colored cafe across the river with money so tight for the two of them. Once when he and Jubilee first started going out, he had taken her on her birthday to the colored side of the truck stop on the highway and bought her a fried chicken supper with rice and gravy. They both decided Jubilee's own fried chicken could beat the chicken at the truck stop any day, so they decided not to waste their money on it any more. But suddenly, he wished he could go to Grapes Camp and buy himself whatever he wanted to eat there. Just sit down and order what he wanted.

By now Jubilee would have his supper ready for him on the little wooden table and Mr. Luke would already be home from Jackson wondering where his colored boy was with the pickup. But he was almost overwhelmed with a desire to forget all that right now and just be free to go down to the cafe with a woman who didn't need anything from him. He could feel something inside him want to cut loose and not care about how things looked. It was a crazy kind of thing and it scared him.

"No. I ain't never had any of they catfish. Uh, I gotta go. I's already late getting home. 'Scuse me, Miss Nan."

"Mr. Benny, you mighty lucky got supper waiting on you. I

always has to go buy mine. But sometimes I wish I could just set down at night across the table from my own husband and children. Yes sir. Jubilee a lucky woman," she said.

"Yes, ma'm. Good evening," Benny said and nodded at her and put his hat on.

And Nan smiled and nodded back and headed on down the street toward the railroad. He watched her walk away, making a swishing sound with the smooth, silky material in the dress and clicking the high heels of the shoes against the sidewalk and carrying the perfume smell along with her.

He climbed into the truck and stuck the key in the ignition. He looked back through the glass of the equipment store and noticed Wynn Owen watching him. He was laughing and pointing at him and Benny looked away quickly and pulled out into the street.

He drove the pickup out of town and headed north back up Highway 51 toward Luke Montgomery's house. His insides were churning and he didn't know exactly why. Maybe it was because Wynn Owen had seen him talking like that to Nan Hawkins. She had a reputation in town even among the whites. Some folks said she had a lover in Jackson that was a white man. He could believe it. She must walk past Owen's farm equipment place everyday. Bet Wynn wished he had him some of her. But his daddy probably wouldn't allow anything like that.

That look on the man's face. Like he was saying, "I know what you thinking, colored boy." It wasn't that she was pretty made him think that. But she always caught your eye. It was the way she held her head when she walked or just stood around talking. She walked down the street like it belonged to her and like she didn't have to be nice to nobody she didn't want to. Like she was saying, "Ain't nobody here good enough for me, white or colored." He smiled to himself. He was glad she looked like that.

He pulled up the Montgomery driveway and left the truck parked in the large equipment garage beside the cattle truck Mr. Luke had taken to Jackson and walked on home in the moonlight to Jubilee and his supper late again.

CHAPTER 6

THE CABIN HAD a warm peace to it when he walked in the door. The smell of food cooked and ready to be eaten, the cabin floor scrubbed clean with lye and water, things as they always were when he came home at night. His mother's painted sugar bowl on the little table, the two chairs pulled up for them to eat supper, everything in its accustomed place. A sense of neatness, appropriateness about things.

He stood in the front room for a minute, letting the effect of it comfort him, till he wondered why he had been so upset in town. What they said, Sam and Wynn Owen, it didn't change a thing. In this place, in Hart County, Mississippi, white people needed coloreds and colored people needed whites and that was really what ran things. The part he played here in Tula, it was solid. He had always known what it was. Could count on it always being the same. Count on Mr. Luke always treating him the same way.

And at night when he left work and came home here to this cabin, to Jubilee? He could count on the way a man and his wife treated one another, everything unspoken, quietly assumed, dictated by this place.

Everybody in Tula understood. That was the key that made things work in the little town. Well, he thought, except for Nan Hawkins. She didn't seem to have the vaguest idea about what her place ought to be. How did you figure a woman like that living around here? With her red fingernails and her shiny lipstick. Right here in the middle of the Mississippi Delta. Right here in Tula. Hell, she grew up just like he had in Hart County, but somehow she never learned the rules that told everybody else how to live. Would most likely be surprised if somebody were to point out to her the way she was *suppose* to act. What colored women in Tula were *suppose* to do. She'd just draw back those big full lips of hers and bare those great strong, white teeth in a disrespectful grin. Clean white ladies' houses? she'd say looking in mock wonder over the lace collar of her bought dress. What you talking about? Yeah. That's what she'd do and not care who got upset or thought she was disrespectful. Maybe you could explain women like her in Chicago or Detroit, or even Atlanta. Maybe. But here in the deep south, in Tula?

When Jubilee called to Benny from the back room it interrupted what he was thinking.

"Benny? That you?" She appeared in the doorway, smiling. "What you so quiet about?"

A wave of guilt passed over him and he didn't know why. But before he could think about it she said, "Come on. I got something to show you," and caught his hand and pulled him toward the back room.

"What you want," he said, resisting her lightheartedness with a frown.

"Wait 'til you see what Sis Riah brought us this afternoon. Look."

She carried the small pile of clothes up to the lamp, so Benny would see how nice they were and admire the embroidery on the little jackets.

"Sis Riah went 'round gathering them up from folks all over the countryside. Look, hon. Just like new."

And he felt some sweetness begin to creep into his chest and it scared him so much he trembled. He mustn't think of the baby too much. Mustn't put too much hope onto such a tiny thing. Mustn't let it count for anything at all.

He turned away from her and walked back into the front room, leaving her alone holding up the little bundle of clothes for no one to admire but herself.

And the other fear began to whisper to his gut, the other thing that scared him for no reason he could put into words and he called back to her, "I'm glad to see you not hanging 'round Deedove no more. You ain't been back there, has you?"

"No, Benny. I just been to work and right here." she said following after him into the front room. He was standing silently again with his hands hooked in his pockets.

"Benny?" she said quietly. "What's the matter?"

"Nothing," he said.

"Then how come you ain't looking at what Sis Riah done brought us? Our little girl gonna look mighty cute in these things. Looka here."

"Girl? How come you all time saying 'girl'?"

His voice was angry; he didn't want it to be, but something inside him kept coloring it like that.

"Something happen today upset you?" she was asking.

"Nawh. I just wants to know why you so dead set you having a girl."

"Women just knows things like that, Benny. You know. It's woman's knowing," she said.

Jubilee put the clothes down silently and went to the stove to dish up the peas. Benny noted the way she held her head and he cursed himself for taking away her smiling. Worse thing anybody could do to somebody. He walked out to the back and she heard him dip water out of the rain barrel into the basin and wash his face and hands. No matter how hard it was, she wanted to make him talk to her.

"Why you so late getting home again? Mr. Luke done come by here asking for the pickup," she called to him.

"Had to go get a tractor part," he called back.

"You go by Owens' to get it?"

He paused a moment. He knew what she was thinking.

"Yeah," he called back finally.

"Oh," she said softly to herself, "that what wrong with you."

"Nawh, it ain't," he said, returning, wiping his hands. "That trash don't bother me none."

Saying it out loud to her like that made the strength he had found when he entered the cabin seem hollow, and the bitterness the Owens had heaped upon him began to rise again inside his chest. But he pressed and pushed until it passed over him.

"Sis Riah bring the things by this afternoon?" he asked.

He was going to be better now. She would be able to hear it in his voice. Not quite soft yet, but on the way. Jubilee would breathe deep again. Not have to be so careful with him.

"Yeah, we drink tea on the porch and sit and talk about the baby. It was real nice talking to Sis Riah like that. She visit after little Anise come on up riding that new horse Mr. Luke got. Seem like a good horse, but if he ask me, I say it be too much for a child six years old to ride all by herself. She be here visiting for a while, then ride on back home. That child a real power to herself, Benny. Not the least bit timid about anything. I hope our little girl be just like that."

As soon as she said it, she caught herself, closed her eyes tight, and then looked up at him with worry hanging all over her face.

"There you goes again. Now you for sure gonna tell me. Where you gets that idea from? It better not have anything to do with Deedove."

She set his supper of cornbread and peas on the table.

"Oh, Benny, ain't nothing. No need in worrying. Come on now and eat your supper before it get cold."

But he stood stock still, while she took off her apron and sat down in the chair opposite him.

"Now, I'm just wondering what all the mystery about," he said watching her.

"I done already told you all they is."

"You ain't been to that old witch's place again, is you?"

"Benny, now don't get mad."

He leaned toward her and put his hands on the table.

"What?" he barked.

"I ain't been back, Benny. It was the other evening when I was late getting home with these here field peas. That's the day she tell me. I ain't been back since then."

"These here peas?" he yelled. She nodded and he swung his arm across the table and the bowl bounced and rolled across the floor scattering the peas as it went.

"What she tell you, Jubilee?"

"Benny, you worried for nothing." She looked straight at him.

"What Deedove tell you about my baby?" His voice was angry now.

"She say something real nice about her. She say she gonna be a special blessed child."

"What the hell that suppose to mean?" He shoved the back of the chair up to the table. Jubilee stood up and looked at him squarely in the eyes.

"I don't know. But make me feel proud to think of it, Benny. I wants to tell you about it right away, but I know you'd just . . . "

He pointed his finger at her and yelled, "Jubilee, you listen to me."

"Benny, please don't be mad," she said walking around the table and putting her arms around him.

He pushed her away from him. "You ain't got the least idea what that ugly old hag up to."

"Then tell me. You gotta tell me. Cause I can't find no reason to stop befriending her. She always been real nice to me. I feels sorry for her, Benny. She don't seem to have no friends, because folks is scared of her."

"You got any idea what she is? You ask Sis Riah about her? She gonna tell you just like me. Now I'm forbidding you, Jubilee. You understand?"

"Oh, please, Benny. Don't say that. I needs to see her. She all alone."

"You coming up against me then? That the way it gonna be. Over that hexing old thing?"

Benny was shouting now and she finally shook her head and looked down at the table. He saw sadness leaning hard on her and he hated himself for causing it to be there. If he tried to explain about Deedove, about what he had seen as a little boy, and afterwards about the questions the white men from the church had come around asking. Were there any other coloreds that had befriended her, that might be involved somehow in her business? No, they said. But still there had been suspicions and women questioned at night even with their men folk home. Questioned and accused. If he tried to explain to her now why they had all turned their heads in caution and left her alone, she would know he was afraid. Then how could she ever respect him again? How could she ever trust him to take care of her?

"I'm sorry for upsetting you, hon," he heard her say softly as she tried to retrieve the unspilled peas in the bowl and place them back on the table. Her effort and the apology embarrassed him.

"Ask Sis Riah. She gonna tell you about Deedove. Ask Sis Riah tomorrow," he said and he sat down at the table and thrust a spoon into the peas. Jubilee sat down across from him with glistening eyes and watched as he ate joylessly. When he finished he got up and said, "Good supper."

He walked out onto the cabin porch and stayed until after Jubilee cleaned up and went to bed.

CHAPTER 7

EARLY SATURDAY MORNING Benny hitched their feisty, little, brown mule to the wagon and he and Jubilee rode into town while it was still a little bit cool. Benny's spirits seemed better today and he didn't mention Deedove on the ride in. The vacant lot between Worthey Brothers General Store and the railroad was almost empty when Benny pulled his wagon up into it and easily found a place at the back near the depot where it was shady. He got down onto the reddish-brown dust and gravel and unharnessed the mule and tied him in the shade under one of the old pecan trees. The lot would soon fill up with wagonloads of scrubbed and starched children excited to get out and join others playing along the railroad in the sunburned sand or over in the shade of the two-story, wood-framed building that was the store.

Benny helped Jubilee down from the wagon, holding her to him for a moment, allowing himself to feel the sweetness of her. When he let her go, she smiled up at him and while he watered the mule she walked around a bit stretching her legs and pressing her hands to her back to ease the tightness there until he helped her back up again. Jubilee stood now in the back of the wagon watching for Sis Riah and Sweet Boy.

She was wearing a pink and white seersucker oversized dress

that she had borrowed from Sis Riah. She looked pretty and Benny felt proud of her. The lot was filling quickly when he left it to go collect their week's pay from Mr. Luke. Jubilee started setting up her wagon for the tea party that she and her friend had planned.

A smartly dressed, young, colored woman came to the edge of the lot and stood for a moment, surveying the rapidly growing din of activity. Women nursed or changed the diapers on fat legged babies, children teased and hollered in glee to each other, mules waited patiently, swatting their long coarse tails at flies. The young woman caught sight of what she had come there to see, a graceful figure in a striped oversized dress standing up in a wagon-bed looking out over the crowd with a slight brown hand held up to her eyes. She stood watching Jubilee for a moment across the clamor. Finally, she stepped off the sidewalk and began weaving her way through the gathering press of people back toward the wagon, her high heels picking up a thin coat of the red dust.

Jubilee was spreading an old quilt out onto the wagon bed to sit on when she noticed Nan Hawkins standing at the end of the wagon smiling at her.

"Howdy. Warm day, ain't it?" the visitor said.

"Sure gonna be," she answered smiling and smoothing out the corners of the quilt.

"Your name Jubilee, ain't it?" Nan asked, smiling back at her.

The young woman in the wagon noticed the silky, blue flowered dress Nan was wearing and she ran her hand down the sides of the seersucker stripes of her own dress.

"That's right," she answered, then added, "You Nan Hawkins work at the dry cleaners, ain't you?"

Nan leaned her arms against the boards and watched Jubilee.

"That's right. I hear about you gonna have a baby. Miz Sis Riah come by asking me about the best way to get stains out of baby clothes. She say they's for you."

Jubilee had planned to get everything ready for the tea party before Sis Riah arrived and she hesitated now at the interruption. Finally, she sat down awkwardly on the wagon sideboard.

"I seen you lotsa Saturdays in town, but I guess we ain't never really met," Nan said.

"I heard about you too," Jubilee said smiling.

"Oh? What folks say about me?"

"They always saying how you real smart. Say you knows all they is to know about dry cleaning. How you could probably run Miz Maude's shop all by yourself with out no help from nobody."

Nan's smile grew broader.

"That what they say, huh? What they mean is, I ain't got no need of white folks or men folks. Ain't that right?"

"I reckon that is what they mean."

Nan noticed Jubilee glance toward the entrance of the lot.

"You expecting somebody?"

"Oh, just Sis Riah. We always tries to meet here on Saturday."

Nan turned her head quickly and saw that Sis Riah was nowhere in sight.

"You mighty smart not to need nobody to help you out," Jubilee said watching the wagons entering the lot.

"Smart?" Nan said.

"You know. Able to make a good living for yourself."

"But you is, too. You making your own money working out at Miz Mary Alice's. You don't need nobody."

"Well, ain't like that exactly."

"What it like then? You working, but Mr. Benny collecting your pay?"

Jubilee felt uncomfortable talking about such personal things. Now she felt she had to explain.

"Well, but you don't understand. Benny not taking . . . "

"No need in explaining. I know what men folks like, honey. Even Mr. Benny."

Jubilee felt that she had somehow been disloyal to her husband.

"Oh, it ain't *my* pay exactly. It belong to both of us. Same as his. Benny just save me the trouble of collecting my pay from Mr. Luke."

"Now that must be the reason I ain't found me no husband yet. Cause I sure wouldn't put up with no man treating my pay like it was his."

Nan saw the worry in Jubilee's face change to a smile.

"There Sis Riah and Sweet Boy," she said waving and calling to them.

"Then I better be going."

"Wait, Miss Nan. I think I give you the wrong idea. Benny the best husband in the world. Sweet Boy, going yonder, be about the only man I know good as Benny Horne."

Nan looked up at the young face and the sweetly rounded belly, promising so much.

"You ain't give me no wrong idea. I know what I know. Maybe we talk again sometime." Nan turned toward the lot.

"Don't go yet, Miss Nan. You welcome to have some tea and . . . "

But Nan had already started back, looking out of place among the frolicking children and flour sack dresses. She nodded to Sis Riah as she brushed passed her and continued on her way through the crowd. Jubilee watched her friend make her way to the wagon.

"Morning, hon," Sis Riah said a little breathless. "What you suppose that woman doing hanging around the wagon lot on a Saturday morning?"

"I don't know exactly. I think she just passing the time. She really something else, ain't she, Sis Riah?" Jubilee said watching the retreating figure as she helped the elderly woman climb clumsily into the wagon.

"She's a woman got no comfort in her life and that can be dangerous," Sis Riah said, giving Jubilee a hug.

"Why you and Sweet Boy so late getting in? You have some trouble?"

"Well, not really. Just took a little time to gather up a few eggs to sell to Mr. Pope. Darn things scattered all over the yard. Chickens got out yesterday. Hateful things messed all over my front porch last night. Scratch up some of my best daliahs. Yard's just a mess. I has to stop and clean my porch off before the sun dry that stuff up into glue. Well, don't matter now. I's here and I's ready for tea and cake in the shade. Lord, was it hot in that wagon. You come down early?" Sis Riah began to settle herself down on the quilt.

"Just about the first wagon in the lot. I got tea and cake for us. Set over here in the shade, Sis Riah. How the chickens get out, anyhow?"

"Through a hole Sweet Boy's new, spotted, coon dog dig under the coop," Sis Riah said. "You gonna tell me what that polished up female bending your ear about? Better do it quick, else I'm gonna die from curiosity."

"Well, I don't know any more than you."

"Funny, she come all the way through a bunch of yelling chillun to talk to you about nothing in particular. Wonder what she up to."

Jubilee got out the lemon cake and a bottle of tea and served some up for Sis Riah and herself.

"I wondered the same thing myself, but I can't think of a thing. It sure ain't wanting my business. I don't reckon Benny or me ever gonna have a thing need dry cleaning."

"Good cake, Jubie."

"Thank you. It's your recipe."

"Then that must be the reason," she teased.

"Sis Riah, I needs to talk serious to you about something."

"Uh, oh. You think you might be gonna have a baby?"

Jubilee laughed out loud.

Sis Riah said, "Shoot away, hon."

"Well, you know I puts a lot a store in what you thinks."

"Shows good sense in you. And you pretty too."

Jubilee's face got serious.

"I wants to talk some more about Deedove."

Sis Riah's sighed and shook her head.

"Ain't no need in clouding up a nice Saturday with that old dark storm, baby."

"I guess I needs to know just how come you done taken such a dislike to her. Ain't like you, Sis Riah. I seen you around folks that nobody can stand the sight of. But you always nice and kind to them anyway. How come you be so down on a old woman like that?"

Sis Riah frowned.

"Please, don't mishear me," Jubilee continued. "I ain't correcting you, Sis Riah. Lord knows. But I needs to understand why."

"It's a long story, hon. You sure you wants to get into it right now?"

"It something done come between me and Benny, so I has to hear it soon as I can."

"Well, gimme some more of that tea before I starts. Seem like just talking about it make the day heavy."

"Here. Take some more tea cake, too."

"Thank you, hon."

Jubilee sat down beside her and watched the small twists and wrinkles of her face and eyes as Sis Riah began the story.

"You know about the mama and grandmama and great grandmama of Deedove?"

"They was midwives?"

"Well, more than that. Everybody say they have special powers. In the slave days, all the women before Deedove knows how to deal in potions that has the power to cause folks to fall in love or lose something they takes value in or they enemies gonna turn up sick or maybe even dead sometime. You know, them kinda things."

"Ever since I first come to Tula, I hear about how Deedove a voodoo or conjure. Something like that."

"Yeah, that's what folks believe. White folks as well as coloreds. Sometime during all them years between then and now whenever bad luck come to folks they begun to say it was because of the women that was practicing the conjure. Was a lot of talk about it. Still is some time. That Deedove's kin the ones brought on all the sickness or ruined crops or such like. They was times in the past they come to deal harshly with the women because of it. Sometime they beats them. Sometime even worse. Some women ain't even kin to the conjure women, maybe just a friend, found to be drowned or burnt up, all cause they suspected of conjuring too."

"That why folks stay away from Deedove? Cause they scared of being taken for one of the conjure?"

"At first that was it, for sure. And I has to tell you. The whole thing with that bunch scare me. It ain't the power the women got alone. It have to do with what happen to Deedove twenty years ago."

"What happen to her so terrible?"

"You ain't never heard? Well, I ain't surprised. Folks shy off talking about it."

"How come?"

"Shamed of they fear. Or scared just the mention of it gonna bring evil down on them somehow."

"What happened to her, Sis Riah?"

"Well, some folks around here still believe the devil give power to the conjure. And Deedove the only daughter of that line left. Church folks been saying it was bad for Christians to have anything to do with the women. The word was that babies brought into the world in the hands of a conjure midwife got a curse on them and folks begun to turn aside from the children brought forth in that way."

"I heard stories about babies that Deedove deliver being marked," Jubilee said.

"It's the truth. Webbed hands or feet. Birthmarks, harelip and such. Some of them cursed, die young by drowning or fire. Signs of the devil. White folks begun to say Deedove bringing all this to pass. Colored women gets in bad with the ladies they works for if they hear Deedove done help with they birthing. So Saphronia start midwifing to take Deedove's place. But she ain't near about as good as Deedove is at it. Lot of babies and mamas don't make it before her, and folks put that down as Deedove's work, too. Cause she jealous. So all the women having babies be scared to even speak to her or look like they knowing her."

"That why Benny so hard headed about me going to Lexington to have our baby?"

"I imagine so."

"Was it true, Sis Riah? Did Deedove really cause them things?"

"Who know the truth except Deedove herself?"

"Do you believe it's the truth?"

"I believe Deedove possess power of some kind."

"How come you think that?"

"Well, when Deedove was young and didn't hide it, everybody knew she could see. You know?"

"It's the truth. She done told me things that come to pass," Jubilee said. "She always been alone like she is now?"

"When she young, Deedove have friends. Later on she be more and more alone as the powers come on her. And then when she too old for such stuff, Deedove shock everybody by coming to be with child."

"Deedove have a baby?"

"Uh huh. And don't you know they's some talk about who the daddy be. Cause long as anybody know anything, she ain't messing around with no man whatsoever. And, of course, Deedove ain't telling nobody about it. She just walking around town with her belly getting bigger and bigger."

"If Deedove have a child where it be now that she need comfort?"

"Don't nobody know for sure, but I reckon it dead."

"Dead?"

"Beat out of her, honey."

"Oh, Sis Riah. How come?"

"Well, like I'm telling you, just about everybody believe she and her line the handmaidens of Satan. So when a white preacher's wife have a badly misshapen child, the people in the church turn on Deedove as the cause of it. And she don't work regular for no white family, so ain't nobody with some say gonna be there to take her side."

"Somebody beat her?"

"White men from the church about twenty years ago. Now you want to know what worries me about all this?"

"Tell me."

"I guess I'm scared somebody gonna mistake you for a conjure. Or something gonna happen to your baby. That's why Benny worried, too."

Jubilee sat silent for a moment.

"Sis Riah, what would happen if I was a conjure? Do her power come from Satan?"

"For a long, long time the power of the conjure and they work was loved and sacred things among us. But Christians say it ain't to be held in no kinda respect by nobody. Everybody scared to take a chance on it anyway."

"What you believes in, Sis Riah?"

"I guess I believes in both of them. I ain't found no reason why both of them, Christians and conjures, can't get along together in this world."

"Then why you scared of me visiting Deedove?"

"Well, I ain't sure what she up to. I don't believe Deedove thinking right no more. She done gone into her house twenty years ago and closed the door to everybody."

"Except me."

"Except you."

There was a long silent spell as the two women finished their tea.

"You think she'd do anything to my baby, Sis Riah? To replace her lost one?"

"Strange idea, ain't it? But it make enough sense to scare me. I just think you need to let somebody else do the befriending right now. Stay away from her until the baby come."

"Thank you for telling me about it, Sis Riah. I knows better now how come Benny so deaf on the subject."

"Ain't nothing to disregard, honey. Hear what I'm saying?"

"I hears."

"Good. Job done." Sis Riah said, clapping both hands on her thighs. She glanced out around the wagon and noticed the crowd had begun to thin out and wander on into town.

"Thank you, Sis Riah."

"Sure enough. Lord, day's getting away from us. I gotta get on out of here. Come on, honey, let's walk around some. See what's in town. Almost good as a picture show. On the way in I sees Miss Minnie Pierce and Miss Lee Daniels out in Miss Lee's old Plymouth and they's just tootin' through town. You oughta seen the folks running up onto the sidewalk out of they way. That white woman drive a car like a blind man behind a runaway mule."

Jubilee giggled. "You go on ahead, Sis Riah. I got some errands. I come find you when I's through."

"Then I see about you later," she said, smiling and grunting as she climbed down from the wagon.

Before Sis Riah could get to the sidewalk three or four women

HOME BY DARK | |71|

had stopped her to talk. And although she couldn't hear their conversations, Jubilee knew they were probably asking her for advice or thanking her for the last bit she gave them.

"She just the kinda woman I wants to be someday," Jubilee said to herself. Sis Riah turned and waved at her and she returned the wave just as her friend disappeared around the front of the store.

CHAPTER 8

SATURDAYS IN DOWNTOWN Tula, Mississippi in the summer of 1949 were alive with people polished by the humid air and smelling of Evening in Paris perfume and Lover's Moon hair pomade, dressed in recently mended, starched stiff, ironed-to-a-patina shirts, overalls, and flowered feed-sack dresses and, occasionally, a light, linen suit and a Panama hat or a rayon dress with nylon stockings. The latter were worn by those few people that had managed to get themselves away from the swamps, the cotton fields, and other small towns like Tula to travel to the north and come back later to the Delta wearing the latest styles from Detroit and Chicago. They learned to talk funny and they bragged about the wealth up there in those distant cities that was just waiting for colored hands to grab hold of it. But often times those that left and came back to boast would extend their visit home and finally just stay and then find themselves having to think up a million answers to the question, "When you going back?"

The wooden side walks in front of the stores, Worthey Brothers General Store, Cook's Dry Goods, Pope's Grocery, were filled with the noisy, jostling people. children in clean shorts or pinafores sucked candy and carried small, half full, brown paper bags full of more candy; BB Bats, Hershey Bells, Orange Slices, and Jaw

Breakers. When old grannies stopped to look down at them and ask, "Well, hi you, Hon?" they ducked their braided, ribboned heads and stuck sticky fingers in their mouths and hid behind the legs of their mothers. When finally released from adult conversation they escaped and ran to find other children to play with.

Young girls with varying shades of chocolate skin clung to the posts that held up the porches in front of the stores, watching the street as they talked to each other, occasionally nudging, nodding in the direction of a young man, then giggling and putting their hands over their mouths and looking at each other and giggling again.

Old colored men sat with solemn, reddened, liquid eyes on the wooden benches in front of Worthey Brothers and Pope's. They chewed tobacco and spat into the street, talking about the crops and what hunting would be like in the fall based on the reading of signs passed on by generations of hunters before them that foretold the population of deer and squirrel in the Big Black swamp. Early spring always meant there would be more critters. Dry summer meant less.

Benny opened the screen door into Worthey Brothers. The smell of pieced goods, flour in printed sacks, crackers, hoop cheese, rubber work-boots, leather mule-harnesses, gun oil, soap powder, coal oil, croaker sacks full of potatoes, horse feed, and the mingling of freshly bathed and powdered bodies drifted around and through him. He saw Mr. Luke sitting at the heavy old desk in front of the safe in the back. He took off his straw work hat and threaded his way through the crowd, that was standing around the candy counter at the front, all the way to the dimly lit back of the store, where saddles and harnesses hung over empty barrels, until he was standing just in front of the man he worked for.

The desk sat on the large, extended, first landing of the stairway that led to the upstairs of the store where extra merchandise was stored. The electric lamp that hung above the desk provided a pool of light to work in. Surrounded on two sides by the stair railing, Mr. Luke could look out over the store removed from the noisy crowd below. Benny stood waiting in line with the other hands that worked for Mr. Luke.

While he was standing there, Mr. Charles Wallace walked up onto the landing by the desk and began talking to Mr. Luke about wanting to raise money to build a swimming pool for the white children in town by next summer. While he talked, the line of waiting people below them stepped back respectfully until the conversation was over.

Something about the patient faces made Benny remember sitting under a catawpa tree in Mr. Matthew's backyard listening to the voices of the young Luke Montgomery and a friend coming from the tree house above him. It was the summer Benny and Luke were eleven years old and they had spent their days designing and building a house in the big tree at the back of the Montgomery lot in Tula.

Luke's voice filtered down through the broad, green leaves.

"Daddy's carrying us to the Big Black this afternoon in the pickup to go swiming. Ya'll wanta go?" Luke was saying to his friend above Benny's head.

'His friend was mad at him for building the tree house with Benny all summer instead of with him.

"I don't know if my mama will let me go anywhere with a nigger lover," Robert Harley Wilson was saying.

"I ain't no nigger lover. Why you saying that?"

"Cause you all time hanging around Benny. Every time I come over here to play, first thing we have to do is run that nigger out of here."

"That's cause Benny's the one figured out most of it."

"Hell. Anybody coulda done what he done on this house. If you hada asked me . . . "

"Oh, sure. Like that mess in your backyard you built? You going swimming with me this afternoon or not?"

"I'm going, but my mama won't let me get in the river with a nigger."

"Nobody's asking you to."

Robert's mama came to pick him up around dinnertime. She pulled up to the curb in the Ford and honked and Robert reluctantly climbed down through the hole, muttering "nigger" under his breath when he passed Benny. When he had gone, Luke called down to Benny to climb back up and help him finish the elevator they had been working on before Robert's visit interrupted them. Benny didn't move from his spot under the big old tree, but sat still there on the ground, his eyes staring at an anthill he'd been watching.

"Benny?" Luke called again and looked down at him from the hole in the floor that was the door.

Still he didn't answer.

"What's the matter with you?" Luke said.

"Nothing. I gotta go. My mama tell me to get on home when it get to be dinner time and finish up my work."

"Your mama didn't say any such a thing."

Luke waited and thought. Benny watched the ants.

"You pouting?" Luke asked finally.

"Nawh."

"Mad?"

"How come you let that boy say that kinda stuff about me?"

"What kinda stuff?"

"You know. Can't swim with a nigger and like that."

"Aw, he just mad cause I ain't let him work on the tree house."

"How come you letting me work on that house instead of him?"

"Cause you know how. He don't know nothing. He'd just mess it up. You gonna help me with this elevator or not."

Luke stuck his head through the hole and looked at Benny.

"I gotta go on home."

"That's a lie. I'm telling you right now, Benny Horne. Get on up here and help me with this."

"How come you ain't ask me to go to the river with you?"

"Don't be stupid, Benny. You know as well as me, white children and colored children can't swim together. That's the way it is."

"How come you to let your friend talk bad about me like that?"

"He don't mean nothing by it. Robert's always saying stuff like that, don't mean nothing. Just don't pay no attention to it."

Benny didn't climb back up into the tree house that day or any day ever again. He got up and walked toward his cabin at the back of the lot and didn't look back no matter how much Luke Montgomery called to him. It was the last day of that thing that some people somewhere might have called a friendship. It seemed to Benny right now that the man that sat at the raised up desk in front of him had no connection whatsoever to that boy he spent his childhood with. Luke Montgomery had changed. Benny had, too.

"You want the whole week's worth or you want me to hold some back for the doctor and the hospital?" Mr. Luke said to him when it came his turn to get paid.

Benny stood holding his hat.

"Hold back a couple of dollars, Mr. Luke, if you will."

"Want to know how it stands now?"

"Yassuh. If it ain't too much trouble."

He watched him turn back a few pages in the ledger and find the right column.

"This'll give you fifty eight dollars. That's a lot of money. Think you'll need that much?"

"Don't know exactly. I'm just saving most I can until the time come."

"I can call Dr. Kitchen's office in Lexington for you if you want and see if he can give you some kinda idea. Of course, you'll have to pay for the call."

"Yassuh. I'd sho' thank you, sir."

He counted out eight dollars into Benny's hand.

"You gonna spray the cotton in the field on the old Nance place on Monday?"

"Yassuh. I is. I done had some trouble with the sprayer again and I had to get a new gasket for the nozzle from Mr. Owen's yestiddy. I had him put the cost on the book for you."

"Sam Owen give you any trouble?"

Benny looked away and laughed nervously.

"Nawh, sir. Not much."

"Not much, huh? Damn white trash. Always got to give some kind of trouble to the nigras. I'm sorry you had to go in there, Benny."

"Yassuh."

"I guess there's always gonna be some of that kind in Hart County to bother coloreds. Best thing to do is just don't let it get to you."

"Yassuh. Thank you, Mr. Luke."

Benny turned away and walked into the dimly lit back of the store. He clenched his fists around the hat brim. Anger rose in his gut like the Big Black that threatened the crops in springtime. What did Luke Montgomery know about "just don't let it get to you"? He thought maybe he better wait back there in the back for a while, pretending to look at stuff, while he calmed down. He could see the bright sunlight outside through the opened back door that led to the railroad station and a public outhouse.

A voice came from the shadows near the back door.

"Well, here you is with that look on your face again."

"Who is it?" asked Benny, looking away from the light and trying to reaccustom his eyes to the darkness.

"It's Nan Hawkins, Mr. Benny."

The voice seemed separated from the din in the place and his nose and head filled with the smell of perfume. He began to make out her stylish dress and hair done close to her head in marcelled waves as she walked toward him from the light. He wondered how long she had been there.

"How you doing?" he said, drawing up his shoulders and turning his straw hat in his hands.

"Never better, Mr. Benny. Never better."

"What you standing back here among the saddles and feed for anyway?" he asked her.

"Studying you," she said with a little laugh. "I been watching you while you was waiting in line for your pay. You look like you fixing to chew a nail. Same kinda look you had yesterday in front of the tractor store. You don't watch out you gonna have a stroke."

"There ain't nothing to watch," Benny said roughly. He frowned and pretended to examine a plow harness hanging on a rough wooden rail nearby.

"Oh, Mr. Benny. You is wrong there," she said walking closer to him. She made a swishing noise when she moved. Benny remembered the sound his hand made on the silk nightgown of a town girl when he visited her for the first time after riding a mule all the way in for that purpose only.

"Well, I'm glad you having some fun out of me," he said to her. The girl had been broad looking like Nan, but he hadn't minded. He turned again to go.

"Wait up, Mr. Benny. You don't have to leave so fast," she said and he heard the silky whisper follow behind him. "You know what I saw?"

"Nawh, I don't."

"I see you standing up in that line of folks waiting, looking like you was thinking real hard about something. And then when it come your turn to get paid, you put on your hang-dog face. Just like you turn into somebody else."

"What you talking about?" he asked her.

"I seen that kinda thing before," she was saying. "Colored men looking different depending on who they talking to. They gotta change they face so many times it make a girl wonder who she talking to. You know, that the main difference between colored men and white men. White man got the same look no matter who he talking to."

"I ain't never noticed," he said.

"You just watch the difference sometimes when you thinking on it. You gonna see it, too. Different folks, different face. But just in men folks. Ain't so true about women."

He looked down at her and then away quickly.

"It always been like that, I reckon," she kept on. "Colored women got to watch they men folks real close. See who it is they be with at the time."

Benny looked over his shoulder at the man sitting in the pool of light, paying Quilla and her daughter, who picked cotton and hoed for him. They tied the dollar bills and change he gave them up in handkerchiefs and tucked them down the front of their dresses between skinny, hard breasts as they walked out of the store. Hippy was getting paid now. Benny studied the face of his friend. Nan watched him and laughed quietly.

"Every thing a terrible gamble for a colored man. And Mr. Luke the dealer in your poker game, Mr. Benny."

It brought him back to his senses.

"I don't know what you talking about. Mr. Luke just the man I work for."

"He the one saying what your face suppose to look like."

Nan was smiling up at him.

"You don't know nothing about me and Luke Montgomery. We go back a long ways. That man a fair man whatever else he be. Don't never try to cheat me out of nothing belonging to me."

"Except maybe your manhood," she said, laughing.

The words struck him like a hand.

"Nothing wrong with my manhood," he said. "I don't know what you talking about. Why you come back here talking to me anyhow?"

Her face tipping up toward him was broad and common like that first woman, inspite of the lip rouge and bought clothes.

"Mr. Benny, did I make you mad? You done misunderstood what I was saying. What I mean is I knows the kinda pressure you under all the time," she said. There was a change in her tone. "You just needing somebody to talk to. Get all that bad stuff out of your system."

"Nawh. I ain't needing nothing I can't get on my own."

"But this ain't the kinda thing you talks to your wife about. Or even a friend, like Mr. Hippy? I was just thinking that it might be a help to come on up the street to the cleaners sometime for a talk? I got a brand new bottle of whiskey hid under my bed and a good easy chair to go with it."

Benny looked down at the smile. He knew what she meant. The thing he couldn't understand was why this kind of woman was coming after him. There were plenty of young men in town who would give anything to be in his shoes right now. But this looking at him, it was a waste of her time.

He had worked too hard to regain some of the respectability his daddy lost when he started doing what he did. He could tell Mr. Luke had always half way expected him to do the same thing, but he'd never been unfaithful to Jubilee since they were married and he never intended to. Running around and getting drunk with his pay check on Saturday night and ending up in jail or waking up Sunday morning in a strange bed after fooling around with some woman all night that he had no business with. He knew all too well where that kind of stuff would lead him.

"I gotta be going, Miss Nan."

"Of course, it'd be just to talk. I know you wouldn't want nobody to see you coming up to my place thinking we was up to something."

She was smiling and he could see her teeth and mouth shining in the dim light. That first woman he had, in the silk night gown slid as easily into her bed as he had slid down a mud bank into the river when he was a boy. He remembered how she felt to him. He swallowed hard.

"It don't matter what idea somebody get. I do what I please," he said, roughly.

"Oowhee, you mighty mad at somebody, Mr. Benny," she said. "You sure got something burning up your insides." She turned around to go. "I gotta get on back to the cleaning shop right now. But if you wants to come by for a little talk, we could go upstairs to my sitting room."

Benny watched her stroll through the crowd laying her ringed hand with the red fingernails delicately on pieced goods and china plates as she passed on toward the front of the store into the light, speaking a greeting here and there until she was finally out the door.

For a moment he stood motionless. Then suddenly remembering himself, he looked around quickly to see if anybody had noticed him back there in the dark. He was trembling. He steadied himself on a pile of feed bags. He breathed in the familiar smells around him and for a moment took some calming from them and the sure, constant way his life was, no matter how distasteful sometimes. And finally after a little while he stood up and left the store after her.

CHAPTER 9

BENNY PROPPED HIS foot on a bench outside Worthey Bros. and rolled himself a cigarette. He headed up the wooden sidewalk smoking it. Several people greeted him as he passed and he covered up his sullenness with polite returns. He knew almost everybody in town. He had walked these same sidewalks nearly every Saturday of his life and he knew downtown Tula as well as he knew his own backyard.

He knew its history. The general merchandise store down by the lot, for instance, hadn't always been run by Edgar and Robert Worthey. Olivia Montgomery's daddy, Frank Russell, had originally built the big, two-story building, making sure its location was handy to the business that would come from the railroad and the river. He knew the small, new town that had sprung up on the banks of the Big Black was going to need a store. To run it he hired two brothers that came into town from outside of Camden with nothing but a little education and some red sand in their pockets to show for themselves. He had a hunch though that there was a lot more to the penniless Montgomery boys than most people could see.

Pretty soon, Matthew, the youngest of the two, had made enough money to buy a big piece of farm land from him down along the edge of the swamp and the older brother, Elijah, who was more of a merchant at heart, was able to buy out all his brother's interest in the store. As the town grew, Elijah eventually moved all his merchandise up the street past the bank and the post office to a newer building with glass showcase windows across the front of it. Further on up the street was the farm equipment store with the lot that separated it from the dry cleaners. After Elijah Montgomery vacated the original building the two Worthey brothers moved in and established another general merchandise store of their own.

When Olivia Russell fell in love with the youngest of the rough, business-savvy, young Montgomerys her parents were not entirely happy. Matthew had the swarthy skin and black straight hair that unquestionably whispered of Indian blood in his family tree. But his uncanny business sense and Olivia's refusal to budge off her affection finally changed their minds. After all Indians weren't Negroes. Later on Mr. Frank Russell left the building to his daughter, Olivia, who by then had married Matthew Montgomery in an elaborate formal wedding in the church her father built for the town.

Benny was in front of the post office when he heard someone call his name. He turned to see Sis Riah hurrying across the street and his bitterness faded as the smiling, bustling figure approached. She had been one of his mother's best friends, so Sis Riah felt like it was her duty to love and advise her friend's orphaned son. And Benny had enough sense not to turn down her affection or her good advice.

"Benny, I needs to talk to you, boy" she called.

"Morning, Sis Riah. Where Sweet Boy?"

"He told me he going to talk to Mr. Cook about some work he want done on his store. Putting on a porch or something," she said, smiling and stepping up onto the walk and puffing as she talked. "But I just seen Mr. Cook setting in the back of the drugstore drinking a ice cream soda. That mean Sweet Boy most probably shooting dice down along the tracks with Hattie Lee's boy, what just got back from up north, pockets just a jangling. I lets him think he gotta hide it from me. Make the game more fun for him that way. Besides last thing I wants is that boy getting in my hair all day long. It's enough I got to put up with him at home all the time."

"Sis Riah, who you trying to fool? Ain't a soul in this town don't know how thick you and Sweet Boy always been."

Sis Riah smiled. "Lord. Don't you know it's the truth," she said, momentarily letting her thinking wander off its mission.

"You needs to talk to me?"

"Oh, yeah" she said. "About Jubilee and the baby and Deedove." She glanced at the crowd milling around them.

"Come on, Benny," she said. "This ain't no place to talk. Too many ears and mouths."

She turned and headed toward the beveled glass door of the Hart County Bank. When she opened the door she glanced behind her to see Benny holding back.

"Well, come on," she said to him.

"What you doing, Sis Riah? Us folks can't go up in there."

"Course, we can," she said. "Come on. Ain't nothing in this here place gonna bite you."

Sis Riah, with her purse over her arm, glided across the cool black and white tile floor of the bank lobby toward a teller at a brass and oak framed window, followed by a reluctant Benny, who had barely enough time to stomp out his cigarette and snatch his hat from his head. He stood back as she cleared her throat audibly in front of the pink, blonde woman standing there.

"I wants to add ten dollars to my savings," she said, drawing out a bankbook and a small leather coin purse from the bag she carried. She counted out ten rolled up one-dollar bills and laid them on the counter in front of the woman. Benny stood speechless behind her.

"Why certainly, Sis Riah," the teller said and she took both the money and the book and disappeared through the door behind her. Benny saw in the back room two heavy black doors in front of a vault that was big enough to walk into.

"For God's sake, Sis Riah, what you doing?" Benny whispered.

"Putting up a little money for my old age." Sis Riah answered and turned a grin toward him over her shoulder. "What's the matter with you? Ain't you ever been in here before?"

"I thought this place just for white folks," he whispered.

"I know. Lotsa folks thinks that. I did, too. 'Til my sister, Etta, you know, the one move up to Philadelphia, sent me a letter going on and on about a lazy no-good son of hers wanting to get a loan from her because he found out something about her bank account. I figured she bragging like she always do. Sometime I don't even read everything she write, she go on and on so. That's the reason I almost didn't notice that part of the letter. About the bank. But when I did; 'Humpf,' I says to myself. 'Etta can do it, I can, too.'

"Well, I comes right on down here the very next Saturday we's in town to see what I can do about a bank account of my own. Hates to let that woman get something up on me just cause she living up north. I figure, worse they can do at the Hart County Bank is throw me out and I can stand that.

"Come to find out they's more than happy to take my money. Teller say the bank use the money folks puts into savings to loan out to other folks and then they turns around and pays you a little something for the privilege."

"They gives your money away?"

"Nawh, hon. They just puts it to work. Don't let it lay around getting lazy."

"You mean, you getting paid to save your money in here?"

"That's what I'm saying."

"How long you been doing this, Sis Riah?"

"About ten years now. I got close to twelve hundred dollars."

"What you say?"

"It's the truth."

"What you gonna do with twelve hundred dollars?"

"Well, I got me a plan. I know it ain't gonna be easy, but one of these days I'm gonna buy me a place of my own."

"You mean like a farm?"

"That's right. A farm."

"You gonna own it?"

"That's what I'm hoping. Don't matter how long it take. How

hard it be to find. One of these days me and Sweet Boy gonna leave Tula, maybe get on down somewhere around Camden, find us a little place way out in the country where we don't have to answer to nobody but ourselves. Make our own way. Gonna find us some kinda little farm with a house on it good enough to live in. Somebody need money bad enough they gonna sell to colored folks."

"Sweet Boy know you got all that money?"

"What you think?"

"How come he ain't never said nothing to me about it before?"

"Cause he don't say nothing about it to nobody. Don't wanta seem like he's boasting. You know how he is."

"A place of your own?" Benny said incredulously almost to himself.

"Look, Benny. Ain't nothing you and Jubilee can't do for yourselves. Ain't you been saving some back for her to go to the hospital when the baby come?"

"Yeah. But that just . . . "

"What you think would happen if you was to take that money you been having Mr. Luke hold back out of your pay check every week and puts it into this here bank? Be just as safe as it be with Mr. Luke. Only difference, it gonna be earning you a little extra besides."

The idea frightened him.

"But Mr. Luke always done that kinda thing for me."

"Well, you a grown man. About time you do it for yourself," she said. "You just keeps on saving the same amount you been saving. Jubilee have that baby you keeps right on saving. You be mighty surprised how soon it gonna add up."

A lightness crept into his chest.

"About how much a house and a piece of land gonna cost, Sis Riah?"

"I knows a couple living right now in Choctaw County done find theyselves a little twelve acre place with a nice stand of loblolly pines and a three room house. Eight hundred dollars. Man own it say it too far out in the country for white folks to live in. That's how come him to sell it to them. Course, I'd settle for some place not quite so big. Anything that's alright for Sweet Boy to raise a few cows, plant a little cotton."

"Eight hundred dollars lot of money to a man ain't got but fifty eight to his name."

"Well, more than most. How long it take you to save that much? Less than six months?"

"But me and Jubilee living awful hard to do it."

"That fine. You doing it for a reason. Not just hard living and nothing to show for it."

"But after the baby come, he gonna cost us something ever now and then, I know. Things gonna come up."

"So you can't save a whole lot every time, you can save something. Sometime little, sometime more. Just what you can. But every time something."

Benny studied the strength of the vault doors in the back of the bank. and he thought of something else.

"Sis Riah, how you know they gonna keep a colored man's money safe back there in that place? They gonna try to say you ain't got no money in they bank when the time come you wants it back."

"Long as I got this here bankbook, federal government gonna see my money safe. I done studied the papers I sign when I first open my account."

"If I was to do something like that how I begin saving my money here?"

"When you gets ready, hon, you just tells them. They gonna show you how. Now, Benny, enough of that. We gotta talk about Jubilee and your baby and what Deedove up to."

"I done already determined to ask you about that, Sis Riah. Deedove got her eye on Jubilee. Jubilee saying she just a lonely old woman. What you think? Reckon I needs to worry?"

"Like a mama bear worrying over a cub. I stop by the wagon a while ago and me and Jubilee talk about her."

"She listen to you?"

"I reckon. But I don't know exactly how to warn her about Deedove. It's mainly just a feeling I got. I done heard stuff and seen stuff so much, until I don't know what the real danger is anymore. I know better than to believe everything I hears about her."

"You think Deedove really knowing how to do that kinda stuff."

"If any of them ever know how to do them things, Deedove know it, too. Deedove come from conjures, Benny. Pass from daughter to daughter. Good Lord knows I appreciates what a hard thing it is to have no chillun. But Deedove a conjure woman. Barren don't just mean she lonely in her old age. Barren mean death to the line Deedove a part of. And Jubilee having a baby. Seem too much a coincidence to me."

"You tell that to Jubilee?"

"Uh huh."

The young, woman came out of the vault room and handed Sis Riah her bankbook and smiled.

"Your account is really growing, Sis Riah. What you plan to do with all that money? I certainly hope you won't spend it foolishly after saving it for so long."

"No ma'm, I won't. Thank you, ma'm." The pink woman went back to work and Sis Riah and Benny walked together across the lobby.

"What in hell do she think I gonna do with it? Buy jaw breakers?" Sis Riah hissed as she stepped down the marble steps to the sidewalk. "You gonna have to put up with some of that, Benny, if you saving your money there. Course, you gonna have the last laugh when you moves out of town onto your own place. Cause they's lotsa white people in this county ain't got that."

"I done put up with a heap more, Sis Riah. That ain't nothing."

"Don't discount it too easy. Anything pore white trash hate it's a colored man got more than they got. You has to keep your smartness hid and use it when ain't none of them watching."

"Sis Riah, I been knowing that most of my life."

"Now, what we talking about? Oh, yeah. Deedove. Well, truth is, I don't know exactly what to tell you. But I feel it in my bones we got to discourage Jubilee from spending too much time with that woman. I can't figure what Deedove thinking, but I know Jubilee gonna have a baby and that just what it is that Deedove want the most in the world. Conjure power or none, Jubilee need to keep a distance from her."

"I already done forbid her to see Deedove."

"What is it about men folk think they can forbid? Lord. Only thing you can forbid is you, Benny Horne. Right now we don't want Jubilee worrying about nothing. And that's your job. Worry the thing press her into buying whatever it is Deedove selling. Tell Jubilee you feel easy if she don't see none of Deedove until after the baby come. Tell her she do it for your sake. Then she will. Tell it to her just like I said it."

Benny stood for a while after Sis Riah left him thinking about her logic. He passed some time talking to some of the men about farming and he watched as people began to desert the sidewalks and return to wagons for dinner so little ones could take afternoon naps on quilts laid out on the bottom of wagon beds or, if necessary, in the shade of the pecan trees. He followed some of them to the edge of the lot and stood for a minute and watched Jubilee setting out the stuffed eggs and fried chicken for their noon meal. He saw the sweet clumsiness from the weight of the child as she moved about in the wagon. And the wonder of her rose from his chest to the back of his throat.

There was absolutely nothing on the earth, he thought, that he would not do, no pain he would not endure, no work he would not take on for her sake. He thought about Deedove and then about the plan of leaving this place that had been home for so long to his people. What would she say when he told her about saving, like Sweet Boy and Sis Riah had done, for a place of their own some day? There would be years of pinching and scrimping ahead. And they already had things pretty good right here and now in Tula. They'd never go wanting for food or clothes or a place to live as long as they stayed right where they were. And nobody could predict just what troubles they might come up against on a place of their own. Would she doubt that he'd be smart enough to work out whatever problems came along? As he watched her now busy in the wagon, he knew what she'd say, because she was the one who had never been afraid. The fear was in him.

He started to head down the lot when he heard Luke Montgomery call his name. He turned around to see him just coming out of Worthey Brothers.

"Benny, tractor's ready to go on Monday morning?"

"Nawh, sir. Not quite. I gotta put on the new gasket."

"That shouldn't take long. Where is the tractor now?"

"Setting down there by the railroad tracks on the Gage Place."

"When it's fixed, drive it on up to the Nance place. And try to get it on over there early while the dew's still out. Oh, tell Jubilee I'll pick her up on Monday morning and take her on in to the house."

"Yassuh. We sho' do thank ya'll for giving her a ride every day, Mr. Luke."

"Well, I'll be awful glad when that baby gets here and Jubilee can walk on up to the house in the mornings on her own again. And, Benny, I certainly hope you let her off of having another one right away."

"Yassuh, that's what we planning. Uh, Mr. Luke?"

"Yeah?"

He hesitated nervously.

"Uh, where you wants me to poison when I gets through up yonder?"

It wasn't really what he wanted to ask.

"Probably the fields by the river."

"Uh, Mr. Luke. There was something else I needed to talk to you about."

"Yeah?"

"Mr. Luke? You keep your money at the Hart County Bank?"

"Yeah, some of it."

"Is your money safe in there, you reckon?"

Luke Montgomery chuckled. "Well, sometimes banks fail, but it's safer than most places."

"Mr. Luke, did you know they let's colored people keeps they money in that bank?"

"Well, yeah, I guess so. If you can keep it that long," he said, smiling.

Benny swallowed hard. "Reckon I ought to keep Jubilee's doctor money in that bank?"

"Why you want to do that?"

There was surprise in his voice, but he didn't seem angry.

"Mr. Luke, now I don't wants you to think I don't trust you none. You always been honest with me."

"Well, I certainly never cheated a hand of mine that I know of. Do you think you can't count on me anymore to take care of your savings, Benny?"

"Oh, nawh, sir, Mr. Luke. I knows you gonna keep it safe for me."

"Then I can't see what you'd gain putting it in the bank instead of having me hold it for you."

"Mr. Luke, I hear the bank gonna pay you little something while your money stay in there."

Luke suddenly understood the logic of Benny's argument. He noted the distress on the Benny's face and he realized how hard it was for him to say these things. He wondered what his daddy would do in this situation. But he wasn't his daddy and Benny wasn't just any colored man.

"Yeah, that's right"

"Then, Mr. Luke, you think it'd be a smart thing for me to put that money in the bank?"

"Yeah, I think it would be a smart thing for you to do."

Benny smiled in relief. "Well, sir, I thinks I wants to do it that way if it be alright with you."

"Want me to help you open an account?"

"Nawh, sir. Miz Sis Riah done tell me how."

"I mighta known all this came from the likes of old Sis Riah."

"Uh, she don't mean nothing uppity by it, Mr. Luke."

"It's alright, Benny. Nobody's gonna bother Sis Riah while Mama's around."

"Yassuh."

"Well, I'll write you a check right now."

"Yassuh."

He took a black checkbook and pen out of his shirt pocket and propped his foot up on the fender of the pickup and wrote out the check and handed it to Benny. He started to warn him not to lose it before it got safely to the bank but decided it would be worse than a needless thing to say.

"Thank you, Mr. Luke."

"See you Monday morning," Luke said returning the book to his pocket.

He got into the pickup truck and Benny watched as he headed out of town. He held the check tightly in his hand. He would go right after he ate his dinner and put the money in the bank like Sis Riah had showed him. His money in his bank account waiting for the time he made the decision to use it. He hurried on to the wagon where Jubilee was waiting for him to tell her about it.

CHAPTER 10

NAN HAWKINS WATCHED the street from her upstairs window for a long time, but Benny didn't come to the cleaners that Saturday afternoon. The picture of a colored man helping his pregnant wife down from a farm wagon and then holding her to him for a fraction of a moment like she was gold was etched in Nan's mind. She sat alone in a big rocking chair holding a doll with blue eyes that opened and closed, whose faded lips and cheeks were framed by a limp organdy bonnet that matched the dress. She held the doll out in front of her.

"You the only family I got, Pearl," she said out loud. "You my only child."

She hugged the doll to her and stood up and walked to the window. She could see the stairs that went up to the apartment and the Saturday crowd on the sidewalk below. She knew the sound his feet would have made on the landing. Just like she did when she was nine years old, sitting in that same old rocking chair in front of the same window watching the sidewalk below.

It would be early in the evening and her mama would be expecting somebody to come visiting soon. A daddy, and he always made the same kind of sound on the landing, heavy and exciting, just like the sound Benny would have made.

And when they heard it, mother and daughter, only one of them didn't know the other thought a thing about it, the mama, Leota, would go to the door and answer the knocking. And there would be the sound of sugar in her voice that made the child feel warm and sweet to hear, sitting quietly, secretly listening to the daddy voice talking low to her mama in the hall.

"Gimme a kiss, Leota," he'd say.

And Leota would giggle. And the child would listen with anticipation for the wet sounds that signaled the daddy had drawn the pretty, dainty body close to his and pressed his wet mouth against the powdered cheek and colored lips. And the child shivered deliciously.

Until, finally, Leota would say, "Stop it now. You gotta wait. Nan still up."

And then the pleading of the daddy voice, "Come on, Leota. I can't wait no more. She gonna hear it sometime, anyway."

Every Saturday the daddies visited her mama walking up the stairs over the dry cleaners. They came sometime bringing her flowers for the table. Nan sat reverently in the chair before them, roses sometime, in a blue glass vase where Leota had set them on the table in front of the window.

Sometime there were presents, like Evening in Paris perfume wrapped up in colored paper and earrings with sparkling glass stones. Things like that. Presents that came begging Leota to bestow special favors on the daddies that brought them. And sometimes the daddies brought presents for Leota's daughter. That's why Nan sat in the old chair breathless with anticipation on Saturday when she knew the visitors would begin to come.

Nan inspected her hands and straightened the ring with the large yellow stone.

"Or nail polish. Sometime she get nail polish. Red," she said out loud.

She turned her hands over, palms up. Great big old things. Her mama use to tell the daddies about them, her big hands, and her head and how it was too big for the rest of her.

"I reckon she looks just like her daddy," Leota would say.

And the daddies would say, "She ain't never gonna be what you is, Leota." And then they'd laugh about it.

The first time she heard her mother say that, it nearly scared her to death. But the older she got, the gladder she was that she wasn't one bit like Leota. She couldn't remember a time in her life when that woman had thought about her enough to feed her a bite, or dress her, or give her a thing she ever wanted or needed.

And there were things she wanted real bad back then when she was little. A child, standing back in the doorway, watching her mother's pretty little fingers as she dressed up for the daddies, aching for the feel of those fingers on her face, running along her cheek, wondering what it must be like for the daddies to have those soft little arms wrapped around them, hugging them.

"But that's just when I's little," she said to herself.

She opened a drawer in the table and took out a small pink plastic comb. She untied the bonnet and began to comb at the faded golden curls of the doll.

"Mama always saying, 'Nan just like her daddy.'"

She never knew her daddy. But she always knew even if she hadn't heard Leota say it that she must be like him. She knew when she stood back behind her mama watching the reflection of both faces in the mirror of the dressing table. And she knew when she studied her own face that it was his face, not Leota's, and she was glad of it.

"Thing about my daddy I come to admire most was that he was gone. Left a long time before I was born." And she was proud of him for that.

It was different when she was little. Back then she use to dream about where her daddy might be. She thought if he knew about her, he'd come and get her for sure. Because she was just like him, dark, strong, big hands, smart because of her big head. Taking care of herself. Not needing anybody. Just like him. Just as if she were a man, too. Then the older she got, she quit caring if he came for her or not. She was simply thankful he'd left some of his strength here with her inside Leota. She quit thinking about all that a long time ago. Even before her mama died.

She figured out early on that she could not depend on Leota to get the money for them to live on. She knew she had to eat and sure as hell she needed this place to live in. So she took it on herself to do all the work Leota had been hired to do downstairs in the cleaners. All by herself. Maude Jones, who owned the cleaners then, didn't care who did it as long as it got done. Every week Nan collected the wages and hid the money where her mama couldn't find it, under her bed in an empty laundry soapbox.

Leota never got up until the middle of the afternoon when she came into the kitchen all sleepy eyed and hungry and ate whatever she could find, whatever Nan had brought home from the store. And while she ate, she yelled at the child about where she got the money to buy that stuff and was she stealing hers. And all the time Nan just stayed quiet knowing Leota would eventually get tired of yelling and go back into her bedroom and spend the rest of the daylight hours drinking and dolling up and waiting for her night visitors.

Leota paced as she waited, into the kitchen and back through the sitting room to the front hall, listening for the sound of footsteps on the landing that meant a daddy was coming up carrying a fresh bottle of moonshine or maybe some cheap wine and a dollar or two. And Nan waited too, as quietly as she could, sitting in the chair by the window. By morning he'd be gone.

That's the way things went up until the day Nan found her mama dead in the front hall. Until then the daddies came and went and most of the time Nan didn't even see them. Except of course the one time when she was sitting in the big chair listening, not knowing which of the daddies had come to Leota's door, but hearing the big hands running up and down Leota's good dress. And the child sitting quietly, hoping Leota wouldn't yell at her too soon to get on out of there and go to bed.

But this one time her mama's admirer came walking right on into the sitting room and kind of stumbled and laughed across the rag rug to the chair where Nan was sitting and knelt down in front of her. His hair was oiled back and smooth and he smelled like the toiletry counter at the variety store and like Leota did when she drank so much she fell asleep and the child couldn't wake her up. The daddy looked up at Nan sitting in the chair and he grinned a big grin.

"I got something for you, baby," he said.

He handed her a brown bag from the variety store. She didn't know what to make of it, so she just held it for a while without moving. His hands rested on her knees warm and sweaty. His eyes and his mouth were kind of wet and he leaned his big grinning face over close to hers. She pressed her head back away from him into the old chair, but the grin came closer.

"Well, open up your bag, see what I brung you," he said. So she did.

In the dark depths of the bag she saw yellow curls shining up at her and she smelled the thick, sweet smell of a bought doll.

"That you, Pearl. I never gonna forget what you smelled like."

The dress and bonnet were crisp and new. Tiny, white socks and black, shiny shoes adorned the little feet. The pink mouth turned up in a little smile. Never before had the child possessed anything like it. She didn't know what to say, so she looked up at the daddy and tried to smile. He pulled her up close to his oily head and held her next to him for a long time after she wanted him to quit.

"That's enough of that," Leota said from the doorway.

But the daddy kept on holding her and rubbing the soft skin of her face with his rough cheek and kissing her with his wet lips. And Leota's voice back behind him in the doorway getting mad.

"Hey, I say that's enough. Come on and get your loving from a grown woman."

She walked across the rug in her high heels and pulled at the daddy until he let go and got up wobbly and turned away from the child and put his big hands on the woman breasts and kissed her loud and wet on the mouth. Leota reached out and grabbed him by the belt and pulled him toward the door smiling sweetly into his face and calling back over her shoulder, "Get on to bed now, Nan. And lock your door."

And she pulled him down the hall to her bedroom laughing.

"First time you sleep with me, Pearl, I remember sniffing your blond, curly hair. It tickle my face. I couldn't believe such a thing as you was mine. I falls asleep holding on to you."

Nan rose and dropped the doll into the chair and walked quickly into the kitchen and stood at the sink filling a water glass with the contents of a bottle on the counter. She took a swallow of the dark red liquid.

"I don't know nothing that night when I goes to sleep, but I know a whole lot when I wakes up in the morning."

She was surprised at first because she thought Leota was in the bed with her. It was still dark and a hand ran slowly along her leg. It was warm and rough and it felt as though that hand loved nothing so much as the feel of her skin, and everything in the child became happy.

"I just push my scrawny little backend right up into whoever it was in my bed with me. Get as much as I can."

The room was too dark to see, but she felt the hands wrap around her bony ribs and pull her back into the chest behind her. The other hand began rubbing up the inside of her leg. She lay still, soaking up the feeling of being caressed. The hand moved slowly up the inside of her thigh until it began to stroke the little girl parts. Still she didn't understand exactly who was in the bed with her. But in the middle of what followed she pretty much figured out it was the daddy.

"First, I holler out to Mama, cause it hurt like hell. Great big old man like he was. Me just a child. Course, nobody hear me yelling except the daddy. And that just seem to egg him on."

The great big daddy hands held the child in place, so there was no way for her to squirm loose. And then in the midst of what he was doing to her, he suddenly became calm and the hurting stopped, so the child lay against the daddy, still and listening to the sound of his breathing and thinking how warm and comforting it felt to lie that close to somebody. And for the first time she felt comfort and she sucked and gnawed at the feeling like a starving dog.

And when he finally let go of the little behind he said, "You tell your mama and you gonna hurt worse'n that." And he pulled away from her and left the bed cold and lonely.

He needn't have worried that the child would tell her mother. She intended to do exactly as she was told. Not because she was afraid of what he might return and do to her. She wasn't afraid at all. She kept her mouth shut when her mama finally drug herself out of bed the next afternoon, because she was afraid Leota would hit the ceiling if she knew the child had figured out a way to get some of the daddy loving. And out of pure spite she might not let the daddy come back and fill the hungry little heart back up again. Leota never did find out. Even though the man came back time and time again to the child's bed.

Nan walked back into the sitting room with the half-full glass and picked up the old doll by the arm and stood at the window as she finished the drink.

"Didn't last long though anyhow. Just up until the morning I find Leota sprawled out all over the front hall with her head busted in. Stick of firewood beside her."

She was past ten years old by then. She wasn't scared a bit. She simply turned and walked down the wooden stairs and caught hold of the first colored person she saw passing by on a Monday morning. Deedove was on her way out to Mr. Bridgeport's place to render lard.

"I think my mama dead," she said calmly.

So Deedove climbed the stairs, the child following along behind. She opened up the door to the front hall, the child standing outside in her nightgown on the landing, waiting, sucking on her fingers, dry eyed, thinking about what was going to happen to her now. Deedove didn't say a thing, just hurried back down the steps, across the street, and walked right into the white waiting room of Dr. Ingram's office. The child stood on the landing watching her until the eave of the roof of the farm equipment store blocked off her view. And still she stood, frozen there on the top landing, thinking and worrying about what would happen now.

"I remember the face of that old white doctor, red and full with big old jowls. He got some kinda palsy that cause his hand to shake as he turn her head over. Leota's eyes wide open, fixed on a spot somewhere on the ceiling, eyes looking so surprised make me look up there, too, see what she so interested in."

Dr. Ingram put his shaky hand on Leota's neck just below her chin and then on her wrist. Finally, he looked up and shook his head.

"Gone," he said to Deedove. And the child heard and understood, but her eyes were dry and she didn't say anything. All she could think about was what would happen to her now.

Nan returned to the kitchen to refill her glass.

But she didn't need to worry. When the time came for her to go back to work at the cleaners, she went, just like she always had. Above her in the upstairs living quarters the undertakers were carrying Leota's body away. The only thing the child felt was embarrassment at the mess she'd left all over the hall upstairs. She never knew who told Maude Jones about it, but she never mentioned it to the child, and she just let her go right on living upstairs by herself and working in the dry cleaners downstairs. Maude had figured out long before Leota died that it was the child who did all the work anyway, and it didn't matter who did it as long as it got done.

The truth was Nan liked the work. Writing out a ticket for a pair of pants or a suit that somebody brought in to be cleaned and marking the clothes before she loaded them into the dry cleaning machine. The smell of cleaning solution and the ironing of the clean suits and shirts until they looked like new. She liked taking in the money at the counter and matching the cleaning tickets with what she'd taken in at the end of the day.

The only thing she missed about her mama being gone was the visits from the daddy. For a long time after her mama died, she half expected to see him turn up some night in her bed, but he never did.

"And just look at me now, Pearl. Nobody in town know I owns this place. Might hurt business everybody know a colored woman own the dry cleaners. But it belong to me free and clear."

She'd planned it that way. She knew after a while Maude Jones would get so she couldn't work any more. And when that happened she intended to be ready.

"You shoulda seen the look on that woman's face, when her colored help offer her cash money for the whole thing from the ground up. She couldn't hardly close her mouth.

"My lord, Nan. Where on earth you get that kinda money?"

What a bargain it was. She got the building, the dry cleaning equipment and business, as well as the upstairs living quarters. And she'd paid cash money. Money she'd started saving long before her mama died. She'd wheedled more and more pay out of her employer as she grew older and took on more of the responsibility of the place. She was diligent to a fault and gave neither time nor money to anything except the dream of owning the cleaners herself and the comfort the dream brought her.

And now that she had done it, . . . now . . . now she felt a kind of pause, a waiting for the next thing in her life to happen. Now that she could begin to take things a little bit easier, start to look around, see what she might have missed on her way to getting here. Just a kind of pause.

Nan stood by the window watching the crowd below her on the street and she thought again of the young woman who straightened out the quilt in the wagon bed that morning. She walked to the hallway and down to the bedroom and stretched out on the clean bedspread and cradled the doll in her arms and hummed softly.

"Wonder what Jubilee do for her comfort, Pearl? Benny her comfort. I got a dry cleaning business and Jubilee got Benny. She think she done won the prize."

Nan smiled because she knew about men. No matter how good they might look for a while, they always ended up taking what wasn't theirs. Taking the coffee you brought them in bed, taking the money out of your purse while you were in the kitchen making the coffee, taking your right to think for yourself, taking your right to try to get whatever you wanted most in your life, then running off and leaving you first chance they get. Some of them, like Benny, looked like they were different for a while. Some of the daddies who came to visit her mama were just like Benny at first. She winced, because they were the ones that hurt Leota the most. They gave her the hope that something good was finally going to happen. The ones like Benny taught Leota the hardest lessons. So Nan always knew to look for her comfort some place else.

"My comfort tied up in being free," she said to herself.

She was free to do whatever pleased her and owning the dry cleaning business shone like a trophy inside her mind that said, 'Nan Hawkins is the freest colored woman in the world." And her freedom was her comfort. But Jubilee married Benny and now she was having a baby. That was the way she found her comfort. And she sure looked comfortable. She was wearing her comfort around like a new hat in church.

"Jubilee got everybody in town believing her comfort a whole lot sweeter than working in a dry cleaning business. Everybody thinking, Nan Hawkins give everything she got for something like Benny Horne. A husband a whole lot better than a dry cleaning business.' But I know about you, Mr. Benny." Still there was something about the way she had seen him hold Jubilee that morning.

Nan got up off the bed and walked to the full-length mirror hanging on the back of the hallway door. Her rayon dress clung to her strong, muscular hips and legs. She looked at her own eyes, at her face, broad and strong. That woman in the mirror didn't take junk off of any man. She had a business of her own and everything in the world she ever wanted.

"But, lord help her, Pearl. She got a hunger inside of her; she gonna have to eat the whole world to get rid of."

She thought of Jubilee's body, delicate like Leota's, but misshapen, now and awkward with the child. And the hunger rose in her throat. She closed her eyes and thought of the big belly under the oversized dress. And she ran her opened hands down over her breasts and across her flat abdomen. Benny's child.

"Ain't no reason I can't get some of that, too. Time come Benny gonna leave I still have the child," she said. The satisfaction of the thought filled her core and made her dizzy.

She picked up the doll and hugged it to her and threw back her head and smiled and closed her eyes.

CHAPTER 11

ON SUNDAY, JUBILEE and Benny rode in the wagon to the little church where Benny had spent every Sunday morning since he was born, except when he was too sick to move. They pulled up into the pine-shaded back yard in the wagon and tied the mule to a chinaberry tree. The grey, weathered boards and batten on the outside of the building had been nailed into place a hundred years ago by the slaves of Mr. Cyrus Nance, when he responded to the nagging of his wife that something had to be done to convert their heathen slaves to God fearing Christians.

Benny and Jubilee walked through the pine trees over the bare, red sand and clay yard around the church to the front door. Through the years the congregation had resisted the urge to paint the outside walls and beautify the yard around it with flowers or junipers that might have softened the harsh effect of the rough-sawn weathered boards rising so abruptly out of the dirt. It wasn't that they didn't love the old place. But something in all of them said to leave it just like it was, so folks who entered the worn front door might be greater affected by the extraordinary interior.

Embraced and protected on the outside by the old gray boards, the inside of the little structure, the walls, the crossbeams above, the alter rail in front, the chairs that the preacher and the visiting preacher and the choir director sat in, the pews, everything that could be, had been carved or painted in intricate and loving detail. The people who sat there every Sunday never tired of looking at the beauty and wondering at it.

The story of the little church with pictures had appeared in the Four County News and later in the Clarion Ledger. The world beyond the walls called the place a perfect example of primitive art. The article had caught the attention of rich people who came from everywhere asking for permission to take pictures of the church. Sweet Boy's daddy had been forced to put a padlock on the door for fear that some of the pieces here and there might come up missing. Some visitors said it proved how well off the slaves were before the civil war; others said it proved just the opposite.

Appearing along with the stories in the newspapers was a faded picture of the artist, Jesse Wilkes, when he was a young man before the civil war. It was the only photograph in existence of him. His granddaughters had found it in some of his things after he died. He was standing in front of a wagon of cotton with some other boys waiting for their turn at the gin. The others seemed vague and shadowy in the old picture, but Mr. Jesse was standing in front of the wagon and he was close enough so you could see the squint on his face as he looked toward the late fall sun. He didn't look like a sculptor or an artist standing there. He just looked like the field hand that he was.

When it appeared in the paper, Benny looked at the picture a long time and tried to read the shadows of the eyes with the memory he had of the old gray headed, bent man. Mr. Jesse use to hobble into church on the arms of his aging granddaughters every now and then when Benny was a little boy. Everybody standing and talking in the aisles would get quiet and move aside, hat in hand, and nod a humble greeting to them as they passed on their way to the front pew. Benny's mama would hush him when he asked her who they were and how come they came in so late and made such a stir.

"Mama, they sitting on the front row," he'd say.

Hadn't they taught him that it was presumptuous to sit up

front like that? But Mr. Jesse and his granddaughters did it anyway and nobody thought it amiss. And when the congregation stood up to sing, Mr. Jesse sang all the old songs from a seated position and the congregation acted like they felt honored that he let all of them sing along with him.

This Sunday, Benny and Jubilee sat as they always did in the pew with Sweet Boy and Sis Riah. Benny gazed at the paintings around him. Mr. Jesse had carved and painted the figures with large, full lips and broad noses, hair tightly curled or tied over with richly patterned bandanas, all African men and women. There was a dark Abraham sacrificing a dark Isaac, a colored Joseph being sold as a slave to the Egyptians, Mary Magdelene, a black woman, caught in sin, the apostles and Jesus all dark. An African Mary held a sweet, dark baby who looked like the babies that always dotted the congregation of the little church. The Garden of Eden was filled with exotic animals that nobody knew the name of and there was one terrible tree, whose great gnarled trunk held spirits and elves with faces both beautiful and terrible that filled the knots and dark hollows of the branches. Benny had seen some of those faces in his dreams when he was down sick or sleeplessly worrying about something.

There were faces and stories that Benny couldn't remember ever hearing before, an old woman in a long flowing robe with a strange emblem on the front of it and a turban wrapped around her head that supported a big basket filled with some exotic kind of fruit. As a little boy, Benny had gazed at that fruit and wondered, when his stomach growled as the preacher talked past dinnertime, what it would be like to have that basket lowered and that fruit offered to him to eat until he was full. Above the altar there were groups of men in frightened clumps that looked outward towards clouds of fire where great mythical beings flew triumphantly toward the skies above them.

Mr. Jesse created the inside of the old church. And he never stopped to ask whether it was correct or in keeping with anybody's idea of the way things ought to be. He just did it.

Benny and all his friends were told the story of the artist as soon as they were old enough to understand. Mr. Jesse was a slave, brought from Africa when he was a boy about ten or twelve years old. He was one of the men that Mr. Cyrus put onto the job of building the church. But the master and his overseers didn't care how well the work was done. What did it matter if the roof leaked or the wind blew through it cold in winter?

"Nobody gonna use it but the darkies," they said.

So they never came around to check on the progress of the church. It was during the slow months; the men had six weeks to finish the job and that was that. And while the slaves sawed and nailed and fit wood to wood on the little building, without the bullying of the overseers at their back, they began to care about what they were doing for the first time. Because for the first time, they were working for themselves.

Jesse Wilkes was put to work on the new church just about the time he thought he wouldn't be able to live any more if he couldn't say what his soul needed to say to somebody. When the pitiful little building was finished everybody left off work and went back to the field. All except Jesse, who was told to finish up the thing.

The master's wife donated all the paint left over from the newly decorated big house. Among the many different colors, in none of the cans was there a large enough amount to paint the walls a solid color. The paint was left outside the door along with the young Jesse Wilkes, who was instructed to finish up the inside anyway he saw fit.

And sometime about then, Mr. Jesse got a vision. Suddenly he started to know what the inside of that place was going to look like. His mind began to dream the shapes and feel the wood that his hands would bring to life for those who were to sit within the walls. The generations of children yet to be born would look into the faces of his saints and see the reflection of their own faces. The congregation that gathered there in the years and years to come would be reminded of what they truly were inside and not what the outside world told them they were. At the same time the board and batten, grayed by weather and time, would keep the beauty safe inside.

The job had come to Jesse Wilkes just in time. And then the master didn't think about the slave again for a while. Mr. Jesse use to say the angels covered him up from the master's mind. So he just kept working every day until he couldn't see to work any more. And even when he started back to work in the field, he came to the little building at night with a candle and painted or he filled the floor with the oak and pine shavings from the carving. Every Sunday when the small pitiful congregation of dirt tired people came through the door they entered the scenes that began to fill the walls.

It was a long time before the master knew anything about the paintings and carvings. None of the worshipers spoke about them, not even to each other. The artistry on the inside of the church was held in mutual silence and reverence. But when the world found out about the remarkable beauty, the world wanted it. Mr. Cyrus right away took Jesse out of the fields and put him to work carving and painting whatever he told him to. And Mr. Jesse was happy to spend his days working like that. But none of the work Mr. Cyrus ordered ever came out like the work he did on the church.

Jubilee was a descendant of Jesse Wilkes. She sat quietly between Benny and Sweet Boy up near the front. They saved a place on the end for Sis Riah when she finished playing the old piano for the singing. The light from the window beside the pew filtered in on Jubilee and Benny thought he had never seen anything so fragile. He swallowed and looked away from her quickly.

He reached over and laid his hand on Jubilee's smaller one. She smiled at him and he saw the kicking of his first child making her dress flutter gently. This child, yet unborn, would grow up studying these walls just as he had and would have that sense of something that was on-going in this place. His firstborn, girl or boy, would hear, too, the something that had called them all together long before his life began and would keep on calling them long after his life was over. His grandchildren and great grandchildren would sit here in this place someday and sing these same songs, look at these same walls of Jesse Wilkes and think and remember, too. Benny's eyes welled up in gratitude.

When church was over Benny and Sweet Boy walked out together right behind Sis Riah and Jubilee. The two women joined a group of women who were visiting in the front yard of the church while the men walked off around back to the wagons.

"How much longer you got, Jubilee?" Saphronia asked haughtily as they walked up.

"Doctor say about three, four weeks, Miz Saphronia."

The midwife stood tightlipped and stony before her.

"Look to me like your doctor done made a mistake. 'Course who am I to know?"

Jubilee tried to defuse her anger. The congregation had just finished selecting Sis Riah and Saphronia to go to an important church conference at Tugaloo College. All the churches in the state were sending delegates to participate.

"Miz Saphronia, you must be mighty excited about going all the way down to Tugaloo next week," she said.

Saphronia's face relaxed in self-satisfaction.

"Might be kinda interesting," she said.

"Brother Woodrow say the meeting about the colored Christian's future in the South. What you reckon that mean?" Jubilee asked.

"Well, I is sure I don't know, but I ain't gonna sit around down there wasting my time listening to some fresh talking boy's uppity ideas."

Sis Riah interrupted. "Now, Saphronia, you just cool off. We gonna keep our heads open. See what we can see. Don't you close up your mind before we even gets there."

Saphronia pulled her purse higher on her arm. "You saying I got a closed mind, Sis Riah?"

"I'm just saying we ain't gonna call nobody fresh and uppity until we know what we looking at. We just gonna hear what being said and bring back the message to this here church in Tula."

"Humpf," Saphonia said.

Sis Riah ignored the roll of her eyes.

"Don't start none of that, girl. Now listen. I'm gonna come on by Miz Olivia's some time this week and we gonna talk about the particulars of the trip. Gonna be fun, Saphronia." She caught Jubilee by the arm. "Come on. Let's get on home."

"Don't have that baby before we get back," Saphronia called after the two women. "Won't be a midwife in town."

"She ain't gonna need one," Sis Riah called back as they walked out of hearing distance. "Lord, that trip gonna be a trial with that woman along."

"What you think, Sis Riah? About when the baby coming?" Jubilee asked her when the two of them got to her wagon.

"You listen to what your doctor say, hon. Don't pay no attention to that old antique." She kept walking toward her own wagon.

"Sweet Boy, let's go," she called.

Her husband grinned at her and touched his hat in a gesture of good bye to Benny.

"I'll see you next week," he said.

Benny helped Jubilee up into their wagon and then he joined her on the seat behind the mule. He signaled the animal into motion. One by one the members of the congregation said goodbye and separated from one another. And wagon wheels rumbled and headed out away from the old building in all directions leaving the church yard silent and dreaming.

CHAPTER 12

AT THE SAME time Sis Riah's church was letting out, Olivia Montgomery walked out the double front doors of the Tula Methodist Church. It was a red brick structure that was built just after the civil war with a newer two story educational wing added on to the back. A large stained glass window donated by the Atkins family covered most of the front and there was a bell in a steeple above it. Children dressed in Sunday clothes ran up and surrounded Mr. Willie Harrison because he always handed out sticks of gum to them after church. Olivia saw her granddaughter, Anise, holding out her hand for a stick of Juicy Fruit.

She paused at the top of the steps to look at the congregation below her, all familiar faces. Mr. and Mrs. Cochran, whose son had polio, and the Bridgeports, they were cotton buyers, and Mrs. Minnie Pierce, who married a northerner who left her after only one day of marital bliss and was never seen or heard from again. She still used his last name, the only thing he left behind. And the preacher and his wife, middle aged now, still struggling with the sorrow of losing their only child years ago, so they never got up the courage to have more children.

She watched her son, Luke, tall and olive skinned, like his Grandfather Montgomery, walk across the lawn toward the Worthey brothers who were talking to her husband, Matthew. Standing just out of the July sun in the shade of the old pecan trees, Edgar and Robert Worthey stood with their summer suit coats unbuttoned and their hands in their pockets jingling change.

"I hear you getting a new bull," Edgar said to Matthew.

"Who told you that?" Matthew answered grinning around a cigar.

"Charlie McKay said he told your boy about one for sale in Illinois and Luke was real excited. Good price, Charlie said."

"I already got a bull. What I want with another bull?" Matthew asked.

"That's not what Luke said," Robert put in.

"Luke knows what I think about raising cattle. Montgomerys raise cotton, not cows," Matthew said, a little irritated but covering it with a smile as his son joined the group under the trees.

"You don't know what the deal is yet, Daddy. Howdy, Mr. Edgar. Mr. Roger," Luke said nodding to the other men.

"Don't matter. I don't need another bull. Already got the best Angus bull in the county. Besides we got more cows now than I want, thanks to you." He glanced at the Wortheys. "And I don't want to talk anymore about it."

Roger Worthey smiled at Luke and spoke.

"You hear Walter Abel lost two of his men last week? Scott and Big Tollie packed up their families and took the train to Detroit. Gonna work in the factories there, I heard."

"Damn fools. They'll be back," Matthew said.

"Yeah, wanting jobs. Somebody to pay their doctor bills. Buy school shoes for their children," Edgar added.

"Well, maybe so," Luke said. "But some of them are staying up there. And let's face it. Some of them . . . like Benny . . . some of them are smart enough to make a go of it, too."

"Benny said anything to you about moving?" Matthew interrupted.

"Not yet, but if he and Hippy took a notion to try their hand up north, we couldn't stop them. Then what would we do?"

"Benny Horne's family been working for Montgomerys long as any body can remember. They ain't going any place," Edgar said.

"There's no law says he can't though. And we'd have to replace them. Takes a lot of people to plant and hoe and pick the size cotton crop we got." Luke looked at the two Wortheys.

"I don't want to stand out here and talk about it," Matthew said again.

"Colored trade's way down this summer. Not as crowded in town on Saturdays as it use to be," Roger said glancing at Edgar. "Hard to say why though."

"Could be anything," Matthew commented.

"Come on. We all know why. Coloreds are leaving the south."

"I don't want to talk business today, Luke. It's my day off," Matthew grinned at the other two men.

"But, Daddy, pretty soon everybody's gonna have to raise cows instead of cotton and then you won't be able to find a good bull anywhere for a decent price."

"I said, I already got a bull"

"Not like this one."

"How do you know. You ain't even seen it. Now I don't want to talk about it any more, Luke. It's Sunday," Matthew said. The grin was gone and he had a scowl that Luke recognized.

"Matthew, your cotton short enough to tractor-poison this year?" Edgar was asking.

"Yeah. Won't make as much as last year, but we'll save some on the cost of poisoning. Benny don't charge near as much as Abbot Lee does to fly over and spray it," Matthew laughed.

"Can't wait long to do it either. I found some weevils yesterday afternoon in the stand down by the river," Luke said.

"Well, Benny won't kill himself hurrying to that job. You never heard such complaining. But then it ain't his cotton," his father said.

"He's got the tractor ready to go early tomorrow morning. Said so yesterday."

Miz Clair Worthey called to her husband and his brother to come on. She was getting hot in the car waiting for them. So the Wortheys left and Luke and Matthew followed them toward their own cars.

"I want to tell you about something that happened yesterday. But I don't want you to get upset over it," Luke said. He stood almost a head taller than his father. "Benny asked me if I'd give him the money he's been saving, so he could open an account in the Hart County Bank."

"Why did he want to do that? Did he say?"

"Well, he mentioned something about getting interest on it. Kinda acted like he didn't know a whole lot about it. Sis Riah put him up to it."

"Interest? What does Sis Riah know about interest? Musta been talking to her sister. How much did Benny have coming to him?"

"'Over fifty dollars."

"That's more money than Benny's ever seen at one time in his life. If he'd got hold of it yesterday, he wouldn't have a penny of it left this morning. Drinking, gambling, cattin' around."

By then they were standing in front of Luke's blue and white Fairlane.

"Maybe Hippy would have done that, but you're wrong about Benny."

"Yeah, I thought his daddy was different, too. Married Sadie Upton. Nice clean nigra. Had a bunch of nice little pickaninnies. Kinda smart. Begun hanging out with that young gal in town, not even old enough to be his daughter. Got her a child. Then soon as it got old enough to work, here he comes wanting me to take the boy on. Nigras just children after candy, boy. No matter what you do for them, they just children after candy."

"But I think Benny put the money in the bank straight away."

"You gave it to him?"

"Well, it was his. I had no right to keep it."

"Damn, son. You do stuff like that, you asking for trouble. Benny won't have the vaguest idea what to do with fifty dollars rattling around in his overalls."

"Daddy, you're wrong about Benny. I bet that money's in the bank right now."

"And I'm saying Benny's no different from his daddy. No matter how much you'd like to think so."

"Well, tomorrow morning first thing, Benny's gonna be sober

and sitting up on that tractor poisoning cotton. Just like he said he would."

Matthew scowled. "Then again, maybe this gonna teach you something about who you dealing with. You just remember Benny Senior. Same tree, son. Same tree."

The churchyard had emptied when Olivia carried a vase of orange and white daylilies across the lawn to the front of the little brick parsonage that stood next to the church. She walked carefully over the sidewalk, so she wouldn't catch the heels of her new shoes in the cracks made by the intrusive roots of the giant oaks. The thought went through her head that she needed to get the colored boy, who did her yard work, to do some cleaning up over here. Olivia always felt that an unkept yard at the church or parsonage was a direct reflection on the Montgomerys, since they were synonymous in the town with the Methodist congregation. She walked past her husband and son and opened the back door of their brand new, black Buick and set the lilies down of the floor. She tapped the horn at Matthew.

"You're asking for trouble, Luke. You putting that poor bastard in a position the good Lord never intended for him to be in. Next thing you know he'll be coming after Mary Alice."

Luke laughed.

"That's ridiculous."

"You think so? I'm telling you, Benny's no different from the rest of them."

Luke shook his head, smiling at his father's scowl. He walked to his car and got in beside his wife. Anise was taking her turn on the front seat between them and Chip was in the back seat brooding over his younger sister's rights.

"Were you arguing with your daddy again?" Mary Alice asked her husband.

"Well, kinda. I told him about Benny wanting to put his money in the bank." Luke started the car and backed into the street.

"Oh. Did he think it was a bad idea?"

Luke laughed.

"You know he did."

"Well, most darkies you wouldn't dare trust with that kind of money," Mary Alice said over Anise's head.

The little girl was chewing her stick of Juicy Fruit and listening to the adults talking. She pushed her head up over the seat so she could look back at Chip. He was silent and sulking. She sent him a sticky smile.

"Mama, make Anise turn around."

"Anise," her mother said.

The little girl quickly stuck out her tongue and turned to face the front.

"Ever since I can remember Dad's always helped the hands on the place with their money. For their own good. They can't do it for themselves. I know that. But Benny . . . You know, we were kids together. Like Mother and Sis Riah. And Benny . . . I always thought he was . . . that he had some sense . . . "

"Mama, Jubilee helped me sew my apron," Anise said, leaning against her mother's arm.

"I know. She spoils you, Miss Priss." Mary Alice smiled and pinched her daughter's nose.

"Daddy, are you going to Jubilee's house to talk to Benny this afternoon?"

"No, we did all the talking we needed to do yesterday."

"Aawwh! Then could I walk across the fields down to her house for a visit? I haven't seen Jubilee all day."

"No, sugar. That's no place for you to be by your self."

"But you let me go on Friday."

"That's because Jubilee was there by herself."

"But you let Chip go down there on Sundays."

"Chip's a boy."

"Yeah, I'm a boy and you're a girl," Chip spoke up from the back seat.

"What difference does that make?"

"I'm not going to argue with you, Anise. Jubilee is having a day off and I'm sure she needs it. You'll just have to wait until tomorrow to see her."

"Yeah, Anise," Chip snickered from the back seat.

Luke Montgomery turned the Fairlane into the driveway at the bottom of the hill that ran up to the two-story Cape Cod style farmhouse. Chip immediately jumped out when the car stopped and ran as hard as he could toward the back screen door, yelling, "I bid the gizzard."

"Darn, he always gets the gizzard," said his sister. "Daddy, why doesn't Jubilee go to church with us?"

"She has a church of her own, Anise," her father said, picking her up and carrying her inside the house.

"Oh," she said. "Can I go see it sometimes?"

"Maybe," he answered, but she didn't think she ever would.

CHAPTER 13

WHEN BENNY GOT to the cotton field early Monday morning, Mr. Luke's daddy was waiting there for him. He was leaning up against his pickup and he signaled as Benny drove the tractor off the highway onto the dirt road beside the field.

"Cut that thing off and leave it here," he yelled. "I need you to help me get a cow and calf back into the pasture down yonder."

Benny felt something in his stomach knot up. Chasing down one of the white-faced cows and her calf would probably take him the better part of the morning. The hot part of the day would be upon him and he would run the risk of not finishing the field that day. Mr. Luke would be upset.

"Uh, Mr. Matthew, Mr. Luke done told me to get on to this cotton quick as I can this morning. Hippy right down the road at his house. Be alright if he help you?"

"I'm telling you to do it, Benny. Hippy's vaccinating calves today. You know that as well as I do. Now get down off the damn tractor and come on."

"Yassuh."

Benny cut off the motor and climbed down. He headed around toward the passenger side of the truck where he always rode with Luke.

"What in the hell you doing?" Matthew yelled.

Benny realized his mistake too late. The hands on the place never rode in the cab of Matthew's pickup. He said they stunk it up when they rode up there with him and he couldn't get the smell out for days. Benny began apologizing.

"Come on," Matthew said. "I don't have time for that. Just stay out of my truck."

For some reason he seemed more irritated today than usual. Benny climbed in the back of the pickup and Matthew backed out of the trail on to the highway. The gears made a grinding noise as they lurched down the road toward Lexington. Benny had to hold on to the sides of the pickup to keep from being tossed out.

Hippy should be taking care of this, he thought, but Matthew Montgomery would never be caught listening to the suggestions of a field hand. With Mr. Luke it was a different matter. He often asked Benny for his opinion. But what was he going to think when he made his usual run by the field to check on the progress of Benny's work later on that morning? Well, he had tried to side step Mr. Matthew, but it hadn't worked. He didn't know what else he could have done.

The truck stopped suddenly, throwing Benny against the back of the cab. Mr. Matthew pulled off to the side and Benny saw the brown and white milk cow and her calf lazily chewing the kudzu along the side of Highway 17. He vaulted out of the back and took a look at the situation to figure out the best way to get the cow back over the hill and into the pasture. Matthew went on ahead to the broken fence.

When the cow saw Benny coming, she took off down the deep draw along the side of the road away from the pasture and the calf followed close behind. Benny ran along the roadside trying to get ahead of the animal, so he could direct her back. She kept trotting farther away, then stopping and grazing casually. Whenever Benny got close to her, she would look up suddenly, wall eyed, and take off again. Finally, he snuck up on the far side of the road until he knew he had gone quite a ways passed her and was in a good position to run the cow back toward the break in the fence.

Just at that moment Matthew topped the hill and looked down the long stretch that Benny had just walked and yelled, "How come you way down there? Don't you know how to run a cow?"

"Yassuh. I's just trying to get on the far side of her," Benny called.

"You were just trying to waste my time," Matthew yelled back. "Hurry, will you? You got cotton to spray."

Wasting time was the last thing Benny wanted to do. He picked up a long stick and started walking down the draw toward the cow and calf, who turned and began moving back toward home. Now it was just a matter of keeping her in the draw and off the road as they ambled nearer the crest of the hill. It was slow going, but Benny knew from experience that if he tried to hurry the process he might find himself back where he started, having to go through the whole chase again.

Finally, he topped the crest of the hill and herded the cow to the place in the fence where Mr. Matthew was standing. The cow, seeing suddenly that her freedom was in danger of coming to an end, lunged past the man and headed down the other side of the hill. Benny used the technique he had employed before and slowly got himself into position to herd her back to the broken place in the fence.

"Mr. Matthew, stand in the draw and keep her from going back down that side again. Wave your arms, so she'll shy away from you," Benny called.

"I don't need you to tell me how to get a cow back into a pasture, Benny," the man yelled back as he walked away from the fence.

This time they were successful and the cow followed by her calf trotted back over the downed fence like it was what she intended all along and began to chew on the green clover growing in the field.

Benny pulled at the fence posts in an effort to stand them up straight. It was the kind of job that would have been much easier if two people worked at it, but Matthew did not work along side the hands. So Benny kept tugging until he got them as straight as

he could and shoved and stomped the displaced dirt and rocks
into the hole under them. The fence wasn't strong that way, but it
would hold the cow and calf in until he could get back out there
and do a better job with the right tools.

"There you go, Mr. Matthew," Benny said to the man sitting
in the cab of the truck.

"You call that fixed. It's going to fall over again first thing that
comes along and you'll have to take the time to do the job over
again. But I reckon that don't matter to you, because it's not your
fence anyway or your stock either. And Luke thinks you got enough
sense to take care of yourself. Get on in the truck. I'll get you back
to the cotton."

"Yassuh."

Benny swore to himself as he climbed into the back of the
truck. Mr. Matthew put the pickup in reverse, backed up and shot
back down the highway to the Nance place where Benny had left
the tractor. He stopped long enough for Benny to get out and
then took off in a cloud of dust.

Benny was tired and sweaty and he hadn't even begun work in
the field yet. He checked the nozzles and spray tanks and then got on
the tractor and headed it down toward the back of the field. Luke was
late getting by that morning. It was just before noon when his truck
pulled up and he got out. He stood looking at the cotton field. Benny
was on the far side and couldn't see the expression on his boss's face,
but he knew by the way he was standing that he was surprised to see
only a few rows at the back of the field finished. Benny knew better
than to complain about Mr. Matthew.

"What's taking you so long? Tractor break down?" Luke yelled
as Benny got off and walked toward him.

"Nawsuh. I ain't been working long."

"When did you start?"

"Just about a hour ago," Benny answered. "Mr. Matthew . . . "

"I thought you were going to get here early this morning."

"Yassuh, I was. I mean, I did. But Mr. Matthew come by and
took me down toward Lexington to help him get a cow off the
road and fix the fence," Benny explained.

"So you just took off and did it. Goddamn it, Benny. Hippy coulda done that. The calves can wait, but this cotton can't. Why in hell didn't you take time to think a little? Taking off to do something like that."

"Yassuh," he said. "Well, I told Mr. Matthew that . . . "

"And now it's right at noon. Hell. The morning's already wasted. Go ahead and eat since you've stopped. And then for God's sake get on back to that poisoning. You gonna be late finishing tonight. Try to stick to it this time, Benny. Don't let anything sidetrack you."

Benny stood with his straw hat held in his hands and watched Mr. Luke get back into his truck and back onto the road and drive off. He locked his teeth and spat hard into the cotton rows. Sweat rolled down his forehead and into his eyes.

When Luke was out of sight he threw his hat on the ground and turned his head away from the road.

"Shit," he said under his breath and then looked at the tree line far down at the end of the field and the gullies beyond them.

"Shit."

This time he yelled it.

How long could he put up with this? How on earth had his Daddy done it for so long? But he knew how his daddy had done it. By cutting loose in the only way allowed him.

He was too mad to notice the sound of the automobile until he saw the old, green Ford coupe pull into the trail and bump along the ruts, kicking up dust to the far end of the field where it disappeared behind a stand of cottonwoods. Benny recognized the car as the one that was equipped with a pole across the back seat to hang dry-cleaned clothes in paper clothes-bags, ready for delivery. He felt a sudden rush of feeling that displaced the anger momentarily. What was she doing out here? Who was she delivering to on that road? Only thing down that way was an empty cabin. Must have turned off on to the wrong road.

He walked back toward the cool shade to eat under the trees that grew by the gullies near where the car had gone. He smelled like the cotton poison that he'd been working with. The fumes from it had gotten into his lungs and stung them in spite of the handkerchief he kept tied around his mouth and nose when he worked. It made him sick to poison the cotton. He would be sick tonight after this day of work. The thought added to his anger. Maybe eating would help him put things away in the right place where they belonged.

When he saw the car parked under the trees he knew where she probably was and he thought he knew the reason she had driven it there where it was, hidden from the road by the thick blackberry bushes and cottonwoods. He knew what the warmth he felt deep inside him was, too. He walked toward the car. It was empty. He looked around. This place out of the sun under the trees, it was a haven, a refuge, an escape from the heat of the July day, from the irksome work and from the other things, too.

Down in the gully he knew there was a pond. He imagined it now, the light bouncing in shivers off the surface. And the thick smells of earth and water meshed so closely together that each penetrated the other. And the heat.

He heard her first before he saw her. It was a splash and then the sound of water washing over arms and shoulders. He started to turn around and go quickly back to the tractor and the poison. He knew that it was what he should do. Instead, he stood still for a moment, waiting, trying to hear what she was doing with the water in the pond.

He did not know when he began to move toward the thick underbrush and follow the narrow trail made by deer until he could see over the blackberry and wild rose bushes. And though he expected it, knew by instinct what was happening ahead of him in the pond, still he felt astonished when suddenly there she was. Her face and body, strong and coarse, divided the water with dark armed grace.

He was struck stone still and silent, as he watched her make her way through the silver liquid to the other side, then crouch and turn back toward him, bare-breasted and smiling, showing the strong, white teeth. Submerging the breasts slowly, she closed the lips and settled the chin back into the water and pushed off from the other side, arms laid out in front of her on top of the coolness, moving back toward him. Her eyes held his eyes, her mouth with pouting lips narrowed into a smile.

He did not remember taking off the shoes and socks, the overalls and work shirt that smelled like cotton poison, the underclothes that Jubilee always washed so carefully and folded and put away for him. The clothes, suddenly, were gone and he walked naked into the pool of water as if he were being baptized.

He was at her in an instant, his mouth open, covering hers, sucking the lips that pouted until she tried to pull away, but he would not let her. And then he sucked the cheeks, the face, the neck, the thick, black nipples until he hurt her, running his hands down her body, numb to the gentle caresses she used to try and calm him. Picking her up, one arm under her shoulders and one arm thrust between her legs holding the strong buttocks above the water, he carried her to the mud along the bank and laid her in its slick, sticky blackness and found her with his hands. She raised her head to slow him, but his hand grabbed her hair and held it back to the mud. He thrust himself into her, stabbing at the anger that had suddenly changed itself into her flesh, until the terrible heat surged from his chest, his gut, his buttocks, and exploded outward into the woman, extinguishing the enemy that raged round about him and the anger slowly receded and then was gone, for now at least, and he could find some quiet inside himself again.

He noticed for the first time that she was crying when he let her go and laid back on the muddy bank. It was quiet crying, just tears and her breath jerking in her chest every now and then. She turned her back to him. She was astonishingly narrow at the waist and he realized for the first time that her body was small, delicate in places and vulnerable. She rose up off the muddy bank and walked slowly back into the pond concealing her body from him and crying silently as she went.

"I'm sorry. I don't know why I did it like that. I'm sorry if I hurt you."

"Then how come you to do it, you piece of shit?"

"Well, what you expect? You was asking for it."

"I ain't asking for nothing."

"Well, what you call it then? Coming out here where there ain't nobody around and letting me find you like that."

He was rinsing off the mud and the sweat now and splashing water on his privates, pulling back the foreskin and cleaning the end like you'd clean a gun, she thought.

"You think I wanted that, what you just did?"

"Well, you sure as hell look like you did."

"You think a woman like it like that? Shit, I don't know why I come out here."

"What in hell do you think you gonna get?"

He was stepping out onto the grass and putting on the clothes and the cotton poison smell again. She stood there turned toward him, her broad nose and heavy mouth, water coming up to her waist, dripping off her nipples, mixing with tears. He felt his body begin to warm again at the sight of her.

"I don't have to take that kinda stuff off of you or nobody else."

She waded out of the pond and stumbled toward the undergrowth, denying him the sight of seeing her put her clothes back on. He listened for the sound of her.

"Nan?" he called.

He stood for a moment, then longer, thinking he would see her emerge. But then he heard the sound of her car starting and only caught a glimpse of the back of her head when he ran after the sound, barefoot out of the underbrush and watched the car bump back down the trail to the road in a cloud of July dust. He caught hold of a cottonwood trunk, bewildered and mad at himself and wondering what had come over him.

CHAPTER 14

JUBILEE WOKE FROM a strange, disturbing dream that left her filled with foreboding. She reached over to tell Benny about it but found the bed beside her was empty. The messed up bed covers and pillow on his side made her feel terribly alone and increased her uneasiness. She sat on the side of the bed in her white cotton nightgown, and, grabbing hold of the iron headboard, she pulled herself awkwardly to her feet. The smell of flowers filled the house.

The early morning sun lit up the clean windows of her small front room and threw another shadow window on the floor and a breeze blew in from across the cotton field. The smells that had so ominously filled her dream now pleasantly filled her house. Cape jasmine and lilies and what else. Then she saw them arranged in a canning jar on the little table beside the open window. Field grass. That was the other smell. She laughed, and leaned over the flowers to smell them.

"You crazy woman," she said out loud to herself. "Ain't nothing to be scared of. Ain't nothing but a dream. It's cause of these here flowers in my kitchen. Just like when I dream I needs to pee, and I wake up and sure 'nuff I do." Well, she thought. Flowers. Wonder what cause him to bring flowers? Must have walked clear over to the old falling down Russell house to pick them. Weeds grown almost waist high in the old forgotten yard, but the flowers still bloomed there. Only place she knew where the sweet scented blooms were available to anybody who wanted them.

"And he know how much I love field grass in flowers in the middle of summer."

And the Rose Bay? she thought. Where had Benny found Rose Bay? She checked the bouquet again. The dream was mistaken; there was no Rose Bay. Just Cape Jasmine and lilies and field grass. She smiled. Must be because of this baby.

"What you think, honey. Your daddy bringing flowers and me about scared to death because of a dream. I hear women expecting babies be a little like that sometime." She patted her belly. "Your daddy gonna take good care of you, little girl. Ain't no green and purple snake gonna bother nobody around here."

She knew by the angle of the sun's rays coming in that it was almost seven and she hurried back into the bedroom to put on her loose work dress and an apron. She was in for a busy day at work. The Montgomery family would be leaving tomorrow morning early for their yearly summer vacation in Florida. She'd be cooking food to take and washing and ironing last minute clothes selections all day, but after that she'd be off work for a week and she could use the time to get ready for the baby.

Every year for a week in the summer Luke Montgomery rented a big house down in Pensacola that sat right out on a smooth white beach. Anise had told her all about it. The little girl always came home from those trips talking about days filled with sand and salty, emerald green water, riding waves and hunting hermit crabs and sighting porpoises just out beyond the swimming area. For days she would be drugged to a honey sweetness from the sun and activity. Jubilee had pictured it in her mind.

"Some day I see to it you gonna see the ocean, too," she said out loud to the baby inside her. "When you grows up a little." She liked talking to the baby. And she did it more and more these days as her time got closer.

And then suddenly she thought again of the terrible thing that had awakened her and the feeling of it swept over her like ice water and she had to stop and tell herself again that it was just a dream. She certainly couldn't let herself be weighed down today, because she needed all the strength she could get for the work ahead of her at the Montgomerys.

"Miz Mary Alice gonna want a caramel cake to take with them. Just like my grandmama teach me when I was a little bitty thing and me and mama live with her in the big house way out in the country. 'Brown the sugar first in the good heavy iron skillet,' she say. Old country kitchen, wooden floors washed with lye until they was white. The place so far out you ain't gonna see nobody for days at a time. When you big enough, baby, you gonna learn to make a caramel cake, too. I pass it on to you."

The house her grandmother lived in and the land around it, the cotton and corn fields, all of it had actually belonged to her grandfather before he died. A colored preacher walked out into the field one day where he was sharecropping and told him his mama's brother, Jesse Wilkes, had died and left him a farm. Easy as that. Mr. Jesse didn't have sons of his own and his daughters had settled up in Memphis. Jubilee couldn't remember her grandfather, but her grandmama talked about him all the time.

After he died, her grandmother and her mother and uncle put in the crops and ran the place. It was the happiest time in her life up until now. But her mama never did like it there. The only reason she stayed that far out in the country was because she didn't have enough money to live any place else.

After Jubilee's grandmother died, her mother and her uncle decided not to say way out there. So they sold the old place for almost nothing to the white man who owned the fields that joined it. Her mother got a little something out of the sale, enough to satisfy her yearning to see the city. Right away she took off to Detroit to look for some work, she said. She left her daughter with a sister that Jubilee had never seen before in her life until then. It was only suppose to be for a little while. That was the last time Jubilee ever saw her. It was the reason she had always wanted a family of her own so badly. Because of being left there in such a comfortless condition.

She never heard what happened to her mother and the not knowing nearly drove her crazy if she thought about it. So she didn't. But she wondered if her mother had ever seen a white beach and a green and purple ocean.

And she stopped perfectly still and the coldness rolled over her again, because she was reminded of the strangeness in her dream of a child playing in a field of white flowers near a green and purple snake.

When she suddenly realized she was standing poised on the steps of her porch almost in mid-step, she smiled and shook her head and walked on out to the highway.

Mr. Luke came to get her in his light green pickup where she stood waiting at the end of the tractor road.

As she sat beside him in the cab of the truck she said, "Miss Anise sho' excited about going to Florida tomorrow."

"Yeah, I know she is. But none of them realize what has to be done on this place before I can leave everything for a week."

Jubilee thought about the mountain of work she had to finish at the big house that day. Just like men folk, thinking they the only ones do anything worth while, she thought.

"Yassuh," she said aloud.

"Benny get to the field early this morning?" he asked her. "I can't believe how slow he was yesterday. When I checked on him at noon, he'd just barely begun poisoning the field. So, of course, he wasn't able to finish. He promised he'd get back on to it this morning first thing."

Jubilee was surprised.

"He ain't got home until late last night, Mr. Luke, and he was up before me this morning. I don't know what time he leave."

And when did he have time to pick flowers and put them in a jar? she wondered. Didn't make sense. She knew Benny and she knew how he was when he came in from a bad day, things going wrong one after another and slowing him up. He wouldn't be thinking about anything else but how tired and frustrated he was. And if the cabin was dark and supper cold and she was asleep because she got so tired from work lately? He'd stomp and fuss around 'til he woke her up and she offered to heat up his food and sit and listen, sleepy eyed, while he let go of some of the steam that accumulated in him during the day.

She was later than usual that afternoon getting home from work. Her lower back ached and her feet were swollen almost out of her shoes. She went inside the cabin and poured some tea into a glass and walked barefoot out onto the little front porch. She pulled some mint leaves for her tea off the plant that was threatening to take over the steps. She sat down in the swing and pushed her body to the end with her back toward the yard and pulled her feet up and leaned her head back and closed her eyes.

While she was at work she had put the unsettling dream out of her head, but now she felt it creeping back. She reassured herself by rocking her knees back and forth while she drank her tea.

"You looking comfortable."

The voice came from behind her.

She started and turned around quickly to see who had come up so quietly. She laughed in relief when she saw who it was.

"Afternoon, Miz Deedove," she said and began to take her feet down off the swing.

"No, don't move. I can set right over here in this old straight chair," she said as she shuffled up the steps on a cane and sat down with a slow painful movement that ended with a hard bump and a grunt.

Jubilee thought she must have seen Quilla's little girl on the way, because the laces on her old field shoes were tied. Deedove couldn't lean far enough over to get at them herself.

"Can I get you a glass of tea, Miz Deedove?"

"Nawh. But I got a little something for you. Good strong stuff. My mama use to always make it up fresh and keep it on hand when she midwifing. Best stuff she know of for expecting mamas," Deedove said and handed her a small clear bottle with amber colored liquid in it.

Without hesitation Jubilee opened the bottle.

"How much?" She looked at Deedove.

"Every bit," was the answer, so she poured the contents into her glass.

"Thank you, Miz Deedove. You a kind woman to take the time to mix this up fresh for me every week."

"Humpf. Sis Riah don't think so. Just because I can't go around get no baby clothes for you. Because ain't nobody in this here county gonna say nothing to old Deedove. But I gots a job. My job see to it you gonna get the tonic." She paused. "Quilla's little girl say Sis Riah and Saphronia going on a trip."

"Yassm. They going to a church meeting on Saturday and Sunday at Tugaloo College."

"Montgomerys gonna be gone until next week?"

"Yassm, that's right."

"Then you rest up, hon. Everything gonna be different next week."

"That just what I'm gonna do, Miss Deedove. I'm gonna rest right here on this here porch long as I can."

"And drink your tea."

"And drink my tea," she said and sipped the cool liquid. After a while she said, "Miz Deedove, what you put in your tonic?"

"What you think?"

Jubilee closed her eyes and leaned her head back again and smiled.

"Lemon grass the main thing. Probably cut the taste of the stuff ain't so good. Tansy ragwort. Water hemlock. Angelica and sea holly. Some stuff I ain't never taste before. Something secret."

Deedove started and looked cautiously at the closed eyes on the calm face.

"What you know about them things?" she asked harshly.

Jubilee's eyes opened in surprised at the tone of Deedove's voice.

"I don't know exactly. I's just being silly, I guess."

Deedove watched her face carefully, reading the lines, the wrinkling around her eyes and mouth. She could see that Jubilee was not aware of how close she had come to the truth. For a while the two women sat silently as they often did.

"I got something else for you this evening," the old woman said, finally, interrupting the quiet. "I got your baby girl's name."

Jubilee sat up in the swing in surprise.

"You do?"

"Her name gonna be Grace."

"Grace?" Jubilee said listening to the sound of it.

"It mean something good come you ain't expecting. It speak about what she gonna inherit."

"Deedove, what you talking about?"

"Time gonna explain it, Jubilee."

"Grace. I likes it. Sho' better than the name in the dream."

"What dream?"

"One I has last night. Can't hardly shake it out of my head; keep coming right back on me."

"Don't never try to get rid of them kinda dreams. Hold on to them until you understands what they trying to say to you."

"I don't understand nothing about this one except it scare me."

"You better tell it to me."

"Well, it begin, I think, with some flowers Benny bring me last night after I's in bed. In the dream I's smelling Benny's flowers with the field grass in them and I smell something else. Like Rose Bay. It just fill up my head. Make me want to get close as I can to whatever it is smelling like that. Breath it in until I be filled up with the smell from my head to my feet. You ever smell something you like that much?"

Deedove sat perfectly still with her eyes wide opened looking at Jubilee.

"Rose Bay? Where Benny get Rose Bay?"

"Oh, no, ma'm. The Rose Bay part wrong. Just jasmine and lilies and some field grass."

"How come you to know what Rose Bay smell like?"

"My grandmama show me a real old, wooden box she get from her mama long time ago. She say she don't know how long that little box been in our family. She keep it on her dresser. Keep funny things in it. Stones, dried seeds and flowers. She say I needs to set that box in my memory. How it smell. How it look. Little flowers of some kind on top made out of shells set down into the wood. She say that box made from the wood of a Rose Bay tree. Long time ago somebody kin to us bring it all the way from Africa."

Deedove was leaning forward in the straight chair, mesmerized by the unexpected innertwining of the tendrils of that power she was born to recognize.

"Go ahead. The dream."

"Yassum. Well, right away all them sweet smells begun to call to me, but I don't know which way to go to find them. And something come up to me, like it was out of a deep river fog. It's the one what was the Rose Bay."

The old woman gasped.

"Deedove, you alright?" Jubilee asked.

"I's alright. You just go on. Tell it to me. All of it."

"Well, the Rose Bay suddenly turn into a woman."

"I knows that woman," Deedove said softly. "I know who she be."

"My grandmama?"

"You woulda known your grandmama right away. Nawh, not your grandmama. Was *my* mama you seen."

"Your mama. But, Deedove, how come I see your mama in my dream?"

"Listen. While she live my mama keep every thing she put on her body in a trunk made of Rose Bay wood. I can't even think of her without thinking of that smell. Ain't no truer sign. What she say to you?"

"She say this baby suppose to be named Delora, because of the sorrow in her."

"Sorrow? What she mean by that? Ain't gonna be no sorrow. How come she telling you sorrow? Then what happen, girl? Tell it to me just like it was."

"Let me see. I dreams I's in a fog, like I say before, so I can't see nothing at all and the Rose Bay that was your mama, leading me on along. I just follow the smell like I would have been following somebody. And pretty soon the Rose Bay lead me out of the fog. Or it could have been daybreak. I ain't sure. And I see spread out before me a meadow in the middle of a pine woods with trees all around it that's alive with spirits."

"What you mean 'spirits'?" Deedove interjected.

"I can't exactly see them, but I can feel them everywhere, like a humming of some kind. And then I hears laughing and I looks around the field and there in the middle of the whole thing is her, the baby. And she just be laughing and playing in this great, old, big field of flowers. I knows that it's her. Funny thing though. I think something wrong cause she ain't got no smell of her own. Just the smell of flowers and grass. And I takes notice of it and remembers it."

Jubilee paused and looked far out over the swamp.

"What else?"

"Next come the scary part. Hard for me to speak in words."

"You go on and tell me the rest, Jubilee."

"Well, all of a sudden, a shiny green and purple snake come forth out of the spirit woods and into the field of flowers where the baby be and slithered up so close to her I can't stand it. And that snake know my baby because it keep calling her by her name, 'Delora, Delora,' and it keep on coming closer and closer to her. It so beautiful in the light my eyes about put out, but a terrible fire shooting out its mouth. All I can think is I gotta keep that thing away from the baby any way I can. And I tries to run towards her, protect her, but I can't move no matter how hard I tries and the snake, still slithering toward her. And all the time I keeps on thinking about smelling the flowers and the field grass and the Rose Bay until they about makes me sick.

And, finally, while the baby playing all around in the flowers the snake raise up its head and begin to puff out its mouth to get it all full of fire. I can't hardly stand to see what gonna happen. I wants to close my eyes and run away. Still she my own little baby out there, so I has to watch.

And then, all of a sudden, fire everywhere, wherever I look, and the baby and the snake covered in it. And the fire flash and lick and eat up everything it touch, the flowers, the whole field. Pretty soon everything in the dream burnt up but me and the Rose Bay spirit.

And my whole soul break apart in crying and sorrow. But then your mama begin to comfort me and say my little girl alright and weren't no more hurt by the fire of that snake than the day time is by the night. She say the baby gone for now but gonna come back to me someday."

Jubilee wiped the wetness from her face.

"And your mama ask me do I understand what I see. And I say I don't. But she say I'm gonna understand all of it by the time it come to pass. It gonna be like coming out of the night into a real bright day. She say then I be able to see lots more things than I can now."

Deedove sat in confusion and shivered. Why didn't she understand what the dream meant and why had the revelation come to Jubilee instead of to her?

"Deedove, you listening?"

The old woman looked as if she had fallen asleep with her eyes opened. Her lips were moving ever so slightly like she was talking very quietly to herself.

"Miss Deedove?"

"Yeah."

"What do it mean? Something gonna happen to Grace?"

Deedove didn't answer for a while, but finally said, "I don't know."

She rose from the chair, slowly shaking her head.

"Don't know near about what I know this morning. I'm gonna get on home, think on this thing a while. Take some time to think on it. Why ain't she coming to tell *me* whatever it is she want to tell?"

"Your mama?"

"Look like she don't want me to know, so she wrap it up in a puzzle. She mad because I'm shutting her out, long with the others. All time saying I done misused the powers. Think they know everything they is to know. She mad at me for that. What business she got with this here girl?"

"Miss Deedove, sometime I can't understand a word you say."

Deedove seemed to come out of a trance and she looked sharply into Jubilee's face.

"They been mad at me long enough. Time come for us to get along."

She walked carefully down the porch steps holding tightly to the rail and her cane.

"I gotta get on home and think on it. Talk to them. Whether they gonna talk back or not. I'm going on home."

She turned and looked back a long moment behind her.

"Miss Deedove, you gonna be alright?"

Deedove looked up at the sky.

"Storm coming," she said. "Don't know if everybody gonna be safe at home when it come or if we gonna lose somebody before it get over."

She shuffled on down the path leaving a confused and worried Jubilee standing on the porch behind her.

CHAPTER 15

BENNY GOT BACK into the fields at dawn on Wednesday morning. He wanted to finish work on the Nance place early if he could. Next week would be unusually busy. The young Montgomerys would be in Florida and as usual he would be in charge of things on the farm. He didn't expect any problems unless Mr. Matthew tried to butt his nose into the work. Nothing Benny ever did was right to that man. It didn't matter how many times he tried to prove to him that he was hard working, Matthew always turned it around into something that made him look lazy or stupid or dishonest. Benny thought it might be because his daddy use to brag all the time about how smart his son was. He'd tell stories to anybody who'd listen, colored or white, about Benny.

Like the one about the hay. It didn't seem like much, but he told that story over and over. Benny must have heard it a million times. He and Luke were sitting side by side in the late afternoon, riding high up on top of a full hay wagon, swinging their legs at the dust the wheels kicked up. It was back when hay was taken in wagonloads from the field instead of bales. Benny watched the men, his daddy among them, forking the hay into the barn, the itchy chaff and sweat mixing in their hair and settling on their faces, working its way down the neck of their shirts with more sweat and wedging into their shoes. His daddy sneezed and scratched at the stuff all night when he got home.

"Daddy, I got a idea," he said one night after supper. His daddy was still a young man then, believing anything might come from this smart son of his. He looked away from the plow harness he was mending and leaned towards the boy.

"About what?"

"About getting the hay in."

"Well, lemme hear it," his daddy said, smiling at him.

"Getting the mules into the trailer's what made me think of it."

"Uh huh."

"You know how ya'll runs that rope sometime around the rumps of the mules when they balks about getting in, and then ya'll sorta pulls them on into it? Into the trailer?"

"Yeah."

"What if before ya'll starts pitching hay up onto the wagon ya'll just runs a big rope all around the inside. Then when the wagon full and the mule pull it into the barn ya'll just lay holda both ends of the rope and pulls the hay out onto the barn floor. Cause it be dry, the hay is, and light, so it'd just slide right on out. Wouldn't it?"

His daddy smiled.

"Might," he said and went back to the harness mending.

"You gonna try it?"

"Might."

The next day his father laid the rope out in the wagon as Benny had described to him.

"What you doing?" the men asked.

"Trying something?" was the answer.

Benny was there with Luke, watching his daddy do it. When the full wagon backed up through the barn door where the load was to be stored he and another hand heaved on the rope ends and the hay sure enough slid out of the wagon and onto the barn floor.

"I'll be damned," the others said. "What made you think of that?"

"Benny, Jr. think of it," his father said.

"Oooh, that boy smart," they said and he saw his daddy's face turn proud.

Mr. Matthew was amazed when he came to check on their progress and found them nearly finished. He didn't know what to say when they showed him how they'd done it and who was responsible for the idea.

"Lucky guess," he said. "Anybody else coulda thought of it. Just a lucky guess."

And the cattle chute. He always told about that, but it really wasn't anything much. Other farmers had done it before, but the Montgomerys hadn't thought to use the idea until he came up with it on his own. He must have been about ten or so and he and Luke were sitting on the top rail of a fence watching the hands riding the horses in the pasture and roping and manhandling yearling calves to the ground to brand or vaccinate or dehorn them. It looked like pretty exciting work to the boys, who were told that they were too small yet to help with this kind of job.

"Daddy, I got another idea," Benny announced as they walked home in the evening. Not that all his ideas worked, but his daddy paid attention to him back then.

"You know when ya'll fighting them calves to do stuff to them?" He waited to see if his father was listening.

"Yeah, whatcha got in mind?"

"Well, ya'll take the time to build a little fenced in place. But you make one side so you can pick it up and move it pretty easy, maybe you and a few others, and then ya'll just run the calves into it. You know, one man on a horse drive the cows up into it and then ya'll could just make it smaller and smaller, make the cows get closer and closer inside until one man just slip a rope around the neck of which ever cow he want to. See what I mean?"

"Well, before it'll work you gotta make it so's the movable part of the fence'll set good and tight and won't just fall over when all them scared cows starts to running at it," his father countered.

In a few days Benny showed his father a drawing of a way to lock the fence to other secured sections. Mr. Matthew grudgingly gave them permission to try it out and even he had to admit it worked.

Later Benny improved the idea by adding a chute at one end that held only one calf at a time with a removable gate to the front and back. When the hands finished branding and vaccinating a calf the far gate was removed and the scared, walleyed animal could return to the pasture easily while another calf was prodded into the chute to take its place.

"I seen plenty of those. What you think so marvelous about a cow chute," Mr. Matthew said. "Luke, how come you always hanging out with this boy? You got Robert to play with. Go have your mama call him to come over."

But the Montgomerys used the chute from then on.

Benny directed the tractor between the cotton rows. Inside his head he allowed a sweet wash of the memory of his daddy's face during those times when he was a little boy. But his memory kept ruining the sweetness of it by reminding him of the time after the test, that dry, hard time. And he would have to think about that for a while, because his memory was merciless.

He kept half expecting that cloud of dust to reappear at the top of the trail and the green Ford coupe to come bouncing down the road. But nothing had come by on the highway all morning. And if he did see the old car turn down the dusty lane what then? If she waited for him at the pond, what would he say to her that he didn't say yesterday?

And what about Jubilee?

The thought made an ache in his chest. He should have seen enough of what his daddy did to his mama to cure him of ever getting into something like that.

But then again he hadn't done anything much. A lot less than everybody in the county expected him to do. Hell, he knew plenty of men who cheated on their wives. Mr. Jim McKibben had a mixed family over in Camden. And Willie Joe Evertson was sleeping around with a thirteen-year-old girl right in town. Got her big. Their wives had to know something about all that. They musta just learned to live with it.

But he knew for a fact there were men in Tula who never did stuff like that. He'd never heard a whisper about Mr. Luke. And he knew Sweet Boy had never cheated on Sis Riah. And he'd always thought he'd be like that, too. Not like his daddy.

So why had he done it?

He had been mad. And she was asking for it. And he had the right. He worked hard. And hadn't he resisted this kinda thing lots of times before, when women threw themselves at him in the past? Women had always liked him. Jubilee was lucky to get whatever part of him he was willing to give her.

But the truth was Jubilee was better than him. He had known it right at the beginning. That he'd married above himself. He knew it when he first laid eyes on her. Not just that she was good looking, but there was a dignity about her. She was real young then and he knew he better act quick before somebody else got her. And somewhere down at the bottom of him he felt an old fear begin gnawing at him again. He always believed he would lose her some day. It made him dizzy to think about it.

It was the reason he'd walked a mile farther down the road last night to the old mansion when he was so tired he couldn't stand up after finishing the field. And then cutting the flowers that Jubilee took such pleasure in with his pocket knife, and walking back through the fields, remembering the field grass right before he got home. He worried now that it was too much. That she'd suspect something. He never did things like that, sweet things for her. He felt like he always had to challenge her. Had to keep on proving to himself that she really did love him.

When the baby came he'd try to do more, maybe take care of it every now and then, so she'd have some time for herself and wouldn't get so tired like his mama had been. Seemed like his mama was always tired. On Saturday nights after she'd worked in Olivia Montgomery's house all week, she'd feed and bath all five children and get them to bed early, so they'd be ready for church on Sunday. No help from anybody. All by herself. Not one of the children more than a year apart. And where was his daddy when she was doing all that at home?

His mama died young. Not surprising. After that his oldest sister waited on his daddy like he was God Almighty and tried to do the same things her mama had done for all of them. Eventually she wound up marrying and bending her back to a no-good man who wasn't attached to any family, but depending on his wife's work to keep him and his children fed and his house clean.

When Benny was nearly finished with the field he saw he was close to being out of poison, unless there was more in the workshop at Mr. Luke's. He should go check. But just to be safe he figured he'd take the pickup that Mr. Luke had left him to use and drive early next morning to town and go into Mr. Sam's for some more poison. And maybe after he'd bought it, he could just walk up to the dry cleaners to tell Nan how sorry he was again, make sure she understood, before he came back to start the Gage place fields. That's all. Just say he was sorry.

He could go early, because the equipment store opened early and he'd get to the cleaners before it opened maybe and what would he do then? Climb the stairs to where she lived above the cleaners? No. He shook his head. He'd wait down stairs and knock on the door of the cleaners. And when she finally answered because he made such a racket he'd say what he came to say, that he was sorry if he'd hurt her, and then he'd get on back to the poisoning.

But he knew how dangerous it would be with this damn heat down in him. He would have to be very careful. He'd just see her again to apologize for his behavior and at the same time remember how lucky he was to have Jubilee. He wouldn't be mad this time and he'd just go to explain that he had taken out his anger on her, nothing more, and that he was sorry. But what if the Owens said something to him again? Made him mad again. He didn't care. He wouldn't let it bother him. He knew he was stronger than that trash. He'd just be humble and polite, play that game to get what he needed and go. But what if she couldn't hear him knock on the cleaners door or maybe if she wouldn't open to him no matter where he knocked? If she were that mad.

All day long while he worked he had fought inside his head, deciding and undeciding, reminding himself about Jubilee and the baby, but then finding himself thinking about the sight of water dripping from the breasts of a woman who required nothing from him, no promises kept or broken. A woman who could have anybody or anything she wanted, but had come looking for him. He'd suddenly catch himself remembering the pond and the water and the slick wet body sliding between the inside of his legs. And then he could hardly stand the heat of it.

He had been thinking so hard that he was surprised when he reached the last plant of the last row and finally turned off the sprinkler. He climbed down off the tractor, wiping his face with the cleanest part of his handkerchief and stood looking back over the even rows with stunted cotton plants just beginning to bole, all alike, same height, same distance apart, well tended and healthy despite the lack of rain in the early summer. And he was proud of what he had done, planted, thinned, weeded, poisoned to make the good stand of cotton that he saw stretching away from him up the gentle hill to the gullies. It would have a good yield in the fall in spite of the early drought. He could tell.

He drove the pickup into Mr. Luke's garage and walked home. It was still light and he knew Jubilee would have supper waiting. He didn't know exactly what he was going to say to her. He thought maybe she'd already guessed everything or that she'd take one look at him and know. So he hesitated. He felt his heart beating in his neck and ears. He turned onto the path and stood waiting for a moment. He had to calm down, think, before he got into the house.

The smell of the flowers reached him as he walked up the wooden steps of his porch. The day had cooled down a little and it was getting dark. The call of katydids and frogs filled the evening. Everything just like it always was. Except for the inside of him.

Jubilee called out to him when she heard him on the porch.

"Benny, you get through early?"

The screen door opened and before he could think she was throwing her arms around his neck.

"Oooh, Benny. I feels like you been gone a week." She started to kiss him.

"Watch out. You'll get poison all over you," he said shoving her back from him. She stood at the door with her arms still raised slightly for the embrace and then turned quickly and followed him into the house.

"Here. Lemme take them dirty overalls and put them in the back yard by the wash bucket," she said. "I already done the pair you wore yesterday. They out hanging on the line."

She followed him into the front room where the smell of the cotton poison blended with the flowers and the fried chicken and green beans cooking on the stove.

"Nawh, you ain't. I do it."

He started taking off his overalls and work shirt in the backroom by their bed. She stood at the doorway, watching him.

He carried his dirty clothes outside and dropped them into the wash tub. He knew she could hear him washing off in the basin of water that stood by the back door. When he came back in wearing his under things, she had not moved from the doorway between the two rooms in the cabin. He looked up and saw the admiration in her eyes and quickly grabbed a pair of old work pants and a shirt from a nail behind the door and began pulling them on. She would try to read the anger in his movements. He had to be more careful.

"Supper smell good," he muttered.

She smiled cautiously.

"I dish it up for you."

She turned quietly in the doorway without saying anything more and in a while he heard the sounds in the front room of her setting out their supper on the little table by the flowers. His mouth went dry.

"How you like the flowers?" he called to her.

He had said it wrong, too nice. She'd suspect something. When he came into the front room buttoning his shirt her back was to him and he watched it for signs.

"Jubilee?" he said finally.

"They's beautiful," she said not turning around. "The flowers beautiful."

He'd upset her. He better say something. Maybe he'd tell her part of it. Not the whole thing, because he didn't know it all himself.

"Jubilee, I's sorry if I acted mad when I first come in."

He sat down at his plate. When he looked up at her face, it was solemn and her eyes were full. Hell, he said he was sorry. What else did she need from him?

"What's the matter with you?" he said, the anger back in his voice.

"I's sorry I come running out like that at you. I knows you tired. But this morning when I wake up, you ain't here. Didn't even know what time you got home last night."

"Well, everything slowing me down yestiddy," he started to explain.

"That the longest time we been apart since we's married. I miss you, Benny, almost more than I can stand. I wake up smelling something good in the house and I get up and find these here flowers setting on the table and I think about you going to pick them way after dark."

"They just going to waste out yonder at that old place. You might as well have them."

"When I hear you out yonder on the porch I just forget how tired you gonna be. That's how come me to run out the door hollering at you."

He looked at her open eyed. She thought his anger was her fault.

"I got to go into town tomorrow morning. I's almost out of poison," he said, not looking at her but at his plate.

"The equipment store? I hate you has to go talk to them people."

"Gotta have that poison early. No need to worry. I ain't gonna let that trash bother me none."

"Benny, Owen's place right down from the dry cleaners. If you happens to see Miss Nan, would you tell her I says, 'Howdy'? I had the nicest visit with her on Saturday at the wagon. She real friendly to me. I's surprised."

Benny looked up at her in astonishment.

"What she doing talking to you?" he asked.

"I don't know. Guess she need friends just like anybody else.

Didn't visit long. She left before Sis Riah got there. I woulda served her up some cake if she hada stayed." She studied his face carefully. "Something wrong in that, Benny?"

"Nawh, nothing wrong. I just wondering who you talking to is all." He looked back down at his plate quickly. "Say you smell them flowers when you wake up?"

"Before I wake up even. I's dreaming about the smell of them flowers. Benny, you reckon they's any truth in dreams?"

"Don't know. Maybe."

"Well, best part is I find out what the baby's name gonna be. Deedove say her first name to be Grace, but the dream say . . . . "

"Where you see Deedove?"

"Uh, here."

"In my house?"

"Benny, don't get mad. It just for a little while. And, Benny, listen. I know what her name gonna be. Our little girl. She gonna be Grace Delora. Ain't that a pretty name?"

"So now you letting that old witch name my baby? Jubilee, what I has to do to make you scared of that woman?"

"Benny, you wrong. You still looking at her with your child eyes what saw something awful long time ago. She different now. Benny, Deedove got a love for me and this baby you don't understand."

"Deedove love what she can make use of."

"No, Benny. Listen. She don't want nothing but good come to us. Grace and me. Every week since she know Grace coming that woman make a tonic out of good stuff she pick fresh herself and bring to me. She make it because she care about . . . "

Benny stood up slowly, his eyes wide and the wrinkles deep across his brow and drew in a deep breath.

"She bring you what?"

"Wait, Benny. It ain't to do me no harm. I be fine. Be feeling real good. Sis Riah say I looks fortified."

"Jubilee, I swear if I ever catch that woman in this house I gonna kill her with my own bare hands. Last words I wants you to say to her, 'stay away from this place if she want to live'. Jubilee, I means it. You know what I'm saying?"

"But Deedove ain't gonna hurt me or this baby no more'n you is. She kind. Love us. You just got to understand that."

He stood before her, silent. What she had said about his hurting her. She was so trusting. What could he say to her now? That she was not safe, not even from him. That he most certainly could hurt her. That at this very moment he was burning with the desire to go into town and do something that would hurt her more than she could ever imagine.

He looked at her for a moment as if he would speak, but turned silently instead and walked out of the house.

CHAPTER 16

JUBILEE WALKED THROUGH the yard gate of Sis Riah's house early the next morning. Sis Riah and Sweet Boy lived in a cabin down the road about a mile toward town from Mr. Luke's. It was more than double the size of Jubilee's and Benny's place. The front room was twice as big and there were two nice sized bedrooms in the back, the smallest of which was kept ready all the time for visiting preachers or other people who needed a place to stay. Sweet Boy kept the outside walls whitewashed and the doors and window trim painted green. Miz Olivia insisted that Matthew should have him instructed on how to install electricity so that the place was purged of the smell of kerosene, and she made Sis Riah agree to have a telephone in case of emergencies.

It was a palace after what they'd lived in before they came back to Tula. Sis Riah had covered the rough walls on the inside with wallpaper and hung curtains in the windows that matched. She made slipcovers for an old overstuffed couch and chair that Olivia had given her and samples of Sis Riah's hand working skills were everywhere. The light linoleum on the floor was always clean and shining and Sis Riah kept fresh flowers in the room even in winter from her own garden.

One of the first things she had Sweet Boy do after they moved there was to fence her in a flower garden just outside the front door. Every woman in Hart County was envious of that garden. Sis Riah could have made a good living off of selling flowers to ladies in the county, but she preferred to give them away to people she thought really needed them for some reason. Like Mr. Jim's grandmother on her eightieth birthday or Quilla's youngest child, who worked so hard to win the school spelling bee, but lost. She never delivered the flowers herself; she sent Sweet Boy to the door with them. And it seemed like the more she cut and gave away the more abundant was the crop.

And their house always had people in it, not because it was so nice but because no matter what their age or condition in life Sis Riah always counted people more important that things. Still she was surprised when Jubilee showed up at her door early Wednesday morning.

"You walk all that way by yourself, gal? What done possessed you to do a thing like that? You wanta have that child along side the road some place?" she said.

"No, ma'm, but I's a little lonesome this morning."

She stood looking at Sis Riah through the screen door.

Sis Riah unlatched and opened the door quickly for her and said, "Well, come on in and set down. You want some coffee?"

"Not right now. But I'd welcome the chance to set down."

Sis Riah was alarmed at the weariness on Jubilee's face.

"Come on back here to the bedroom and lay down, honey," she said.

"Oh, no, ma'm. Setting be fine."

"Nawh, come on now. I's packing up some things to take to Tugaloo with me." Jubilee obediently followed her back to one of the bedrooms. "You know, I gotta try to keep up with Saphronia down there. Why don't you lie down right here on the bed, get your feets up, help me decide what to take," Sis Riah said.

Jubilee sat heavily on the bed and Sis Riah took her legs and gently pulled them up onto the crocheted spread.

"Wait. My feet gonna ruin your covers," Jubilee said.

"Don't matter. You look about done in, honey. How about a cool glass of water?"

"That be real nice. Thank you."

Jubilee laid her head back on the clean pillow. Sis Riah came back in a minute with a flower-painted jelly-jar glass full of water.

"Now you listen here, honey. I don't want to hear nothing about you walking out like this in the hot morning no more. You putting yourself and this baby in danger. I'm gonna get Sweet Boy to take you home after he come in for his dinner."

"Ain't no need to bother. I be alright," Jubilee said with her eyes closed.

Sis Riah looked at the young face carefully. Her mouth was shut and drawn tight over her teeth.

"What you worried about, hon?" she said.

"Aw, nothing much."

Sis Riah didn't say anything. She watched as Jubilee's face slowly softened into calmness against the pillow. Finally, she picked up two dresses and held them in front of herself.

"Which one you thinks I oughta take?"

Jubilee opened her eyes.

"That one nice," she said pointing to a blue and white, floral print.

"Ain't it too bright? You know I gonna be with some high nosed folks down there. Swanky clothes. What you think?"

She was looking at herself in the wardrobe mirror with the dress held up in front of her. Jubilee smiled.

"Try it on so's I can see how it look with your navy blue hat."

"I don't know. I's afraid that dress too showy. I sho' don't wanta look proud. Saphronia gonna do enough of that for both of us."

"Where you get it?" Jubilee said as Sis Riah wriggled out of her house dress.

"Olivia. She sent it to me for my birthday last spring. I never woulda dreamed of buying a dress like that for myself. I never had it on except in the privacy of my own house."

"Miz Olivia give you that?"

"Uh huh," she said slipping the dress over her head and backing up to Jubilee to zip it up.

"Try the hat on with it," Jubilee said.

Sis Riah put the hat on and looked at herself, then tipped it forward and to the side a bit to give herself a look of smartness.

"Oh, alright. I can't turn it down. Olivia sho' do know what I like."

"I wish I was going with you." Jubilee said as Sis Riah turned her back for unzipping.

"I do too. Some day we do things together like that. Alright, now you rested a little. Time to talk to old Sis Riah. What you feeling lonesome about this morning?"

Jubilee didn't answer but watched her get out of the dress and put her housedress back on.

"Well?" Sis Riah asked again.

"Benny brung me flowers Monday night," Jubilee said quietly.

"You worrying about that?"

"He went and got them for me after he work in the field all day."

"And that what got you bothered?"

"Yassum. Sound foolish, don't it?" Jubilee said, but Sis Riah wasn't laughing.

"Doctor say everything gonna be fine, girl?"

"Yassum. I ain't worried about that."

Sis Riah sat down on the foot of the bed and with her large smooth hands began rubbing Jubilee's ankles and feet.

"You thinking something wrong between you and Benny maybe you don't know about?" she asked carefully.

Tears formed under Jubilee's lashes.

"They was cape jasmine and lilies from the old Russell house. And field grass. That what I like the most."

Sis Riah got a clean handkerchief and handed it to Jubilee and then sat back down and returned to rubbing the swollen ankles.

"I remember the very day Olivia's mama, Miz Helen Russell, planted them cape jasmine bushes, one on either side of the front steps of that house. She say she's planting them there so Olivia have cape jasmine in her wedding bouquet. Olivia just about five years old then." Jubilee giggled through the tears. "Them bushes done real well there. But Olivia married Mr. Matthew right after

Christmas time and she had to carry holly because it was a cold winter and nobody even had camelias blooming yet."

"That the truth?" Jubilee asked smiling.

"Sho' is. Miz Helen never done forgive Matthew Montgomery for that winter wedding. 'Course, she never thought to blame Olivia for it."

"Oh, Sis Riah. I knew if I could just get over here you gonna make me feel better."

"Feeling better fine but don't solve nothing, do it, hon?

"No, ma'm. Maybe ain't nothing really need solving," Jubilee said.

"Well, why don't you just tell me what you worrying about? You know I gives away lotsa free advice. You can sho' have your share this morning if you wants it. You worrying cause Benny brung you some of Miz Helen's cape jasmine?"

"Ain't that silly?"

"Only you know in your heart if it silly or not, honey."

The warmth and kindness in Sis Riah's hands made Jubilee begin to cry again.

"Brung them while I's asleep. Turn out I didn't even get to see him to say thank you for another whole day because he busy with the poisoning."

"Now, now, honey. Maybe that just the problem. Maybe you lonesome cause Benny having to work so hard right now."

"Could be. I so glad to see him when he finally get home last night I coulda eat him up."

"Bet he glad to see you, too. Huh?"

"Well, I don't know. He acting real hard. Wouldn't let me touch him, not even to help him with his overalls."

"Most pro'bly the man was wore out," Sis Riah said.

"I know that the truth, for sure. But then the very next thing he say to me be nice like he feel bad he talk harsh to me. Then pretty soon he all hard again. First fussing, then nice, then fussing some more. That how it go all during supper until he just up and leave and don't come back until I's asleep."

Jubilee rubbed her hand along the bumps Sis Riah had worked

into the crocheted bedspread, feeling the progression of holes that radiated out from each round crocheted ball. Sis Riah's face was thoughtful, but she didn't say anything.

"I keep on wondering how come him to bring me them flowers," she said, "if he mad?"

"Bringing flowers a kind thing unless they got snakes in them," Sis Riah said with a little laugh.

Jubilee let out a little cry of alarm and sat up.

"Snakes?" she shuddered. "How come you to say something about snakes?"

"Wait, honey. I just teasing you."

Jubilee sat on the bed rigidly with her eyes opened wide looking at Sis Riah.

"It just a saying, honey," Sis Riah said, putting her arms around the young woman and rocking her gently. "Calm yourself."

"Sis Riah, something bad happening," Jubilee cried.

"Shhh, now, honey. Don't get yourself upset. You listen to old Sis Riah. Nothing matter now except that little old baby and you. That what you gotta take care of. Nothing else important. Anything wrong you can tend to it later. Right now you ain't gonna think of nothing except your job. You and that baby."

"I just can't do that, Sis Riah."

"Now, listen to me. Somewhere inside you a place that strong, not soft and weak. Somebody done left you some strength to draw from. My strong place come straight from my mama. And I know you strong, too."

"When you have to draw strength? Seem like you and Sweet Boy happiest people I know."

"I'm gonna tell you something you has to believe. When me and Sweet Boy first married us both working hard for trashy people down by Canton. Bad stuff happen to us there. I ain't going into no details."

Jubilee looked up at her in surprise.

"What happen?" she asked.

"Don't matter what happen. But we both hurt bad. And I has to thank Olivia for helping me out when I couldn't help myself.

Weren't nothing I could do about it. Nothing Sweet Boy could do
neither, except get hisself killed over it. Then I wouldn't ahad him
no more. Don't think I coulda stood that. I told him so."

"Sis Riah, I always thinking you never did have no problems."

"Ain't no more'n lotsa other folks had. But I had to look down
inside myself and I hear my mama saying, "You do what you got
to do. When things come around bad you just stand up and go
on.""

"My mama ain't like that. She answer her problems by leaving."

"You got strength come from somewhere, hon. I know it."

Jubilee thought.

"Maybe my grandmama. She like that."

"Then draw on her, honey. She waiting inside your memory
to give you some strength."

"And you, too, Sis Riah. You giving strength, too."

Sis Riah got a cool, damp washcloth from the other room.

"Now, wipe your face off," she said and Jubilee obediently did
so.

"I be alright now," she said.

She got up and walked to the window and looked out at the
pecan trees in the back yard. Sweet Boy was mowing the grass
with a push mower that looked like a toy in his big hands. She
smiled as Sis Riah watched her from the bed.

"Sis Riah, what you know about Nan Hawkins?"

"Well, I think most people feels kinda shy of her. She a real
good business man, though," Sis Riah laughed.

"I hear she got a white boyfriend in Jackson."

"I hear that, too. Don't know if it true or not. You know how
folks loves to talk about stuff like that. But I knows one thing. She
don't take nothing off of no colored man. Don't have to. Make
men folk feel like she above them kinda. I reckon all her men
friends leaves after a while cause they can't stands a woman got
every thing they got except one of them things 'tween they legs,"
she laughed again.

"Reckon she rather have a business than a husband?"

"She ain't got no choice. She too strong for a husband. She

ain't never gonna find a man around here willing to look up to a wife. Least ways, I sho' ain't never seen him. Most men folk I know gotta have a woman kinda scared of them all the time."

"Benny ain't like that."

"Yeah, he is."

"I ain't scared of Benny, Sis Riah."

"Honey, you not as smart as I thought you is if you believe that."

"Is you scared of Sweet Boy?"

Sis Riah smiled at the thought of anybody, grown or child, man or woman, scared of the kindly giant she was married to.

"Lord, no, honey. That man got so much tenderness and sweetness in him, he don't like to run the combine in Mr. Matthew's oat fields for fear he gonna run over a rabbit litter. He never could even go hunting with his daddy and brothers. Couldn't stand to shoot nothing. Barely tough enough to be a man. That's how come God make him so big. So living things gonna naturally respect him without him scaring them into it."

Jubilee looked back onto Sis Riah's back yard. It was the kind of yard that needed children to play in it with a swing tied up in one of the big old trees. Her own yard was rows and rows of cotton plants clear down to the Big Black swamp. She watched a bright red cardinal come to a pile of breadcrumbs Sis Riah had thrown out onto the grass. She felt better now. Lighter.

"I wouldn't trade Benny and this baby for all the rayon dresses and polished fingernails in the world."

"Now, ain't that the truth."

"Sis Riah, Sweet Boy ever run around on you? I mean when ya'll was younger?"

"Well, honey, I sho' never did know about it if he did. I pro'bly kill him if I find out about it. Her, too, I imagine. Jubilee, that what you worrying about?"

Jubilee turned and started for the door.

"I don't know."

"Honey, Benny done seen too much destruction brought on by his daddy by that kinda stuff to ever get messed up in it hisself.

Now, hon, you needs to concentrate on putting off your worrying for a while."

"I'll try. Thank you, Sis Riah. You like a mama to me." And she started for the door.

"You going?"

"I expects I better."

"And I expects you better stay here until Sweet Boy take you in the truck."

"I be alright. Walk feel good. It cloudy and cool and I go slow."

"Well, I can't make you wait for a ride. You know, Saphronia gonna be gone through the weekend. That woman try the patience of a saint, but she pretty good at getting babies into the world."

"Doctor say first baby take a while to get here, so I has plenty time to get up to Lexington to the hospital."

Jubilee walked out onto Sis Riah's porch.

"You sure you has to go. I gonna stop packing in a minute and fix some ice tea."

Sis Riah stood on the inside of the screen door and talked to Jubilee through it.

"It be noontime soon. I better get on home. I done already got what I come for, anyway. Thank you again, Sis Riah."

Sis Riah stood at the screened door and watched as Jubilee walked down the bottle path to the gate and slowly left her range of clear vision. As she continued down the road she met up with someone who was shorter than she was, humped over, it seemed, and walking with a cane. Sis Riah squinted through the screen, but she couldn't tell who it was. She saw the walker reach out her hand with something to Jubilee, but she pushed it gently away, and shook her head. She tried to continue on, but the something was offered again and this time Jubilee accepted. The two women continued on their opposite ways along the road and Sis Riah finally recognized the walker when she passed her gate.

"Morning, Deedove," she called.

"Humpf," was the return greeting.

Sis Riah turned away from her front door filled with all kinds of worry.

CHAPTER 17

IT DIDN'T TAKE Benny but twenty minutes to walk to Mr. Luke's house early Wednesday morning because he cut through the fields to shorten the distance. He timed himself, so he'd know exactly how long it would take to reach the pickup when Jubilee's pains came on her. As he walked up the driveway, Hippy was coming from the backfield with a full milk bucket in his hand.

"What you gonna do with the milk this week while Mr. Luke's family gone?" Benny asked him.

"Mr. Luke don't care what get done with it, long as I keep that old cow from going dry. You want some of it?"

"Sho' do. Lemme get a quart jar off the back porch. I can't drink no more'n that. Sho' is a lot of milk."

"Mr. Luke always see Quilla get some. Mr. Matthew generally get some of it, too. He be by directly for his share. You going into town today?"

"Yeah, I gotta go down to get some more cotton poison for the Gage place," Benny said dropping his eyes.

"Don't Mr. Luke got poison in the tractor shed?"

"Nawh. Look like he all out."

Benny filled a jar with the warm milk and drank it as he walked back toward the garage.

"Don't take nothing from Sam Owen, you hear?" Hippy said as he carried the milk to the back porch.

When Benny tried to start the truck, the engine sputtered and died at first, but he turned the key again and this time it caught. He backed the pickup out and waved as he passed Hippy walking toward the highway.

Benny had lied to his friend about checking the tractor shed for more poison. Hippy was suppose to vaccinate calves today, so Benny hoped he wouldn't have any reason to go by there. He felt ashamed. What was wrong with him anyway? He wasn't going to do anything in town today that wasn't exactly what he ought to do. He'd pick up the poison (They'd need it sooner or later anyway and he wouldn't have to worry about running out on a Saturday.) and then go quickly by the dry cleaners and apologize to Nan Hawkins. Jubilee, herself, had told him to go by and speak to her.

Benny didn't see Sam or Wynn Owen when he went in for the poison and the white lady that kept books for them came out of the office when she saw him waiting at the back counter and wrote down the cost of the stuff under Luke Montgomery's account. Benny wondered what Luke would think when he saw he'd bought more poison. He put the poison in the back of the pickup that was parked in front of the store and folded the receipt into his shirt pocket and walked up the street.

The cleaners was in a two story building that use to be an old boarding house back in the late 1800's. Across the front were two big windows separated by the door that customers used. The last coat of light blue paint on the clapboard exterior was beginning to peel away from the wood. The stairs along the outside wall that led to the upstairs living quarters were in need of some repair. Miz Jones ought to keep this place up better, he thought. Along the front was a painted wooden sign that read "Tula Dry Cleaning and Laundry."

Benny tried the knob on the door. It was locked. He had checked the time on a clock on the wall of the equipment store. It was almost seven o'clock. He thought Miz Jones probably would expect

Nan to be up and working by now in the back of the shop where the cleaning equipment was. He knocked and waited, looking up and down the street for anyone he knew who might be passing by. He told himself it was all right to be here.

He knocked again on the door. This time louder.

What would he say when she answered? He thought about it. "Miss Nan, I just wanted to say again . . . " He'd call her *Miss* Nan. He'd say he didn't know what had gotten into him. He was sorry he'd (What would he call it?) hurt her. She would smile at him and he would feel (What would he feel?) nothing. He knocked again and called.

"Miss Nan. Miss Nan. You there?"

The business was dark inside. He could see through the glass at the top of the door that she was not downstairs yet. If she was to hear him from the upstairs living quarters he would have to knock and call her name louder. He looked again at the street and saw that there was nobody around to misunderstand what he was doing, knocking and yelling at her door so early in the morning. He might have to explain that he'd been sent by his wife to speak to Miss Hawkins.

One last time he would call. Then if she didn't answer he would be on his way to get to the cotton and tractor. He needed to be going about now anyhow. He didn't really need to apologize to her. He had apologized that afternoon after it happened. And, after all, hadn't she thrown herself at him? He certainly wasn't wrong about that. Swimming out in the pond that way.

He knocked again, rattling the door and calling her name at the same time.

There was no answer. He lost hope in the possibility that she could hear him from upstairs. He turned away and walked back toward the pickup in front of the equipment store unwilling to climb the stairs and knock. His disappointment was overwhelming. It was a good thing she hadn't heard him; his feelings were a lot hotter than he thought. He was glad he hadn't seen her. Maybe in a few weeks when he had cooled off. After Jubilee had the baby and all his attention was on them.

"Mr. Benny?"

He almost didn't hear it, the voice was so low. He turned and looked back at the cleaners. She was standing on the landing of the second floor holding a flowered robe pulled tight around her, her legs and feet bare. He stood looking up at her for a moment not knowing whether to yell the apology or maybe motion for her to come down the stairs to him.

"I just needed to talk to you a minute," he called.

She stood there waiting. He looked up and down the street again and seeing no one near by he walked to the bottom of the stairs.

"Could you just come on down here a minute? I don't wanta yell up this here stair."

She didn't move, but stood clutching the robe to her.

"I ain't got my shoes on," she said. "Come on up here if you want to say something to me."

He didn't want to argue with her out there and without really deciding what to do he found himself climbing the stairs toward her. When he got to the landing she had gone into the living quarters and was holding the door open to him.

"I can't come in. I just wants to tell you again that I's sorry about the other day."

She laughed, releasing her hold on the robe and letting it fall open. Underneath he could see her pale pink, satin nightgown. He had never seen anything like it before. She turned and walked away from him into the sitting room where she sat years ago and listened to her mama and a suitor talking and giggling in the entrance hall. She crossed the room and pulled a cigarette from a package on a table and lit it and picked up the faded, old doll. She sat down in the upholstered chair by the window and draped her bare legs over the arm.

"Now tell me, Mr. Benny. What you sorry about, huh? Sorry you see me driving down that tractor trail to the bushes back of that field? Sorry you catch me taking a dip in that pond without no clothes on? Or is it the next part you sorry about? Sorry you been fucking round with somebody else beside your wife. Huh, Mr. Benny?"

She looked at him with a half smile that teased and mocked him at the same time. He stood in the doorway to the room.

"Miss Nan, I can't stay. I just . . . . "

"What's this "Miss" shit? Don't gimme none of this 'Miss Nan' business. You just come right on out and tell me why you come to my door this morning knocking and yelling, Benny Horne. Tell me what you sorry about."

She blew smoke at the ceiling and swung her bare legs back and forth gently, smiling. Benny had never seen a woman smoking before. He could feel the heat in his thighs and he knew he had to leave quick, bolt out the door that was still opened behind him and run. Still he stood there. She waited for him, drawing on the cigarette again and tilting her chin and blowing the smoke upward.

"Well?" she asked again.

There was a long pause. Benny watched her smoke the cigarette.

"I gotta go. I got work to do," he said remembering.

"Yeah, you got work to do."

She swung her legs to the front of the chair and stood up with her back to him, dropping the doll into the chair and mashing the cigarette out in an ashtray on the table. He felt his legs begin to move him to her.

She turned quickly and put her hand up to his chest, holding him away from her.

"Whoa, Mister Benny. Hold on. You ain't answered my question yet. What you sorry about? You tell me right now."

He pressed his chest against her hand expecting to feel it give way. But when it didn't he said, "I's sorry for hurting you."

He hesitated, waiting for the pressure on his chest to relax. She still held him away from her, looking up at him, smiling at him and teasing. He spoke again.

"And I's sorry if you didn't really want me to do what I done, that I done it."

The arm remained rigid.

"Yeah, and . . . ?" she prompted. He paused again. She held him still. "Let's us have the truth here, Mr. Benny. You tell me what you sorry for now. Every bit of it."

"And . . . and . . . I's sorry for doing something like that to Jubilee," he said softly, reaching for her.

She smiled and relaxed her arm and slid her hand up his chest and around his neck and drew his face to hers and kissed him for a long time. His hands came up from his sides and found their way under the flowered robe to the boyish waist and down her backside, cupping her full buttocks in his hands and pulling her up toward his mouth. She backed away from him, but kept hold of his sleeve and pulled him toward the entry. He thought she was going to push him out the front door, but instead she closed it and led him down the hall into the bedroom.

"Mr. Benny," she said, "what you gonna be sorry for after today?"

And she smiled at him and slowly unbuttoned his shirt and drew his bared chest to the pink satin nightgown and pulled him down with her to the bed.

When Benny left, Nan stood alone again at the window of the sitting room, watching him walk down the stairs and up the street toward the farm equipment store. The house was silent now and empty. She reached into the old chair for the comfort of the doll and picked it up smiling and clutched it to her chest.

CHAPTER 18

THE NEXT DAY Jubilee picked up her bucket and walked over to the Nance field early in the morning to pick some blackberries from her favorite vines. She intended to spend the rest of the day making jam to spread on hot biscuits on cold winter mornings. She had started out in the cool before the sun was high and finally stood looking at the field spread before her. The land rolled gently upward toward the back of the cotton field where a line of green untamed growth sprang up before the red sand gully that held in its bosom the secluded little pond fed by rain and spring water. Nobody ever came to that thicket to pick the berries, so the largest and sweetest the vines could produce would be waiting there for her.

She imagined Benny in this field a few days ago with the kerchief tied over his nose as he guided the tractor between the rows of cotton. She walked over to the side of the trail and took the nearest cotton plant in her hands, moving the leaves gently aside and inspecting the bolls underneath carefully. They were still tight and secure against pillage.

No weevils here.

She smiled with satisfaction and pressed her hand into the small of her back for a moment and then continued on toward the berries.

When she reached the vines that circled the pond she saw

what she had expected. The berries hung in shiny black readiness. The vines caught and tugged against her clothing and scratched her arms and hands as she pulled the ripe berries away from the red and green ones that needed a little more time to hang in the heat and sun to be worth anything to anybody.

There were some evils connected with blackberry picking. The briars, of course, and even now along tight arm and waist bands, tiny red insects, too tiny to see or feel almost, were making lines of small, itchy welts on her skin. But the berries were worth it. The only sounds were the thump of the bucket slowly becoming muted with berries, and the rustling of small animals and birds whose nests were hidden in the underbrush.

She finished on the field side of the mass of vines and began to move away from the road toward the pond side. The vines rose up all around and above her head giving her the feeling of being in a secret outdoor room. She continued to pull and the berries dropped into her juice and blood stained hands.

As she moved to the lower vines, she was surprised suddenly to discover a small white bundle folded carefully and lying on the rich, black loam underneath. She bent over and reached her arm through a maze of older, woody vines. Finally, when she had it in her hand she stood up straight and unfolded the thin cotton batiste and lace. It was a dainty, lady's camisole. The neck was edged with fragile lace beading and blue satin ribbon to be tied when worn, gently enclosing the breasts of some slight woman. She looked down at the ungainly bulkiness of the front of her and for the first time since she realized she was to have a child, she yearned to retrieve the thin beauty and subtle curves of her own body.

She wondered how the beautiful little piece of clothing had come to be there. It had not been there long, since there was no sign of weather on it. Maybe yesterday. Or even early this morning. Had it become an expendable layer when on the way to town the hot sun and humidity got too intense for its owner? Jubilee imagined her leaving the dusty road and creeping behind these vines, where she had taken off a summer dress or dropped it to the waist and removed the camisole, folding it up carefully and hiding it under the berries, with the plan to retrieve it later?

Or perhaps the delicate ribbons that now hung wrinkled and undone were pulled roughly apart by masculine hands urged on by the hotness of new love? The thought made Jubilee smile.

She wondered if the owner was white. But she couldn't think of any reason a white woman would remove an undergarment out here in the middle of a cotton field. At the same time she couldn't imagine any colored woman she knew owning such a delicate thing. She stood gazing, holding the piece to her chest over her own breasts that had grown uncomfortably large.

Benny might have seen the wearer while he was driving the tractor through the hot fields and stinging from the poison. She would have been headed into the cool thicket where the little pond lay or perhaps smiling and walking more quickly out of it again. If he'd seen her he would have wondered what she was up to.

As she picked the berries, she thought she would ask him that evening, if she thought about it, to help her solve the little mystery if he could. Suddenly as a breeze blew off the pond the fragrance of rose bay filtered past her. She paused for a long moment, wondering until she became aware that her back had begun to ache, reminding her to get on with the job, so she could finish picking and get home to rest.

When her buckets were filled, Jubilee walked down the dusty field trail and turned off onto the highway and headed toward home. She had not gone far when she heard an automobile behind her turn off the highway. She looked back expecting to see the pickup of Mr. Matthew or Luke and was puzzled to see the dry cleaning delivery car throwing up dust as it sped through the ruts down the same trail she had just walked.

"Wonder where she headed?" she thought out loud and then turned back and wearily walked the rest of the way to home.

CHAPTER 19

ON FRIDAY AFTERNOON Sis Riah stood in front of the bus depot impatiently waiting with Sweet Boy. Saphronia was late. In one hand Sis Riah held her nice purse and in the other hand the grip that contained the flowered dress. Tucked into a side pocket of the purse were two bus tickets to Madison, Mississippi, bought with the money the Mississippi Colored Missionary Association had sent to cover the traveling expenses of the Hart County Church delegates.

The Trailways Bus Station sat like a slice of pie at the north end of Tula on Highway 51 right across from the back part of the lot Mr. Frank Russell gave Olivia and Matthew for a wedding present. When the state ran the highway through Tula, it cut off the back corner of the lot and eventually the Montgomerys sold the disenfranchised, triangle to Dub Presley for the Standard Oil Service Station and Bus Depot. At first people in Tula laughed about the strange shape of the filling station, but it had been there so long now nobody noticed it anymore.

"Where is that woman?" Sis Riah said exasperated and she looked across the street into the back pasture of the Montgomery place. A line of red crepe myrtle bushes hid the back parcel where Olivia had instructed Matthew to build a four-room house for Saphronia.

Sweet Boy took the grip his wife was holding and smiled down at her. "She gonna be here in time, honey. We's early."

"You see the bus coming?" Sis Riah fretted.

"Nawh, baby. It ain't suppose to get here for another ten minutes. Chances are it gonna be late besides. You ought to go on back to the wagon and set down. I wait here and come getcha when it show up."

"I can't set around in no wagon right now," she said standing on tiptoe to see around the bushes across the road.

"Now, Sissy, quit fretting about Saphronia. Bus ain't here yet, and she so close by, anyway, she don't have to do nothing but step out the door to be here."

Sis Riah put her hand up to her eyes to cut out the sun, so she could look up at his face. She saw his smile.

"What you grinning at?"

"You, in that hat."

"What the matter with this hat? Too proud?"

"No, just right. Make everybody see what a pretty woman I got."

"You crazy thing," Sis Riah said jabbing at him with her elbow. "Now tonight we gonna be at Saphronia's cousin's place in Madison and tomorrow morning she gonna take us on into the college."

"Sissy, what you know about this here cousin of Saphronia's?"

"She fine. She the president of the Missionary Society down there and that congregation three times the size of ours. She gonna be nice unless she like Saphronia. Don't worry. She going to the conference, too. Everything gonna be fine and I be back Sunday evening before you can get into any trouble by yourself."

"You know I ain't gonna get into no trouble. House clean, clothes washed, put away, enough food to last me until next year." She reached over and squeezed his arm with one gloved hand.

"Wish there was a way for you to stop by and take a look at that little piece of land in Camden I saw advertised in the paper," he continued. "You be so close to it. Maybe we just take the wagon over there next Saturday. I needs to see if the fields too dry in summer to raise good corn. Wish I knew more about buying land."

"Too bad Mr. Matthew ain't the kind of man got a mind to help us."

"All he ever say to me when I try talking to him about it, 'What a illiterate colored boy like you gonna do with a piece of land of his own.' I always wants to tell him, 'Same thing I do with yours.'"

"Don't let that old prickly pear bother you none. He just don't want to lose you working for him. He know you one of a kind."

"Still and all, I wish I could get some kinda advice before we risk spending that much money for a place ain't worth nothing. No telling what it'll do." He looked down at her earnestly. "But I wants the right of doing things on my own piece of land so bad I can smell the dirt. Thinking and figuring out the way things oughta be done, then rolling up my sleeve and working them on out. Sweating and getting wore out over my own crops."

"Both us wants that. House on a place like that gonna need lots of work, I imagine."

"You been saving a long time for some land and a place, Sissy."

"*We* been saving for it. We still a ways from being there. But I believe we needs to go take a look at any place don't cost no more than that one."

"That's because it be too far out in the country for white folks to live. But that make it just right for us, huh, baby? Maybe we ask that man what's selling it if he let us live on it and work the balance off."

"I don't know. I sho' hates to owe money to a white man I don't know nothing about."

Sweet Boy grinned and pointed toward the street. "Sis Riah, look yonder. Here come Saphronia, totin' her grip and wearing a hat bigger'n yours. Wait right here. I'm gonna run go help her. I bet she got everything she own in that thing."

Sweet Boy put Sis Riah's suitcase down beside her and hurried across the street to intercept the figure in the large flowered hat coming toward the station. She could see Saphronia smile when her husband grabbed the grip and walked along beside her, leaning over and talking as he walked. Sis Riah knew Saphronia was beside herself with joy. Ever since she first laid eyes on him when she was just a girl, she had wanted nothing in the world as much as Sweet

Boy. The frustration of that yearning over the years had made the nature of the woman who was coming toward her sour and critical and she never had married.

When Sweet Boy was around, Saphronia turned into a different woman, sweet and girlish. But her adoration had never bothered Sis Riah a bit. Over fifty years ago when she was a young wife that man had promised to love her forever and he always did what he promised. That's the way he was. Constant to a fault. Like the way he kept on taking stuff off of that cranky, old skunk Olivia was married to. Any other man in the world would've left that job a long time ago.

Saphronia waved at Sis Riah. She was wearing white gloves up to her forearm with seed pearl flowers embroidered across the top of the hand. Her navy blue suit was pulled tight across her bosom and hips. She wore white pumps with the toe out and she wobbled a little on the thick high heels that jabbed at the black top of the street. The petals of the pink roses on her hat shook above the grin she directed up at Sweet Boy.

As they approached the crossroad, Sis Riah looked north up the highway and saw it was empty except for a wagon and mule in the distance coming toward town. Saphronia and Sweet Boy followed her glance and then crossed the road to the station.

"You got the tickets?" Saphronia asked as she walked up, holding Sweet Boy by the arm.

"Yeah, I got the tickets. Let go my husband, you hussy," Sis Riah said laughing. "Go find a man of your own."

Saphronia returned her smile. "No more in Hart County worth having."

"Ain't you worried that hat gonna be too floozy," Sis Riah teased.

"You talking about floozy? You look at yourself in that window yonder. I'm ashame to get on that bus with you looking like that."

The bus was only a few minutes late and after their suitcases were installed in it's belly the tall, buxom woman and the shorter ample one boarded and made their way past white travelers back to the colored seating section. Sweet Boy stood like a monument in front of the gas pump. He already seemed a little lost as Sis Riah pulled down the window and motioned him to walk back toward them.

"You gonna be alright?" she asked.

"Oh, yeah. Now, Sissy, don't forget nothing you hear down yonder. I wants to know all about it when you gets back," he said reaching up through the window.

"I ain't gonna forget, honey. You the one oughta be going on this trip," Sis Riah said leaning out toward him.

"I got too much work to do for Mr. Matthew right now. I'm glad Miz Olivia let Saphronia go with you. Take a good look at that young preacher, so you can tell me what you think when you gets back Sunday evening."

The bus driver boarded at the opposite end of the bus and the doors closed with a sigh. In a little while the motor roared into gear. Sis Riah stuck her hand out to Sweet Boy who caught it in his own.

"Check on Jubilee if you has a chance to tomorrow afternoon."

"She be fine, Sissy. Don't worry about her."

"Well, I can't help but be uneasy. Go by for me, will you?"

"Alright. I go see her or else talk to Benny. Don't worry."

The bus began moving. Sis Riah let go of her husband and, putting her gloved fingers to her mouth, motioned her hand back toward him with a wave. The service station receded slowly as they pulled away. Sweet Boy was standing in front of the pump waving to her. Soon Sis Riah was too far down the road to watch her husband turn and head around back of the station to the wagon and start on home.

CHAPTER 20

WITH JARS OF blackberry jam still warm on her shelves, Jubilee was tired Friday night when Benny came in. She didn't meet him at the door like she had before. All during the evening he seemed almost like he was somewhere else and she couldn't seem to get there no matter how hard she tried. Then again, she was too tired to try very hard. So she didn't talk to him much and after she served him his supper she cleaned up her little kitchen and went off to bed before him, hoping the ache in her back would go away as she slept.

The bed was cool and clean and she gave in to her tiredness. She thought of the small bundle of white lace that she had discovered that morning at the blackberry picking and the delightful puzzle it caused in her head. She thought again of its owner unbuttoning a bodice and dropping the sleeves of some stylish dress, so she could remove the little undergarment and fold it carefully and push it back under the vines. And standing on the bank of the pond hidden from view, enjoying the coolness of the gully, leaving her breasts unclothed to the fresh, cool air and then what? Maybe pulling her dress back up and making herself presentable again before she left the thicket. There was really nothing wrong with taking unnecessary clothing off in the heat of a Mississippi summer, even though Jubilee would never have the nerve to do it outside like that.

Jubilee smiled, because she understood. Somewhere inside her, too, was that kind of woman, if she weren't so tied down. Tied down? she thought with surprise. Was she tied down?

Or if there was someone with her. A lover maybe, who helped her untie the ribbons, she might have been embarrassed at that. But Jubilee doubted it. They would have arranged to meet there, she supposed, out in the open. She smiled to herself. The surprise about it was that they would choose Mr. Luke's field to meet for loving. Didn't want anybody to know about it. She smiled deliciously with the thought and turned over and nestled into the clean covers.

She heard the creak of the screen door.

"Benny, you going out?" she called.

"Yeah. Just to cool off. You go on to sleep."

"Be careful of snakes if you goes down toward the swamp."

"Yeah. I know."

She heard the thunk, thunk of the porch steps under his foot and then there was silence in the cabin except for locust and cricket songs thrown into the night from the swamp and the fields. Jubilee turned again heavily in search of some coolness. The stillness Benny left in the cabin caused a thickness in her chest that she needed to relieve. She floated inside her head, looking for an opiate that would comfort her. Her mind began unconsciously forming the image of round, filled cheeks on the inside of her closed eyelids, a wet, opened mouth, a girl-child's filled eyes crystallized with delight and wonder. She moved her hands along the largeness of her stomach and her whole body began to fill with the incredible sweetness of it. The extraordinary expectation, the wonder that would reveal for the first time the cloven living, breathing part of her own body that she could soothe and caress and feed in exactly the sweet filling way she had always wanted to be soothed, caressed and fed. She would be her own mother. And she would not stop until she filled up to overflowing that hungry place of emptiness that her mother had left unfilled inside of her.

She imagined the fragile weight in her arms. Walking, rocking, comforting. The embracing of her own. No longer hungering for the aunt, who reserved the meagre crumbs of her miserly caring for her own flesh and blood, or the cousins, who clung to their scanty store of motherly affection and carefully preserved it against starvation, or a mother, who had gone away forever kicking up a cloud of dusty road behind her, or a husband, who ached and ached and would not let her comfort him. This movement inside her belly belonged to her.

Round soft skin laid against woman skin. Warm.

Rocking through sweet misty places into almost sleep.

Her calling to the child.

"Grace. Where you, Grace, honey?"

And the child whimpering, lost, calling without words, calling out of the dark, and the whisperings of women anxious, anxious about a child. Searching for the path. Searching for a way to rescue. And the white lace thing and blackberry thorns in her fingers as she calls to the child, and, finally, an answer on the other side of the blackberry vines.

"Here I am, mama. I's coming."

And a rustling of the vines heavy with briars and fruit parting into a path. And suddenly emerging from the parted bushes a green and purple snake.

Benny walked off the porch and through the cotton field toward the swamp. The night was soft and warm and he walked into the warmth, toward the fecund depths where river met bank. He was remembering a time when he looked up into his daddy's face that was smiling and proud.

"Exel, you know my boy, Benny Junior," he said to the man who had greeted him in the street.

Exel was his daddy's best friend since they were boys. He reached his grown man hand out to shake the small one.

"Mighty fine looking boy," he said. "Look just like his mama."

Benny Junior shook the hand and said, "Howdy, Mr. Exel."

And Exel laughed and it made the boy feel uncomfortable.

"Mr?" And he laughed again, cause he liked being called that.

"He smart," his daddy said. "Smart as a grown up man." It made Benny feel better. "Smarter'n you and me both."

"That right? Well, you must ain't had nothing to do with him then if that be the case."

"Boy gotta good mama and that's the truth," his daddy answered.

"Ain't nobody around here gonna argue with that. Yep, you got a fine boy here."

Suddenly there were tears in Benny's throat. He shook his head and looked up at the stars and made a vow to himself that no matter what happened in this world he was gonna take care of his children better than his daddy had taken care of him. No matter what.

He reached the deep trees and turned without thinking down the path that led along the river to the highway. He drew in the cooling night scents of the swamp and dusty field that still smelled like poison. He sat down on a fallen tree that blocked his path and looked back up at the stars filling the clear summer night sky. He could smell the river's musky invitation and he wished he was on it, sitting in a wooden row boat, paddling down stream and heading for a place he had never gone before. He would go where the river went, without a mind to think of the past, without skin, without wife or child.

Or maybe there wasn't a boat. Just him. Just blood and muscle and bone. Uprooted from this place. Pulled up out of the quicksand, sucked out and swept down stream to the sea. Washed through and divided into a million tiny particles like sand. So lost that he never would be able to get back again, that nobody would ever be able to collect all the pieces to put him back together. Tiny pieces of what use to be him in another time spread to the outer most parts of the world, carried by the waters of this river. He let his mind run on that for a long time until his head cleared and he felt a little bit of peace come back.

But soon, without realizing it, his mind began leaking in thoughts of the afternoon and Nan, the sweetness of her body, the strength of her. The kind of woman he had never known before, like a new country he was exploring for the first time with strange new vegetation and surprising landscapes. The coarseness of her spoke confidence and rebellion. She reeked of freedom. She didn't need people like most people did. It seemed to him like she wouldn't have known where to make room for anybody in her life except for a short time.

But this afternoon when he asked her what she wanted from him in the midst of their love making she had said, "Gimme a baby, Benny, like you give Jubilee. That what I want from you. Plant your seed deep down in me and give me a little baby, too, Daddy Man."

The thought almost made Benny pull away from her. The possibility had not crossed his mind before and he felt his father in him and he remembered seeing the little boy, who held innocently onto his mother's skirt. His half brother. His father's nastiness and filth. That's what Tula thought of the child, anyway, the whole time he was growing up. He remembered seeing him often, smiling shyly on the Saturday streets of town, but Benny never looked him in the eye or smiled back at him. He was a constant embarrassment. Proof to everybody in the county that his daddy was weak and promiscuous. Benny had no idea where that boy was now. Soon as he could, he left Tula and never came back, not even to see his mama. Benny didn't want a child of his to ever have to live that way.

But Nan Hawkins.

"Shit," he said into the night.

He closed his eyes tight and clenched his teeth and he ached with wanting.

"Shit," he cried again. "Daddy, look what you done."

But the sounds of the night went on and the light of the stars remained above his head. His daddy was dust by now. His mama, too. What was going on right now with him was his? Sitting on the fallen swamp tree, here, now, breathing the sensuous night air and seeing the stars and remembering with guilt and then with passion the heat caused in him by the hot, sweet inside of Nan Hawkins. No matter how hard he fought, a part of his mind had already begun working out a way he could get to her. In twenty minutes he could be in town. His hands remembered the slim waist sliding between them and his mouth wanted to taste again the breasts, small and childish.

In twenty minutes he could surprise her with a knock on the upstairs door. She would wake up slowly, hating to leave the silkiness of her bed. When she came to his knock she would be wearing the nightgown and seeing him there framed in the glass of the door, she would put her hand to her mouth and gasp in mock surprise and then pull him in and give him a taste of her skin. The deep muskedine bittersweetness of her skin. Without realizing it he had already walked to the road and was headed toward the highway and town.

Jubilee woke in the middle of the night with a cry. While she had slept the snake that crawled from under the blackberry vines lunged suddenly and bit her in her low back as she turned and tried to run away. The poison entered her spine and worked its way around her abdomen, choking the child within her and making her whole body rigid with pain. And then the whispering of the women choir had risen and overpowered the snake and the pain receded. And the women brought her cape jasmine and day lilies and field grass and rose bay to comfort her and then told her the pain would return for the child was descending in birth. And the pain began again slowly at first in her back then wrapped itself cruelly around her. That was when she awoke.

The ache was more intense now. She thought at first she must have been lying funny on the bed. She tried to change her position and move quietly to keep from waking Benny until she realized he wasn't sleeping beside her. What time was it? Had she slept long? She listened to the dark for some sound of him.

"Benny?" she called.

There was no answer. And then the pain began to overtake her again. She grabbed hold of the mattress and pushed her teeth together. Her mind raced. Were the women telling her the truth? Was it time? Was this the way it happened? And then the edge of it and then it faded and she relaxed her hold on the mattress.

"Benny," she called now louder, more insistent.

There was no answer. Where could he be? Still out walking?

"Benny," she yelled again feeling a panic in her throat. She had to get up, light a lamp, get to him somehow.

She pushed herself up out of the bed and walked into the front room and lit the lamp. Things calmed down. She had panicked for a minute, but she was alright now. She went to the screen door.

"Benny," she called.

She cupped her hands around her mouth and called toward the swamp. She waited and listened deep into the dark. Nothing. Only night sounds. Where in God's name was he? Should she go out to look for him or was it better to stay here in the house? Dr. Kitchen had said it would take a while for the first one. She needn't be anxious. Benny had just taken a little walk and he'd be right back. She realized she was standing on the porch of the little cabin trying to see down the path to the road.

She went down the steps carefully holding on to the porch post as she went.

"Benny, where you gone to? I needs you." she said to herself.

It started again as a vague ache in her back just below her waist and as her stomach muscles turned to iron she was overcome and had to sit down in the road until it passed.

"Oh, my Lord," she said. "Benny, please let me find you."

She knew now that her time had come. She got on her all fours when the pain was gone and managed to get to her feet again. By the time she reached the highway she was well into another one. She knew she could go no further and she also knew she couldn't get back to the cabin.

"Benny," she called again. "Somebody. Anybody, help me."

But the road was deserted and nobody answered.

CHAPTER 21

DEEDOVE REMEMBERED LONG ago as a child running frantically in the late afternoon toward the swamp, hoping she could out run them, hoping maybe the conjure women inside her head would not be able to find her there where it was so dark and so far away from home. She didn't run from fear but weariness. Maybe the ancestors had been filled with too many admonitions that day or had argued among themselves as they sometimes did over the best way to advise her. She didn't remember exactly why. She realized now how foolish it was to run. She believed most of the women before her had prized the wise council so readily available to them. But each individual descendant reacted differently to the ancestors and on that day their eternal meddling had finally sent her gasping and diving through the thick woods, wild blackberry vines and drooping Spanish moss on ancient oaks tearing at her face and arms.

In a midnight part of the swamp she crawled quickly along deer paths to the scratchy underneath of wild rose bushes and sat panting on the cool black dirt. The familiar smell of sluggish river water and decaying vegetation surrounded her. The women's hushed and unabated mummurings and mutterings continued. She shook her head to quiet them and cried out and clasped her hands tightly over her ears. They had always been there. In her whole life there had been only short spans of time when there was relative silence, but the women were so numerous they could not all remain quiet for long no matter how much she begged them to.

To be truly alone, to be locked inside her own head like other children were, to have possession of the only key that opened that lock, to be lonely, to hear only silence within and without, what bliss it would be. But her mind since birth had been utterly laid open to legions and on that day the noise of it had sent her fleeing into the swamp.

Finally she had dropped her hands from her ears and looked around. She was alone and it was very dark. The sounds of animals she did not recognize began to echo through the shadows and she was frightened for the first time in her life. She crawled back out the way she had come in and stood up and tried to get her bearings. Nothing was familiar and the light was fading fast. It was then she realized that finding her way in the dark would never be a problem as long as she had the women to lead her back home.

*　　*　　*

Deedove awakened suddenly in the middle of the night to the sound of her mother calling her name.

"Mama," she demanded. "You here?"

Make us some fire, came the answer.

"Fire? In the middle of July? My house already too hot," she argued.

She waited and listened as the breathing continued insistently. Finally, she groaned and got up stiffly from the homemade cot with the corn shuck mattress she'd slept on for years and shuffled her knotty misshapen bare feet across the rough wood floorboards. She followed the breathing noises to the stove where the firebox of dying embers from the greens she'd cooked the night before still produced warmth to her touch.

"What ya'll wanting fire for anyhow?" she called out and waited for the sensation of words and meaning that crept through her head when the women talked to her.

The breathing continued. The women required a sign, a gift, to show them she was not going to be hard headed and that she was willing to listen to what they had come to tell her. They knew she would be curious about what they were up to. She peered into the firebox and reached down and picked out a stick of pinewood from a bin at her feet and shoved it into the stove. The fire caught up immediately and as the flames broke forth the breathing became a sigh, a whispery host of female voices. The ancestors loved fire and drew themselves deliciously toward it.

"What ya'll come here for middle of the night waking me up?" Deedove asked the empty corners of the room.

As the fire rose the sigh of voices increased and then faded back into the night. The women wanted more.

Deedove frowned and stuck out her lips to the room, but finally added several more sticks of wood that caught on and burned to a height barely safe within the confines of the small firebox of the stove.

More, they demanded.

"I can't build no more. I burn up my house," she said to the flames.

She waited, but the women were silent except for the sounds of breathing. They were playing a game with her. They certainly hadn't congregated here just to get her to carry firewood for them; they had come to tell her something. She was sure of that. She could tell they were excited, but she would not hear the news until they were good and ready. So she'd just have to play the game until one of them who could bear the suspense no longer blurted out the secret.

She turned toward the ancient brick fireplace. She could build a bigger fire there. Grunting with effort, Deedove brought in some firewood from a stack on the porch. She pulled a burning stick out of the cook stove and held it to a pile of pine logs she had laid on the bed of cold, damp ashes.

The voices tittered with happiness and shushed each other and breathed again the command for more.

"You gonna get more. But it gonna take me a while. Ain't been no fire here since way last March."

The wood began to smoke and she watched the first spark

shoot out from the logs. Tiny tongues of hot light began to lick and curl around the wood, then burst into full flame and burn greedily and the sighing, whispery voices that had awakened Deedove became a full delighted chatter all through her head and Deedove stepped back away from the fireplace and smiled with satisfaction at the blaze. It was good to have them here.

"Who all in my house?" she said.

The smoke and smell of rose bay filled the room in curls and waves of warm resonant being and the voices began to hum and murmur to each other.

"I know your smell, Mama."

The words echoed teasing inside her head and then drifted about the room. "I know your smell, Mama. I know your smell." Deedove smiled and took in the delicious odor and let the sweetness of it float to her head. She held out her arms and, eyes shut, turned slowly in a full circle reveling in her ability to see without her sight and catch the teasers recklessly revealing themselves here and there like pipes playing and the distant thump, thump of drums. And swaying and reeling to their music Deedove began to dance. Finally she sat down in happy exhaustion.

"What ya'll wants?" she asked.

Laughter rang in her head and she heard the voices singing her name the way they did when she was a baby.

"Deedove. Deedeedeedeedovedovedovedovedove . . . . "

The sound of it filled her up.

"Mama, I'm glad ya'll here," she said.

The voices sighed milky sweet in reply.

"I know ya'll always with me. I can feel it even when none of ya'll saying nothing to me."

She thought of the reason for their long time of silence.

"Everybody still mad at me cause of what I done, Mama? I been grieving over it for twenty years now. Ya'll was right. Nothing work out like I plan it. I done a terrible, selfish thing."

It was the first time she had ever said it to them.

"Ever since it happen. Sometime I hear her crying and I know I's the one has to get her home safe even if I has to die to do it."

The voices sighed and wrapped around her. The flames popped and hissed in the fireplace and the smoke rose in the room like gauzy robes.

"But I was getting so old, Mama, and I's scared if I didn't do something the conjuring gonna end when I die. I can't stand before all ya'll carrying that burden.

"Then one day I see this here young girl and I know I's looking at the line. You know, another one. So now I think I got it figured out. Tell me if it gonna work this time. I'm about at the end of my rope, Mama. I can tell."

And just as one lights a lamp in a dark room, she knew why the women had come back to her to celebrate. Tonight once again they would be about their most ancient and joyous of tasks. She got up quickly from the chair and put on her old coat. She had to hurry. The night sounds of frogs and locusts invaded the room. She stood before the dying flame waiting for a moment, her head filled with their anticipation. They had told her the message they came to tell. She must hurry and get herself to Jubilee's cabin as quickly as possible. The baby was coming and the young mother needed her.

CHAPTER 22

WHEN BENNY LEFT Nan, the summer night was turning into dawn. He hurried. He didn't want Jubilee waking up before he got home and asking lots of questions about where he'd been.

He had almost run the two miles from town and he was right near the place where the path led off the road when he heard the sound. At first it seemed to him the whimper of a kitten, soft and plaintive. But then it swelled into a wail. He stood stock still for a minute, trying to see in the direction the cry had come from, searching along the side of the cotton rows in the early light. A bundle of something white lay piled up just off the road. As he moved closer to see what it was a shiver of recognition raced along his spine. He leapt the side ditch and stumbled over the plowed dirt to where she was.

"Jubilee, what in God's name you doing out here?" he called as he ran.

"Benny, is it you? Is you alright?" she called.

She was half lying, half sitting at the edge of the field. Her skin was cold and damp and she was shivering violently.

"Oh, dear Lord. Jubilee," he said as he bent down over her.

"It started," she said, gasping as a pain came on and then subsided. "She done started coming and I come out to find you.

But I couldn't go no further and I couldn't get back to the cabin. Benny, is you all right? I so scared you been hurt in the swamp somehow or in the river or something."

What I done? he thought as he put his arms under her gently and picked her up and began to carry her down the path toward the cabin. She rested her head against him and was overcome with the comfort of seeing him and being able to lay the burden of herself and the baby on him.

"Benny, you is alright," she whispered. "You is alright. I scared something bad happen when I can't find you. Where you was?"

He kicked open the door and walked with her to the bed.

"That don't matter right now. We gotta get you to the doctor in Lexington. I'm gonna have to leave you here for just a little while and run go get the pickup at Mr. Luke's," he said putting her down gently and pulling the quilt up over her.

"No, Benny. Please don't leave me. I so scared. The baby gonna come pretty soon. I can tell."

"But we got to get you to Lexington, like we done planned. To Dr. Kitchen."

"No, Benny," she pleaded grabbing his arm. "Promise me you ain't going nowhere."

Benny knelt down beside her and took her hand in his.

"Jubie, it ain't gonna take me but twenty minutes to get to that truck, just a few more to get back here. Then we gonna get on up to Lexington. Everything gonna be fine. Just like we plan."

"Benny, what I gonna do if she come while you gone? Please, Benny, please."

Right now she needed him to take charge of things but for the life of him he couldn't figure out what he ought to do. The fear in her eyes alarmed him.

"I stay with her," said a soft voice from behind him.

Benny turned around to see Deedove standing in the door. The hair on his neck stood up and he was terrified. She shuffled right on into the room carrying a wrapped up bundle.

"What you doing here? You get out of my house right now," he said rising and stepping toward her.

"Ain't no need to be afraid of nothing. I knows what to do if need be. I seen my mama bring a hundred babies into the world. Whole lot of 'em I brung myself. Ain't as many as Saphronia, but enough. Go on, boy. Get the pickup. Your wife be alright. Old Deedove stay with her."

She began carefully unwrapping the bundle.

"Benny, you go on. I be alright if Deedove here," Jubilee said from behind him.

"I ain't leaving you with none of that. I say get outa my house right now before I throws you out," Benny said almost yelling. "And I better not see you hanging around outside nowhere neither."

She looked directly at him with a steady, steely face and then began gathering up the bundle again.

"I'm going. Something bad happen to that girl the blame on you," she said turning and shuffling toward the door.

"Please, Benny. I needs her. Let her stay," Jubilee pleaded from behind him and she began rocking her head from side to side and moaning. Benny turned toward her in alarm when the moan turned to a cry. The sweet face framed by the pillow was distorted with pain. He felt fear and guilt mixing together in the pit of his stomach.

"Old woman," he called out.

The bedroom door filled again with the bent gnarled figure.

"How long she got?" he asked, his eyes fixed on Jubilee who was now rigid with pain. "You better tell me the truth."

She smiled slightly and moved closer toward the bed.

"Long enough, boy. Go on, now. Get the truck."

He hesitated a moment trying to think, trying to figure out what he ought to do and then he turned and bolted out the door and was half way down the path running for the road before he asked himself what he was leaving. He would be quick. She wouldn't have time to do Jubilee any mischief. In only a little while he would be back with the truck and take her on up to Lexington. Dr. Kitchen had said it would take a while for the first one. He wished now they hadn't planned to do it like this. It would be so much easier to get Saphronia from town. And then he remembered with desperation that both Saphronia and Sis Riah were gone.

He cut straight across the pasture past the barn running toward Luke Montgomery's big house. It seemed to take him much longer than when he timed it before. He ran up the hill to the house that sat silently dreaming and deserted in the early morning light. He shot past it to the garage and jumped into the driver's seat of the truck and turned the key. The motor sputtered and died. He turned the key again.

"Please, please," he said aloud.

It sputtered and died again.

"Damn," he yelled looking up in frustration and waiting for a moment. He was almost overcome with the rank press of urgency. Again and again he tried the ignition but the truck refused to respond. Finally, he jumped out of the cab and raised the hood. It was hard to see in the dark garage. He peered down into the depths of the motor, but he didn't know anything about fixing automobiles. He shook the ignition wires and then the battery cables and got back into the truck and tried it again. This time the motor answered with a cough and a rattle and then a quiet confident purr and with a sigh of relief he backed out of the garage and headed toward the intersection of the Lexington highway and old 51 that ran in front of his house. He mashed on the brakes at the stop sign and then in alarm he heard the motor cough and sputter and die again. He turned the key. The engine chugged briefly and then quit for good. The night sat silently waiting around him.

He cursed and got out and ran around to the hood and, lifting it, he peered again into the motor. Nothing looked wrong. But what did he know? Mr. Luke always took his automobiles down to Presley's to be fixed, because he wanted it done right, so the hands on the place had only learned to work on the tractors and other farm equipment. If he hadn't been so upset and had time and light enough he would have been able to translate his tractor knowledge into the language of the truck motor, but he could only think of the minutes going by and Deedove at the cabin with Jubilee all this time. He jiggled the cables of the battery again frantically and hurried around and turned the key. The motor remained mute.

"God, please," he begged aloud to the early morning.

He looked down the road for somebody coming and wondered what to do now. He could go back up to the Montgomerys' (He knew where a key was hidden.) and go inside the house and find the phone and call somebody. But who would he call at this time of day. Sis Riah had a phone, but she was gone. Then he thought that Sweet Boy would be at home, and he knew a little more than Benny did about gasoline engines.

He ran back to the big house and cautiously let himself in. He had never been inside the place before. The first thing that struck him was the smell of it. There was no odor of lamp oil or kerosene. And everything was terribly clean. He looked around for the phone and finally found it at the end of the dark hallway that led toward the back sitting room. He located the light switch nearby and dialed Sweet Boy's number and stood nervously waiting for him to answer.

He looked around him at the flowered wallpaper and matching carpet. Being inside the house frightened him. He felt like he must be breaking some terrible law that might bring severe punishment by daring to come right up into Mr. Luke's house like that when nobody was at home. But he didn't know what else to do. He wondered what he'd say if Mr. Matthew showed up right now. His heart jumped at the thought. But the house was silent and empty.

"Yeah? Hello?" he heard a voice on the other end say.

"That you, Sweet Boy?"

"Yeah. Benny?"

"Yeah, it's me. Uh, Sweet Boy, Jubilee done started having her pains and I can't get Mr. Luke's old truck to go. You got any way of getting out here to help me fix this thing?"

"Where you at?"

"I'm up at Mr. Luke's using his phone. Truck down at the intersection where it quit on me."

Benny could hear the panic in his own voice.

"Alright, boy. Just calm down. I get something on and be right over there."

"How long it gonna take you?"

"I got Mr. Matthew's old Ford out front."

"Would you hurry, man? I'm about scared to death," Benny said and laughed with nervousness.

"Don't worry. I'm coming."

And then there was a click and a buzz. Benny put down the receiver and left the house as quickly as he could, locking it carefully after him, thankful to be outside again. He ran back down the road to the truck and, puffing for breath, he looked more carefully at the inside of the motor, trying to make sense of what he saw there, thinking all the time about Jubilee back at their cabin with Deedove. He had to hold on to the sides of the truck to keep from shaking, so he could stand up. Too much time had gone by. He knew it. The sky was lighting up now and he could see more clearly.

He forced himself to calm down and sit in the truck and wait. He thought about Nan Hawkins still asleep in the dim bedroom above the cleaners. Last night she had begged him to sleep with her there in the bed. He knew he oughta get on home, but she held him by the arms and pulled him back to her when he tried to get up and go. So he gave in. And when he woke in the early hours of dawn he knew he had been away too long, so he left quietly without waking her and ran most of the two miles back to the cabin. Then suddenly he realized what he was thinking about and he jerked his head back to the thing he had come home to.

"Oh, God," he said. "What have I done?"

He jumped out of the truck again and slammed the door. He was just about to bolt for the cabin when Sweet Boy drove up in the old pickup and stopped it across the road from Benny. When he looked under the hood of the old truck he shook his head.

"Don't seem like nothing wrong to me. Got plenty of gas?"

Benny checked the gauge.

"Yeah," he called. "Sweet Boy, you gotta hurry. We gotta get this thing started right away."

"Might be corroded ignition wires. Get in and try it again," he said.

Benny climbed hurriedly back into the cab and turned the key. The sound of the motor trying to catch made him jump with hope, but then he heard the slurring sound as it died again.

"Lemme try something," Sweet Boy called to him. And then, "Try it again."

Benny turned the key. The sound of the starter working uselessly with the battery rose and fell again, and then with complete despair he heard the thing slowly grind into silence and refuse to make another sound.

"Look like we done for now," Sweet Boy called.

"Can't we do something?"

"Presley's have to do the work, Benny. I ain't got no idea about it. Could be the battery, maybe worse. Be another couple of hours before they opens."

"She can't wait another couple of hours, Sweet Boy. What I gonna do? You know who she with right now? She with Deedove. She down at that house with her right now."

"Lord, Benny. You left her with Deedove?"

"I didn't have no choice. Jubilee ain't gonna stay alone; she scared the baby coming right away. And I has to come get the truck. Sweet Boy, I gotta get her to Lexington."

"Now listen, boy, you just scared because this your first one. First time take a while. You got time to get the truck fixed and get on up to Lexington. Old Zee at Presley's do a rush job for you soon as they opens this morning."

"But that just the trouble, man. Jubilee been going on a long time now. I reckon most of the night."

"How come you ain't taken her in sooner?"

"I didn't know about it. I weren't home."

"Where you be, man?"

"Some place I ain't got no business being. Sweet Boy, what I gonna do now?"

"Look like to me you gonna have to take the help of Deedove and be thankful the good Lord ain't left you high and dry."

Benny felt tears well up in his eyes and he was embarrassed for Sweet Boy to see them so he turned his head away and looked down the road in the direction of the cabin.

Sweet Boy kept talking. "Ain't nothing I see for you to do but go on home. I'll get back to town and get Mr. Matthew's permission to take this old thing up to Lexington. He don't never use it no more, but I don't know for sure if it'll make it. He sho' won't let me take that new pickup of his. Don't worry about Mr. Luke's truck. I see about it. You at your house, maybe you can keep a eye on Deedove. Come on. Get in. I take you on by home."

Sweet Boy slammed the hood down. The two men ran across the road and Benny climbed in beside Sweet Boy. They rode silently in the early morning light until they reached the head of the path that led to the cabin and Sweet Boy stopped the truck.

"You needs me to come in with you?" he asked.

"Could you? You could just park along side the road here for a minute and come on down," he answered.

"Sho' can."

There was a strange calmness about the place and the first rays of morning sunlight were gilding the outside of Jubilee's clean windows. The air was cool and sweet with honeysuckle. They could hear the slow rhythmic tuk tuk of the old wooden rocking chair in the front room before they got to the porch. Benny hesitated at the door, listening. It was quiet except for the rhythm of the rocker. He took a breath and opened the screen door slowly and walked in.

The place seemed peaceful and tidy. The morning sun was throwing a shadow of window onto the floor. Across the room, with her head tied up in a clean bandana, the old conjurer was sitting in the chair, bent over a tiny wrapped up bundle in her arms and she was humming low and rocking in the early sunlight.

CHAPTER 23

"ABOUT TIME YOU get back here," Deedove said without looking up.

"Where my wife?" Benny demanded.

"Just where she suppose to be. You got yourself a baby girl, Benny Horne," she said.

"What you doing holding her? Where Jubilee? What you done to her?"

"Nothing to beat what you done to her," she answered without looking at him. And then after a pause she added, "Jubilee sleeping."

"She better be all right or you going to be in some bad trouble," he said.

Everything seem alright, Benny," Sweet Boy offered, standing in the doorway.

Benny strode quickly across the room and opened the bedroom door. Jubilee was in their bed with the cover tucked neatly around her.

"Benny?" she called weakly to him. "You seen her?"

"First thing I gotta see is you," he said leaning down over her.

"Us fine. You got no need to be unsettled."

"Jubilee, that old witch do anything funny to you?"

"No, Benny, no. Deedove done help me. Take both us together

bring Miss Grace Delora into this world. But everything fine now. Go on and look at her. She so pretty. When I first see her I about cried."

"Here, you wants to hold her?" the old woman said from behind him pushing the bundle toward him.

Benny took the baby awkwardly at first. She lay sleeping in the folds of the blanket, the tiny face peaceful with eyes shut tight, lips pursed, skin pale as coffee milk. He felt the small, warm weight against his arm and chest. The miniature lips sucked contentedly in sleep. And an ache welled up in his chest.

"She beautiful, ain't she?" Jubilee said softly.

He could hardly speak. He waited until the lump in his throat eased.

"She alright? All her parts alright?"

"Uh huh," Deedove said and turned back toward the front room. She had heard something she hadn't expected from the inside of Benny Horne. The man had been struck down with love for the child and it was a force she hadn't reckoned on. But there was still fear there and a great lot of anger, too.

"Sweet Boy, take a look at my girl."

Benny pulled back the corners of the blanket. The big man walked awkwardly and gently into the room and peered into the tiny face.

"Lord. Ain't she pretty. Sis Riah gonna die because I the first one seen her. Uh, Benny, I's kinda worried. Reckon I better get on now, see about the truck?" Sweet Boy said.

"Oh, yeah. I forgot."

"What you doing out here so early anyway, Sweet Boy?" Jubilee said, pushing herself up a little.

"I couldn't get Mr. Luke's truck started," Benny began to explain.

"Don't matter now. You tell Sis Riah about the baby first thing for me, will you, please, Sweet Boy?"

"I sho' do it, Miss Jubilee. Well, I better get on now." And he left, ducking out the front door followed by Benny carrying little Grace.

"Thank you, man," he said rocking the baby gently back and forth in his arms.

"Jubilee gonna need some help. You gonna stay home today?"

"I reckon, but I got the farm on me while Mr. Luke gone."

"Sissy be back tomorrow night. I imagine she be right on over here."

"I feel a whole lot better about things when she get home. Deedove still give me the creeps."

"Hey, man, I sho' don't aim to tend to your business, but us gotta talk about what it was keep you away from here last night. I hates to see you ruin what you got here with something ain't nothing but foolishness."

Benny was ashamed to look at his friend.

"You don't have to worry about none of that. Nothing ever gonna drag me away from this here again."

The big man nodded and turned and walked up the path toward the truck.

Deedove stayed around during the morning for a while and did some house work and Benny bent himself to taking care of Grace and Jubilee, because he couldn't bear for the old conjurer to do for them.

"I's going now," she said finally and walked down the steps holding on to the rail, carefully taking one step at a time.

"I reckon you thinking I'm gonna thank you for what you done, but I know you up to something and time gonna tell me what it is," Benny said from the porch swing where he sat with the sleeping baby in his arms.

"Uh huh," she said not turning toward him, but pausing a while, and then finally saying, "Well," and nodding and starting down the path. Pretty soon she turned onto the highway and walked on out of sight.

He would not have her in his house again no matter how much he needed help before Sis Riah got back. He rocked the baby gently in the swing, thinking and leaning to touch her forehead with his lips. The skin was incredibly soft. He studied the tiny child in his arms and then leaned back against the chain.

The morning around him lay cool and light. A strange sense of wellbeing rolled over him. He was finally free from the presence of those watery, old eyes that pierced his skull right through to his brain and picked away at whatever he happened to be thinking. All morning long he had felt them prying and watching while all the secret things in his life kept creeping into his thoughts no matter how hard he tried to keep them out. Every now and then during the day he'd find himself reaching out in his mind for the hunger of the night before and a silver shudder would overtake him. And then he'd catch himself and look at her and she would be looking at him and smiling. But now she was finally gone.

The fragile arms and hands of the baby in his lap began to wave and grasp at nothing in her dreams. She was so tiny, so fragile, so dependent on him. Anger rose up in him and made him hate what Nan Hawkins was doing to him. Goddamn it. In just a short time she had threatened everything he'd built up for himself. And he hadn't asked for a bit of it. Never dreamed of it. He had been minding his own business. This was all her fault. Her doing. Seeking him out in the store, coming way out to the cotton field like she did, letting him see her in the pond like that. He allowed himself the freedom to think about her for a moment. The crude toughness of her, the rank independence, her haughty attitude. Begging for trouble.

And then he thought there wasn't a man in the county who wouldn't burn up to be in his place right now. And what on earth made her go after him? He thought about that for a while and his pride began to speak to him and sooth his anger. But the baby's waving hand came in contact with his and she clutched his finger and brought him back to her.

He bent over and raised the little hand to his lips. The ache inside him returned. Lord God, he had to do right by her if he never did anything else right in his whole life. Somehow she had to get a better chance than he had. Not all the time feeling bad about who she was. He couldn't stand to watch her grow up with nothing. Grow up working too hard and living on somebody else's land like he had. Always feeling like every time he put his foot down it was on dirt that belonged to somebody else. And him, even as a little boy, all the time feeling like he owed somebody something for the privilege of breathing. If Sweet Boy and Sis Riah could get a farm of their own so could he. A farm for her. For Grace.

And nobody knew what he had done except Sweet Boy who was his friend and maybe Deedove, though she hadn't really said anything about it. He still had Jubilee's respect, fear, even sometimes. He'd just go on like nothing had happened. Deny it if anybody were to ask. Right out in front of Nan if he had to. People would believe his word over hers any day.

CHAPTER 24

THE BABY BEGAN a little squirm and wrinkled up her face and gave a cry that was somewhere between a kitten's mew and a cough. Benny got up carefully, jiggling her on his arm as he carried her back into the bedroom where Jubilee was sleeping.

"Jubilee, you awake? I think Grace hungry," he called quietly.

She opened her eyes. He helped her put his pillow behind her and then stood by the bed watching her unbutton the top of the nightgown and bare her nipple to the hungry baby who nuzzled until she found it. Benny smiled and pointed to the side of the baby's face working along with the sucking. Jubilee remained silent and ran her finger along the tiny jaw line.

"I been swinging her on the porch," he said. Still she did not look at him. Suddenly, he felt very afraid.

"You all right?" he asked her.

"Just fine. How about you?"

"Well, I sho' am happy about her," he answered. There was a silent pause. What was going on?

"It be all right she ain't a boy, Benny?"

"Oh, she just fine," he said, suddenly grateful that she was a girl and wouldn't have the struggle of being a black man. Jubilee glanced up at him and then back down, but in that moment he saw the pain that filled her face.

"What's the matter? You sure you all right?" he asked again.

"Well, I been trying to think, Benny. I don't know should I say anything about it right now or not. Maybe it just go away on its own. Some things better left unsaid for a while at least."

"Then don't say nothing," he said.

"We didn't have Grace I guess I never would. But I have to say it because of what me and you always be wanting for her, Benny."

"What the matter with you? Ain't nothing wrong."

He let the old familiar anger tinge his voice, but it didn't discourage her like it usually did.

"Something going on with you," she said.

"What you mean, something going on?"

"I's talking about where you was."

"When? Last night? That what you worrying about? Well, ain't nothing. I just got lost in the swamp walking. Spent about half the night finding my way back home. Where you think I was?"

She looked up at him. There was something in her face he did not recognize. He was afraid for her to speak.

"Benny, you been over every foot of that swamp a hundred times since you was old enough to walk. You'd a come quicker losing your way in my front yard."

"But I's in the dark."

"Benny, don't do that."

"Well, then what?"

She looked down at the baby, because she was afraid to see the language of his eyes.

"I think you was in town."

He put his hands at his waist and looked out the window. Here it was. Well, maybe it was better for it to come on out right now. He just wouldn't admit anything. No matter what. And if he asked the questions first, they might not scare him so much.

"In town? What business I got in town in the middle of the night?"

"Benny, I got a idea who you was with."

What was she doing? Didn't she know what he was fighting to save here? If she would just quit asking all these damn questions about it right now.

"What in hell you talking about? I ain't been with nobody."

"Benny, yesterday when I was picking blackberries I find a piece of lady's underwear up under some vines. I been thinking on that little bitty thing all night long. While I was puffing and sweating and pushing this baby into the world I kept seeing it laying under them vines, talking to me, trying to tell me something."

"What was it you say you seen?" he asked her.

"A fancy piece of lady's underwear. I found it when I went blackberry picking in that gully on the Nance place, right where you poisoned the cotton that day you brought me them flowers. Night I had that dream. It was right by the pond way up under the big vines setting on the ground. I wondered how come somebody to leave it there. And last night while I's laying out there on that road, scared I's gonna bring Grace into this world on a cotton row, that little old thing come into my head. But it weren't until this morning I finally understand. If I hadn't a been so blind trusting, I'd a figured it out sooner. Benny, you know I ain't foolish."

Her voice had gained some kind of strength he'd never heard in it before.

"I ain't never said you foolish," he said.

"I ain't Nan Hawkins neither.

Now she had done it. Said it so it couldn't be taken back. He didn't know what to answer. The anger he usually used on her had become useless. But it was all he had. Behind it he was nothing. He heard his mouth speak loud and rough.

"Nan Hawkins? What Nan Hawkins got to do with this?"

Jubilee didn't need to look at him to know she was right. The truth almost frightened her into silence, but she realized that sooner or later she had to confront him with it and she sensed that somehow her strongest moment with him was now with Grace nursing at her breast and him standing there beside the bed watching.

"Jubilee, I don't know what you talking about. Look, I know I ain't always been what I wanted to be for you, but . . . . "

His voice was thin with control. It would have been better if he'd hit her. But she would not stop.

"Benny, this the most blessed morning of my life, because I finally got something of my very own, gonna be mine forever. This here little girl. I think I kill somebody with my bare hands that tries to hurt her.

"Good God, Jubilee, don't you think I feels the same way you do. Whatever I do or say making you worry about something . . . . "

Suddenly, he began to change a little in her mind to something weak and ordinary. He saw the thought flicker across her face and shuddered at what it meant.

"Hey, nothing different," he tried to say. "Come on now. What you think different? Things gonna be like we been planning all along for her. Better even. I got some good ideas. Wait'll you hear. How about us gets us a piece of land just like Sis Riah and Sweet Boy gonna do? You know. Keep on saving like we been doing."

"No, Benny. Hush now. Listen to me. You her daddy. The only one she ever gonna have. And you my husband. But most important thing, you a grown man. And, Benny, you strong and free no matter what some folks'd have you believe. Nobody in this world can take away your freedom, unless you done already give it up to them."

"This don't have nothing to do with freedom," he began.

"Benny, I can raise this here baby by myself, way most colored babies raised around here. But she deserve a mama *and* a daddy to raise her up. We plan it that way long time ago. Even before we know we gonna have her."

"Goddamn it, Jubilee. You know I wants that for her, too. What you talking about raising her by yourself?"

"But I needs to tell you," she continued, "if her mama can't have every bit of her daddy, she don't want none of him at all. I don't intend for her to spend one minute of her life worrying about whether you gonna be there when she need you or not. She gonna know who she can count on in this world right from the beginning."

"Jubilee, if it kill me to do it, I'm always gonna be there for this child. What done got into you? You crazy or something?"

"Shh, listen. My mama done thrown me away first chance she get, but nothing in this world ever gonna take me away from this little girl long as me and her alive. You understand me? I ain't putting up with nothing less than that for her either. She gonna get all or nothing of you, Benny Horne. You understand?" Her voice was steady and strong. "I ain't giving you a warning or trying to play on your feelings. I'm just telling you what is the God's truth inside of me."

"Jubilee, what you think I'm fixing to do?"

"Sis Riah tell me your mama put up with your daddy catting around for a long time hoping her love and understanding change him and bring him back to her, but he die in another woman's bed. So it's a waste of time me trying the same cure on you. You gonna have to decide right now whether you gonna keep hanging around Nan Hawkins every time you gets the chance or whether you gonna be here for me and this little girl all the time. You ain't gonna be able to do both."

"Jubilee, I can't believe you talking like this."

She looked at the baby in her arms.

"I's taking my chances now, Benny. I figure this the strongest I gonna ever be with you."

"What you want me to say?"

"Ain't nothing you can say right now make a dime's worth of difference. It's what you gonna choose to do. Time gonna have to tell the truth about things."

"What you want from me?" he asked, angry again.

Her voice was even. She looked straight at him.

"I wants every bit of you, Benny Horne, or none at all."

Grace began to grow restless and fret, so Jubilee put the baby on her shoulder and patted the small rounded back gently.

"Jubilee, you don't want to get into this kinda talk right now. It ain't good for you. We talk about it later. I put your fears to rest then."

Her eyes were filling with tears, making him want to yell at her and fill her up with so much fear she'd never again dare to touch the deep place inside of him where she was now.

"Nothing left to say about it," she said.

"Don't I get to defend myself?" Benny asked, but she did not respond and he turned and walked out of the room. She heard the screen door open and shut and then the house was silent.

CHAPTER 25

ON MONDAY MORNING Grace was two days old and Jubilee couldn't stand to lay up in bed another day. Sis Riah would be there soon and she wanted to be clean and dressed when her friend arrived. She had never needed her council and comfort more than she needed it now.

Since the night the baby was born Benny had been amazing. He had cleaned the house, cooked their food, and picked up the baby when she cried. But she and Benny had not looked at each other or talked beyond simple necessity in two days. Benny had slept on a pallet in the front room, so she could be more comfortable in the bed, he said, and the pressure of it hovered over them like a dark, heavy, storm cloud that threatened to break out in rain at any moment. The kind of cloud that made you wish it would go on and do what it had to do, so you could quit waiting and watching and get on with living.

Finally this morning Benny had asked her if she felt good enough for him to go see about the work on the farm that Luke had left him to do. He said he would look in on her about ten o'clock. Then he left. The cabin was clean and quiet, and Jubilee expected the storm cloud to retreat for a while with Benny gone. But she soon realized it was far more upsetting when he was out of her sight than when he moved quietly around the cabin doing the kind of things she never dreamed she'd ever see him do in her lifetime. She kept wondering if he really had gone to work in the field that morning. Or maybe if all the cleaning and cooking he'd been doing for Grace and her freed him from any guilt he might feel over running to town to see Nan Hawkins as soon as he got free of the house.

While Grace was peacefully sleeping in the back room, Jubilee could not rid herself of the panic that vandalized her peace of mind. She thought crying might help, but her eyes were bone dry, burning almost. She had never gotten much comfort from tears. She sat down at the little table and took a deep breath. She felt sick. She put her face in her hands and reached in her mind for something that might comfort her enough to get her on to ten o'clock.

She heard someone call her name and she answered.

"Somebody there? Sis Riah, that you?"

But there was no answer.

Well, now that she thought about it, she hadn't really heard it exactly anyway.

She shut her eyes and sucked at the turmoil inside herself, forcing calm through her chest, stomach, arms, legs, the back of her neck until she forced the release of some cold hand that grasped the spirit deep within her. After a while Grace woke up and she felt a small measure of ease come over her as she fed and rocked the baby.

Ten o'clock crept and crawled into existence and Benny came up the porch steps sweaty and serious.

"How you doing?" he asked.

"Everything just fine. What you do this morning?"

She watched his face carefully. Nothing.

"Got on to the last of the poisoning," he said.

He walked through the house and drank water from the dipper hanging on the water barrel in the back. When he came back in he went directly to the basket where Grace was sleeping and looked at her carefully touching her face gently with his rough forefinger.

"You look like you getting some strength back," he said to her.

"I been getting good care," she answered smiling at him cautiously.

He smiled gratefully back and asked if she needed him to do anything for her. When she said, "Nothing", he said he'd check back in on her about noon and get her some dinner. And then he left again.

She thought again for the millionth time about what she'd said to him the night Grace was born. She didn't know the woman that said those things. She realized for the first time that there was steel somewhere in the center of her. But had she already begun to let him off the hook a little? She felt the oppression begin to creep back over her. He had been working, she reassured herself. She could smell the cotton poison on him. But then maybe he put some on his clothes on purpose to fool her. Good Lord, she thought, she was really thinking crazy. She needed to talk to somebody sane right now. Where in God's name was Sis Riah?

"Call her," a voice seemed to say.

The sound of the words directed every nerve in her body to attention. It was the second time she believed she had heard someone talking to her this morning when nobody was there. Was this how it was when people lost their minds?

Her thinking was interrupted when Grace began to fret and she hurried to the basket and picked her up and changed her and took her to the front porch to rock and nurse her. Sis Riah would approve of this, she thought.

Benny appeared on the tractor trail at a quarter past twelve just as she was beginning to be sure he would not come. This time he smiled when he saw her rocking with the sleeping baby in her arms on the front porch.

"Wish I had me a picture of that," he said as he climbed the steps. "Sis Riah been by?"

"Not yet," she said hiding her worry.

When he left with a promise to come back at two o'clock she managed to say that it really wasn't necessary and that he should just keep on working until dark. She said she knew the interruptions were eating up his time, and she appreciated his worrying about them, but they'd be alright. And then when he walked out to the pickup and drove out of sight of the cabin the old worries came right back and sat on her chest again. By three o'clock she was just about out of her mind and pacing the kitchen floor. She thought if Sis Riah didn't come soon, she'd just have to wrap the baby up and try to walk over there.

When she heard the voice for the third time she knew she wasn't imagining it. She stopped in wonder and stood stock still in the front room.

"I know somebody calling me," she said and then waited for it to come to her again. It did.

"Jubilee, call Sis Riah."

She located the source of the voice this time. It came from the inside of her own head, and though she did not understand how, the sound of it did not issue forth from her own thinking. It came again, whispering gently, kindly, coaxing her once more.

"Jubilee, call Sis Riah."

Although it was not her own voice, it was a familiar one and she was surprised that in spite of the strangeness of it, somehow it didn't scare her.

"Who is it?" she thought and as quick as lightening in her head, before she could echo it aloud in her mouth and on her tongue, the room was filled with the smell of rose bay.

"Deedove's mama," she smiled and she drew in a hungry breath and filled every particle of her body with the sweet undeniable essence of the conjure women. There was something secure and unchanging about the smell. She closed her eyes, wrapping her arms about herself and swaying with the sudden release of peace that the smell gave her. She recognized immediately the music in her head. It was what she had listened to so many times in Deedove's cabin when she thought it was just her imagination. Something terribly significant was happening to her and she wondered at the easy way it came upon her. She felt like a child welcoming her mama home after she'd been away for a long, long time. The comfort, the joy, the security of that. And the women felt the joy, too. She heard their laughter and their rejoicing in the welcome that she offered them, the kind they had sought so long from Deedove and never found.

She opened herself to them, a little at first and then more and more of her. The darkness and sorrow of her life and the joys; she offered it to them. They flooded through every cell of her. They threw open the gates of her consciousness. The windows of her house became more than windows, they were great portals that let in wide rivers of light and warmth. It seemed she was swirling in a pool of laughter and knowing and conversation and awareness the likes of which she had never known before.

At first she wondered if she was dreaming. She could feel part of herself holding back as it watched the silver whirlpool engulf her with its intensity. But another part of her joyously welcomed the coming at last of ancient and trusted friends and it gently coaxed the fearful, hesitant side of her nature to partake of the new world that she was merging into. Jubilee knew instinctively what was happening to her. It was as if since the day she was born she had known this day was before her. She knew she would never again be completely alone. She was no longer a motherless child, but a child of many mothers. Her life would never again be as it had been before.

"Call her," the voices said. The sound was sweet and inviting inside her head. "Call Sis Riah."

How wonderful, she thought. The women recognized that even with their overpowering presence she still needed her old friend.

"How?" she asked simply and then as quickly as she had said it she knew.

She dropped immediately to her knees and unclenched her hands and rested them; her palms lay gently in her lap opened upward. Relax, they instructed, and she allowed her mind to travel over every part of her body testing and coaxing the muscles to give in and go slack. She allowed her head to rock back and fill up with thoughts of Sis Riah sitting in the swing on her porch visiting and talking to her. She felt her thinking become solid and mobile and drift away from her, filled with the power of her desire and directed by her will. Suddenly, she wasn't on the porch anymore, but inside Sis Riah's kitchen listening as she talked to Sweet Boy about the meeting she had gone to with Saphronia over the weekend. Jubilee listened for a while and then whispered softly, "Sis Riah, come see me. I needs you." That's all she said, but she knew it was enough.

CHAPTER 26

"COURSE, I WAS planning to get on out here anyway, soon as I could," Sis Riah was saying. She sat in the swing, rocking and patting Grace and looking into the baby's beautiful little face. "Soon as Sweet Boy get to feeling better. But his stomach be so tore up, wouldn't been no sooner than tomorrow before I get here. But then we be setting talking this morning, and I just right out hears you calling my name, clear as if you'da been setting right there with us. So I tells Sweet Boy what I done heard, and I says, 'You gotta get me on out to Jubilee's right now. I don't care what ailing you. Something going on with her. So he go outside, sick and all, borrow Matthew's old truck and here I is. Now ain't that some kinda story?"

Jubilee was sitting on the porch steps, leaning against the front post, carefully watching how the older woman held Grace, trying to memorize her movements and the way she patted and kind of half talked, half crooned to her. In her head, the conjure women murmured and sighed.

"Benny proud of her, Jubilee?"

"Yessum, he real proud." With the mention of Benny she felt the great dark cloud move in and cover up the sun Sis Riah had brought with her.

She turned away and began breaking off pieces of the mint plants at the porch edge. She crushed them in her hand and raised her palm to her nose to smell the rich summer scent. Sis Riah watched her.

"What the trouble, hon?" she asked.

Jubilee looked at her friend, who had only a little while earlier heard her mystical call for help with the ears of love and had come running to her side. She felt her eyes begin to fill with gratefulness. Inspite of the women she needed to talk to Sis Riah, but her tongue felt as useless as a wet stick of firewood.

"I wants to tell you, but I don't know if I can right now."

"You begun already, hon. Just keep going and take your time. I'm here to listen."

There was a long moment, silent except for the creak of the porch swing moving gently back and forth and the summer bird songs drifting up from the swamp. The conjure women hushed in recognition of the wisdom of this woman who was not one of them. Although they understood the hurt in Jubilee's soul right now, they could not help put things aright as Sis Riah could.

Sis Riah leaned back patiently as if she intended to sit right there all week if need be. Jubilee took a deep breath. She searched for a place to begin that would start the unburdening.

At last, she spoke, stumbling at first and then breaking forth into the thing. About the night when she woke needing Benny and he wasn't there, about finding the camisole and later making the connection between it and Nan Hawkins. How she confronted Benny after Grace was born and what he had said. The determination she felt for Grace and herself. And the loss of something perfectly sweet in her life that she believed she would never again regain. And the women listened.

She stopped, finally, and looked at Sis Riah who still rocked the swing gently with Grace lying in her lap, the little head propped on her knees. With calm assurance the older woman smiled down at the small, wide-opened, black eyes. Jubilee was comforted to tears to see the gentleness on that face and to know the world was still on its assigned path through an orderly universe.

"What Benny say when you talk to him about it?" she asked.

"He say it ain't true, Sis Riah. Then he slam out of thee house and don't come back for a long time when it get real late and me and Grace asleep."

"What about since then?"

"We ain't talked much. Just necessary stuff. Thing I don't understand the most. You wouldn't believe your eyes to see him with that baby. He seem to love everything that has to do with her. If she begin to cry he take her up every time, hold her. She wet, he change her diaper, fretting, he walk around with her, inside or out. Talk to her while he walking. Hardly put her down when he able to be home, even if she sleeping."

"That the Horne in him," Sis Riah said keeping the steady rock, rock of the swing going. "And how he be treating you, honey?"

Jubilee felt the conjures listening and soothing her in her head.

"Well, he ain't never been kinder to me since we first meet. I can't tell is it because of the baby or he just feeling guilty. But, Sis Riah, I don't want none of Benny's guilt. I wants him doing all them things because he love me and because he want to."

The baby whimpered and Sis Riah made soft little clucking sounds that comforted Jubilee again to tears.

"This put me in mind of Benny's daddy," Sis Riah said. "How much you know about that family?"

"Some. Benny ain't never said a whole lot, but I done met his eldest sister live in Goodman, the one more or less raise the children when his mama die. She seem real nice, but I sure don't care for her husband none."

Grace began to fret in earnest, so Jubilee moved to the swing and sat down beside her friend and began unbuttoning the oversized man's shirt she was wearing.

"Benny ever talk about his daddy?"

"Little bit. I know his daddy cat around and Benny say he ain't never gonna be like that. But yet that just what he doing."

Sis Riah nodded. "Well, but you know, Big Benny weren't meant to be that kinda man. He don't start out that way."

"You mean when Benny little?"

"Uh huh. From the outside looking in, Big Benny and Sadie Horne had theyselves one of the finest families in this part of the county. Two of them working hard for Matthew and Olivia Montgomery and raising up six children easy as weeds growing up beside the road. Benny the first boy."

Sally the oldest child? The one I meet?"

"Uh huh. Then come Tessy, then Benny. Then three more after that. Children like stair steps, one born about every year and a half. Pretty mess of children. Tessy dead now from a fever and the others scattered everywhere. Big Benny work real hard for Matthew Montgomery and us know that ain't easy. Them children don't know how lucky they is. Benny Horne love his babies the most anybody ever see in a man. Always going around town carrying one of them over his shoulders. You know, just enjoying them."

"Benny never tell me about that. You suppose he remember it?"

"He remember alright. But Big Benny change, hon. He mostly remember that."

"How come?"

"Well, a whole lot of things. Everything just seem to beat the hope right out of him. Last thing was the test Little Benny take. State test."

"But Benny done good on that, didn't he?"

"Just like everybody knew he would. First day your Benny big enough to get into school, teacher saying he some kinda smart. His mama and daddy always saying he going to college. Tugaloo. But they ain't got no money for college."

"Benny don't ever want to talk about that test none."

"Well, the whole thing just be a hurt for him in the end. Everybody watching to see what that boy gonna do. Big Benny think he done come up with a way to solve the money thing."

"How?"

"Every year the Lions Club give prize money to the child in the county make the highest grade on the state test. Up until that year some white child in Tula get the prize. Ain't no colored folks cares who gets it one way or another. Colored children don't never take the test, no how."

"How Benny come to take it then?"

"His daddy do that. Big Benny go to Matthew, ask him can Little Benny take that test along with Luke."

"He ask Mr. Matthew? That take some courage," Jubilee said smiling.

"Well, because if he win he be able to pay some for college with the prize money. Course, Matthew 'bout kill hisself laughing. He say that be just the thing gonna finally stop the talking about that little nigger having so much sense."

"Sweet Boy tell me one time that Benny beat the stew outa everybody on that test, including Mr. Luke," Jubilee added.

"That was about the maddest I ever see Matthew Montgomery. And Lord, Big Benny and Sadie be proud of that boy. And they begun waiting for the prize money to come, so they can send it on ahead to the school in Tugaloo."

Grace finished nursing and Jubilee laid the small bundle against her shoulder and gently stroked her back.

"So what happen when they get the prize money?"

"Didn't never get it. You know Matthew high up in the Lions Club. Next thing anybody know, they announces in the Four County News they ain't gonna be able to award no prize money that year because the price of cotton real low and they sure sorry for it. Gonna give out a certificate instead."

"Certificate? That ain't worth nothing to nobody," Jubilee said.

"Cruel to that child. And then I don't know what happen. Seem like Big Benny just cut loose."

"That when he stray away from Miz Sadie?"

"I think he finally come to believe nothing ever gonna change. Stuff he have to take off of Matthew Montgomery all the time, the babies he love so much gonna have to put up with the same thing when they grows up. They whole lives. He can't do a thing about it. I think nobody know, except Sadie maybe, how sad it make that man to know that. Big Benny have to make his life bearable somehow. He have to say to the world and hisself that he don't care what happen to all of them. Only way he be able to stand such a thing."

"That's why he change?"

"I think maybe."

"Sis Riah, I hear about Benny's mama."

"Sadie Horne? She didn't know what to do. So she keep on doing what she been trained all her life to do. She know somehow she have to help him. So she shut her mouth and take it. Big Benny be home, want his dinner, she give it to him best she can. He want to sleep in the bed with her, she let him. He want to be her husband for a while, she let him. And nothing ever come from that woman's mouth about what a terrible state her husband done come to. She acting around the place like everything be just like it always was. Nothing change."

"I know. I been hearing folks talk about Miz Sadie ever since I come to Tula."

"Everybody love her. But she die from the burden of it before her time. Then Sally take over and use her mama's ways as the way a colored woman suppose to live. She wear her fingers out doing for the other children and her daddy whenever he around. And she marry a no account man, because she don't expect nothing more."

"I see that. But what happen to my Benny?"

"He believe that test cause all the trouble in the family. But ain't nobody in Hart County ever blame Benny for it. You knows how folks think of that boy. They respects him."

The conjure women whispered to Jubilee and a vision of Benny flashed in her mind showing her something about him. She thought she might explain the voices to Sis Riah, but she knew the time was not right. So she spoke as if the idea were her own.

"Benny meant to be a guide to others," she said out loud.

"Uh huh. Unless they lose respect for the man."

"What I have to do?"

Sis Riah smiled at Jubilee and shook her head slowly.

"You don't have any idea what you is, do you, honey?"

"What you mean?" Jubilee asked. She wondered if Sis Riah knew about the voices of the conjure. But there was no sign of the knowledge on her friend's face.

"I mean, you like the first prize at the turkey shoot. Benny musta felt like he the king of the world when he get you."

"Then why he head for Nan Hawkins door?"

"Maybe just because it was open. Or maybe because he think he not good enough for you. Pretty soon you gonna get tired of him and leave anyway. Maybe both."

"Nan Hawkins too strong for me, Sis Riah. She got too much to offer Benny."

"Don't belittle what you offering, honey. A family living together, loving one another, raising up children. No man brought up in the Horne family gonna discount them treasures. They born to it."

"Then what I suppose to do."

"You already on the right track. Don't put up with one minute of what he doing right now. It ain't alright and it ain't just fine. His mama did what she had to do and I don't fault her none for that. But you gotta show her son he gonna have to give that stuff up to have you. And somehow you gotta look like you ain't winning some kinda war while you doing it. Make him understand that he the one winning the war."

Jubilee knew what Sis Riah was saying was true. But the thing that made the doing of it hard was the risk. If he left, what then? What would she do with the icy chunk of fear her mother had thrust inside her chest when she left. She shivered at the loneliness Benny's absence would cause her.

"Sis Riah, I's scared."

"Well, you gotta hang on until the turn come and I believe it will. Hold your ground. I be here when you needs me to help shore you up."

A horn blew from the road and the two women shaded their eyes and looked out and saw Sweet Boy waving at them. Sis Riah waved back.

"I gotta go. You let me know how things are going. I be right here," she said to Jubilee. She leaned over and kissed the baby's head and Jubilee's cheek and then stiffly descended the steps, holding on to the rail as she went.

Hang on until the turn come, Jubilee repeated to herself as she watched her friend walk on out to the truck. But how was she to know when that happened? And how hard was it gonna be to hang on?

Or maybe Grace's birth had made the final difference and the crisis was already over and she didn't have anything else to worry about. She listened for a moment for her new voices, but they were silent on the subject. She'd just have to wait to hear what time would tell her.

CHAPTER 27

THE COMFORTABLE, TWO-STORY, white, frame house where Luke Montgomery's family lived sat on a hill that began its rise down along the river and rolled up to a gentle crest alongside the Lexington highway. The hilltop was high ground and, therefore, a dwelling place for many generations of men long before the young Montgomerys cleared it of blackberry bushes and cottonwoods and built the house. Now it looked out across a wide front yard filled with young silver-leaf maple trees and magnolias.

At night the family sat out in the front yard and watched lightening bugs glitter under the trees. Anise and Chip caught the insects and put them in canning jars on their bedside tables to use as night lamps. Mary Alice told them the legends that man has devised through the centuries to explain the night sky. She pointed out the Milky Way and the big and little dipper and how to find the steady North Star. They talked about how far away stars were and how the sky never ended. She told them that even as they sat there with everything so serene around them, the earth was whirling dizzily around in circles and speeding around the sun that did not go out at night, but was at that moment lighting up the children on the other side of the world. Everything that seemed so quiet and fixed in the night sky was in reality in constant motion, a graceful and intricately choreographed dance.

Anise struggled to wrap her understanding around the ideas as she and Chip lay on the ground on their backs, listening and watching for falling stars, and she and her family became in her mind tiny specks of dust in the universe.

On the morning after the family got back from Florida as soon as she woke up Anise ran into the bedroom where her mother was working.

"Mama, please, can we go now to Jubilee's house?"

She stood watching her mother sort clothes on the bed, picking out cream colored shells from among them and brushing grains of white sand off onto the floor.

"We have to wait until Jubilee's ready to have some company."

"But I know Jubilee wants to see me. She hasn't seen me for a whole week. I bet she's mad because I haven't come to visit her yet."

"Anise, how could you possibly have visited her before now. We didn't get home until ten thirty last night. You think we should have gone to see her then?"

"No, ma'm, but now it's daytime, and she'll be expecting me pretty soon."

"Well, we'll see. I've got lots of things to do today, because Jubilee's not here. Would you take this stack of clothes into your room, and put Chip's on top of his chest of drawers? And put yours away in the right places, too."

"Yessum. Mama, who's going to work for us while Jubilee's away?"

"Daddy sent word for Mandy to plan to come on in for a while."

"I can't stand for Jubilee to be gone. Couldn't she just bring her baby with her? I could take care of her. Huh, Mama?"

"Oh, Anise, that's the silliest thing I ever heard of. You taking care of a colored baby. Now get on out of here with those clothes."

When she came back after accomplishing the task her mother gave her, she said, "Mama, can we?"

"Can we what, Anise?"

"Can we please go see the baby this afternoon?"

The little girl sat down on the bed beside her mother holding a funny little doll in her hand. The ruffle around the neck of Anise's pale pink cotton sundress was turned up and her mother reached over to straighten it.

"Alright. But just for a little while, because we don't want to wear Jubilee out and make it even longer before she can come back to work."

"And can we take a birthday present for the baby?"

"Well, I have that little baby dress all wrapped up that I showed you."

"Mama, what color are little nigra babies?"

"Oh, honey, I guess kinda light brown. I'm not sure, though. I don't guess I've ever seen a new born colored baby."

"Are they just like white babies only they're brown?"

"I guess so."

"You mean that's the only difference. They're brown instead of kinda pinkish?"

"Well, at first, maybe."

Anise held up the doll in her hands and looked at the painted face.

"Mama, will I ever be a colored person?"

"No, honey. Your mama and daddy are white, so you'll be white all your life."

"I think Jubilee is beautiful. Don't you?"

"Yes, I suppose so."

"Her skin's not as dark as Benny's. And Hippy's skin is almost black. Does that mean he's more of a nigra than Benny and Jubilee?"

"No, Anise. People are either colored or not. There's no such thing as being more colored or less colored."

"What makes Jubilee's skin lighter than Benny's, Mama?"

"Probably has some white blood in her."

"Does white blood look like colored blood?"

"Yes."

"Then how can they tell the difference?"

"Oh, Anise. I don't know. Hand me that towel."

"How does the white part of Jubilee's blood turn into colored blood when it's inside her?"

"Lord, you ask a lot of questions. I don't know."

"If I had colored blood in me would it turn into white blood?"

"Anise, shame on you. Don't say things like that. You have absolutely nothing but white blood in you. Don't you ever say a thing like that again."

So the little girl sat silently for a while, thinking and watching her mother, because she wasn't exactly sure what she had said that was wrong.

Whenever Anise went with her mother to Worthey Brothers on Saturday afternoon for bread or something, she watched the colored children on the sidewalk as they laughed and played with each other. Sometimes she knew the games they played, and she wished she could get out of the car and play with them. Sometimes they'd stop for a minute from their running and laughing to stare at her and she stared back.

She wondered if Jubilee liked being a colored person. She stretched out her hands in front of her and looked carefully at the fingers and arms that were browned from the Florida sun. Maybe if she stayed out in the sun some more she would slowly turn into a colored child. Or maybe if Jubilee stayed out of the sun she would become white.

Most of the time Anise was glad her skin was white. In Jackson in the back of Kennington's Department Store stood the old, rust-stained, "colored" water fountain. She was glad that she had somehow managed to join the group that had at sometime in the past gained the right to drink from the nicer, shiny one. But Anise envied the fact that colored people got to sit in the balcony at the picture show on Saturday afternoon in Tula. When she watched them filing up the stairs, she thought how fun it would be to sit way up high like that and look down on all the white people's heads below who watched the same Tarzan or Roy Rogers movies they did.

Waiting that day for her mother to say it was time to go see

Jubilee and the baby was torturous. Finally, at three o'clock she threatened to run alone across the two big pastures that separated her house from Jubilee's cabin if Mary Alice didn't hurry.

Finally, she sat by her mother in the blue Fairlane. Her gift for the baby, wrapped in white tissue paper with a pink ribbon, rested on her lap. She held her legs stiffly and primly together. When her mother turned down the little dirt trail and cut the motor off Anise jumped out, slamming the door behind her, and took off down the path. Mary Alice followed her walking carefully and noticing the last of the flowers that Jubilee had planted back last spring that lined the way, thinking that it was the colored woman's way of copying her own flowered walk.

"Jubilee," Anise started calling as she neared the house. "Jubilee."

Mary Alice saw the young woman open her screen door and step out on to the porch and wave at the little girl. Anise bounded up the steps and wrapped both her arms around her and then held the present up for her to take. Mary Alice had just gotten to the bottom of the steps when Jubilee finished unwrapping the gift.

"That's real nice, Miss Anise. Grace gonna thank you for that doll when she get bigger," and she hugged the little girl again.

"Is that her name? Grace?" Anise asked.

"Yessum, that's it. Grace Delora Horne. That be her whole name."

"How are you, Jubilee?" Mary Alice asked.

"I's fine, Miss Mary Alice. Thank ya'll so much for coming."

Mary Alice handed her the other present from the bottom of the steps. Jubilee reached down to take it.

"I hope you can use this," Mary Alice said.

"Oh, yessum. I'm sure I can. Thank you, Miz Mary Alice."

"Please, Jubilee. Can I see her now?" the little girl said, jumping on her toes and peeping through the screen in an effort to get a glimpse of the baby.

"You sho' can. You and your mama just make yourselves comfortable on my porch. I'll go in and get her. Here, Miz Mary Alice. Set here in the swing."

Mary Alice sat down stiffly and Jubilee disappeared into the dark back of the house. Anise peered through the screen door.

"Calm down, Anise. You don't want to scare the baby, do you?"

"Oh, here she comes."

Anise quit jumping and held her hands up to shade her eyes, so she could see through the screen door better. When the door opened she stepped back, covering her mouth so nothing like a squeal would jump out before she could check it. Jubilee sat down in the straight back chair across from the swing and held the sleeping baby for Anise to see.

"Oh, Mama, look at her little hands and her ears."

Mary Alice leaned forward to see. She didn't know exactly what to expect and she gasped with surprise, because Grace was the most beautiful baby she had ever seen. Her skin was smooth and ivory colored and the black lashes already beginning to grow, curled against the tiny rosy cheeks.

"Oh, Jubilee," she said. "She's beautiful."

"Is she too little for me to hold, like Kitty Montgomery's kittens?" Anise asked.

"You wants to hold her, Miss Anise? That alright, Miz Mary Alice?"

"If you trust her."

"Sho'. I trusts her," she said, smiling at the little girl.

The young mother stood up and Anise climbed into the chair and sat straight up with her arms extended waiting for the precious bundle to be delivered to her lap.

"Now, hold still," Jubilee told the little girl.

Just as she set the small bundle in Anise's arms the baby stirred in her sleep.

"Oh, mama, she smiled at me."

Anise leaned over and kissed the crown of the little head and then laid her cheek against the soft forehead.

"You need anything, Jubilee?" Mary Alice asked.

"No, ma'm. We got diapers and clothes for her. Sis Riah done gone around to folks in the county and brung me some things. We all fixed up."

"I'm sorry we came to visit so soon. Anise about drove me crazy this morning wanting to come over. I held her off as long as I could."

"Yassum. I wanted Miss Anise to see her. I know she want to."
There was an uncomfortable silence.

"Ya'll have a nice trip, Miz Mary Alice?"

"Marvelous. The children found a horse shoe crab on the beach one morning. You'll be glad to hear we didn't bring it home. And Chip learned to water ski. We're trying to figure out how he can do it on the Gage place lake right now."

"That sound like fun for the children."

Anise looked up from the baby for a minute.

"Jubilee, when can you come on back to work? Can it be soon? Old bad Mandy is gonna be working for us until you get back. She won't ever let me help her. She always says, 'Never mind. I do it, Miss Anise.'"

"Anise, that's not nice now. Mandy does a good job. Course, nobody can take the place of you, Jubilee," Mary Alice said.

"Yessum. I don't know exactly, Miss Anise. Maybe in a few weeks."

"Couldn't you just bring Grace with you? I could take care of her while you did the work."

"Don't be silly, Anise. You don't know how to take care of a baby," her mother said.

"But Jubilee could teach me and then I'd know. Couldn't you, Jubilee?"

"Yessum, I expect I could."

"We want Jubilee to take all the time she needs, Anise. She needs to rest and not have any little girls bothering her for a while."

"Oh, no ma'm, Miz Mary Alice. Miss Anise don't never bother me none. She always real good."

Jubilee smiled down at Anise.

"Then I could take care of her some?" the little girl pushed.

"Well," Mary Alice said.

"We'll just have to see how things works out, honey," Jubilee said.

"Anise, we better be going. Remember I said we couldn't stay too long," her mother said, getting up from the swing and walking across the porch.

"Mama, look. You can see the top of the hay barn from here. I could walk straight across the pasture, over the hill and pass the barn and come home by myself later on."

Mary Alice glanced at Jubilee.

"She welcome anytime she wanta come over, Miz Mary Alice," Jubilee said.

"I need to talk to your daddy about it first, honey. If he thinks its safe and all. But we gotta go on now," she said.

Anise got up from the chair with the baby and rocked her gently back and forth in her arms.

"Miz Mary Alice, if Mr. Luke think it alright, I be happy for her to come across the pasture whenever it be alright with you."

"You sure she wouldn't bother you?"

"No, ma'm. Anise don't bother nobody. It be real nice to have her around some."

"Well. Come on, darling. I have to fix supper tonight. Tell Grace bye."

"Bye, Grace."

She kissed the baby again and handed her to Jubilee.

"Bye, Jubilee. I'll come back and see you again soon," Anise called over her shoulder as she hopped down the steps.

Jubilee watched the mother and daughter walk hand in hand down the path. She watched Anise climb into the car and slam the door. Mary Alice turned the Fairlane around in the highway and headed back toward the intersection. Jubilee waved until they were out of sight.

She hoped she'd looked all right to her guests, not upset or anything. Trying to look normal on the outside while her insides were turned upside down. She thought of the time she stood with her aunt and two cousins on a porch like this one, waving and watching her mother drive away in a car with a man friend, who was taking her as far as St. Louis. The car had rumbled on out of sight while she stood on the porch behind watching motionless and silent, wrapping her anguish in an appearance of serenity.

CHAPTER 28

THE BELL OVER the door of the dry cleaners jingled as Luke Montgomery came in and walked over to the counter. Nan Hawkins was at work in the back. He could see her moving with assurance among the confusing array of machinery. A young colored girl up toward the front threaded brown paper clothes bags up a chain attached to the ceiling and with her other hand hooked a cleaned, pressed garment to the lowest link and slid the bag down over it. Then she labeled the bag and hung it on a rack with other bagged clothes.

When she saw him she stopped her work and came to the counter to wait on him.

"Yes, sir, Mr. Luke?"

She was young, twelve or thirteen, and her hair was braided into three parts. Her dress was clean and pressed and nicer than he would have expected. He recognized her as one of Quilla's girls.

"Well, it's Izzie, isn't it? How long you been working here?"

"Be about a week now, Mr. Luke," she said hesitantly.

"Well, good for you. Maybe you gonna follow in Nan's footsteps."

She ducked her head and laughed nervously.

"Nawh, sir. I's just bagging clothes and minding folks that comes in."

"Well, that's fine. Mighty fine. Uh, Miz Mary Alice sent me in here to pick up a blue party dress of hers."

"Just a minute, Mr. Luke. I see is it ready."

Izzie walked back to the rack where she had been hanging the clean, bagged clothes and began reading the labels. The bell on the door tinkled again behind him and Luke turned to see his mother's cook, Saphronia, come in and stand away from the counter respectfully until Luke had finished his business. She smiled agreeably and nodded at him.

"How you, Mr. Luke?" she said.

"Nice to see you back, Phronie. You and Sis Riah have a good trip?"

"Yassuh, sho' did."

"Lot of talk about that preacher ya'll heard down yonder. Article about him yesterday in the Jackson Daily. Hope he didn't put any crazy ideas into your head."

Saphronia fidgeted nervously with her purse.

"Nawh, sir. Sho' didn't, Mr. Luke. Sho' didn't. That stuff ain't nothing I got no business with." She sniffed and lowered her voice. "But they's lotsa folks at that meeting just lapping up every word he saying. Freedom this, freedom that."

"Well, that's dangerous business, Phronie. You and Sis Riah better steer clear of that stuff."

"That's just what I say, Mr. Luke. But they done elected Sis Riah to be one of they state committeewomen. Course, our church gonna be proud of her, but I tells her she getting herself into some mighty hot water. Lord God, I wouldn't be none of that if somebody paid me."

"Well, I hope she knows what she's doing. She sorta rules the roost up here because of Mama, but she'll be pretty much on her own down yonder in Jackson."

"I say the same thing to her. And she ain't no spring chicken neither," Saphronia said.

Luke looked back toward Izzie who seemed perplexed.

"Miss Nan," she called toward the back. "Miz Mary Alice's dress ready yet?"

Nan looked up toward the cleaned clothes and bags at the front. "Yonder it is, waiting for a bag," she called over the sound of the machines.

Izzie looked back at the man across the counter. "I's sorry, Mr. Luke. Be just a minute."

"Take your time."

Saphronia spoke again.

"Mr. Luke, you see Benny's baby yet?"

"Not yet. I hear it's a nice little girl."

"Come sooner than expected. I tell that gal last Sunday she ain't gonna wait no three weeks like the doctor in Lexington say. But she ain't gonna listen to none of Saphronia."

"Mary Alice and Anise been to see her. Anise can't quit talking about her. We having to tie her to the bedpost to keep her from going down to Jubilee's cabin every day. She thinks that baby is hers."

Saphronia chuckled politely.

"Well, I reckon I won't get to see her 'til Sunday. Jubilee probably have her presented then. We usually does it like that."

Izzie had finished bagging the dress and brought it to the counter. "Here it is, Mr. Luke," she said.

"How much I owe you?"

"Dresses be fifty cents."

"Good Lord. Fifty cents to clean one dress. Maude Jones is robbing this town blind."

Izzie dropped her eyes to the counter as Luke reached in his pocket for the change. He picked up the bag and turned to leave.

"Tell Mother I'll be by sometime this afternoon for some of your chess pie," he said to Saphronia who smiled and nodded.

Izzie sorted the money into the coin drawer below and was about to wait on Saphronia when Nan came up from the back and interrupted.

"Never mind, Izzie. You finish bagging the clothes. I wait on Miss Saphronia."

Izzie's face became anxious.

"Yassum," she said and she turned back toward the work behind her.

Nan smiled at her customer.

"Morning, Miss Saphronia."

"Morning, Miss Nan. I come in to see is you got the stain out of my nice dress. Like I told Izzie when I bring it in, I don't know where in the world I pick it up. First time I notices it is when I climbs off that bus from Tugaloo."

"I think I remember we done got that out," Nan said as she moved hangers along a bar and read tags tied to them. "Here it is. Tag say, 'Stain Removed'. You wants to look at it? See is it alright?"

"I sho' do."

Nan slid the brown paper bag off and held the dress up for inspection.

"Well, Lord bless me," she said. "I can't even see where it was. That some mighty fine cleaning. Was ya'll able to tell what it was?"

"Seem like coffee or tobacco juice."

"Oh, Lord," Sis Riah shuddered. "I sure hope it was coffee. Anyway, I do love this dress."

"It's mighty pretty."

"It'll do. But ooh, Miss Nan, you shoulda seen the clothes on the women down at that conference me and Sis Riah went to. And hats. Oh, my Lord, the hats. I got some good ideas for this fall." She grinned and put one hand on a hip. "Not that me and Sis Riah didn't add a little color to the gathering."

"Miss Saphronia, you always been a good dresser."

"Not good as some women around here," she demurred. "Where you find your clothes at, Miss Nan?"

"They's a store in Jackson carry nice things for coloreds. La Paree. Down on South State."

"Ready made? Bet they cost you something."

"Not too bad."

"You lucky you got this here good job. Miz Maude ever come down here to the business any more?" Saphronia looked around.

Nan hesitated. "Well, she don't very much. She pretty near leave it up to me, now. You know she ain't well." She saw a thought flicker over Saphronia's face and added quickly, "Course, I always ask her before I do anything new."

Sis Riah smiled again. "You better watch out being so smart. Men folk ain't gonna want a woman smarter than they is."

"Thank you, Miss Saphronia. I'll remember what you say." She smiled back.

"Well, I know you ain't got no mama to tell you such things. You a nice looking woman. But you gonna have to play dumb to get a man to the preacher," she said.

Nan smiled and nodded at the woman who seemed oblivious to the fact that she had somehow never managed to capture a husband for herself.

"Did I hear you telling Mr. Luke about Jubilee's baby?"

"Sure did. And, honey, they's some kind of talk going on around town about it, too. Sis Riah let it slip when she come by Miz Olivia's this morning for some beans."

"What about?"

"Something about Benny not being home when Jubilee begin to get her pains. And, honey, it was in the middle of the night when she come down with them. Now where you reckon Benny Horn get hisself off to in the middle of the night."

"When it be born, Miss Saphronia?"

"Friday night or rather early Saturday morning. Little girl name of Grace Delora."

"She still in the hospital in Lexington?"

"Lord, no, hon. She never get to no hospital. I hear she about had it in the field, because that's where she go looking for Benny when she wake up and find he ain't in the bed with her." Nan looked away quickly as Saphronia continued. "If it weren't for old Deedove, I hear tell, Jubilee have that baby all by herself right out there in the middle of the cotton."

"Deedove receive the baby?"

"Honey, yeah. Can you imagine letting that crazy old thing deliver your child?" Saphronia leaned closer to Nan across the counter. "I wants to tell you, I'd rather bring my baby into this world all alone out in the middle of a swamp than have them hands on her. And ain't it justice. Jubilee and Benny bragging how they planning on going to the hospital when her time come. Like she some kinda queen. That's what pride bring you. That them Hornes for you," she clucked.

Nan thought for a moment.

"Miss Saphronia, what time your church start on Sunday?"

"Say what?"

"I's just wondering. I hear ya'll got a real good preacher. I been thinking of coming on out there some Sunday and hearing me a sermon."

"Get over to our church?" Saphronia asked, her evangelical spirit rising.

"Yassum, you think that be alright?"

"Why sure, Nan," she said and smiled broadly. "Ain't never too late this side of the grave to come to the Lord. We be glad to welcome you. Start around ten; sometimes don't let out 'til one, if the preacher get wound up. Course, you sit at the back, sneak out early if you wants to. Everybody expecting Jubilee and Benny to have they baby presented this coming Sunday."

"Well, maybe I come and see it."

"That be real nice. I be hoping to see ya'll then. Well." She looked thoughtfully at Nan. "Oh, how much I owes you."

"Fifty cents, Miss Saphronia."

"And I think it be a small price to pay for saving my dress. Don't know why Luke Montgomery so tight fisted with his fifty cents." Saphronia folded the bag over her arm. "Well. See ya'll on Sunday morning then."

She gave Nan another studied look and walked out of the dry cleaners.

Nan watched Saphronia cross the street and disappear into the corner drugstore. Her mind slid back to Friday night, Benny turning up at her door, waking her up out of a sound sleep. The two of them together just like she had dreamed it. His hands on her silk nightgown. Pulling up his shirt and kissing his stomach. The smell of the leather belt and then the buckle undone and the zipper and sliding the pants off his hips. Her hands running down the muscles of his buttocks. It was good, too good for him to forget soon.

But now if he was feeling guilty about not being with Jubilee when she needed him. Nan had to get to him quick, keep him hot, add some more wood to his fire. She needed to find out where he was working, get a message to him. Better still, she could just show up there, surprise him like she had that day at the pond.

"Izzie, I's leaving for a while," she called as she walked out the door. "Just finish bagging the clothes and wait on the customers. I be back by dinner."

The door jingled shut behind her. She looked up and down the street. Luke Montgomery was coming out of Sam Owen's place with what looked like a part of farm machinery, maybe for a tractor. If the tractor had broken down, Benny wouldn't be in the fields. She climbed the stairs to the living quarters. She'd change into something pretty, something light and low-necked and maybe wear her high-heeled shoes. Benny always said something about her shoes. She'd just take a little drive out by Mr. Luke's place and see if she saw him anywhere.

CHAPTER 29

NAN DROVE PAST the cotton and corn fields to the tractor shed that Mr. Luke had set up for the hands to use when they needed gas or equipment. There was no sign of anyone there. She noticed the big barn up on the hill across from Mr. Luke's house. She got out of the car and walked across the pasture toward the structure. The ground was uneven and she had to watch her step to keep from ruining her shoes. A jersey milk cow and a few Angus brood heifers grazed and swatted flies with their tails in the sultry morning sun. She raised her eyes again toward the weathered, old, hay barn at the top of the rise. She looked and listened, but there was no sign of anyone around, only birds flying in and out through the upper openings.

By then she was hot and sticky and out of breath and when she got to the door, she stepped inside to rest and cool off a bit before she started back to the car. The blinding morning light filtered to a gentle haze inside. She was surprised to hear the lazy quiet of the barn's interior interrupted occasionally by the sound of a pitchfork biting into hay followed by the swish of it being picked up and thrown. She walked quietly toward the sound to get a look at the worker before he could see her. She would have a hard time explaining to Hippy or Mr. Luke what she was doing in

such an unlikely place. But at the same time the fear of discovery
excited her. She imagined her dress up to her waist and Benny's
hot sweat mixing with hers while Luke Montgomery watched their
heat secretly from behind one of the hay bales.

She crept quietly through the milk barn into the large hay shed
where she spotted the shirtless worker with his back turned toward
her. She recognized his neck and the bare muscles of his shoulders
bent over a full pitchfork. As he turned to fling a load above his
head onto the top of a nearby pile he caught sight of her. His face
went rigid.

"Hi, Benny."

"What you doing here?"

"I come to see how you getting along."

"Mr. Luke see you hanging around his barn I'm gonna catch
hell."

She bristled at his anger.

"Don't make a nickel's worth a difference to me what Luke
Montgomery find in his barn."

Benny pushed past her to the door and looked out toward the
house across the highway and then back toward Nan's car. He
turned back toward her, his face calmed. She laughed.

"Ain't nobody out there, silly."

He rubbed his face on the inside of his sleeve.

"What you doing, coming out here?" he said turning away
from her.

"Ain't seen you lately. Been missing you, Daddy Man."

"Yeah, well, I . . . uh, Jubilee done had the baby and I been
busy."

"I know. Heard about it this morning in the shop. Saphronia
tell me."

"Yeah, well . . . "

There was a pause. Benny turned to pick up another mound
of hay in the pitchfork. She watched him for a moment.

"I hear she real cute. Look like you," she said.

She walked clumsily on the high-heels around in front of him
and leaned against the rough wall. The morning sun striped the

floor through the wallboards and lit the dust flung up with the hay.

"That baby ain't none of your business," he said as he delivered the hay on the fork to the top of the stack.

She stepped closer to him, getting in his way.

"Well, Mister Daddy Man, what is my business then?"

He looked down at her teasing smile for a minute and let her slide both her hands underneath his belt in the back and work them down over his buttocks and press her breasts against his chest.

"Come on, Nan. Don't do that. Get away now. I'm through with that stuff. I got me a baby now and I wants to be a good daddy for her."

"I show you how to be a good daddy, Benny Horne."

She rubbed the silky material of her dress against the sweaty front of him.

"Damn it, Nan. Don't do that. If Mr. Luke catch us here in his barn . . . "

"What difference it make if Mr. Luke know you fooling around with the cleaner woman? What he do?"

"Won't be what he do make no difference. Be what he think."

"Oh, and long as he don't know what you been up to, he gonna keep on thinking how his Benny something different from most nigger men. Smarter. His Benny a good, smart, upright nigger man. What the good in that?"

She stood solemn waiting for an answer.

"I just don't want . . . "

Benny shook his head.

"Aw, Benny, honey. Ain't nothing you do gonna make no difference. Besides, nobody gonna catch us in here anyway. It smell so good and it so cool. Just put your arms on around me now. I needs me a daddy man so bad right now."

She stood on her tiptoes and kissed his chin and his face and his lips. He dropped the pitchfork and cursed and grabbed her face fiercely in his hands. Just as he did there was a sound from behind them at the barn door.

"Benny?"

They were apart before Anise and Chip Montgomery came around the haystack and found them, Nan smiling, Benny fumbling for the pitchfork.

"Hi, Benny," Anise chirped.

The two children stood looking at them.

"Uh, hi, Miss Anise. Mr. Chip," he said grabbing the fork back up and jabbing it into the loose hay on the floor.

"Benny, daddy said we had to come help you clean up the hay off the barn floor since we broke it all loose when we built . . . "

She looked back and forth between the two people.

"Hi, Nan Hawkins. What you doing in our barn?"

"Shut up, Anise," Chip hissed.

"You shut up, Chip Montgomery. I can say what I want to," she said, punching him in the side with her elbow.

"Excuse me," Nan said brushing passed the two children and walking on out toward the barn door.

"Benny, what was she doing in our barn?" Anise asked again.

"Anise, I told you shut up," Chip said.

"You're not the boss of me, Chip Montgomery," she answered.

Benny began to recover a little.

"Well, Miss Anise. Mr. Chip," he said smiling. "Ya'll come over to help me? That sho' is nice."

"Did you cover up our fort?" Anise asked.

"I don't know. Where is it?"

"Well, the front door is hidden over here by the wall."

She walked to the far side of the stack, climbed up a few feet and then disappeared into the hay.

Poking her head back out again, she said, "It's fine, Chip. The secret room is still here."

The boy, tall for his age and skinny, walked over to the opening, trying to hide the smile on his face from Benny. He climbed up to the hole in the hay and disappeared from sight. Benny stood staring at the place where the two children had disappeared into the hay. He knew that Chip understood what he had seen. Would he explain it to his little sister? Maybe say something about it to Luke?

"Get out of the front hallway, Chip. I wanta get out. The hay is sticking my legs," came Anise's voice from somewhere deep inside the stack. There was a tussling noise and the stack shook as Anise reappeared at the side opening.

"Alright, Benny. I'm ready. What you want me to do?"

"I don't know exactly, Miss Anise."

"Daddy said for us to carry the loose hay over to you so you could put it back on the stack," Chip said emerging.

While the two children began gathering up armloads of hay and dropping it in front of Benny, they kept up a steady stream of bickering. Chip teased his younger sister about how little she was, how slow she was, how inept in general about everything. Anise answered his verbal assaults with insults and punches. Benny wondered if he had been like that with his own sisters.

He could hardly look the boy in the face while he worked, so he kept his eyes down and concentrated on the lifting and stacking. When the job was finished the two children picked hay off their clothes and walked toward the door. Benny was about to breathe a sigh of relief when Anise stopped and turned toward him.

"Benny, how come Nan Hawkins was here?" she asked again.

"She come to ask about the baby. She done heard Grace been born and she want to know how she be."

"She came all the way out here from the cleaners? I don't see why . . . . " Anise was interrupted by Chip.

"Come on, *Anus*. We're gonna be late for dinner."

Chip grabbed her arm and pulled her toward the highway and the house.

"Don't you dare call me that. I'm gonna tell mama you called me that and she's gonna give you a whipping. That's a real bad thing to say to me, Chip."

Benny watched the children climb under the barbed wire fence and run toward home. He prayed Anise would forget what she had seen and not mention anything about it to Jubilee. He looked around back toward the tractor shed for the car. It was nowhere in sight. He was amazed at his feeling of disappointment. He had to get control of himself. And then he began to tremble with the thought of what had almost occurred. What would have happened if the children had not come in when they did? He was wildly thankful that their entrance had not been a few minutes later, making them witness to something he dared not even think about. But he knew while he stood there in the silent barn that she was waiting for him to come to her the first chance he got. He shook his head slowly feeling the grief rising steadily up in him, because he knew deep down that sooner or later he would not be able to stop himself from going to town.

CHAPTER 30

THE CHURCH WAS filled with the subdued murmurs of people that worked from daylight to dark in the blistering summers of rural Mississippi. Sis Riah's flowers, dahlias and snapdragons, overflowed a large vase in front of the preacher's pulpit. The flutter of pasteboard fans beat the still, humid air. The protest of infants too young to understand the constrictions of church going and the punctuations here and there of moved believers mingled with the drone of the preacher's voice as he spoke about sin and sacrifice and hate and love.

Jubilee sat beside Benny listening to the preacher and holding the baby who was wearing a delicate, handmade, long, white, christening dress. Saphronia had brought it to the cabin a few days earlier after Jubilee sent her word at Sis Riah's prompting to come see the new baby. Jubilee had seen the christening dress before. It was an old tradition in the church for every baby to wear it to their first church service where they were the object of everybody's attention.

Sis Riah had told her the story behind it, that years ago it had belonged to the wealthy Macon family, who once owned most of the land on both sides of the Big Black in Hart County. The dress was made of the finest handmade lace and cotton batiste by nuns in New Orleans and bought for the youngest Macon child to wear at her christening. Before that event could occur, however, a night fire destroyed the Macons' huge old Georgian mansion that stood atop a bluff above Deedove's cabin. Saphronia's grandmother, one of the Macons' house slaves, passed by silverware and jewelry in her confusion and snatched the garment up and carried it out of the burning house as though it were a rare jewel.

When she brought it to the old master, who stood dazed in the smoky turmoil of the yard, he said, "Is that all you could get?" And he slapped her hard across the face and then cried as he watched the last of the family mansion go up in clouds of black smoke that darkened the starry night sky.

So Saphronia's grandmother pulled herself up, tucked the extravagant thing under her apron and never said another word about it to the Macon family. But from that time on, it was worn by all the babies who were presented at the old colored church.

Grace wore the dress now as she slept quietly in Benny's arms through most of the service. And Jubilee kept a calm look on her face with her eyes on the preacher as he delivered the morning message. She did not change her expression when the conjure women whispered to her a few minutes after the singing was finished that Nan Hawkins had crept in late to the service and had quietly taken the nearest empty seat by the back door.

Jubilee reached back with her mind, reading the thoughts of the other woman and felt the force of Nan's desires and discomforts rush over her. She heard the frightened, wistful voice of the child-Nan whispering hunger and jealousy and yearning that tumbled toward Grace, then Jubilee, then back to the baby again. She reached out to comfort the child-Nan, who like herself had no mother, and she heard the woman-Nan, who feared there would never be babies for her.

She felt Nan's hunger caress Benny, who knew nothing of her presence in the back. And Jubilee listened to the thoughts of her husband, thoughts of love for her and Grace and anger at himself when he thought of Nan. She could feel the power of the things that drew him to her and she knew her power was greater. But there was a trial ahead. A terrible trial that they must all go through.

Benny didn't know Nan was in the church until the end of the service when the preacher walked to the back to pronounce the benediction. He turned with the baby in his arms and saw her standing there, head bowed like everybody else. The sight of her made him jump and he found it hard to breathe. He was sure Jubilee had seen her, too.

What in hell was she up to anyway, sashaying into church for the first time in remembered history on this particular Sunday? To his knowledge, she had never set foot in the place before. Why now? He was angry and scared of what she might do next. If she spoke to him after church, how was he suppose to act? What would he say? If she wanted to see the baby, hold her, what then? If she spoke to Jubilee, could he act like she was just any body who'd come to church that day? Or would his face or his actions somehow reveal the truth? Would someone seeing him guess what had been going on between them? In the field. In her house. Sis Riah, maybe, or Saphronia.

Oh, God, he had to get out of there. Get Jubilee and the baby and himself home. He glanced nervously at his wife, who was calm with her eyes straight ahead. The congregation was alive with talk and movement. He saw Nan pass the preacher and say something to him as she shook his hand on her way out. Everybody spilled out of the little stucture into the sandy yard under the old pine trees. They began to gather a few at a time around the young couple to look at the baby. Grace lay in her father's arms and well-wishers passed by bending down for a closer look at the sweet little face, remarking on who she looked like and how anybody could see Benny sure loved that baby. And Benny fought to keep a calm smile on his face.

At first he didn't see her and he thought with relief that she must have hurried to her car and left. But he knew her well enough to know better. She'd never leave and miss this. She would enjoy his discomfort and the power it gave her. She knew when she stepped in the church door that morning what it was going to do to the inside of him to see her there. Goddamn it. What did she think she was doing?

But Nan Hawkins was not feeling powerful or smug. She stood at the edge of the disassembling crowd for a few minutes only half hearing the welcoming greetings of people she knew and of church officials who were glad she had joined them this morning. She moved cautiously closer, keeping out of Benny's sight, and listening to the talk about the pretty baby and her parents. She could hardly keep herself from walking over casually and looking into the folds of the blanket to see the baby, imagining what it would be like to hold her, and most urgently, how it would be if the baby were hers.

When the crowd began to thin in front of the church and Jubilee took Grace to the wagon to feed her, Sweet Boy came over to Benny and took his hand and shook it.

"You a lucky man, Benny Horne," he said.

"Thank you, Sweet Boy. I knows it," Benny answered, trying to keep an eye on where Nan might be and seeing her suddenly standing in the side yard talking to Mr. Jack Taylor.

"I don't deserve them," he said, his voice thick with emotion.

"You right about that. Tell me what I can say to get you away from that stuff you into."

"I don't know what you talking about."

"Come on back into the church. It be quiet in there and I needs to talk to you about some things."

"Not now, Sweet Boy. I gotta go. Jubilee need to get Grace on home."

Benny began to walk down the front steps, but his friend caught his arm.

"This afternoon?" Sweet Boy persisted. "I bring Sissy by. We walk out in the field.

Benny nodded. Sweet Boy let go his grip.

"Fine. I see you then."

Benny turned and hurried across the nearly deserted yard, his eyes nervously scanning the area. Nan was nowhere in sight. He breathed a sigh of relief. Jubilee was waiting in the wagon cradling Grace in her arms. She was silent as Benny climbed up and took the reins and hollered to the little red mule to get going. They rode in silence under the pines down the gravel road to the Lexington Highway. She read his anger and confusion, but there was nothing more she could do. She tried to look ahead, but the way was blurred and she couldn't see. She ached to reach out and touch him, but she knew that he was the one who had to come to her now. So she sat silent and unmoving with the baby in her arms.

When they reached home, Benny turned to help her out of the wagon and found that she was crying.

CHAPTER 31

THE AIR IN the house seemed hot and still. Benny and Jubilee ate Sunday dinner without talking. Neither one of them seemed to be able to break through the silence. Benny knew Jubilee had seen Nan at the service, but he thought if he brought it up, it might seem more important to him than it was. Than it was? Hell, it had almost made him throw up right there in the church.

After dinner Benny went out on the porch to sit in the swing. Jubilee had just finished washing the dishes up when she heard Sis Riah's whoop from the yard. She folded the dishcloth quickly and walked to the screen door. Benny was already greeting the couple on the path to the house. He watched as Jubilee walked out on the porch and down the steps into the ample arms of the older woman and his heart was humbled and grateful.

The two women sat down in the porch swing together. Benny heard them talking about what a good, quiet baby Grace was during church. Jubilee's voice lightened and he became hopeful.

It was a hot time of day. He and Sweet Boy walked along the rows of cotton plants and out of habit they examined leaves and bolls for signs of insects.

"Look pretty good," the older man said.

"Yeah. Short, but full of bolls," Benny responded.

"Let's us head down toward the swamp. Be cooler down yonder," Sweet Boy said.

The two men walked through the fields toward the thick shade. They stood together by a fallen log on the edge of the Big Black swamp. Sweet Boy was the only man in Tula who was taller than Benny, but the larger man's kind demeanor was gentle and reassuring. He was still dressed in his Sunday shirt. He was taller than Benny by half a head and he must have out weighed him by fifty pounds though he was not what anyone would call overweight. His heavy, dark face glittered with perspiration that ran down his thick neck and onto the collar of the shirt. His eyes, fringed with laugh lines, were solemn.

"What you want to talk about?" Benny said.

Sweet Boy looked at him a moment before he began. "What you think I'm gonna talk about?"

"Look, Sweet Boy, if this about the night Grace born . . . "

The big man began shaking his head. "Benny, listen. Be still and listen. I don't make it a habit to put my say into somebody else's business unless I's asked. But you my friend. Hey, you like a son to me."

"Wait, ain't no need to talk about it no more. That's done with."

Benny turned away, so Sweet Boy couldn't see his face, and looked back up in the direction of the cabin. He watched the two women rock the swing on the porch. They were too far away for him to hear what they said, but Sis Riah's laughter rang across the field occasionally.

"If you done with it, what she doing in church today?"

"Anybody say anything?" Benny asked.

"Just that they surprised she there. Nothing else. Not even from Saphronia."

"Do Sis Riah know about it?"

"Jubilee talk to her some," Sweet Boy answered.

"Damn. I hates her to think bad of me."

"What you expects her to think? Lots better than what everybody else gonna think when the word get around."

"What she say about it?"

"She just don't understand what you doing. Nan Hawkins a poor substitute for Jubilee."

"I know that, man. God almighty, I know that. Jubilee see her today, too," Benny said.

"What she say?"

"Not a single word."

"What that woman doing there in church anyway?" Sweet Boy asked.

"Hell if I know. Seem to me like she wouldn't want to be where Jubilee and the baby be."

"Sissy say she jealous of Jubilee."

"I don't see how she come to that. With all that woman got."

"Yeah, but Sissy say with all she got, she ain't got a husband and a baby."

"But she don't want none of that, Sweet Boy."

"Then how come her to be in church today. Just when ya'll presenting Grace to the congregation."

"Grace none of her business."

"Benny, you ever think about what you doing gonna cause lots of people hurt. Not just Jubilee and the baby. Me and Sissy what loves you and lots of folks in Tula."

Benny laughed. "Lots of folks in Tula?"

"People look to you, Benny, boy. Respects you. The way you lives."

Benny shook his head and squatted and picked up a handful of dirt.

"Look who you talking to. A man live in a rundown cabin on land belong to a white man. I ain't got a hope in the world past what you see right here."

"What if I tells you that ain't true?"

"I reckon I wouldn't believe it."

"Well, me and Sissy up to something gonna change that. Listen here. We been saving us some money for a while, so we be able to buy us a place of our own someday."

"I know about that. Sis Riah tell me ya'll saving for a farm. But ain't much hope of finding a farm somebody sell to a colored man."

"No, listen what I'm saying. Other day us read in the paper about a little house on a piece of farmland way out in the country from Camden up for sale. White folks don't want to live out that far. Man what owns it wanting bad to get rid of it. We hoping to go see it real soon. If it look good, Sissy have a idea about ya'll maybe getting something close to us. Sissy love to have Jubilee and that baby to fuss over. Then us could leave off working for the Montgomerys."

"Well, it be a long time before I has the money to join you."

"But it could happen some day. Me and you do good together. Help one another out."

"Well, I's too tied up to leave any time soon. I got Jubilee and the baby to think about. And Mr. Luke depend on me. It something I has to think about."

"Look, son, none of this gonna happen right away. Just keep it all in your mind. Talk about it. See what Jubilee think about the idea."

Benny looked at the face of his friend, sincere and warm.

"I believe Jubilee love to be anywhere Sis Riah be. And I think I couldn't find no better man to work with than you."

"Same here, boy. Now keep in your mind what I say. About the farm and also about that woman. Give that thing up right now before you look back and discover the price you done paid for it."

They had begun to walk back through the field away from the cool shade of the swamp and the smell of the river up the low rise to the house. On the porch, Sis Riah was holding Grace and singing to her while Jubilee sat on the steps and joined in when she knew the words. Benny walked slowly to give himself time to take in the sight and to listen to the sounds coming from his house. His eyes filled as he watched his wife in that moment. And it occurred to him then that there was something about her he had almost missed in the last few days. Something different. It was as if she could drop into his thinking anytime she wanted to like a summer shower finding its way through the giant leaves of a catawpah tree.

CHAPTER 32

JUBILEE OFTEN SMELLED the rose bay now and her head was filled with the conjure women most of the time. This background chorus was hard at first for her to get use to, but now she hailed them as a group of intimate friends that she could talk with whenever she needed to.

Their presence gave her a new power. She could remember and understand more of the past and sometimes have glimpses of the future. She often knew what Benny was going to say before he said it. And she knew that what he said sometimes didn't match the truth she could hear in his mind. It seemed to her as if she had been looking at him through a dirty window ever since they met. Now she could see him clearly as if the window had been washed. Sometimes she saw his daddy and his granddaddy standing right behind him with a sadness on them that sucked the life right out of her. The sorrow of those men seemed to lay her heart wide open. At those times she could forgive her Benny any of the terrible, dangerous mistakes he was making right now.

She could see the strands that ran through the fabric of their lives, the beginnings of wonderful paths, any one of which might lead Benny into a deeply fulfilling future. But between then and now, like a coiled water moccasin waiting in the shallow water along the edge of the river, something terrible waited, too terrible to think about for even a minute, something that would grieve them for the rest of their days.

. . .

She sat now in Sis Riah's wagon headed for town in the middle of the week with a three-week old baby in her arms. Grace was rocked to sleep with the motion of the wagon and Sis Riah and Jubilee without speaking to each other watched the progress of the mule plodding down the highway, giving no attention to the occasional cars that passed by. Jubilee looked into the face of the child in her arms, listening to the profound silence that surrounded her that the women in her head refused to talk about. But by using her own prophetic power she had discovered something hidden within the silence. The child seemed empty like an abandoned house and a fierce darkness surrounded her and someone in a rayon dress looked past white organdy curtains fanned by the wind.

She had come to Sis Riah's cabin early in the morning with the baby in her arms and told her friend that she had to get to town without Benny knowing anything about it. Sweet Boy and Sis Riah were hesitant to help Jubilee when she told them what her purpose was. Sweet Boy said he was sure Mr. Matthew wouldn't let him off work to drive them into town without a good reason. And neither of the two women could drive. But Jubilee said she'd walk if she couldn't find another way, so Sweet Boy rigged up the mule and wagon so the women could take it on in.

"How come you think it gonna do any good for you to go talk to her?" Sis Riah said, when Jubilee tried to tell her why she had to go. "That woman got a high spirit. Ain't easily scared off of what she want."

"I don't intend to scare her. I got to make her understand. I can't tell you how I know what I know, but she gonna hurt my baby in a way she don't have any idea about." She looked at Sis Riah and her eyes filled. "She gonna hurt us all, Sis Riah. I gotta go try to do something."

"Why won't you try to tell me more about it, hon? I gonna be on your side no matter what. Just let me help you think. Don't seem in no way like this the right thing for you to do."

"Sis Riah, this ain't just a jealous wife talking to you. I know about some things you don't know a thing about and I can't tell you how I know. You just laugh at me."

"Aw, honey. You know I ain't gonna laugh at nothing."

"But you'd disbelieve me, I know. And I wouldn't even blame you."

"Honey, I can't stands the thought of you going into that cleaners by yourself. Taking that woman on alone. Seem like you ought to let me go along with you."

"I ain't going in to fight nobody and I can't risk Grace in that place. You gotta believe me."

"Not even if I got hold of the baby?"

"Not even then."

"How you think she gonna get hurt just 'cause she in that place, honey?"

"'I don't know exactly. But I know it be a terrible place for her. You promise you take care of her for me. You ain't going back on your word, is you?"

"Nawh, hon. I say I keep her in the wagon for you and I will."

They passed the city limits sign and took the road that led through Tula toward the stores downtown. The mule plodded along past the graceful old homes of the wealthy landowners of Tula that had been built by slaves before the Civil War.

The wagon rolled past the church and right on into the downtown. The street was almost deserted in this hot part of the day except for some white folks who had driven in to pick up a few things. Jubilee felt the worry rising in her. Sis Riah spoke.

"Wish we'd a had Matthew's old truck to use. Woulda made this trip a whole lot cooler and quicker."

"The wagon fine, Sis Riah."

The older woman drove the wagon into the vacant lot beside the general store. She got out and tied the wagon in the shade under the pecan trees and Jubilee climbed carefully into the back and laid Grace down on a clean blanket and covered her completely with a light quilt.

"There she be, Sis Riah. She gonna sleep 'til I come back. I ain't gonna be gone too long."

"Do what you has to do, honey. I gonna take out my knitting. I be right here when you gets back."

Jubilee climbed down carefully over the side of the wagon and straightened her cotton print dress that was still too tight for her across the middle, so it had to stay unbuttoned in the back at the waistline. Even in the heat she put a shawl over her shoulders to cover the misfit. She felt ungainly and awkward and, looking down at herself, she shook her head and began walking toward Worthey's.

"Jubilee," Sis Riah called.

The young woman turned back.

"I gonna be praying, honey."

Jubilee nodded and smiled. Sis Riah watched her until she was out of sight.

CHAPTER 33

WHEN JUBILEE GOT to the cleaners there was nobody around. Even the ring of the bell over the door had not summoned anyone from the back where the dry cleaning machine whirred and bumped. The air was hot and oppressive in the place and the smell of cleaning fluid made it hard to breathe.

"Miss Nan?" Jubilee called.

No answer.

"Anybody here?"

She heard a back, screen door creak open and bang shut and Izzie, came puffing in and hurried up to the counter.

"Oh, Miz Jubilee, I's out back. Has you been here long?"

"You work here, Izzie?"

"Yassum. Sorry I make you wait. When things gets slow in here Miss Nan don't mind if I goes down by the river."

"I bet it's nice down there right now."

"Yassum, it is. I keeps a fishing pole on the bank, see if I can bring some fish home to Mama."

"Well, I hopes you don't lose none 'cause of me."

"Oh, no, ma'm. What you need, Miz Jubilee?"

"Well, I's looking for Miss Nan. She anywheres around today?"

"Yes, ma'm. She upstairs at her place."

"Thank you, Izzie. You get on back to your fishing. Sorry I bothered you."

"Oh, no, ma'm. That's fine."

Jubilee climbed the steps outside the cleaners. She knocked on the door, and in a minute she heard someone coming. Before she could think Nan Hawkins was standing in front of her wearing a white satin slip and smiling broadly. When she saw Jubilee her expression changed, and she grabbed a robe from behind the door and pulled it on.

"Morning, Miss Nan. Can I come in and talk to you?"

Nan quickly disguised her shock at seeing Benny's wife at her door and smiled as she stepped back for Jubilee to walk past her into the front hall. Her visitor was prettier since she had the baby. Her face almost glowed and there was an unexpected confidence about her as she stood in the front hall looking into the sitting room.

"You has a nice place, Miss Nan. Flowered wallpaper. Nice rug on the floor. Colored glass things in the window, light coming through them. You got a pretty place."

Nan closed the door behind her and stood in the hallway forcing a smile and wondering what she was up to.

Jubilee looked carefully around the room and saw that it was filled with misty remnants of Nan's past life. Her new gifts of sight revealed, in a far corner, the shadowy presence of a little girl, sad and lonely, a child who could not afford the luxury of being a child, who was, instead, her mother's mother. The child drifted waiflike and seemed to stand in front of Nan shielding her from the visitor.

"Not many folks seen it. I don't have no family nor friends drop by." Nan said hesitantly behind her. "But that be fine with me. Visitors always asking questions."

Jubilee heard Nan's fear beneath the thin cover of haughtiness.

Nan walked quickly past her guest into the living room and motioned an invitation to Jubilee to join her. She picked up a cigarette and tapped it on the table. She shook another one out of the pack and offered it to Jubilee.

"No, thank you."

"You don't smoke? Rich white man in Jackson got me started

when I's about sixteen years old," Nan said. "Well, now. What can I do for you? Mighty hot time of day for you to be out in town just visiting."

Jubilee sat down on a small straight chair where she could watch the movements of the little ghost-girl. The face of the child was needy and afraid and falsely smug all at the same time. She drifted toward an easy chair by the window where Jubilee noticed a faded old doll propped up against the cushions.

"Oh, I loves dolls," she said.

"Something my Daddy give me when I's little."

Jubilee saw the daddy come into the room where the little girl stood now and her own heart mirrored the things the little girl felt, the desperate hunger for a mother's caress, the longing for the comfort of family. She turned her attention to the grown up Nan sitting there in front of her with the same child-hunger in her eyes, the hunger that had led her to Benny.

"Miz Maude sho' fix up a nice place for colored help," Jubilee said. "You mighty important to her. Running her business and all."

Nan looked at her carefully. Jubilee knew she was trying to read her face to see how she meant the compliment. Then apparently satisfied, Nan settled herself down across from Jubilee on the old overstuffed chair and blew smoke toward the ceiling.

"Yeah, but, I done all this myself. I likes a nice place to live in. I ain't got nothing else to spend my money on except myself."

Jubilee saw her begin to relax her defenses, so she reached out with her mind into Nan's thoughts. She knew now that Nan was the owner of the business and this place above it. She felt the painful saving up for years, the child-woman doing without things she wanted or needed, so she'd be able to buy it when the time came. Jubilee felt the deep satisfaction Nan had in all of this, even though the pale thin face of the ghost-child still wore a worried expression.

"How your baby doing?" Nan asked.

Suddenly Jubilee felt an icy pricking at her heart, but she remained calm on the outside. The ghost-child in the chair saw her fear and leaned a bit closer toward her.

"She fine."

"I don't know much about new babies, but I's surprised you able to leave her somewhere this soon after she born."

"Sis Riah taking care of her for me for a few minutes."

The two women sat looking at each other for a moment in silence. Jubilee's eyes swept the room again.

"What was it you come for?" Nan asked.

This was not the place. She knew that, beyond a doubt. But there were other rooms. She looked at the child for clues, but the little ghost was only a shadow of the past and did not know the future.

"Miz Jubilee, I said . . . "

"I always done loved organdy curtains," Jubilee interrupted. "You got any in your house?"

Nan gave her a puzzled look.

"In my bedroom. Match the canopy over my bed. You care to see them?"

"Yes, ma'm. I sho' would."

"Come on along then," Nan invited.

She led her visitor down the hall toward the back of the house to her bedroom, the one she and Benny shared the night his child was born. If these walls could talk, she thought. But Jubilee had already read the room and she knew it all without talking walls.

In the bedroom white organdy billowed from the windows and hung in long feathery clouds from the canopy of the old four poster bed. Four candles, partly burned, sat on the bedside table. The thing that would happen would not be planned. It would be an accident. Jubilee's heart froze and she pushed back the tears that suddenly filled her eyes.

"This the place," she said softly.

Nan was caught off guard by the comment, but couldn't resist a smile.

"What place you talking about?"

Jubilee knew that Nan had misunderstood her.

The sun filtered through the organdy and fell in patches on the pale bedcovers. She must choose her words carefully if she were to somehow keep the unspeakable thing from happening.

"Miss Nan, I gotta say something to you and somehow I gotta make you understand."

Nan took a step back toward the darker hallway.

"Maybe you be more comfortable in the living room."

"This fine here. Maybe just the place we suppose to talk."

Jubilee sat down on the clean white spread, sliding her hand over a spot near the middle of the bed and studying it with her eyes and Nan stepped back inside the doorway and stood against the flowered wallpaper.

"I ain't got any idea what you needing to talk to me about."

The little ghost-girl stood in front of the grown-up-Nan, her eyes opened wide and her hand up to her mouth.

"I wanta talk about you, Miss Nan."

It was the last thing she expected Jubilee to say.

"About me?"

"And my little girl."

"I don't understand."

"Come on and set right here," Jubilee said, inviting her in.

Nan walked over hesitantly and sat down in a cane-backed rocking chair by the dresser. Jubilee could see her own reflection in the mirror just behind Nan. She spoke to the child and the grown up Nan.

"I understands why you wants my Benny." Nan laughed, but Jubilee continued. "I understands the longing in your soul for something to hold on to. Something gonna give your child-self some ease. I know ever since you born you been desperate for somebody to love you, take care of you, so you know you worth taking care of."

Jubilee searched for the right things to say. She knew it was the shadow child she was speaking to.

Nan bristled. "What you talking about? What give you the right . . . "

Jubilee put her fingers to her lips to hush Nan.

"Hear me out," she said. "I can't stay much longer. I know you done seen for the first time in your life, with your soul's eyes, a man got the strength to satisfy the hunger in you. And you right about what you see in Benny. But you gotta know you breaking apart the very thing in him you need so bad."

"You a strange woman. You know that? I don't have to . . . "

"Listen, Miss Nan. You break apart the man, he be weak and worthless to everybody, including you. Benny suppose to show folks here how to go about making a good life for theyselves. Even your little boy ain't gonna be able to do that if Benny don't do it first."

"What little boy you talking about?"

"I didn't come to talk about that. What I gotta make you understand is you gotta let go of Benny. For my baby's sake you gotta let go of Benny."

"Jubilee, I ain't intending to take Benny away from you."

It was the truth. Nan believed at that moment that she only wanted a child from him, but Jubilee knew better.

"Nan, listen what I'm saying. Somebody gonna give you the peace you looking for, but Benny ain't the one. Ain't nothing for you and him but sadness and sorrow. I can't just sit back and let that happen without trying to make you understand."

Her voice was soft but strong and the look on her face scared Nan with its intensity. She sat staring at Jubilee in surprise at her boldness.

"You crazy woman. You know that?" Nan said.

"If I don't speak now, the sacrifice gonna be terrible. You and Benny gonna be ruined. All the broke things be burnt up. And he the one have to live with the ashes."

Nan stood up as Jubilee continued.

"This the last thing, then I got to get back to Grace. You gonna have somebody, Nan. Make your child-self whole. But Benny ain't the one. I can't explain how I come to know all this, because you wouldn't believe me. But I know that the truth."

"You putting a hex on me, woman? That what you trying to do?"

"Ain't no hex, Miss Nan. It just what gonna be if things don't change, sure as tomorrow. I'm begging you for my baby's sake, stop what you doing before it's too late."

Nan stepped toward her.

"Listen here, you cotton-picking, colored maid. You think you can scare me into something you don't know who you dealing with. You hear that, girl. Now I think you better get your pitiful self out of my house."

The sunlight reflecting in the mirror behind Nan seemed suddenly to turn to flames and Jubilee saw a shadow on the bed grow smaller and smaller until it finally melted into light.

"I'm going. Ain't nothing else I can say. End of it rest on you."

She rose and walked out of the bedroom back into the hall and left the place, clicking the front door shut behind her.

By the time Jubilee got back to the wagon she was nearly broken down with sorrow.

"Oh, honey, what happen?" Sis Riah said when she saw her coming around the corner. "You look like you done seen the dead. I know you should've let me go with you."

"It be alright, Sis Riah. Everything done that can be done. But it weren't enough."

She climbed into the wagon and picked up the sleeping baby and looked at her carefully while Sis Riah untied the mule and turned the wagon around. She was so beautiful, this child with so much silence around her. She was too perfect to last.

CHAPTER 34

JUBILEE KEPT QUIET all the way out of town and her friend sat beside her trying to think of something to say to get her attention away from Nan Hawkins.

"Jubilee, Quilla's youngest come by while you gone. Say she think Deedove real sick. She say she go by her house last night wanting to sweep her yard out for her and she don't come to the door but just holler from the bed. Say she don't care if the yard swept out ever again and to go away."

"Sis Riah, can you spare the time for us to turn back and go see about her? I know how you feel in the past, but . . . "

"It be fine, honey," Sis Riah interrupted. "Sweet Boy tell me how she help you that night when they weren't nobody else around. Let's us turn around at the Yarborough road."

Ever since Grace was born Jubilee had felt powerfully connected to Deedove. Whenever she smelled the scent of the rose bay floating about her cabin, she knew Deedove's mama was there. The conjure loved Jubilee, because she welcomed them so freely. But the more the conjures stayed in her head and taught her about the power, the less they were with Deedove and the old woman's power had weakened because of that.

Deedove's cabin sat below the ruins of the burned down Macon mansion situated on a bend in the Big Black River. The remaining skeleton of the house rose out of kudzu and oak trees reminding poor descendants that the fields spreading out along the banks had once been part of the prosperous plantation.

The wagon stopped just before noon in front of the lone cabin that sat in sight of the ruins. The bare dirt yard in front of Deedove's cabin was sun baked without even bitterweed growing on it. The weeds and undergrowth that had taken over the field, however, were making a steady assault on the yard and overtaking the cleared dirt in front of the porch little by little every year. The cabin looked like nobody lived there. Jubilee put Grace up to her shoulder and the two women got out of the wagon and walked to the door.

"What you reckon done happened, Jubilee? I ain't never seen the place looking this forsaken."

"I don't know. I be here a few weeks ago. Things seem much better kept up then. Seem like it wouldn'ta run down so fast."

"Deedove?" Sis Riah called.

There was no answer. The cabin door was ajar and the screen door was hanging off to the side on a broken hinge.

"Miss Deedove, you in there?" Jubilee called.

"You suppose she already dead?" Sis Riah whispered.

"I know she ain't, but her spirit very low."

Grace began to stir and fret and as she did they could hear raspy breathing coming from the dark interior. Jubilee pushed the door opened gently.

"Doodove, it Jubilee and Sis Riah. Quilla's youngest girl say you sick," Jubilee called picking her way through the gloom to the cot in the corner. At first there was no response.

"Deedove," Sis Riah called.

A husky voice came from the cot. "Sis Riah in my house?"

As the two women got closer they could make out a form huddled in the bed, face to the wall and covered completely with an old quilt.

"How you suppose it so dark in here this time of day?" Sis Riah whispered from behind Jubilee. "And close. Lord, what that smell?"

"Hold Grace for me," Jubilee answered. "I gonna light the lamp, so we see better."

The older woman took the baby and stood back, waiting for the light.

"Deedove, how you feeling? You sick?" Sis Riah said gently.

"Sis Riah?" came the rough voice from the darkness.

"That's right, Deedove. It's me."

"Lord, Lord. Sis Riah in my house," Deedove muttered.

"Deedove, look here. I got little Grace. Turn around, so's you can see her."

"You gots the baby?"

Deedove's voice sounded like dry brush battered in a windstorm.

"Don't you want to see how she doing?"

Grace began to fret, so Sis Riah rocked and patted her. Jubilee found a match and lit the lamp.

"Look here, Deedove. Grace. Look how she growing."

There was a slight movement from the bed.

"Sit on up, now, so's you can see her."

Jubilee started a fire in the wood stove and straightened up the things that had been left in disarray about the room.

"Miss Deedove, when you eat last? This stove stone cold," Jubilee called across the tiny room.

"Ain't been hungry. Ain't been nothing," she answered.

"Sit up, Deedove, and I put the pillows behind you, so you can hold this baby," Sis Riah coaxed.

Jubilee returned and folded back the dark quilt from the grey head. She sat on the side in the dimness and ran her hand under the cover along Deedove's arm. It was cold and dry.

"Come on, Miss Deedove, you gotta help us some. Turn your head around and take a look at my pretty, little girl."

There was a silent pause and then the head began to turn toward the room. The skin was wrinkled and ancient and the eyes were dull and swollen.

"Good morning. You wants a little tea?" Jubilee asked.

She put her hand under the shoulders and gently pulled Deedove up. Sis Riah laid the bundled up baby on her lap and propped the pillows behind her.

"Now, you gonna tend to this baby whilst we tends to you," she said.

"Where your tea, Deedove?" Jubilee asked.

She found it in a can on the shelf and filled the old dented teakettle with water from the back rain barrel and put it on the stove. Sis Riah had begun straightening the sheets and quilt on the cot.

"You got some clean sheets, Deedove. These wrinkled and hot. Smell musty. Some fresh ones feel nice on your skin. Make you feel better."

"In the trunk yonder," she said as she watched the baby who was looking up at her.

Sis Riah got sheets and a pillowcase out of the trunk.

"These nice, Deedove," she said.

"Belong to my mama."

"Lord, they smells good. What kind of sachet you use?"

"Rose bay. Jubilee tell you about it. I been saving them because of the smell. I hates to use it up."

"Can't you get no more?"

"Don't seem like it. Not like that."

"Alright if we uses them then?"

"Make no difference now."

"I ain't never learnt how to make a bed with somebody in it. Can you walk, Deedove?" Sis Riah asked.

"If I wants to."

Sis Riah helped Deedove to her feet and the two women and the baby traveled carefully across the room to a straight chair at a small table. Sis Riah shook out the sheets and put them on the cot, folding in the corners to make them hold tight in place around the corn shuck mattress. She tucked one of the pillows under her chin and slipped on the sweet smelling case. And plunked it up at the head of the bed.

"I'll take these and wash them for you," she said gathering up the dirty things.

Deedove sat at the table holding the baby and watched her two visitors with amazement. The light of the lamp seemed brighter and the stove sent warmth out into the room. Jubilee found three cups with saucers and wiped them clean and set them on the table for the tea.

"Sis Riah, I gonna get the biscuits and blackberry jam we brought with us in the wagon. They go nice with the tea.

"Wants me to take the baby now?" Sis Riah asked Deedove.

"No, she just fine. I hold on to her."

"You feel strong enough?"

Deedove nodded.

Jubilee returned and put the biscuits in the middle of the table between them and sat down with the other two women.

"Let's have us a little blessing," Sis Riah suggested.

"Blessing?" Deedove asked

"Uh, huh. God done give us a gift to bring us to your house today and He give us this here sweet little girl to look at while we eating."

"Lemme say it, Sis Riah," Jubilee offered.

"Go right ahead."

Her heart was suddenly filled with some pure sweetness that made her eyes fill.

"Thank you," she said and paused to get control of her voice. "I thank you for hope and things that makes us happy. I thank you that we ain't never gonna know everything they is to know. I thank you for making us so's we can know a little something about you." She hesitated for a moment. "Thank you for my little girl. Do with her what you will. Amen."

Deedove sat open eyed, looking at both women with eyes closed and hands folded. All about her drifted the sweet ordor of her mother and all the conjure women, so strong she had to remind herself that it was only the sheets that surrendered the smell up into the room. She looked down at the baby whose black eyes sparkled in the lamplight.

"You there, child?" she called silently.

But there was no answer. And she could not see in the little face the slightest sign of the child-spirit that she had worked so hard to rescue. If the child-spirit and the baby she held had become one, Grace would not be so silent. Instead she had caused the terrible emptiness and silence to the beautiful form in her arms. She had failed. All her power had not been enough to retrieve the wailing little soul that wandered alone in the darkness. The old woman suddenly cried out and rose up from the chair and thrust the baby away from her into Jubilee's arms. Deedove stumbled and wailed back to the cot and dropped clumsily down, pulling her knees up and lying down with her face to the wall again.

"Deedove, what's wrong? You sick?" Jubilee cried.

"Go away. Lemme alone. I just wants to lay here until the rose bay all gone and breathe in the smell of my mama before I dies."

And then Jubilee saw in the room the familiar rose bay spirit that she first saw in her dream, standing at the foot of the cot smiling at Deedove.

"Deedove, look at the foot of your bed. See who there," Jubilee said.

"I can't see nobody no more," Deedove muttered, her head still turned away.

"Then I see for you. Deedove, your mama there."

Sis Riah walked quietly forward and took Grace from Jubilee's arms and stepped back.

"What you mean?" Deedove said.

"Your mama standing at the foot of your bed looking at you," Jubilee said. "She say she got a terrible great love for you. Look for yourself."

Nothing moved in the cabin. The silence was deep and strange. Sis Riah stood back watching and trying to understand. And then the old head began to turn away from the wall again and the cloudy eyes reached out into the room, scanning every corner and board.

"Where she be?"

"She still at the foot of your bed. She coming to hold you, Deedove."

She didn't move, only kept looking with the opaque eyes. And then the legs unfolded and the arms began to move outward away from her toward the room.

"She moving up to you now, Deedove."

The old woman began to cry.

"She got her arms . . . "

"Never mind, Jubilee. I knows. I can feel her now. She got her arms around me, ain't she?"

The old woman rocked back and forth and sobbed, her arms hugging her breast and her face turned up and wet like a child.

"Oh, Mama," she said sighing deeply. "Mama where you been for so long?"

"She say don't worry; she here now," Jubilee said.

There was only the swaying and the quiet sound of crying for a while. Sis Riah and Jubilee stood back and witnessed the reunion.

"Deedove, she say all the conjure women here, too. Oh, my lord, Deedove, I sees them. They goes back far as I can see."

"Look at Grace, Jubilee. Tell me what you see," Deedove said.

"Just a pretty little girl," Jubilee answered.

"Oh, Mama," she moaned. "How come the baby ain't here? I done everything I know how to do. How come she still in the dark?"

"She say time ain't come yet. Your work gonna pay off soon. But because the child so scared she have to be drawn.

Her voice was drained of emotion.

"Then what now, Mama. I'm wore out. I ain't got no more power. What gonna happen now?"

"She say you ain't to worry about nothing. She say the conjure women gonna work everything out just like it suppose to be. She say we gonna be a strong nation of conjure women and you gonna be part of it."

"But, Mama, I be so weak. My powers all gone."

"She know, Deedove. She say your job was just to find me."

"You part of the line, Jubilee. You know that? I knew you was first time I sees you in Mr. Luke's back yard. You one of the conjure."

"How?"

"Somehow through your grandmama. What Mama saying now?"

"She say you gonna come to them pretty soon, but you gots to pick yourself up and be strong before that time. She say you still got work to do. She say, she give you the power when you needs it."

Then Jubilee heard, like the skies washed clean after a storm, the muddy voices of frogs and lizards singing, and the calling and chanting of exotic birds and wild animals she didn't know the names of. The swell of thunder and the responding flashes of lightening and finally the sounds of rain drumming at the tin roof above them. The conjure women rose up and sang the song together. Sis Riah also heard the music and rose to her feet and held Grace high over her head.

"Praise God," she sang. "Amen. Amen."

And she gave freedom to her lips and let them form what music they would and she opened herself up so the miracle within the room could move through her. They sang until they were hoarse and the joy inside them was again manageable. And when the last notes of the song disappeared and the very air shivered with the memory, Sis Riah stood with her eyes closed, still holding the baby above her.

"You hear it, too, Sis Riah?" Deedove asked her.

"Lord, yes. I hears it. Praise God," she answered, her eyes still closed.

"Cause she believe it," Jubilee explained.

"Then they gonna use her somehow, too," Deedove predicted.

Jubilee looked at the old conjure woman. Her face shown.

"I's still a part of them, Jubilee. And you is, too," she said.

"And Sis Riah hear them," Jubilee said.

"Cause she willing to. When the time come, when I needs her, Sis Riah be the good neighbor to me no matter what we been in the past. The women honor that."

"What about Grace, Deedove?" Jubilee asked hesitantly.

"I don't know, honey. I thought she gonna have the power. Instead you got it. But I can't seem to see nothing no matter how hard I looks."

"What we do now?" Sis Riah asked holding Grace close to her again.

"I reckon, just be happy. Be happy and get ready," Deedove answered. "Now, I's getting outa this bed and eating me some biscuits and butter."

She unfolded stiffly from the cot.

"Ya'll better come on, too. You gonna have work to do. Better eat."

Jubilee and Sis Riah looked at each other and laughed and Grace fretted and began to wrinkle up her face. Jubilee took her and began unbuttoning her dress. Sis Riah sat watching, filled with wonder at what she had heard and seen. And she knew her life would be changed forever by the forces set in motion around her. And the women sat together in the little cabin and drank the tea and felt the strength that comes to women from putting aside and gathering together.

CHAPTER 35

WHEN SIS RIAH finally got home in the late afternoon, Sweet Boy was out by the road waiting for her and when she drove up he climbed into the wagon.

"What happen?" he asked her before he was in the seat.

Sis Riah tried to tell him as well as she could what she'd witnessed in Deedove's cabin.

"I don't know how to make you believe it," she said after she'd told him about the music.

"You don't even have to try, baby. I ain't never heard you tell nothing but the truth," he said. "But it do seem strange."

"Sho' do. I don't know if I believes it myself. And that coming right after Jubilee have that talk with Nan Hawkins."

"How did that go?"

"I got no idea. Jubilee wouldn't talk a bit about it."

"My heart hurt for them two right now, Sissy. Maybe if I weren't so easy I could say something to that man make him see that thing like it is."

Sis Riah patted her husband's arm.

"I likes you easy. Reason you able to put up with me all these years," she said and kissed his cheek. "What you get done today?"

"Well, wait 'til you hear what news I got. Mr. Pierce ready to sell his land in Camden to us."

"You mean it, Sweet Boy? You wouldn't be teasing me none, would you? How you know?"

"Got a letter today. He gonna meet us there at noon in Camden on Sunday. We look the place over, see what we can work out with him."

"What you think make him wanta sell the place to us, Sweet Boy?"

"Need the money and we the only ones interested in a place that far out from town. When I wrote him we interested, I ask him when it be last planted and he say three years ago. That mean the weeds and pines ain't taken over yet. Won't be too hard to plow. But one thing we got to look careful at. Can it grow cotton?"

"And the house. I wants to see the house. We don't need no mansion, still this place got to last us the rest of our lives. I needs a nice place for my flowers to grow close by, too. How much he want for it? He say?"

"Nawh, and I's about scared to ask. That kind of white man most the time know he got the colored man over a barrel when it come to land. Colored man gonna have to pay more whether he can afford it or not. But if it ain't no white man wants it we in luck. That be the case, us can haggle. How much we got all told?"

"I put in three dollars this week. Bring it up to twelve hundred and thirty one dollars all together."

"Last time we hear from him, he asking eighteen hundred."

Sis Riah smiled up at her husband.

"We work something out," she said.

On Sunday they borrowed Matthew's old truck and headed across the Big Black Bridge and drove for nearly and hour toward Camden. They followed a map Mr. Pierce had sent them and finally turned off a dirt road down a narrow driveway lined with cottonwood trees. Mr. Pierce was not there yet. Sweet Boy cut off the motor and they sat in the truck just looking at the house and the land around it.

The front yard was large with the old wood frame house set back behind overgrown shubbery. There was no front porch, but off to the side they noticed a large screened porch. Two chimneys that rose from each end of the house seemed in good condition. Weeds and junipers had almost obliterated a brick walk that ran across the front of the house out to the driveway.

"Look big," Sis Riah said.

"And like it need a lot of work," Sweet Boy commented.

They got out of the truck and walked closer to the empty house. The windows were bare of curtains and Sis Riah climbed passed the rank growth beside the walk and stood on her tiptoes to look through a set of double windows in the front of the house. Through the dirty glass she could see a large room.

"Oh, lordy," she said in surprise. "It so big." She turned to look at Sweet Boy who was leaning down to examine the soil in the overgrown flowerbeds across the front.

"Well, the dirt'll grow weeds. That's for sure."

He rubbed a handful of soil between his fingers. Sis Riah waited and looked at him expectantly. He nodded. She smiled.

"Good?" she asked.

"Pretty good," he answered.

She knew that was his cautious way of being encouraged. They walked toward the back of the house and Sis Riah continued to peep into windows along the way while Sweet Boy left her and walked on out passed the small pasture and barn. Mr. Pierce had said the two fields in back of the house were part of the deal, too, and there were fields just beyond the distant line of cottonwoods that could be rented reasonably and worked. There was close to twenty acres with the house and barn, a good well, and the house already had electricity and running water.

He climbed through the rusty barbed wire fence and grabbed another handful of dirt and noticed the plow rows still visible running in a ridged pattern across the land. He examined the dark soil in his hands and threw it down and walked toward a dip in the pasture where a small grove of hawthorn had sprung up. He could hear the stream before he finally stood on the bank looking at the clear water that crossed the field and ran on down toward the house. There were some things he needed to ask Mr. Pierce. Did the stream ever flood? Had the field ever produced cotton? And when? He would need to walk over the boundaries of it carefully and think hard to be sure he wasn't making a mistake. But he had a feeling about the place. It felt good to him.

Mr. Pierce was a small spare man with gray thinning hair. He climbed out of a new pickup and walked toward Sis Riah, who was standing on the front walk of the house.

"Is you the nigger interested in buying some land?"

"Yassir, me and my husband," Sis Riah said.

"Where is he?"

"'Round to the back, looking at the fields. You Mr. Pierce?"

"Who else be way out here on a Sunday afternoon?"

"You suppose I could see the inside of the house, Mr. Pierce?"

"I reckon it'll be alright. I'll have to open the front door for you. Now don't go messing around with stuff you don't know nothing about, hear? I don't want to spend time and money fixing something I don't have to."

"Yassir, I hear."

"And don't use the toilet," he said as he disappeared around the side of the house.

Sis Riah was too excited about getting into the house to be mad. The front door opened straight into the large double room with an arch just to the left of the front door that separated the living room from the dining room. The floors and walls were filthy. Every thing was in need of paint and repair. Wallpaper peeled from the walls in some places and she could see large water spots on the ceiling here and there where she suspected the roof leaked.

Behind the dining room was a little breakfast room and then the kitchen. Sis Riah gasped when she saw it. It was a big country kitchen, the kind she had always wanted, with room enough for a nice sized kitchen table right in the middle. The cabinets and walls were covered with a layer of grease. She tried the faucets.

Water slightly tinged with rust poured out and into the stained sink below. She dipped her hand into the water and sucked a little out of it. May not be so good to wash clothes in, but it tasted fine, she thought. A small, screened porch led off the back to the yard. The screen was torn and old newspapers and canning jars cluttered the floor.

A narrow back hall led to three bedrooms. She could imagine them with clean windows and curtains and fresh painted woodwork. She was glad things looked so bad in the house. It would make it less attractive for any other buyer.

Passed the bedrooms the hall led her back to the living room. At the far end of the room she noticed two small steps going down to a room-sized screened-in porch. She flipped the light switch by the door but nothing came on. Electricity must be turned off, she thought.

She was standing in the middle of the living room thinking how much she wanted to clean the big double windows and cut back the bushes so the light could get in and she could look out and see the front yard. She heard Sweet Boy and Mr. Pierce come through the back door. She called to them and they found their way through the kitchen and into the front room.

"Well, what did you think of the house?" the white man asked her.

"It need a whole lot of fixing, Mr. Pierce," she answered.

"But it's a far cry from a sharecropper's cabin, ain't it? Your man here liked the fields. Right?" He looked at Sweet Boy.

"Well, the land look pretty good. If the stream don't flood every year and take away the crops."

"That stream ain't never flooded long as I've owned this place."

"Mr. Pierce, how come you selling it?" Sis Riah asked.

"Well, it belonged to my wife's people. We ain't never lived in it. Just rented it out. My wife was raised out here in the sticks, right down the road a piece. She don't want nothing else to do with the country though. Love living right in the middle of town. Hard to rent out to folks these days. Nobody but niggers wants to live this far out from anything. I reckon it won't bother you folks none though."

"How much you asking for it, Mr. Pierce?"

"Well, for you folks, two thousand."

"Two thousand? Your ad in the paper say eighteen hundred."

"Yeah, but I hates real bad to sell the place to coloreds. My wife gonna have a fit. She don't know I'm out here showing it to niggers. But I says ya'll's money just as good as white folks' money. But you gonna have to make it worth my while."

Sis Riah and Sweet Boy looked at each other.

"Mr. Pierce, we ain't got that much. Be another three years before we could pay you two thousand dollars. All we got is twelve hundred."

"Twelve hundred. You expect me to give it to you? Goddamn." He slapped his hat against his leg. "Waste my time getting me out here to offer me twelve hundred for this place. Goddamn, nigger. I shoulda known you wouldn't have nothing."

"I'm sorry, Mr. Pierce," Sweet Boy began. "We hoped you might be willing to sell it to us for that."

"You work for Matthew Montgomery, don't you? You wife here grew up with Olivia. Why don't you ask him for a loan?"

Sis Riah shuddered. She knew what it would cost Sweet Boy in pride to ask Matthew for a loan to buy a house.

Even Olivia wouldn't understand why they would want to buy a house instead of working for somebody else and go risk living on their own land and working it for themselves. Hadn't they been happy living in Tula?

"He ain't gonna ask Mr. Matthew for no money. We just have to find another place don't cost so much," Sis Riah said and motioned to her husband and started for the door.

"Wait a minute. Ain't you got some other connections loan you some money?"

"I don't reckon we have," Sis Riah said and opened the front door to leave.

"You wouldn't lower your price some, would you, Mr. Pierce?" Sweet Boy said.

"Well, I wanta help you folks but twelve hundred . . . "

Sis Riah said, "Come on, hon. We better not take up no more Mr. Pierce's time."

"How about eighteen hundred?"

"Sis Riah, reckon the bank loan us some?"

"Not no six hundred dollars. Not to colored people."

"Look like that's it then, Mr. Pierce. We sorry to have bothered you," Sweet Boy said and walked out the door with Sis Riah.

"I'm sorry, hon," Sweet Boy said when they got back in the pickup.

"Too early to be sorry. We ain't heard the last from that man. And we got plenty of time."

"What you mean?"

"Look to me like that man wanting to sell this place mighty bad. Ain't nothing but poor white trash gonna be willing to live this far out from everything and them kinda folks ain't never got nothing. And there ain't coloreds on every tree can offer to pay somebody twelve hundred dollars in cash for something. We ain't heard the last from that man. You mark my words."

"Sis Riah, I got me a smart woman."

"Yeah, and I got me a sweet, good man." She leaned over and kissed his cheek. "And I know just the kinda curtains I'm gonna put in my living room."

CHAPTER 36

ANISE MONTGOMERY LAY in bed trying to delay sleep as long as she could.

"Mama, can I go see Jubilee tomorrow?"

"Maybe, Anise. You go on to sleep now. I don't want to hear another peep out of you," Mary Alice said, turning off the light and walking out of the room, leaving the door opened a bit behind her so the little girl wouldn't get scared.

She crossed the hall to the large master bedroom. There was a fireplace at one end and a comfortable loveseat and matching chair arranged in front of it. A vigorous Boston fern filled the fireplace during this time of year when no fires were necessary. Luke Montgomery was sprawled in the chair. His eyes were closed and his head tilted back on the flowered slipcover. He still wore his work clothes, dirty khaki cotton trousers and shirt. The high-top lace up leather boots lay off to the side on the rug; his socked feet stretched out in front of him. His hands and face were permanently tanned from working outside all year, rain or shine. He was a good looking, big man, well over six feet tall with large rough hands and crinkles around his blue eyes. His black hair was thick and combed straight back from his forehead.

"Luke, hon?" she said softly. "You look tired. Why don't you get on in bed?"

"Too early yet. Besides I'm not sleeping, I'm thinking."

"About what? The crops doing alright?"

"Yeah, well, pretty good if we could get a light rain in about a week. The crops are fine," he said opening his eyes and looking at the portrait above the mantel of the grandfather he was named for.

"You sound so serious," she said picking up a dress she was working on for Anise and sitting down across from Luke.

"No, not really. I just heard something today from Sam Owen. Make me kinda sick. Said he'd seen Benny going into Nan Hawkins's place upstairs over the cleaners."

"Oh, Luke, really?"

"Don't know how much I trust Sam. He's always saying things about the darkies. Loves to get ahold of stories like that."

"Chip and Anise came home the other day with a story about Nan being in the barn with Benny when you sent them over to help clean up that hay they got into."

"When did they tell you that?"

"I don't remember what day it was. I assumed she had some business with him or something. I didn't imagine anything else was going on."

"Damn. I thought Benny had more sense than that," Luke said sitting up straight on the edge of the chair and leaning toward the fireplace.

"Doesn't have anything to do with sense, Luke. Lots of reasons people cheat on a marriage."

"Still it's so dumb for Benny to get sucked into something like that. His daddy did the same thing. Ruined that family. Gives credit to what people like Sam Owen love to say about colored men. I really expected more from Benny."

He closed his eyes, rubbed his palms over them and leaned back in the overstuffed chair and was quiet for a minute.

"Luke?" Mary Alice said quietly.

"Yeah."

"I've always wanted to ask you. You've never mentioned it. You don't have to talk about it if you don't want to."

She waited a minute. He opened his eyes and looked at her. "What?" he said.

"What did you think when Benny beat you on that state test and folks teased your daddy about it?"

"Well, to begin with," Luke said, sitting up and looking at the fireplace, "I wasn't the least bit surprised. Daddy shouldn't have been either. I knew Benny would beat me. He'd always been able to think rings around me."

"Like how?"

"You wouldn't believe the great things he'd think up for us to do when we were boys. I mean, I loved playing with him when we were little, because he always thought up these great ideas to do. I've wondered since then what Benny would have done with himself if he'd been able to go to State like I did. But, of course, you know . . . And he's different now. Not cock sure of himself like he use to be back then."

"But you've never treated him . . . I mean, you treat him like he's just another hand on the place. I always thought you did it to kinda get even, you know?"

"No, no, not at all. I never felt bad because he was smart. Smarter than me. But after we grew up . . . Well, how else could I treat him? This is Tula."

Luke's voice had more anger in it than he intended.

"But if he's that smart and you two were boys together . . . "

"Well, Mama and Sis Riah grew up together, too. You don't see her treating Sis Riah any different, like she was white or something."

"Oh, no. I didn't mean you ought to . . . But maybe if you could give him some encouragement."

"I do. I give him encouragement. Got more leeway on this place than any other colored man I know of. And that hasn't been easy for me to do. God, you know how Daddy is. Always getting on me to be tougher on him. I get worn out fighting Daddy about it. He never has recognized the facts about Benny. I mean, Benny's a smart man, but he never is gonna stop being a colored man. And this new thing now."

"Isn't there something you could say to him? Keep him from making such a mistake?"

"Lord, Mary Alice, I wouldn't begin to presume to tell Benny how to run his life. Look, he just works for me. All I care about is if he gets the work done."

"I don't believe that, Luke. You weren't sitting here thinking about Benny just because he works for you. And Jubilee. I can't think how bad this is going to hurt her. You think she'll wind up raising the baby alone?"

"I doubt Benny would go that far. But I seen lots of men get pulled off the track by a two bit woman."

"Luke, please try to talk to him."

"Mary Alice, that's Benny's business."

"But isn't Benny something like a friend? I know sometimes Jubilee is. Please, Luke, just try."

"Well, maybe. If I get the chance."

CHAPTER 37

EARLY IN THE morning after Mandy had come to work and fed her breakfast, Anise crossed the pasture where the barn slumbered in the humidity of midsummer and ran down the gentle slope toward the tractor shed and then, finally, to the highway. She wore her sandals instead of going barefoot because of the possibility of stickers. She ducked low under the last barbed wire fence right across the highway from the trail to Jubilee's cabin. Anise could see her sitting on the porch talking to someone she couldn't make out so far away.

"Jubilee," she yelled. "Can I come visit?"

"Miss Anise? Your mama know where you is?"

"She said I could come if it was alright with you."

"Alright. Come on then."

Anise looked carefully both ways before crossing. There was not a car in sight as was often the case on this stretch of highway. She ran down the path and as she got closer to the cabin she recognized the colored woman who stirred the pot in the backyard when her daddy and Benny and Hippy killed and butchered a hog.

"Hi, Deedove," she said as she walked up onto the porch.

"Miss Anise," Deedove said and began to stand up out of the straight chair. "You wants to sit here?"

Anise looked at Jubilee who was holding Grace and rocking her in the swing.

"Can I sit by you, Jubilee?"

"Sure you can. I'll move a little and give you some room."

The swing was a little high for her, but Anise climbed in and settled herself close to Jubilee.

"You wants to hold her, Miss Anise?"

She nodded and Jubilee placed the baby in the little girl's arms and rocked the swing gently back and forth. Anise bent close to the little face and smiled. Deedove rose.

"I gotta be going. Remember what I say. No need to be sad. Nothing be lost."

"Don't go yet," Jubilee said.

"I has to. You got other company and it be best you look to her. Thank you for seeing for me what I can't see no more for myself."

"You know you welcome. Any time you needs it."

Jubilee stood up and hugged Deedove before she carefully walked down the steps and up the path.

"Can't Deedove see anymore, Jubilee?"

"Some things she have trouble with."

"Oh," Anise said and then looked down at the baby in her arms.

Grace was about the same size as the doll Anise had gotten a few Christmases ago. She was holding her now in the swing the way she'd held Francis. That's what she named her. Everybody noticed and smiled at how much the little girl loved that doll. She fed her, dressed her, carried her carefully with her everywhere she went, just as if she were a real baby.

"Can you show me how to change Grace's diapers?" she said now to Jubilee.

"She not wet. We gotta wait 'til she need it."

"Well, what does she need right now?"

"Just to have you set there and sing to her. She love singing."

The face looking up at Anise was serene and flawless like a china cup. Her skin was light brown and black curls circled her head. Anise felt the curls and ran the back of her hand down the baby's cheek. The little head turned and the mouth reached toward her hand. Anise laughed.

"Is she hungry?"

"Don't think so. Ain't been long since she eat."

"Does she take a bottle? I could give her one."

"No, I nurses her."

"Oh, Mama told me about that. Jubilee, will her skin get darker the older she gets?"

"Might will," Jubilee said.

"I like skin that's a little bit darker. The color of your skin."

Jubilee smiled and left the two on the porch and went to get a cookie for Anise from the kitchen. Anise sang softly and bumped her arm to the music and the corners of Grace's mouth turned up.

"Oh, Jubilee, she smiled."

"What?" Jubilee called from inside the cabin.

Anise slid out of the swing carefully and walked with the baby through the screened door.

"Watch," she said walking up behind Jubilee.

The young mother jumped and turned quickly.

"Oh, Miss Anise. You mustn't walk with her. You might drop her."

"But I'm being really, really careful with her."

"You know, Miss Anise, she a real baby, not a doll."

"I know the difference, Jubilee. You think I don't know the difference? I told God if he'd just let me have a real baby again to take care of like Francis I'd show him how careful I would be."

Several months after Anise got the doll, she left her outside overnight. It was the kind of thing any child would do. But that night a rainstorm blew up from the gulf and it poured down in buckets all night long. The next morning first thing when she got up, Anise started looking for her doll.

Jubilee remembered a terrible scream coming from the backyard that sent her and Mary Alice running out to see what awful thing had happened to Anise. They found her standing in the middle of the gravel driveway, screaming up at the sky with both her arms clutched tightly around the doll. When the two women got closer they could see that the painted plaster head had bubbled and warped and the cloth body was sodden and muddy.

"It's alright, Anise. Don't cry. It's just a doll, darling," Mary Alice comforted. "We'll get you another one."

"She's not a doll. She's real. She told me she was real. The rain killed her. I left her outside and the rain killed her," Anise cried.

"Anise, baby, everybody makes mistakes. You didn't mean to leave her outside. Don't cry so hard, honey. She was just a doll. Not a real person. We'll get you another one in Jackson."

"God will never, never, never let me have another real one again, because I didn't take good care of Francis."

And she continued to cry so hard that Mary Alice picked her up still clutching the "dead" doll to her and carried her into the house where she sat rocking her. Jubilee got a damp cloth to lay on her head and finally got her to eat a little chocolate pudding. She never asked for another doll even though birthdays and Christmases had brought replacements. All of them, arranged by her mother like the icons of saints, sat untouched on one of the shelves in her room.

Jubilee watched as the little girl brushed her lips along the baby's soft forehead.

"I waited a long time for you," Anise said softly, "I mean you aren't mine, but I can pretend you are."

Jubilee watched with concern as Anise rocked gently back and forth and sang "Onward Christian soldiers, marching off to war . . . " softly to the baby. Another worry added itself to the weight in her heart.

CHAPTER 38

JUBILEE WENT BACK to work for Mary Alice when Grace was four weeks old. One of Quilla's girls, Eugene, was taking care of the baby for her. Benny would bring her to Jubilee several times a day, to be fed. Matthew gave Benny permission to use his old pickup.

So about half way through the first morning back, Benny drove up with Grace and Jubilee went out under a tree in the back yard to nurse her. Anice stood at the window waiting, not being permitted to be any closer. When Jubilee finished she took Grace inside and put her in Anice's arms.

"There she is, Miss Anice. Ready for some holding."

The little girl carefully cradled Grace and walked away to show her mother.

Benny was waiting patiently in the backyard for the baby's return when Luke Montgomery drove up. He rolled down the window of the pickup and called Benny.

"When you get through with your daddying job I want you to go to town and run some errands for me. I got a list. And see if you can find Sweet Boy. I think daddy has him working at their house today. Painting or something. Tell him I got a message from a man name of Pierce out in Ocala County say to tell him he'll take fifteen hundred for the land. You know anything about that? Sweet Boy and Sis Riah looking for land to buy?"

"Yessuh, I done heard that."

"What they gonna do with it?"

"Farm it I reckon, Mr. Luke."

"And leave Tula?"

"Yassuh, I think so."

"Where'd they get the money?"

"Miz Sis Riah been saving it."

"Where abouts is the place?"

"I hear way out in the sticks."

"Well, there're problems come along with something like that."

"Oh, yassuh, I knows it."

"What they gonna do if something happens and they need money? Tractor breaks down or doctor bills? No white man gonna loan money to an independent darky."

"I know that's the truth, Mr. Luke. But seem like if you think about a problem some, they be some way to figure it out."

Luke patted his fingers gently on the steering wheel.

"Benny, you got savings at the bank now, don't you? You saving for some land, too?"

"Well, I been thinking about it."

Luke was looking out toward Mary Alice's rose garden in the backyard.

"Don't know what on earth I'd do without you here."

"Yassuh."

"We go back a lotta years. Your people and mine."

"Yassuh, I knows we do."

"Sure as hell would miss you," he said and turned and looked at Benny. "Anyway, take Sweet Boy the message and I wouldn't give it to him in hearing distance of Daddy or Mama. Give him a chance to let them in on the news his own way. Then you can pick up the things on that list. I want you to go by the machine shop at Presley's and see if Abbot Lee has that piece off my water pump welded yet."

Luke put the truck in gear and backed down the driveway.

Benny watched him turn up the hill toward Lexington. He couldn't believe he had just told Luke Montgomery he planned to buy a piece of land someday to live on.

Jubilee walked out on the porch with the baby and kissed her cheeks and handed her to Benny. She must have heard what he said to Luke through the open kitchen windows. It was the first time he'd seen her smile since Grace was born.

"You better be on your way, hon," she said. "Tell Eugene to wash out her diapers for me and let them be drying. I fold them when I gets home."

Benny laid the baby in the big laundry basket he'd wedged between the back of the seat and the dashboard, so he could watch her out of the corner of his eye as he drove into Tula. He pulled up in the back of Mr. Matthew's house and got out, taking the baby with him.

Sweet Boy called out to him from the top of a ladder where he was painting shutters on the large two-story brick house.

"Hey, there, Benny. What you up to?"

"Baby sitting," Benny answered, grinning up at his friend. "Got a message for you from a Mr. Pierce in Ocala County."

"What? Mr. Pierce?"

"Yeah, Mr. Luke say he . . . "

"Wait. I come on down. This ain't the kind of thing I wants hollered up at me."

He looked out until he located Matthew Montgomery's figure down at the barn behind the house and then hurried down the ladder as fast as his large frame would allow. He ran puffing across the yard toward Benny.

"Well, what did he say?"

"Mr. Pierce call Mr. Luke. Tell him to tell you he take fifteen hundred for the place."

"Lord, lord, lord," Sweet Boy grinned and shook his head. "Sis Riah right. That woman sharp as a tack."

"Mr. Luke ask me right out what you planning on doing. I tell him you gonna farm the land. He know I got savings, so he ask is I planning on doing the same thing."

"What you tell him?"

"I say I reckon I is."

He laughed and turned back toward the ladder.

Benny's mind was buzzing when he left to go by the machine shop.

CHAPTER 39

MR. ABBOT LEE'S machine shop was in an old double garage that leaned against the backside of Presley's Service Station, hidden from the view of the gas pumps around front. The wide front doors of the garage were opened. The short, stout, bald man was on the phone when Benny drove up and he waited in the truck with the baby until the man got off the telephone. The machinist yelled to him as he came toward the front of the garage.

"Morning, Benny."

He got out of the truck and called back.

"Morning, Mr. Abbott."

"Luke send you?"

"Yassuh."

"It's fixed. I'll go back and get it for you"

"Yassuh."

He went into the little office off the shop. Benny looked around the place. It was filled with tools and machinery that were all a mystery to him. At the far end of the place was a motor of some kind that puttered and hummed and clanked occasionally. He walked back outside to check on the baby. She lay quietly in the basket, her wide eyes fixed on him.

"Now if you was a boy, you could learn all about this kinda stuff. Give up farming all together," he said to her.

"Benny?"

He turned quickly, recognizing the voice.

"Nan? What you doing here?"

"Getting my car gassed up. I see you back here when I come out the colored bathroom. What you been doing? You glad to see me?"

A flood of excitement and anger and fear came over him. He kept his eyes on the baby.

"Why ain't you come to see me anymore, Benny? I misses you."

"What in hell you mean coming into church like that?"

"What? Why, Benny, you mad?" She grinned and put her hands on her hips. "I was thinking a little preaching do me good. I didn't think any body'd mind."

"You know damn well what I'm talking about. The day Grace presented?"

"I just wanted to take a look at her." She giggled. "When you coming back to see me, Benny?"

He looked back toward the office and then behind him toward the street.

"I ain't. Not like that anyway."

Grace began to fret and squirm. He picked her up and held her close to him.

"Benny, let me hold her," Nan said.

"Nawh you don't. I gotta pick up something for Mr. Luke and get her on back to Eugene."

"Please, Benny." Her voice had changed. "Lemme hold her for just a minute. Nobody gonna know. We way back here. Nobody gonna see."

"Alright, but she need changing right now and she fussy."

Nan took the baby and held her close, feeling the gentle weight, nuzzling at the baby scent with her face down near the baby's face and brushing her cheek against the soft forehead.

"Here's the part, Benny," Mr. Abbott said coming from the office. "I'll send Luke a bill." He glanced at the bundle in Nan's arms. "Pretty little pickaninny you got there," he said mistaking Nan for the mother.

"Thank you," she answered softly and smiled to herself and held the baby curls close to her face.

When Mr. Abbott had gone back into the office Benny held out his hands for the baby and Nan reluctantly gave her back to him.

"Please, Benny. Bring her by my place for a minute. I got something for her."

"Nawh, I can't do that right now."

"But you could change her there and clean her up, get her comfortable again. Look, she fussing, cause she don't want wet britches on her no more. You want her to cry all the way home? Come on, Benny. You can just change her and be gone. Come on. I'll meet you there right away. Alright?" she said and took off running back around the station before he could say no.

Benny watched the green coupe drive off toward town. He had Mr. Luke's list to take care of before he could get Grace back to Eugene. Might as well take her by Nan's long enough to change her. He felt a quick stab of excitement.

Benny followed the green coupe down town and parked the truck back behind the cleaners where Nan kept her car. It would be hidden there from the street in front. Grace began crying when he cut the motor off and he picked her up and grabbed a clean folded diaper from the basket. He didn't have to knock on Nan's door. She opened it just as he got to the top step.

"Come on in here and put her on my bed," she said, disappearing into the dark hall.

Benny knew the way. He carried the crying baby down after her. When he laid her in the middle of the bed, she wailed harder than he had ever seen her cry and he frantically unpinned the wet diaper and put on a clean one. Nan quietly watched the care he took with her, talking softly and gently. But Grace didn't stop. When he was finished before he could object, Nan picked her up and began walking and singing around the room, holding the small head against her shoulder.

"Oh, Benny. I wants me a baby just like her. I wishes she was mine," she said and hummed and swayed back and forth.

But Grace kept wailing and Benny got more and more frantic.

"It's too dim in here, Benny. Light that little candle by the bed. I bet she like that."

He switched on the overhead light.

"No, no. That too bright. The candle be better. Put it on the table. While you at it open that window up a little, so she have some fresh air, too."

He did and a gentle breeze blew in rustling the organdy curtains. Slowly, Grace began to leave off crying and closed her eyes and went to sleep on Nan's shoulder. It was a pretty sight seeing Nan Hawkins in the soft light holding his baby. She still had a lot of power over him.

"There now. You feeling better," she said in a voice he'd never heard from her before. She put the sleeping baby down in the middle of the bed and covered her with the light blanket she had been wrapped in.

"I gotta go, Nan."

"Aw, Benny. Not now. Let her sleep a little while. She so peaceful now and she cry so hard. You don't want her to get all upset again, does you? Just let her sleep a little while."

"But I got a list of things I got to do for . . . "

"You go on and do them then. I watch her for you?"

"Nawh, you ain't. I don't want you . . . "

She walked to him and picked up his hands and put them at her waist and slid her arms up around his neck.

"What's the matter, Mr. Benny? You act like all you wanting today is to get out of here quick as you can. You scared of me?" She teased him with a smile. "Nothing to be scared of. Does you still want some of me? Or is you got cooled off since last time you was here?"

Benny looked down at her. It was the old powerful Nan that held him. The coarse face below his was strong and impudent.

"You still want me, Daddy Man?"

"Don't matter what I want." His voice was hoarse.

She smiled. She knew his feelings had changed, but she knew how to heat him up again. She had to get him away from the baby.

"One last time, Daddy Man. Do what you do one last time."

She pulled his mouth down to hers and sucked greedily at it. He let his hands slide up over her breasts and then around her shoulders. And then she stopped him.

"Benny, wait. Not here. I knows a place down by the river. I been dreaming of having you down there. A secret place. Nobody gonna see us. Be like the first time. Remember? Outside? By the river."

"I can't leave the . . . "

"Aw, come on. Daddy. She gonna be alright. She sleeping in the middle of my bed. What gonna happen? Come on. May be your last chance at me. If this the last time, least do it like I wants you to."

He let her lead him out of the bedroom and through the door and out of the house. The street was empty and Benny followed her down toward the river to a densely grown thicket of willows where a concealed path led down the riverbank. He looked back in the direction of the cleaners, but all he could see was the thick vegetation around him.

CHAPTER 40

WHEN DEEDOVE WOKE late that morning she felt a sweet stirring in her head and she wondered if maybe her mama and the conjure women had changed their minds and were giving her powers back. If it were true there had to be a plan in it. Maybe she was going to work with Jubilee to bring the power to Grace. She smacked her lips and smiled and began singing an old song.

It was a happy song and the first one she had sung in years. If the conjure women could forgive her bull-headedness she reckoned she would, too. She tested the happiness. She touched carefully with cautious fingers deep down in her soul. And when she discovered no monsters she flung open that part of her like the windows and doors of an old dead house. She felt a lightness inside her chest that she had not felt for years. But today, this morning, it was singing and shouting deep inside her.

"Oh, lordy, new day," she sang to herself. "What I gonna do with it?"

She began opening windows and doors and letting the light come in. She put a pot on to boil outside. She would bleach out the curtains and the sheets and mop the floor with lye. She felt the warmth of the sun and she looked up the ridge where the ruined mansion hovered over the river. She could see a splash of color in what use to be the rose garden. She grinned suddenly and took off up the hill toward the ancient, charred skeleton. The bushes that once graced the yard were covered over with weeds and kudzu and she had to pick her way carefully to get to where she had seen the bright red from the cabin. She pushed her way through the undergrowth and came out right in front of a rose bush that trailed up an ancient trellis and reached toward the blackened bricks of the one remaining wall. Deedove breathed in the smell of the flowers. She picked a handful, watching for thorns, and scrambled back down the hill. Looking toward the cabin she saw smoke rising from the chimney. And she heard singing.

"Oh, my lordy. Mama," she called out and she began a shuffling scurry toward the cabin.

When she burst through the door they were all there.

"Oh, Mama," she cried.

And her head filled with their song. Her time had come. Now she must do what she had to do. This last thing. She must hurry into town. She must go now.

"What you want me to do, Mama? About Grace? Little, pretty baby? Silent little Grace?"

It was about the baby, but different somehow than she had thought. She was suppose to what? Bring her? Where?

"All of you, tell me. It ain't clear. I got to know what you wants me to do?"

She was to . . . was to . . . follow . . . what? Smoke?

"Don't know what on earth you talking about, but I do it," she said as she put on her old straw sun hat and went out the front door. She squinted and looked hard into the distance in every direction and then toward town and she saw it.

Rising, curling, gray against the smooth round blue of the sky. She waddled off the porch and down the path and out toward the road that ran through a bunch of cabins. And today she remembered. It was the same road the men dragged her over twenty years ago before they beat her. She was so scared they would hurt the baby.

She saw the smoke in the distance and she walked faster, because it was getting darker and thicker and she knew what was ahead. What she had left to do. Bring them the baby. Follow the smoke and bring the baby.

She didn't know it was the dry cleaners until she got half way up the main street and heard folks begin to yell that something was on fire. But she kept up her funny awkward run, on up the street until she stood with a gathering crowd in front of the dry cleaners. At first she didn't know why she had to get upstairs and locate the room where the billows of gray smoke were pouring through the window. She simply knew in her head that she had to go. Something important to do there. She heard the baby crying as she hurried up the stairs.

The song in her heart, the sound of the joy of her childhood, echoed inside her head. She felt like she was going to a circus, not standing outside, because she was colored. No, this time she was going right on in. And it wasn't going to be some plain old circus, it was going to be the biggest, most brilliant circus anybody on this earth had ever seen.

She pushed open the same door Nan had opened for Benny a little while ago and when she did smoke poured out of the hallway. She heard the child-spirit voice now, afraid and lost and she followed the sound into the darkness inside.

"I'm coming fast as I can," she called to the baby. "Old Deedove coming, honey."

The voices of the fire called to her, made fun of her, told her that she would never find the child, that the baby had already been taken away into darkness forever, that she would only die here for nothing. But the song in her heart told her to keep on going. She could see in the dark. She knew where the happiness was. Straight ahead of her. Down the dark hall. And then she couldn't breathe. And as she choked she fell to the floor.

"Mama, help me find her," she whispered.

The flames licked at her, but she rose and kept pushing down the hallway, only this time she was strong. She didn't choke or fall and then the air changed and it was cool and she floated toward the flames ahead of her in the bedroom.

The hysterical cries came from straight ahead. But it was not Grace's cries alone.

"Baby, here I is. I come after you."

The sobbing softened.

"Baby, come out of the flames, so I can see you. Flames can't hold you. Come on out to Mama."

"This a bad place. Filled with bad things."

"I know it is. Come on now. Just come over here to the sound of Mama's voice."

"Mama?"

And then suddenly there she was, the child. Deedove cried out with joy and wrapped her arms around the child-spirit and soon they were outside in the cool air and the conjure women were singing and shouting and waiting to greet them both as they rose up from the burning inferno. Up, up, away from the street, the town, away from the river and cotton fields, away from the county, the country, forever.

~

Sweet Boy had finished the shutters and was climbing down off the ladder when he smelled smoke. At first he thought someone was burning trash until he saw the dark gray cloud billowing up over the pine trees that stood in front of the old Burton house near town. He walked fast to the corner and then broke into a run when he saw the crowd gathering out in front of the dry cleaners.

"Anybody inside, Mr. Sam?" he yelled.

"Saw that old witch woman go up a few minutes ago. Ain't come down yet. She ain't worth risking your life for," he said smoking a cigar and standing out in front of the place like he was watching a good movie.

Smoke was pouring out of the windows as the big, colored man pushed past the white folks standing in awe on the street and ran up the stairs. The smoke and flames at the opened door stopped him for a moment. He put his arm over his face, shielding his nose from the scorching smoke. Flames rippled and danced around him.

He could just make out the form lying stretched out on the floor of the hall.

"Deedove?" he called.

He jumped the flames licking at the door and ran headlong into the fire and smoke.

~

Nan lay on the bank of the lazy river smiling with her eyes closed, listening to the sound of the water. Benny sat on the ground beside her.

"What in hell am I doing here?" Benny said standing up slowly. Nan opened her eyes and smiled up at him.

"Oh, come on, Benny. You know you can't live without some more of that good stuff. Listen to me." She propped her head up on one arm. "I been planning something for a long time. I'm leaving Tula, Benny. Soon as I can. I got money in a bank in Detroit. I wants you to come with me. We could do whatever we wants with the money."

"What you mean?"

"I always plan on leaving this place. Detroit. Chicago. Boston, maybe."

"Nan, you talking foolish. I ain't going no where. I got a wife and a baby looking for me to take care of them here in Tula. I don't intend to let them down."

"Hey, look to me like you already done let them down."

She sat up and began straightening her clothes. He watched her and shook his head.

"There ain't nothing alive can make me leave that baby. Not you or nothing."

"Oh, Benny, I see how you love her. But, honey, you and me, we gonna have babies of our own. And we gonna have them somewhere else. Somewhere folks don't treat them like dirt. Jubilee want to raise that baby here, she welcome to it. And if you feels like you oughta, you can send her money to help out. That's all she need from you anyway."

"That what you really think, ain't it."

"Aw, honey, this talk too serious. Just come on with me. We'll live good."

The rising sound of excited voices filtered into the thicket.

"What that?" he said looking up toward the cleaners.

"Ain't nothing. Somebody in a fight."

"Nawh, it ain't. Something else. Look yonder. Above the willows."

"What?"

"Smoke. Something burning. Something on fire. Oh, God. You don't reckon it's . . . "

His mouth kept the "oh" it had begun to form as Benny jumped up and ran through the willow thicket, bare-chested, leaving his shirt behind. Just as he got to the street the upper floor burned through and fell to the lower floor and when the flames hit the cleaning fluids in the back the whole building exploded. By that time most of the town was standing around watching the show, but nobody was trying to get into the place. It would have been suicide.

~

The next day people said around town that you could hear him yelling all the way to the cotton gin. A bunch of the white folks standing around had to hold him down to keep him from running into the flames. They kept on telling him it wasn't any use. When the closest fire engine finally got there from Lexington, the firemen just directed the hoses onto the neighboring buildings to keep them from catching fire and burning down, too. Nan Hawkins came up from the back of the place carrying Benny's shirt and looking stunned. The crowd started to leave when the fire fighters packed up their hoses and drove the truck back to Lexington. Nobody knew who got word to Luke Montgomery. He just turned up and walked up the street to Benny as if his childhood friend were a white man, put his arm around him and led him back to his truck and they drove off leaving the smoke and ashes behind them.

CHAPTER 41

SIS RIAH ALWAYS remembered that Saphronia had dropped by her house to read her a letter she had gotten from her cousin in Madison. Years later she would tell it over and over again to Jubilee, stopping in time for a moment, forgetting where she happened to be, what she was supposed to be doing and, suddenly, stabbed with memory, would feel like she was right back there again, sitting in her front room with the summer sun lighting up the plants that filled their house. As she crocheted a pink and white afghan for Grace she talked to Phronie about the organized unrest that was beginning to boil up in the country.

She'd remember that she had served fresh coffee in her china cups that her mama had left her, because Phronie was always so impressed by them. The cup she drank out of had a little chip in the delicate pedestal that it stood on, but nobody ever noticed it. Saphronia had warned her on Sunday at church that she was going to drop by today, which Sis Riah appreciated since she always liked to have things fixed up a little for her visits. The house was ready as it turned out for the hordes of people that would parade respectfully through it, bringing covered dishes, the men with their hats in their hands, the women white gloved and whispering. And as it turned out, though she always felt a bit stiff with Saphronia and they often disagreed, on occasions, bitterly, she never forgot that her sometimes friend had stayed there all that day and was the rock that Sis Riah rested on when she couldn't stand up anymore by herself.

It was Olivia who had actually said the words to her. She knew something was bad wrong when her childhood friend and Matthew had arrived in Olivia's Buick with the colored preacher stiffly sitting in the back seat. She was almost too scared to open the door. Olivia was the one who told her. But she really didn't need to. Sis Riah knew it was the only reason that Matthew Montgomery would come to her house.

"Sissy, it's Sweet Boy," Olivia had said.

"Hurt?" Sis Riah tried to read her face. "Oh, my Lord Jesus. Just a minute. I'll get my nice shoes on."

And she had pulled herself away from Olivia. She knew somehow there was no use for her good shoes. She just hoped that she was silly to think the worse right away.

"No, Sissy, honey. Not hurt," Olivia said so very quietly that Sis Riah had to look at her hard to see if she had heard right.

By this time Saphronia had gone to the preacher who was whispering in her ear and then she had gasped and tears began rolling out of her eyes and down her full cheeks and she was trying to catch them with the back of her hand.

"Then what is it if he ain't hurt? What, Olivia? Tell me." By that time there was a dead heaviness behind her face.

"He's gone, Sissy."

"Gone? Like to town. Or to Canton maybe?" She paused. Looking at their faces. "Gone?"

"No, Sis Riah. Sweet Boy died this morning."

She would always remember that and tell Jubilee's second girl how Olivia had taken her so gently by the arm and led her into the bedroom and helped her on to the bed, hers and Sweet Boy's bed, and taken her shoes off with her own hands, the old dirty ones that she would have been glad to change if she had needed to go somewhere, if Sweet Boy had been hurt and in need of her instead of dead and not in need of anybody anymore.

Her friend, for as long back as she could remember breathing, pulled up a chair beside the bed, close, and held her hand and talked quietly about when they were girls and what they'd wanted to do when they grew up and how different life is when you're looking at it from that direction than it is when you see it from where the two of them sat right now.

She didn't remember when Olivia left and the folks in the county began to drop by with food. Seemed like she was in the bed trying to get a hold on the idea of nothing being there beside her, the profound silence on the other side of the bed, and then she was walking into the front room and it was no longer her front room, but a solemn, formal place where people were trying to come to grips with a loss they could never have imagined.

And Jubilee's second daughter would say, "What was Papa Sweet Boy like, Grandma Sissy?"

"Big mostly. He was big. Big in body and generosity, in love and in caring about other folks. You remember that now. Tell your children some day. What folks always say about him. 'One thing about Sweet Boy I'll always remember, he sure was a big man.'"

CHAPTER 42

ANISE WAS IN the maple tree in the front yard, hidden by leaves, when Luke drove up in the pickup with Benny in the seat beside him. Jubilee looked out the kitchen window and saw them and wondered what had happened. Matthew's old pickup must have broken down. The men got out and went around toward the front yard and Jubilee didn't think any more about it.

From Anise's hiding place she saw Luke open the big front door of the house and usher Benny inside. It was the first time she had ever seen her father ask a colored man into the house. She climbed down from the tree and ran in through the back. She hurried to a place just behind the living room door and sat listening to her father quietly offering Benny a chair in the living room.

The quiet, formal dignity surrounding him went unnoticed by Benny. He didn't notice that he sat now in torn, soot-covered work pants on a brocade Victorian chair Luke had offered him. He didn't notice the marble topped, cherry table beside the chair with a crystal lamp on it that Luke quietly turned on, causing the crystals to shake and tinkle. He just remembered looking down at his shoes and worrying if they were clean enough to be on that rug.

Luke left quietly through the dining room door that led to the kitchen. In a moment he walked back in, followed by Jubilee who had a small, fixed smile on her face and he offered her the matching chair across from Benny, whose face bore no expression at all.

She knew, of course, what had happened. She had seen it first in the dream before Grace was born and had always hoped the unbearable loss would somehow be prevented. The conjure women had spared her from knowing exactly when the thing would happen, so she could be relatively calm for as long as possible. But nothing had prepared her for this moment. This unthinkable moment.

"Benny?" Jubilee spoke quietly.

He rose and opened his mouth to speak it honestly to her, but he discovered he couldn't say anything. If he had allowed any noise to come out of his mouth, it would have been a long and terrible wail that would have crowded all his words back into the black pit inside him. He sat silently back down onto the chair and stared at her.

"Mr. Luke?" she said.

"Dry cleaners caught on fire somehow."

"She was up in the bedroom? Sleep?" she asked, noticing how the soot on Benny's face made him look old.

"I don't know exactly," Luke said. "Deedove went in to try to save her and . . . "

"Oh, Lord, Mr. Luke. Deedove?"

Luke's voice was quiet, serious.

"And Sweet Boy, too. He ran up from Daddy's and went in way after there was any chance of saving anything."

"Sweet Boy go in?" she said searching his face. "Sweet Boy and Deedove and my pretty little baby?" She sank into the chair across the table from Benny. "That place take all three of them?"

"I'm sorry," Luke said.

He had just started to say something else when Anise ran into the room.

"What's wrong?" she cried to her father. "What happened?"

"Nothing for you to worry about, Anise," her father said and he stepped forward and put his arm around her, but she wiggled away from him.

"Where's Grace? Is she with Eugene?"

"Anise," her father said.

"Why is Benny crying, Daddy? Did something bad happen to Grace?"

He picked her up and carried her toward the door.

"No, Daddy, put me down. Tell me what happened."

Luke pushed open the dining room door and carried his struggling daughter into the back of the house. Jubilee heard Mary Alice coming to see what the trouble was. Then the crying calmed and she could hear the quiet voice of her father telling them about Grace and the others. She heard Mary Alice gasp and then there was a scream from the little girl.

"No, that's not true. She can't be burned up," she cried and burst back into the room. "Jubilee?"

Jubilee tried to speak, but words could not get through the flood of tears in her throat. She nodded her head.

Anise ran to her and buried her face in her lap. Benny watched numbly as his wife's tears spilled onto the little girl's light brown hair. He could tell by the slump of her shoulders she was trying to wrench some calm from herself, so she could comfort the child. Mary Alice handed Jubilee a handkerchief and knelt down in front of her. She stroked her daughter's head and spoke to Anise gently.

Anise looked up at Jubilee. The eyes and face that she knew so well were different now. The little girl climbed up into the familiar lap where she so often found comfort and wiped the face with her hands. Jubilee put both arms around the little girl and held her close for a long time.

"Please don't cry, Jubilee," Anise said.

But Jubilee didn't know if she'd ever quit crying. She looked to Benny and was moved to the core by the terrible sorrow in him, but she turned her head away, because she did not know if she'd ever be able to forgive this tragic wrong.

Finally, Luke said, "Benny, let me take you and Jubilee on home."

Benny looked at him as if he had spoken in a foreign language. It was Jubilee who answered finally.

"Thank you, Mr. Luke. We'd appreciate it."

CHAPTER 43

ON THE FRIDAY after the fire, they had one funeral for all three, Sweet Boy, Deedove, and little Grace. At the front of the old church were two large coffins made from the pine trees that grew all over the county and one small coffin made by Grace's father. The outside had been sanded down until the surface felt like the top of the baby's head. He painted the inside white, so she wouldn't be so afraid. Benny had worked night and day on it, smoothing the wood and shaping it, carving her name in the top.

On the morning of the funeral, crowds of colored and white mourners filled the little church and the yard in front. Flowers that banked the front of the church were later piled in heaps at the site of each of the fresh graves dug in the cemetery in the back. All the Montgomerys were there. Anise sat by her mother and leaned against her. The colored choir sang some of the old songs of the church and Sweet Boy's favorite, "The Beautiful Garden of Prayer". The preacher spoke words of comfort. And then it was all over, even the thoughts expressed at the gravesides, and people walked away, whispering their sorrows in hushed tones to each other and went on home. Jubilee turned to Sis Riah as she left the little cemetery and put her arm around the older woman.

"How you doing, Sis Riah?" she asked.

"All right, I guess. How you?"

"Can't quite think about it yet. You know. Can't believe it. But I got the rest of my life to do that."

"I know, honey. I know."

The two women walked together away from the fresh graves.

"What do your women say about all of this?"

"The child-spirit safe. I'm happy for that. It was what Grace was here for. Deedove bring the baby to them and they thankful to get her home before it be too late."

"Hard for me to understand exactly how that work."

"Me, too. But the child-spirit was drawn out of the dark by my Grace and the fire somehow."

"What gonna happen to the baby now?"

"She have another time. They'll know when it come and help her get here safely."

"Can they . . . ? Do they talk about other people passed on?"

"You mean Sweet Boy?"

Sis Riah nodded.

"I don't know about that exactly, but they know about the brave thing he done."

"Sometime would you ask them?"

"You know I will."

"How about Benny, honey? How he doing? Don't look too good."

Jubilee shook her head and tears came again to her eyes.

"Only one in the world can comfort him right now is me and all I can feel is the guilt and blame and grief like a great cold river between us."

"Do you really wish him comfort, honey?"

"I think so."

"Then when the time come you'll give it to him."

"I hope you right."

"Jubilee, I got some things I gotta decide on. Don't know exactly what be best. You reckon Benny be willing to advise me?"

Jubilee looked back at her husband still standing by Sweet Boy's grave.

"Aw, Sis Riah. He need to do something like that right now. He'd lay down and die for you if you needed him to."

"When you reckon be a good time to come talk?"

"We come by your house whenever you wants us to."

"Sunday after church be alright?"

"We be there," she said and put her arms around the older woman and kissed her cheek.

"I'll be looking for you," Sis Riah said and walked away toward Olivia and Matthew's Buick that stood waiting for her in front of the church.

The ride home in the wagon was silent and it made Jubilee feel like she had a raw wound somewhere inside her chest. She couldn't look at Benny or speak to him, so she kept her eyes on the road ahead. When they got home, Benny helped her down from the wagon and unhitched the mule while she went on in to make some coffee. When he'd finished outside, Benny walked through the front room as if he were in somebody else's house instead of his own. Jubilee waited and listened to the women. When the coffee was ready she walked back to the bedroom to tell him. He was doing something with his back turned toward her. She couldn't make out what it was until she got closer. Then she could see he was folding the little clothes Sis Riah had brought them before Grace was born. He stood frozen in one position carefully inspecting the little gown. She walked to his side and saw that he was crying. She stood beside him for a moment and quietly reached for his hand and held it tight. It was the first step they would take toward being healed.

CHAPTER 44

THE DAY AFTER the funeral, Saphronia told Sis Riah that Nan Hawkins was planning on leaving Hart County for good. She had no friends in Tula, so there was nothing left to keep her there. She was planning on catching the noon bus to Memphis on Friday. Before the ashes of the dry cleaners had cooled off, Sam Owen had offered to buy the place, so he could keep more farm equipment in stock. She knew it was the best she could do. She didn't go to the funerals. In fact, during the time since the fire, she had not left the tiny room she'd rented above Grapes Camp except when she absolutely had to.

On Sunday, Benny and Jubilee walked to Sis Riah's cabin. It felt good to get out of the house and breathe fresh air. The conjure women had encouraged Jubilee to lean on Benny and let him have the business of taking care of her. They had hardly left each other's side during the time since the fire. The sorrow was like a bridge between them, joining them forever, soul to soul. It was their words and their constant concern for each other.

Sis Riah met them at the door and ushered them into her front room.

"Sit down, honey," she said to Jubilee and motioned Benny to a chair.

The house had the same comforting feeling it had always had.

"Can I get you some coffee and a little something?" Sis Riah asked.

"Yassum," Benny said. "Thank you, Sis Riah."

"Let me help you," Jubilee said rising a little from the chair.

"Nawh, honey. Rest yourself. I already got everything ready."

In a few minutes she brought coffee and some slices of Mandy's blackberry jam cake and sat down at one end of the overstuffed couch across from them.

"Benny," she said finally. "I need some advice. I don't know exactly what to do and I'm sure Sweet Boy would have told me to talk to you about it."

"I be glad to help you if I can."

"You know Sweet Boy and me was planning to buy us a little piece of land out from Camden and Mr. Pierce sent word the day of the fire that he would sell it to us for fifteen hundred dollars. We was a little short of that. I shouldn't even be thinking of it. Oughta give up that idea, I know. Sure can't run the place by myself. But it was Sweet Boy's dream and it such a nice house and a good piece of land with it. Coloreds don't get a chance like this very often. I wondered if you and Jubilee might be interested in it instead of me."

"Sweet Boy talk to me about it the day of the fire. But we ain't got that kinda money. All told we got about a hundred dollars. That's it."

"Well, it was just foolishness, I suppose," she said smiling. "We plan it for so long I just can't see myself staying here the rest of my life, you know?"

"Sis Riah, what would you think of Jubilee and me buying into the deal with you? We ain't got much money, but we could work off our share of it if you'd have us. How much more you need?"

"Lord, that just what I's hoping you'd say. We be short about two hundred just to buy the place. And Benny, the house need some stuff done to it. Some things can wait, but Sweet Boy say it need a new roof right away."

"I don't know nobody got two, three hundred dollars they be able to do without for a couple of years. Except maybe the Montgomerys," Benny said rubbing his forehead.

Jubilee had been sitting quietly listening to the conversation. But suddenly she began to see ahead of them again.

"Benny, I wants you to ask Mr. Luke for some help. They's something different about the way he been treating us since the fire. He gonna understand why we has to go. I wants you to talk to him right away," she said confidently.

"Honey, if you say so I gonna do it. But I don't hold out no chance of getting it."

"Don't go to him in weakness, Benny. Go in strength, knowing you deserve that kinda trust from him. You make that much and more for him over the years you work this land."

"I don't believe he worry about getting the money back. He know I be good for it," Benny said. "He ain't gonna want us to leave though, Jubilee."

"It's alright. He expecting it," she said.

"Good thing you ain't needing to ask old man Matthew for it. Be a waste of good words," Sis Riah said.

Benny and Jubilee walked home in the twilight holding hands and talking softly to each other about what this new place would mean to them. He was a different man with her now. Not like when they were courting or even after they were married. He was new, like the skin that heals a cut. Jubilee said that she knew the farm was their future. Benny didn't ask how she knew. But he believed her.

They didn't say a word about Grace for a long time. Benny had packed up most of the baby things in a box. Jubilee said they'd need them again and it was the first spark of hope he felt since the fire. They hadn't talked about Nan either. She knew they didn't need to.

When he went to talk to Luke Montgomery on Sunday afternoon, Mary Alice invited him into the everyday living room and offered him a chair and said she'd tell Luke he was there. He shot up when Luke came in, but he was told to sit back down and Luke sat on the leather couch across from him.

"Mr. Luke, I come asking for a loan," he said emboldened by the confidence Jubilee had given him.

"I see," Luke said. "First time you ever asked me for money, Benny. What you need it for?"

Benny explained his plan to Luke. He was amazed at himself as he heard the words pouring out of his mouth without hesitation. It was as if he had returned suddenly to the innocent seven-year-old that had a white friend the same age. The fire had seared Benny with the greatest agony he would ever feel and it had rendered him fearless in its heat.

Luke was silent for a moment when Benny had finished. He got up and walked to the fireplace at the end of the room and stood leaning on the mantel and looking out the window that overlooked the pasture to the back of the house.

"Benny, how long our families go back together? You know?"

"Nawsuh, I don't. My daddy. Grandaddy. His Daddy. I don't know back beyond that."

"But your people never been slaves to my people. Your ancestors were free men working the land and getting paid to do it."

"That's what my daddy always tell me."

"We about to break two family traditions, aren't we?" Luke said.

"I think so, Mr. Luke."

"You have always called me that, even when we were boys. I use to like it when we were young that somebody as smart as you had to call me 'Mister'. When I got older I just didn't seem to hear it any more. It's the way every colored man in Hart County addresses a white man, even Sam Owen. Mr. Sam."

"Yassuh."

"Benny, my baby girl still crying over that loss of yours. Broke her heart."

Benny felt a dangerous catch in his throat.

"I'm sorry, suh."

"I know. Your wife means a lot to her and I think she looked on the baby as being partly hers somehow. Benny, things aren't gonna be nearly as easy for me with the two of you gone. Won't be easy for any of us. But it's way passed due. Should've happened for you a long time ago. How much you think you gonna need?"

"Three hundred, Mr. Luke."

"You need something to fix up the place and plant next spring, don't you?"

"Yassuh, I was planning on worrying about that when I got there."

"I don't want you worrying about it. I want to loan you five hundred if you give me a percentage of the crop next fall."

"Mr. Luke, I don't mean to be disrespectful, but I don't want to have the money based on the crop. I been doing that kinda business long enough. I wants to pay you back in two payments. One next fall and one a year after. I hope you ain't mad at that, but that's the way I wants to do it."

"Then that's the way it'll be. I'll write you a check. You can get it cashed on Monday at the bank. Would you and Sis Riah like for me to call old man Pierce?"

"Nawh, suh. We take care of that at Sis Riah's house."

Luke walked out of the room and returned in a few minutes and handed Benny a check.

"When do you think you'll be going?"

"Depend on what Mr. Pierce say, but probably by the middle of the month. Thank you, Mr. Luke."

Benny rose to go and Luke led him to the back door. He nodded to Mandy working in the kitchen as he passed. Luke held the screen door opened for him.

"Benny," he said as he closed the door behind him. "I don't ever want you to call me 'Mister' again. Just Luke will be fine from now on."

"Yassuh, Mr . . . . uh . . . Luke."

He walked down the driveway toward home.

CHAPTER 45

IT WAS GOOD for Jubilee and Benny to have the packing and planning to do. They had taken stock of what they could actually claim as their own and found they weren't nearly as poor as they thought. Benny owned twenty cows and Luke had promised to sell him a bull out of next year's crop that looked promising. And Luke had promised the loan of his cattle truck to transport them to Camden. The little red mule in the back pasture was his too, and would pull the moving wagon to their new home.

They had already made one trip over in Sis Riah's wagon with a load of her things and Jubilee got to see the place for the first time. If she hadn't just known it was the perfect place right away, the conjure women, including the spirit of Deedove, had filled the place with rose bay scent when she walked in the door.

When the final packing was loaded into the wagon and the mule was hitched up and Jubilee had walked through the empty, bare, little cabin for the last time, they climbed onto the wagon seat and Benny gave the command for the little mule to go. They were almost out of sight of the cabin when Jubilee heard a far off child's cry coming from behind her.

"Jubilee, stop."

Benny pulled the mule to a halt and Jubilee turned to see

Anise Montgomery running down the pasture hill and crawling under the barbed wire fence and getting up and running toward the wagon yelling all the way.

"Jubilee, I forgot something. Wait. Wait for me."

In a few minutes the little girl caught up with them and stood breathless on the highway looking up at Jubilee in the wagon.

"Jubilee," she said breathing hard. "I forgot to tell you something. I forgot to tell you that I love you."

"I loves you, too, honey," Jubilee said smiling at the little girl.

"I'll never forget you ever," she said. "Bye, Jubilee."

"Bye, honey. Be good," Jubilee said.

And Benny gave an order to the mule and the wagon moved slowly forward down the road and the little girl stood and waved until she couldn't see them anymore.

The End